GOOD MAN FRIDAY

Benjamin January's search for a missing man takes him into a dark world filled with grave robbers and slave stealers.

New Orleans, 1838. When Benjamin January suddenly finds that his services playing piano at extravagant balls held by the city's wealthy are no longer required, he ends up agreeing to accompany sugar planter Henri Viellard and his young wife, Chloë, on a mission to Washington to find a missing friend. Plunged into a murky world, it soon becomes clear that while it is very possible the Viellards' friend is dead, his enemies are very much alive – and ready to kill anyone who gets in their way.

The Benjamin January Series
from Barbara Hambly

A FREE MAN OF COLOR
FEVER SEASON
GRAVEYARD DUST
SOLD DOWN THE RIVER
DIE UPON A KISS
WET GRAVE
DAYS OF THE DEAD
DEAD WATER
DEAD AND BURIED *
THE SHIRT ON HIS BACK *
RAN AWAY*
GOOD MAN FRIDAY *

* *available from Severn House*

GOOD MAN FRIDAY

A Benjamin January Novel

Barbara Hambly

Severn House Large Print
London & New York

This first large print edition published 2014
in Great Britain and the USA by
SEVERN HOUSE PUBLISHERS LTD of
19 Cedar Road, Sutton, Surrey, England, SM2 5DA.
First world regular print edition published 2013 by
Severn House Publishers Ltd., London and New York.

British Library Cataloguing in Publication Data

Hambly, Barbara author.
   Good man Friday. -- (The Benjamin January series)
   1. January, Benjamin (Fictitious character)--Fiction.
   2. Free African Americans--Fiction. 3. Private
   investigators--Fiction. 4. New Orleans (La.)--Social
   conditions--19th century--Fiction. 5. Detective and
   mystery stories. 6. Large type books.
   I. Title II. Series
   813.6-dc23

   ISBN-13: 9780727897022

Severn House Publishers support the Forest Stewardship Council™
[FSC™], the leading international forest certification organisation. All
our titles that are printed on FSC certified paper carry the FSC logo.

Printed and bound in Great Britain by
T J International, Padstow, Cornwall.

For Jasmine

PROLOGUE

'I told you to fetch me a doctor, boy, not some damn nigger!'

The servant who'd brought Benjamin January to the yard behind the Turkey Buzzard saloon started to stammer an explanation, but January bowed to the man who'd sent for him, said politely, 'I've had training as a surgeon, sir.' And tried to make it sound as if he weren't fighting not to knock the arrogant little feist's teeth through the back of his head.

The arrogant little feist in question was white, as was at least half the crowd that jostled around the scratched 'stage' at the end of the yard in the brittle winter sunlight. The fights, advertised by word of mouth for weeks, had been going on since noon, and by this time – three o'clock – most were drunk. January knew if he punched Ephriam Norcum, the outcome wouldn't be good.

Aside from the law that said that no black man, slave or free, could strike a white one under any circumstances whatsoever, for three weeks now Norcum had been January's steadiest and best-paying employer. Since Twelfth Night had opened carnival season in New Orleans, Norcum had held lavish balls in honor of his wife's birthday,

7

his mother's wedding anniversary, and the engagement of his sister to a man who owned four steamboats and a cotton press. In a city reeling from the effects of last year's bank crash, six dollars for an evening's work playing the piano wasn't to be sneered at. Most banks in the city were closed, including the one in which January's slender funds had been housed, and a third of the population of New Orleans was either out of work or begging for day-labor on the half-empty wharves.

So when Ephriam Norcum slapped his face and snapped, 'Don't you fucken lie to me, boy!' January folded his hands, kept his eyes on the man's gold vest-buttons, and tried to ignore the rage that scalded his neck and ears.

'No, sir.'

For good measure Norcum turned and struck the servant who'd fetched January from the house where he'd been giving a piano lesson: not even Norcum's own servant, but – January recognized him vaguely – the planter Jed Burton's valet, who'd probably come to the fights to hold his master's horse. 'I send you for a doctor and you get me some damn piano-player—'

'I was trained in France, sir, begging your pardon,' January explained in his most diffident tones.

Norcum stared at him as if he'd just announced that he'd recently been elected President of the United States. *Even the FRENCH*, his expression shouted, *ain't THAT crazy...*

A man yelled, 'Your boy gonna fight, or ain't he, Eph? I got a hundred-fifty dollars on him—'

'Hold your goddam bladder!' Norcum yelled back. 'He'll fight all right!' And to January, 'Over here.'

The Turkey Buzzard was a two-story barn of a building constructed – like most saloons in the 'back of town' – from old flatboat planks, unpainted and weathered grimy gray. Along one side, amid scabrous piles of shattered liquor-crates and thigh-deep weeds, a sort of green room had been established for the fighters. Here the men moved about – nearly a dozen, all told – keeping themselves warm between matches, or sat on packing crates, heads back to stanch bloody or broken noses. There was no such thing, here, as real rest.

Not until it was too dark to fight. Even then, January had known such gatherings to prolong themselves into the night by torchlight.

Some had their masters with them, or their masters' overseers: sharp-eyed men with the watchfulness of those who've bet large sums and fear to see it swept away unjustly. The fighters were mostly field hands, men chosen for their size; mostly African-black or close to it. Light-skinned boys were more often taken into house service, and with luck would have too much time put into their training as cooks or valets by the time they got big enough for the master to think, *He'd make a fightin' nigger*. Most were naked – the way they'd fight; a few had put on the cut-down pants that men wore in the cane fields over their regular clothing to protect against the sharp edges of the leaves. Two had blankets over their shoulders, against the bitter,

9

bright February chill.

Strips of pickled leather wrapped their hands, bloody from earlier matches. Their faces – scarred from years of battle, sometimes – wore the blank look of those who dare think of nothing but keeping strong for the next fight.

A bench stood against the saloon wall, where, by the smell of it, customers pissed when they were too drunk to find their way to the privy in the nearby trees. Two men in the threadbare coats and coarse 'quantier' shoes of field hands knelt beside it, but got quickly to their feet at Eph Norcum's approach.

January read bad news in their faces before he knelt by the bench himself.

Shit. He touched the prostrate man's icy hand. *Shit.*

'Get the fuck up, Gun.' Norcum stood over the man on the bench. 'Look alive. You, Mr French-Ass Nigger Doctor – you put my boy back into shape for his bout and be quick about it. There's a lot ridin' on it.'

January felt the glance the two field-hands traded. Gun – a man as ebony-black as himself, with 'country marks' scarred into his face such as January recalled his African father had borne – was drenched in clammy sweat, his eyes shut and an ashy pallor to his flesh. His lips were swollen and bleeding, his puffed nose crusted with gore.

There's a man been hurt in the fights, Jed Burton's valet had said to him, when he'd knocked at the kitchen door of James Thorley's house. *Needs a doctor right away.*

10

January had known then that it could be anything.

He hated nigger fights and stayed as far away from them as he could.

But since long before he'd taken his first training, at the age of fifteen, from a free colored surgeon named Gomez, he'd never been able to turn away from someone who needed help.

'Does this hurt?' Even the slightest brush of his fingers on the fighter's rigid abdomen brought a hissing intake of breath, and the swollen lips squashed tight to suppress a sob. The man Gun was a few inches shorter than January's massive six foot three but heavy-muscled as a bull. By the scars on his shaven head, and the thickened flesh of his ears, January guessed he'd been a fighter in these slave-on-slave bouts – staged for the masters to bet on – since puberty.

''Course it hurts,' Norcum answered for the slave, and spat a line of tobacco into the weeds. 'That nigger Ulee of old man Peralta's got a kick like a goddam mule. I thought Gun was never gonna get up from that one. But Gun beat him in the end.' He grinned with savage pride. 'Gun's tough as a jack bull. Once you get him on his feet—'

From the yard, a man shouted in anger: 'You callin' me a liar, you pussified French pimp?'

'I call you a dog, and an Irishman, and a thief, who stole money from every man in town when that whorehouse bank of yours closed—'

As he'd passed through the yard, January had noted that as usual the crowd was divided,

11

Frenchmen with Frenchmen, Americans with Americans, a representation in miniature of the vicious animosity that had, not quite two years previously, resulted in the whole town splitting itself into three 'municipalities'. By the storm of curses that now broke, he wondered how long it would be before the spectators who'd come to bet on black men fighting started in on each other with canes, boots, and bowie-knives.

The man Gun's eyelids creased.

As if he knew it was time for him to get up...

'This man is in no shape to fight.' January rose and faced Norcum. 'He's bleeding internally. He needs—'

Norcum gaped at January, incredulous. 'I didn't send for you to ask your goddam opinion, boy! I sent for you to get my boy ready for his next fight!' He spat again. 'I got ten thousand dollars ridin' on him layin' out Bourrège's Pedro–' he pronounced the French planter's name *Boo-reg* – 'and I ain't pullin' him out of it on the word of some nigger witch-doctor!'

'Then I strongly urge you send for a white physician, sir. I'm sure he'll come to the same conclusion when he's seen this man. I saw Dr Barnard in the yard there—'

'Barnard?' Norcum jeered. 'That French nancy's got five thousand dollars on Pedro! You bet he's gonna come to the same goddam conclusion as you do, boy!'

'Norcum!' A group of men appeared around the corner of the saloon. January recognized them, from having played at their balls, parties, musicales in years past, when everyone in town still had money to entertain lavishly in the carnival season. The Lafrènniére brothers owned four sugar plantations between them, mortgaged to the eaves to cover operating costs when buyers had offered half of last year's prices for this year's crop; Francois Delaup owned the *New Orleans Bee*, the largest French newspaper in the city. Armand Roffignac – with a hotel and a cotton-press – would have been a rich man, in any times but these. Among them was the planter Louis Bourrège and, with him, a tall young man naked to the waist and sheened with sweat despite the day's sharp cold.

Pedro. Bourrège's fighting slave.

'Are we to have a bout or not, M'sieu?' Smugness tinged Bourrège's voice. 'My boy cannot stand about like this in the cold, waiting for you to forfeit.'

'I ain't gonna goddam forfeit!' Norcum's weather-reddened little face grew dark, and the two or three Americans who had followed the French planters all took up the cry in a way that told January that they, too, had money on Gun. When January opened his mouth to speak, Norcum grabbed him by the arm, shoved him against the saloon's wall.

'Don't you say one goddam word, boy.' Brown spittle flicked January's shirt front. 'You get my boy on his feet and into that stage—'

'He can't fight.' January's voice was hard now. 'He is badly injured. Another fight will kill him.'

Norcum waved the words aside. 'Shit, Gun's won fights with a goddam broken leg!'

A man named Fry came over to them, a land-

13

speculator who, like Norcum, was one of the few businessmen in the city still able to afford such things as parties, music lessons for his sister, and a subscription to the much-reduced opera. Without so much as a glance at January, he whispered to Norcum, 'You ain't gonna scratch, are you, Eph?'

'I am not gonna goddam scratch!' Eph Norcum thrust January away from him, strode back to where his slave lay. January saw him drag Gun up sitting.

'Now you listen to me,' said Norcum quietly. 'I don't care how bad your belly hurts. You can lay down when you won that fight.'

'Sir, I can't—'

'You gonna. I got ten thousand dollars ridin' on your black ass, and every man I know got the same. You know where's the only place I can get that money back if you don't get in there and win? By sellin' that wife of yours – and both your girls – to the dealers.'

January drew breath to protest, and the servant who'd fetched him grabbed his arm, tried to pull him away. *You're in New Orleans*, January reminded himself with an effort. *Not Paris...*

Paris where he'd spent sixteen years of his life, Paris where he'd trained at the Hôtel Dieu, Paris where a surgeon could protest blackmail and murder without being beaten by outraged white men for his temerity...

In Gun's eyes January saw the knowledge that this was exactly what Norcum would do.

His voice low, Norcum went on, 'You kick that Pedro's French-nigger ass or you're gonna be

14

the sorriest nigger in this state. And your wife's gonna be the sorriest one in Missouri.'

Gun closed his eyes for a moment. 'Yes, sir.' He didn't weep, the ability to do so having been beaten out of him years ago. Only put out his hand – massive as an ox's hoof – and the two young field-hands who'd stayed near ran up and helped him to his feet. He barely staggered when his master, and Harry Fry, and half a dozen other Americans crowded around him, slapped him on his back and yelled things like, 'That's the spirit, Gun!' and, *'Now* we gonna show them sissy-ass French...'

January knew he'd better go. Yet he sank down on to the bench where Gun had lain and sat there while the other three slaves ran around the corner to watch the fight. He heard someone shout the names of the contestants: Norcum's Gun and Bourrège's Pedro. 'No interferin' with the combatants ... no man to step over the lines into the stage ... a round is called when a combatant's knee touches the ground ... thirty seconds between rounds...'

Nothing, January reflected, about no biting, no eye-gouging, no recourse to what were politely termed 'foul blows'. This wasn't a white man's fight.

He remembered telling his fellow musicians in Paris about these fights, as he'd told them of the other 'customs of the country' into which he'd been born: of the quasi-genteel arrangements of free colored plaçage and of 'Blue Ribbon' balls, and of the manner in which well-bred young white girls were taught to ignore the fact that

15

their husbands were tupping the female slaves. Of the means by which 'portly' slave girls were 'put with' the most 'portly' of their master's slave men, whether the girls wanted to breed by those men or not. He could afford then to display such curiosities, like the decorative mutilations of savages, for he'd had no intention of ever returning to Louisiana.

Nor would he have done so, he thought, if he'd had anywhere else to go, when the epidemic of Asian cholera had taken his first wife a good deal farther away than Missouri...

In the yard, voices rose to shrieks. Jed Burton's valet came racing around the corner of the saloon. 'Best you clear outta here, Mr January,' he panted. 'Mr Norcum, he mad fit to kill.'

'Is Gun dead?' In his heart he already knew.

The servant nodded. 'That Pedro fetched him a blow in the belly, an' seem like he throw up all the blood in his body. I think he's dead 'fore he hit the ground.'

January closed his eyes for a moment and saw again the fighter's face when he'd stood up and disappeared straight-backed into the crowd.

He hoped someone would tell Gun's wife – and his daughters – what this man had done for their sakes, or tried to do.

'Thank you.' He picked up his satchel, filled with the simple piano-pieces that he taught the children of those few – all of them whites, these days – who had the money to pay for it. In it he generally carried a few paper twists of basilicum powder and willow bark, laudanum, and a scalpel or two, tools of the surgeon's trade that

16

neither whites nor free colored would hire someone as black as himself to practice. Even the
darker-complected among the *sang melée* found
it inconceivable that one who looked so much
like a hulking coal-black field-hand would have
either education or skill.

Even in France – that land of *liberté, égalité*,
and government informers – it had been the
same.

He'd learned a long time ago that music paid
better.

Unless, of course – he reflected as he ducked
between the Turkey Buzzard's outhouse and
woodpile and into the swampy semi-wilderness
of tree stumps and squatters' shacks that lay
beyond – you happened to get on the bad side of
one of the few white planters still rich enough to
be holding entertainments in this impoverished
carnival season of 1838.

Then you'd better start looking around for
some other way to feed your family and heat
your house through the chilly months to come.

ONE

January was not terribly surprised to receive a cold letter from Eph Norcum's business manager the following day, informing him that his services at Mr Norcum's Valentine's Day ball, Washington's Birthday ball, and the bridal musicale in honor of his sister were no longer required. He hoped the planter's ire wouldn't extend to telling his friends, 'I don't want to see that murderin' nigger incompetent so-called doctor on any future occasion...' – meaning on the orchestra dais of *their* Carnival celebrations – but in the course of the next several days it became clear that it did.

'Either that, or they all had money wagered on Gun as well.' He dropped to the worn planks of the gallery floor the equally frosty dismissal from Harry Fry's new wife.

It was the most recent of nearly a dozen, starting with Norcum's – nearly a week ago, now – and including not only those who had hired him for Carnival entertainment, but also the fathers of most of his few piano-students as well. From the assurance of a moderate income through the carnival season, and the hopes of picking up a few more students to eke his family through the starving summer, January found himself facing

19

having his small savings exhausted by Easter, with no prospects for anything beyond.

'The wretched man *would* have his thumb in every business in town that still has its doors open,' remarked Rose dispassionately. She set aside the slate on which she'd been double-checking her husband's budgetary calculations and put on her spectacles again.

In palmier days – before President Jackson had taken it upon himself to dismantle the central bank of the United States and precipitate last year's financial collapse – Rose and January had run a small boarding-school in their big Spanish house on Rue Esplanade. Their students had been mostly the daughters of plaçées, those semi-official mistresses of white planters, brokers, bankers and landowners whose mixed-race children had for well over a century made up a caste of free colored in the town. These girls, of whom Rose herself was one, were traditionally schooled to be what their mothers had been, trained in deportment, music, a little sketching, and given sufficient familiarity with literature to be pleasing companions to the men who'd negotiate contracts with their mothers to give them houses and annuities. In contrast to most other girls' schools in the city, Rose had offered all the things she herself had hungered for as a child: mathematics, science, history, languages modern and arcane. The sort of learning that no girl – white or colored – was supposed to understand or want.

It was, as January's widowed mother had not been slow to point out, a foolish waste of time and capital and a good way to end up bankrupt. ('And don't expect ME to provide for you when you do...')

The times had proven her correct in this. Even parents willing to provide such an unlikely education for their daughters in good times were now forced to make hard choices. Invariably, they saved what funds they had, to educate the sons who would, with luck, bring in money to the family as a whole. The girls would have to wait, as girls always did.

'Mama says Norcum's still rich because he's a slave-smuggler.' Gabriel, January's fifteen-year-old nephew, emerged on to the gallery through one of the long French windows on the heels of Rose's remark. 'He brings them in from Africa through Cuba to Texas, Mama says, for half what Virginia slaves cost—'

Mama was January's sister Olympe. Two years younger than himself, like nearly everyone in New Orleans Olympe was struggling to provide for the children in her household too young to work. When circumstance had made it impossible to hire even a little help in keeping up the big old house, January had taken in Olympe's two older children – Zizi-Marie, seventeen, and Gabriel. Gabriel could make two handfuls of beans and rice into a banquet gods would stand in line for, and Zizi-Marie helped Rose with the housework when she wasn't at her father's shop learning the upholsterer's trade. Olympe's husband – Paul Corbier, a highly skilled upholsterer – hadn't had a commission in over a year, and the family was living on Olympe's earnings as a voodooienne and herb-doctor.

'Well, then we can all have the satisfaction of knowing he'll go straight to Hell when he dies.' January turned Rose's slate around right-ways-up toward him and considered the neat columns of figures: taxes, food, fuel. Repairs on shoes, new sheet-music so that January could stay *au courant* on his work, provided he could get any. Small articles like new gloves and cravats, for who would hire an entertainer who looked shabby? Modest provisions for the church and the 'burial society' – a social and benevolent organization – to which he belonged.

In three weeks it would be Lent.

He looked at the figures on the slate and felt like a farmer who sees locusts descend upon his corn.

'He can't tell the French not to hire you, can he?' Gabriel scooped up Baby John from where Rose had left the infant – now three months old – on a blanket in the mild winter sunlight.

'He can't,' agreed January. 'But he hired me – and the other Americans hired me – back before Christmas, so the Destrehans and the Marignys and the Roffignacs all hired Damien Jouet or Marc Paillard to play for them.' He named the other two best-known piano-players in New Orleans. Like himself, they were the sons of free colored mothers, whose white protectors – in their cases, the boys' fathers – had paid to have them taught.

Like himself, he knew that both men were living on the edge of disaster. In better times, every musician in town subsisted on private

22

lessons. These days, French Creole and American newcomer families alike were all having their sons and daughters instructed by whatever Aunt Unmarriageable happened to be either living in their households or at least eating at their tables three or four times a week.

'Well, beat that with a chain,' grumbled Gabriel. 'Maybe I could quit Maître Clouard and look for work—'

'You'll do nothing of the kind.' Five days a week, Gabriel assisted the principal chef at the Hotel Iberville, learning the art and science of French cookery. This exchange of service brought in no money, but January's instincts told him it would eventually provide the youth with a handsome living.

'I think—' January bent sideways in his sturdy willow chair to pick up Mrs Fry's discarded note – 'I need to speak to Lieutenant Shaw.'

Rose glanced from the slate, eyebrows lifting. Silent.

'City Guards won't hire a black man,' Gabriel protested.

'I should hope not,' Rose remarked. 'Considering the number of runaway slaves we've hidden under this house in the past year.'

January shook his head. 'But I've worked with Shaw finding missing people, or solving puzzles...'

'Like last year,' agreed Gabriel enthusiastically, 'when you helped him get the man who killed his brother—'

'You were away for six months.' Rose gathered Baby John from Gabriel's arms and didn't look at January. Between them the words hung unspoken: *You almost didn't come back.*

'He may know someone who needs a job done. A job they can't ask the Guards to do.' January extended a finger to his son, marveling again at the infant's tiny perfection, as if he'd never seen a baby before. Baby John – no one would ever think of calling that miniature professor of philosophy *Johnny* – was already taking after Rose's slender build, his coloring halfway between January's nearly-pure African 'beau noire lustre' and Rose's quadroon café-crème. The brown eyes that looked back into January's were wise, and solemn, and a thousand years old. *If I have to be gone another six months*, reflected January, *or get myself shot at or half-drowned in the river or poisoned or blown up in a steamboat or all the other fool things I've been mixed up in to get money for this house, these people whom I love ... Men have done worse.*

And he remembered the fighter Gun's face, when he'd gone walking among the white men to a fight he knew he wouldn't survive.

Abishag Shaw, Lieutenant of the New Orleans City Guard, agreed to keep his ear to the ground for unofficial work, when January finally ran him to earth late the following afternoon. 'Dang little around,' he added, and spat tobacco in the general direction of the sandbox in the corner of the Cabildo's watchroom. His aim was far worse than Norcum's, and the worn granite of the watchroom floor was fouled with brown dollops – like vaguely sweet bird-droppings – for yards.

'Carnival ain't a time when folks plot murder in the dark, bein' mostly too drunk to work out the details—'

Two sturdy Guards entered the watchroom from the Place des Armes outside, dragging a gaggle of flatboat ruffians and two black prostitutes, all shouting at one another at the top of their lungs: 'Sure as I stand here as an American, I will not be cheated by the likes of you—'

'You lyin' sheep-stealer! I shit better Americans ever' time I pull down my pants...'

'I'll listen around.' Shaw unfolded his slow height from behind his desk, like the improbable love-child of a scarecrow and a gargoyle. 'Won't be anyone who owes Eph Norcum money, though. 'Scuse me, Maestro...'

Two river-rats had broken free of their captors and – ignoring a clear path to the Cabildo's outer doors – had thrown themselves upon one another like rabid dogs.

January stood back by the desk and watched as Shaw knocked heads together, tossed the largest man effortlessly into a corner and assisted the other Guards in subduing the rest. The whores added their mite to the fray by leaping on to the backs of the peacemakers, shrieking like harpies. When blood started to flow, January made a wide circuit of the confusion to reach the corner of the sergeant's desk and collect a confiscated bottle of rum.

'That little one got a fine set of teeth,' remarked Shaw, returning after a few strenuous moments holding a bloody wrist. He already sported a strip of sticking plaster above his left eyebrow and a bandage on one hand – by this point in the carnival season, most of the Guards were looking pretty shopworn. 'An' I would warn you,' he added as January mopped the tart-bite with rum and bound it up with a clean bandanna from his pocket, 'that most of them that would seek to hire you, the job would turn out to be you goin' to some deserted bayou in the middle of the night an' gettin' slugged over the head, an' wakin' up on the auction block some-place in the territories.'

January gritted his teeth, knowing the Ken-tuckian was right. Slaves were the one thing that hadn't gone down in price, and nobody much cared where they came from or if they insisted they were actually free men who'd been kid-napped...

After letting his words sink in, Shaw added, 'You know Norcum tried to swear out a warrant on you for murder.'

'That's ridiculous! Sir,' he remembered to add, as the desk sergeant – returning through the courtyard door nursing a cut lip – gave him a frosty glare. Shaw was, after all, white, though January's mother wouldn't have had him in her house.

'Well, he lost a sight of money on that fight.' Shaw flexed his bandaged wrist. 'Thank you, Maestro ... An' you needn't worry none. Captain Tremouille's brother-in-law had money on the other fella.'

'That sound you hear,' said January grimly, 'is my heart singing with joy.' Only three dollars remained in the household cache behind the bricks in the cellar, and he was getting desperate. The next stop would be the wharves, or the cigar-rolling shops on Tchapitoulas Street.

'Thought you'd like to know.' Shaw spat again. 'It'll blow over. Most things do.'

This January knew to be true.

'But it's damn little comfort,' he said to Hannibal Sefton, when he encountered his friend the fiddler two evenings later among the brick pillars of the market, 'to think that as a trained surgeon, and a trained musician, the only thing I'm really valued for is the twelve hundred dollars I'd fetch as a cotton hand.'

'Di tibi, si qua pios respectant numina–' Hannibal handed him the cup of coffee he'd fetched from old La Violette's coffee-stand – *'praemia digna ferant ...* No, *amicus meus,'* he added, and pushed back the nickel January laid on the table, 'permit me to expunge the guilt that overwhelms me every time I play for Norcum or his sycophantic friends.'

He carried also three pink pralines on a square of clean newspaper, which he set before January. 'It's the least I can do ... And believe me, I will always do the least I can.'

'Far be it from me to let a man welter in his guilt.' January inclined his head magisterially. Hannibal, January's oldest friend in New Orleans, was the only white man in town who would be seen publicly eating and drinking with blacks, for which the white population regarded him as rather degenerate.

Sugar-grinding season was over, the fields burnt. Farther upriver, the cotton was all picked.

27

In curing-houses upriver and down, rack after rack of wooden molds dripped slow threads of molasses for the edification of armies of cockroaches. In slave quarters, men and women repaired garments and fingers sliced by sharp-cut cane-ends, or torn by the stickers of the cotton plants, and marveled at the wonder of being able to rest with fall of night.

The planters came to town to bargain with factors over this single, massive pay-day of the year; to settle up the year's accumulated debts. To meet other planters, relatives, friends; to attend the theater and hear music other than the field-hollers of their slaves and the amateur recitals of their neighbors' daughters. To see something other than endless fields of whatever crop they depended on: dark-green sugar, or brownish-red cotton starred with white. To enjoy newspapers less than a week old, or books that hadn't been read threadbare over the course of the year.

New Orleans stirred to life. Mardi Gras parties spilled masked revelers out on to the brick banquettes, improbably clad as French aristocrats or Turkish warriors. Both opera houses presented Auber and Mozart and spectacles more vulgar – *The Castle Spectre* and *All For America!* – to bring in Kaintucks' money.

The wives of planters cried out that they didn't care that cotton was down to fourteen cents a pound – it had been thirty-two the year before last ... if they were to convince people their credit was good, they couldn't do so in dresses three years out of date. If they were to find suitable husbands for their daughters, young Marie-Celeste or Marie-Anne or Marie-Thèrése would *have* to appear in the latest style...

Looking out from the shadows of the market to the line of barn-like white steamboats beyond the levee, smokestacks dark against the twilight sky, January reflected that had he not recalled what the wharves looked like in flush times, he could have been seduced into thinking that times were getting better. Slave gangs chanted the old hollers, in language they'd learned by ear from their parents, as they hauled on the cranes or manhandled the crates of purchased goods – cheap shoes, coarse cloth for slave-clothes, all the salt and cheese and cane knives and blankets that those isolated kingdoms would get for the next year.

In the winter of 1836–7, each wharf had been four-deep in steamboats, stacked with dirty-white bales to their roofs: cotton, which had sold for over twice what it brought these days. In the winter of 1836–7, captains and supercargoes had cursed their way along the bustling wharves in search of stevedores, instead of the work gangs loitering in the hopes of a cargo. In addition to the regular gangs – smaller than they had been, because the men who rented their slaves to the dock gangs had often sold a man or two – there were men January knew as bricklayers, drovers, clerks even, hanging around or going from gang to gang: *Can you use another man? I'll work for a nickel a day...*

A nickel would get you beans and rice, with maybe an onion thrown in for lagniappe.

'At least you have the comfort of knowing that your carcass is worth money,' added Hannibal, and coughed. He seemed in better health than he had earlier in the winter, though skeletally thin; he had acquired a new waistcoat, and had put up his long hair in a pair of tortoiseshell combs, by which January deduced that he had a new girlfriend somewhere.

'A reflection I signally lack,' the fiddler went on with a sigh. 'It used to be, I could get work grading students' Greek compositions for d'Avezac's "College" for boys – not to mention earning a dollar or two writing those same compositions for the more enterprising scholars. Now every boys' school that's still open, the master has a brother or a cousin who does the same work for food. Hence my willingness to betray you by making music in Norcum's tobacco-boltered halls—'

'I depend upon you to wreak what petty revenge you can beneath his roof.'

'I presented both his nephews with pennywhistles,' mused Hannibal. 'They're seven and eight years old, and will be living in his house for the next three months. For good measure I left the advertisement for that shockingly expensive shipment of lace that's just come into Broussard's where his wife can find it. But, I must say, like an ancient Greek hero his own actions have called vengeance upon his head: *Se ludice nemo nocens absolvitur*. This late in the season, the only pianist he – or any of his friends – has been able to find to replace you is that German fellow Hatch who plays at the Blackleg

Saloon. Last week Hatch made an attempt upon the virtue of Arabella Fry – I can only assume he was drunk – and arrived at last night's bridal musicale so incapacitated he couldn't make it through the Moonlight Sonata; not that he's ever had much success with it sober, mind you. But even in the worst of my drinking days–' Hannibal coughed again, and pressed his hand to his side – 'there wasn't enough alcohol in the *world* to induce me to kiss Arabella Fry.'

January laughed, though the thought of being replaced by Hatch made him seethe. 'I'll find something.' He tried to sound as if he believed it. 'If nothing else, I suppose I can apply to fill Mr Hatch's place at the Blackleg—'

'Shotwell pays him in drinks.' Hannibal shook his head. 'Which I assure you does nothing for the quality of his performance as the evening progresses. I think a season of his – I cannot precisely call it *music* – is all the inducement Norcum's friends will need to re-hire you come fall.'

January suspected this as well. When the fiddler left him to proceed to his evening's work, January made his way home through the chilly twilight along the Rue Esplanade. The street's double width made it a popular promenade for flower-decked carriages filled with maskers, all banging tin pans and blowing flour into one another's faces, their festivity jarringly alien to his mood. From the open French doors of a dozen little cottages, music and laughter and the smells of burned sugar drifted into the night.

Lamps glowed softly behind the closed shutters of the old Spanish house on Rue Esplanade. As always, merely seeing the place made his heart lift: his house, Rose's house, ramshackle as it was. He climbed the steps to the gallery – it was built high off the street, the ground floor serving no purpose but as a cellar – and found, to his surprise, the parlor occupied not only by Rose, but also by an enormously stout white gentleman only inches shorter than himself, and a tiny fair-haired lady, like a bespectacled mermaid wrought of blown Venetian glass.

'M'sieu Janvier...' The gentleman rose from his chair and held out a hand like a pudgy flipper; January grasped it cordially. 'I'm glad we didn't miss you.'

'M'sieu Viellard.' January turned to bow deeply over the little lady's delicate gloved fingers. 'Madame. I'm glad also.'

And although he didn't say so, bemused and surprised as well. Henri Viellard owned half a dozen sugar plantations and one of the largest private libraries in the state – and was the lover of January's youngest sister Dominique. Henri's wife, the cold-faced little lady clothed, like Henri, in the stiff satins of the French Court eighty years ago, blinked at January from behind enormously thick lenses and said, 'The pleasure is ours, M'sieu. Rose was just now telling us that if we were to put a proposition to you for employment for the next three months, you probably wouldn't turn us down.'

January bowed again. 'Whom do I have to kill, m'am?'

'Oh dear, nothing of the kind!' Henri Viellard

looked up in shocked consternation from the platter of Gabriel's best petit fours that Zizi-Marie had just brought in, warm from the kitchen.

Chloë Viellard's prim mouth tucked into a very tiny smile as she picked up her coffee cup again.

'I'm not sure at the moment,' she said. Her husband's eyes – mild and brown behind his own thick spectacles – flared further in alarm, and he appeared momentarily so horrified at the suggestion that he couldn't even select a pastry. 'And I very much fear, in fact, that the man we wish to locate may already be dead. We don't know about that, either.'

'Rose—' January turned to his wife. 'When I get ready to accompany M'sieu and Madame, please be sure to pack my shovel. When you speak of employing me for a few months,' he went on, 'do you mean here in town, or down at Bois d'Argent—?'

'Neither,' said the young Madame Viellard. 'I'm afraid our dear friend Mr Singletary disappeared in Washington City, and it's there that we need to go, to pick up his trail again.'

'It should be perfectly safe,' Henri Viellard hastened to assure him, and wiped powdered sugar from the gateau off his fingers with finicking care. 'I am told that last summer you undertook a rather dangerous expedition to the Rocky Mountains, but this is nothing of that sort. I'm sure there must be some simple explanation for Mr Singletary's disappearance. He is a rather absent-minded soul. Ah!' Bliss transformed his face as Zizi-Marie returned, with a platter of

33

pralines this time: coconut-white and cochineal-pink as well as the traditional golden. 'Exquisite! But as for our search—' His attention returned to January. 'How much peril could one encounter in our nation's capital?'

TWO

Passage had been booked for them on the British merchantman *Anne Marie*, en route from Havana to Baltimore and eventually back to Liverpool. Henri Viellard chose the vessel because neither its captain nor its owners had any objection to assigning a cabin to a couple of color and their child, if they could pay for it.

January only wished that the 'wife' and child he was to accompany to Washington were his own.

But when hands had been shaken, and preliminary arrangements made for the payment of one hundred and fifty dollars to Rose – half of the agreed-upon fee – Henri took January aside and whispered discreetly, 'If you would, M'sieu, I should be personally very much indebted to you, should you consent to act as escort for your sister. She'll be accompanying us to Washington as well.'

January reminded himself that *personally very much indebted to you* meant *in the event of financial disaster, you can come to me for help,* and refrained from moaning aloud.

The sister Henri meant was not Olympe – mother of Gabriel and Zizi-Marie – but their younger half-sister Dominique: frivolous, beautiful, privileged since birth as the daughter of a white sugar-broker, and Henri Viellard's mistress. January was dearly fond of Dominique and understood why this fat, scholarly mama's-boy of a planter would want to bring her on an expedition in which he had been included merely because respectable wives did not travel unaccompanied. But he understood also that his duties as sleuth-hound and henchman would now be expanded to include posing as Dominique's husband, sharing the minuscule cabin with four trunks containing her dresses, and vacating it whenever Henri arrived for a visit.

Not to mention listening to any amount of his sister's non-stop prattle of dresses, hats, gossip about fellow-passengers and the myriad perfections of her beautiful daughter Charmian, who would – along with her nurse and Dominique's maid – also be part of their little shipboard household.

The voyage to Baltimore took almost three weeks. The weather in the Caribbean was stormy; in the Atlantic, the ship rolled in high seas under an almost constant pelting of sleety rain. Henri remained in his cabin in an agony of seasickness, and because Chloë was impervious to the ailment – and had the maternal instincts of the average garden-spider – Dominique spent most of every day at his side.

January walked the decks when he could, his

muscles screaming for exercise, but many days Captain Fancher issued orders that the passengers must remain below, out of the way of the struggling crew. The only other passengers were three German businessmen and the seventeen-year-old son of a Mexican grandee bound for school in France – and all their respective valets, who, along with Henri's valet Leopold, slept and ate with the crew. All of them fell immediately and violently in love with Dominique. When the pitching of the ship permitted, January and Herr Rosenstein teamed up on piano and concertina so that everyone could take turns dancing with the two ladies, vigorous waltzes that for most of them constituted their only physical activity for days on end.

January forbore to mention to his fellow passengers that 'dancing the slaves' was precisely how slave traders kept their cargo 'in trim' on the long voyage from Africa.

Dominique's maid Thèrése, Chloë's maid Hèléne, and Musette – Charmian's nurse – remained below.

Afterwards, when Dominique took her daughter to bed and Captain Fancher's man came in with the tea, January fleshed out his information about the disappearance of Mr Selwyn Singletary in Washington City the previous fall.

'I've corresponded with M'sieu Singletary most of my life.' Chloë took the teacup that January brought her, from the gimballed urn on the saloon's main table where Herren Coppert and Franck had settled to their usual game of picquet. The lanterns swayed with the motion of

36

the ship, and rain spattered the windows as if hurled from a bucket.

'He was president of the British Mathematical Society, of which my Uncle Veryl is a member, though uncle's hopeless with numbers.' Madame timed her sip to the roll of the ship. Her marriage two years previously to Henri had been considered a phenomenal coup by the Viellard family; what she felt about it, she had never said. 'I've always been very good with them, so starting when I was nine, Uncle Veryl had me write his letters for him. I've never actually met M'sieu Singletary.'

'Can you describe him?' January collected Charmian's alphabet blocks from the low table beside the sofa where they sat, keeping the words together that she'd spelled out, everything from *Anne Marie* to the name of Captain Fancher's manservant, which was Skorsmund.

'Uncle Veryl says he's "about" his – Uncle Veryl's – height, which is five foot eight or nine. But of course he describes Henri the same way, and Henri is over six feet tall.' She rearranged the blocks, changing their upward faces so that instead of spelling out *pineapple* and *piano*, they made neat rows of the alphabet. Chloë was fond of Charmian in her precise way, and fast friends with Dominique, a situation which bemused January but which at least would not result in murder before they reached Baltimore. 'When I asked him, "Are M'sieu Singletary's eyes blue?" he said yes, he thought so. When I asked, "Are his eyes hazel?" he agreed that they probably were. And as he only met M'sieu Singletary

37

once, twenty years ago, he wouldn't know if he was bearded or clean-shaven, though he hadn't the slightest idea what color his hair was...'

'It's probably gray by now,' said January. 'A lot of people are unobservant that way.'

Chloë sniffed, as if this were something that she would arrange, were she ever to find herself in the position of ruling the world.

'How would he have been dressed? Was he a wealthy man?'

'I believe his family was quite poor. He never had much formal schooling, which is probably just as well. From what I gathered from his letters – those that weren't entirely preoccupied with proofs and theorems – he had a sort of self-taught genius for mathematical relationships, the kind of thing I only glimpse now and then, when I see waves break on the bow of this vessel, or how a loose rope will swing from a mast. Uncle Veryl describes him as shabby, though the Virgin and all the saints know what that means, considering the kind of things *he* wears. "Shabby and old-fashioned," he said.'

'*Old-fashioned* could mean anything from a narrow-cut coat, to small-clothes and a cocked hat.'

'Or trunk-hose and a slashed doublet, knowing Uncle Veryl.' Chloë sighed.

'What does he do? Teach, I assume.'

'Oh, no. At least, he does so now ... or that's what he came to America to do.' She rearranged the alphabet blocks again, trying to reverse the letters of the alphabet without moving any block from its original place. A small frown printed

38

itself between her pale, delicate brows. In her gown of gray silk, severely cut and relieved only with the thinnest of ivory piping, she looked like a child dressed by grown-ups to counterfeit adulthood, thin and solemn behind her round spectacle-lenses.

'For most of his life M'sieu Singletary has done the accounts for banks. Five or six in various parts of England, two in France, and one in Amsterdam. Most of his time he spends traveling between them. I suppose it's why he's such an odd man: no family, no friends, but hundreds of correspondents through mathematical and scientific societies, like me and, it turned out, Henri.'

'I didn't know Henri was mathematical.'

'He's not. But M'sieu Singletary is also interested in insects, and Henri wrote to him after reading a monograph M'sieu Singletary published on cockroaches in Bordeaux. The correspondence flourished. Many people admire Henri's collections of butterflies, but he has found few to share his enthusiasm for Dictyoptera.'

January said, 'Hmmn.' In the cottage that Henri had purchased for Dominique on Rue Dumaine, where Henri himself lived three or four days a week in carnival season, he had seen the planter's collections of insects, shells, and flowers exquisitely desiccated in sand. His medical training appreciated the other man's fascination with those delicate variations in the forms of organic life, but he'd lived too long in New Orleans to take any delight in trays of preserved roaches. Dominique – Minou, the family called her – wouldn't even go into the room.

'Be that as it may,' Chloë went on, 'last year the University of Virginia offered him a year's post. Henri and I both had to write assuring him that Americans were not barbarians and that the United States was a perfectly safe place to visit if one refrained from playing cards in waterfront taverns.

'To do him justice,' she added, 'while I don't think M'sieu Singletary capable of telling a scoundrel from a Presbyterian minister, he dislikes human company so much that I can't really see him blundering into trouble that way. Yet something has undoubtedly happened to him.' She sat back on the sofa, folded lace-mitted hands. 'Quite apart from the affection I feel for him, I feel responsible for encouraging him to come. I meant it for the best...'

'Does he play cards?'

'Not as most people understand playing. He's written to me more than once that games as such bore him, as they bore me. You have no idea what a relief it was to hear from someone who understood about working out mathematical probabilities when you're playing copper-loo with idiots who think they're being so daring, playing cards behind the nuns' backs. Indeed,' she added wistfully, 'to write to *any*one about *any*thing other than how my music lessons were progressing, not that a single member of my family can distinguish a nodal pattern from a cat's cradle.'

She smiled her precise cut-glass smile. 'Even when I was little – and he deduced quite quickly

40

that I was a ten-year-old girl and not Uncle Veryl – he'd send me long treatises on the algorithmic probabilities generated by shuffling – he hadn't the slightest idea of what little girls were interested in, of course – exactly as if I were an adult member of the Mathematics Society. He always assumed I'd be able to follow him, though he was perfectly ready to explain if I couldn't. You can't imagine what that ... that assumption of intellectual equality meant to me when I was eleven, and bored to the screaming-point surrounded by the other girls in the convent. And he always did write. That meant a great deal to me, too. My aunts never did. His letters always came. I lived for them.'

In the swaying lantern-light her heart-shaped little face looked older than her eighteen years, and sad. Looking back, perhaps, on that tiny heiress, surrounded by the expectation of what a good French Creole girl should be. A pious wife, a doting mother, an accomplished hostess. And not able to understand why she wasn't it.

Reason enough, reflected January, to travel nine hundred miles, to pick up a trail months cold. So that the old man, who had opened for her that door to the world of the mind, should not be forgotten, or left to die unheeded in a foreign land.

Even if it meant hauling along her husband to lend her countenance, and her husband's mistress to keep *him* company, and the aforesaid mistress's brother to pretend to be a husband so that he could lend *her* countenance, plus the mistress's child, the child's nurse, and the mistress's

41

maid, like so many lapdogs on a single leash ... all pretending they had nothing to do with that cold little fair-haired lady sipping her tea in the shifting lamplight.

'*Darlings...*' cooed Dominique's sweet voice from the doorway, 'thank you *so* much for seeing me here safely.' She tossed back the oiled-silk hood of the cloak that covered her dress and smiled meltingly up at Captain Fancher, to whose arm she clung. 'The violence of the sea must be nothing to you, after years of striding across it like a conqueror, but it *terrifies* me.'

Then she turned and touched young Señor Calaveras lightly on the biceps, her smile like honey and velvet. 'But you don't seem to be bothered by it at *all*, and it's your first voyage...'

And all of it, reflected January with an inner smile, perfectly sincere. At four years old, Minou in a tiny gown of lace, like the Christ Child on a Mexican altarpiece, would always go to the most distinguished visitor first, whether it was their mother's lover St-Denis Janvier – Minou's father – or whichever of his guests it was most vital to impress.

'And it's just as I feared,' she continued, smiling. 'Benjamin has lost no time in finding another woman—'

January said, 'Fie, woman!' and all the men laughed heartily, since no one on board would take seriously the remotest possibility that a respectable white lady like little Madame Viellard would enter into an intrigue with a black man – not even a dusky-hued Caribbean Creole, and certainly not a man so extremely black. Dominique kissed her 'husband' lightly in greeting, and immediately embraced Chloë Viellard as well.

'Darling—'

'Sweetheart—'

The next instant little Herr Coppert was at Minou's elbow with a cup of tea in one hand, a small plate of sweet biscuits in the other, and adoration in his eyes.

And indeed, with her silky brown curls no longer confined in the tignon which Spanish law in New Orleans had once mandated for any woman of color – and which tradition in that city still demanded – Minou could easily have passed for a Spanish or Italian lady, as did many *gens du couleur librés* when they traveled north. January's presence as 'husband' put paid to that illusion, but his perfect French and educated English, coupled with the cost of Dominique's dresses, his own well-bred tailoring, and his ability to hold his own in a chess game with Herr Rosenstein, made him in the eyes of the Europeans acceptable company – particularly since accepting him would include the lovely Minou in their midst.

In fact, the color bar only appeared at mealtimes, but at least the Janvier family dined at a small table in the saloon at the same time as the white passengers, rather than being obliged to eat with the servants. On an American ship they'd have been sleeping in the cargo hold and eating with the crew.

'I was telling M'sieu Janvier,' said Chloë, when Dominique dismissed her suitors and settled in an enormous sighing of lace petticoats on the sofa, 'how poor M'sieu Singletary came to set sail for the United States after spending the first sixty-five years of his life adding up figures for Hurlstone and Ludd's Private Commercial Bank. He wrote to me from Baltimore in the first week of October, to say he had just set foot on American soil and was setting forth for Charlottesville by way of Washington the following day. But he never reached Charlottesville.'

'Had he enemies?' Dominique, her many-colored teacup cradled in slender hands, leaned forward eagerly. 'People who might have lain in wait for him? Or lured him to some private place where they could make away with him?'

In addition to gossip and millinery, Dominique was deeply fond of sensational fiction, of the Venetian daggers-in-the-dark variety. 'As a man who audits the books for banks, he must have *thousands* of enemies!' The dim lamplight glowed in her lovely brown eyes. 'Those who have embezzled money and fear detection; or whom business reverses have driven mad. And if the wife of one such man committed suicide from despair at their ruin, I can easily see that the husband would have followed him on shipboard, waiting for his chance—'

More reasonably, January inquired, 'Did he know anyone in Washington or Charlottesville?'

'Well, Dr Applegrove on the University board,' said Chloë. 'Though they – like he and I – had never met. Another of his correspondents was a bookseller named Deaver in Charlottesville, whom I did know of to write to, when I didn't

44

hear from M'sieu Singletary in three weeks. It wasn't like him, not to write. By the time M'sieu Deaver's reply reached me, saying that M'sieu Singletary had never arrived, I had also received letters from a Dr Woolmer, who runs a boys' school in Georgetown near Washington, and from a Mrs Bray, the married daughter of one of Mr Singletary's banker employers, asking if I, as another of his correspondents, had heard anything of him? It was at that point,' she said, her spectacle lenses flashing as she turned those large, pale-blue eyes back to January, 'that Henri and I decided to speak to you. But by then he'd been missing for over ten weeks.'

'Does he drink?'

'Not that Uncle Veryl had ever heard of.'

'I suppose,' said January thoughtfully, 'that if he did, one of his correspondents – Applegrove, or Mrs Bray, or Dr Woolmer – would have mentioned it as a possible explanation for his disappearance. Did he have any illness that you know of? Something that might have flared up unexpectedly?'

Her smile was like the glint of chipped glass. 'Considering the detail with which he described his *mal de mer* on the voyage over, I assume had anything else been amiss I would have heard of it.'

'What about women?' asked Minou. January had been dying to bring the subject up, but it was not a question that even a white man could ask a white lady, let alone a black one. 'You say he was one of those odd old bachelors, but you know, dearest – or maybe you don't...' She

45

frowned worriedly. 'About how old gentlemen turn into *complete* imbeciles over pretty young girls?'

Chloë tucked her smile away again, like a cat: 'Only old gentlemen in someone else's family.' Her glance did not so much as flicker toward Herr Franck, whose snowy beard and numerous grandchildren did not deter him in the slightest from gallantries toward both women. Then the amusement faded from her eyes. 'I'm not certain whether it's something he'd write to me about. I did ask Uncle Veryl about it – in Latin, to preserve the proprieties: *lascivia puella, et fugit ad salices, et se cupit ante videri* – but he was horrified that I should even *think* of such a thing in connection with the President of the British Mathematical Society. And I did write to the Chief Constable of Washington, several times.'

'And heard nothing?'

'Congress is in session,' said Chloë, who was one of the few women January knew who read newspapers regularly, 'and will be until June or July. Heaven knows what the town is like at such times. It is very close to the North.'

Yes, he thought as he rose and offered Dominique his arm against the slow roll of the ship. It was very close to the North.

He had been to Europe, and he had been to Mexico, nations where, to one degree or another, he had been regarded as a man among other men and not twelve hundred dollars' worth of cotton hand walking around asking to be kidnapped.

He doubted he could return to France. Even after almost five years back in Louisiana, the

46

pain of the loss that he had suffered there – the death of his first wife in the great cholera, which had torn the heart out of him in ways that he suspected might never be healed – was still too great to face, even with Rose at his side. And in Mexico, that land of peril and violence, he had learned that though there was no slavery, black men were almost as little regarded as they were in the United States. It was not a land in which he wanted to bring up his children.

Increasingly, neither was Louisiana.

As he made his way through rainy blackness to the companionway, clinging to the guy rope stretched along the waist of the ship with one hand and to Dominique's slender waist with the other, he thought about the North.

The other half of the United States. The world of factories and traders, where men either worked their own farms or paid a wage for the labor of others. The world where slavery had been outlawed. Where men of color, if they were not permitted to vote or serve on juries or hold office, at least were permitted to choose their own jobs and raise their families without fear of being sold off like cattle when 'Michie' needed some extra cash.

Where he did not know a soul.

Rain smote his face. The ship fled on into darkness.

THREE

When January was not quite eight years old, the smallest of the other boys in the 'hogmeat gang' on Bellefleur Plantation had come running out to the chicken runs where the gang was assigned to clean that day – it was spring, and already hot. He could still smell the reek of chicken guano. The boy had said, 'That man's buyin' your mama, Ben!'

He'd seen 'that man' arrive two days before, a sugar broker from New Orleans, St-Denis Janvier. January – only his name had not been that then, only Ben, or Livy's Ben – knew he'd be whipped for leaving his chores but he'd run to the house anyway, sick with dread. On the back gallery he'd found Senja the cook, and she'd confirmed it: Michie Fourchet had sent for Livy from her work in the laundry, and the three of them were in the plantation office. 'Don't worry, Ben.' Senja had hugged him, a compact woman of Yoruba ancestry, smelling of sweat and molasses. She had a kindness for Ben because he'd cut kindling for her and never seriously tried to steal food. 'Michie Janvier live in New Orleans. That's just a little ways down the river. You can walk it 'fore sunrise an' be back home for breakfast.'

Desperately, he pushed back the tears that burned his eyes. All his short life he'd lived in terror of this moment. Obscurely, he knew, in his heart, that once his mother was gone she'd never bother to walk the short distance from New Orleans out to Bellefleur. She was like a cat, which in her leggy disinterested grace she resembled. Give her her dinner, and she wouldn't pine long if you drowned her kittens.

When she'd emerged from the office – one of the line of *cabinets* that extended from the back of the main house to form a U that funneled the river-breeze – he'd had enough sense of self-preservation not to run to her there. Instead he'd gone roundabout to the two-room cabin they shared with three other families and found her lugging water up from the bayou to wash.

She'd said, 'Ben, fetch your sister,' as she dumped the water into the trough outside the cabin.

'Did he buy you?' Ben had fought to keep the agony from his voice.

She'd pulled off her tignon, regarded him with those enormous brown eyes, like a sibyl's. Dense brown hair, the hue of the hulls of hazelnuts, braided around her face. Her father had been white – presumably a sailor on the ship that had brought her mother from Africa – and she was proud as Lucifer of the sharper features, the higher cheekbones he'd bequeathed her. She worked in the laundry, having displeased Michie Fourchet in some fashion, but Ben knew Fourchet still bulled her and lent her freely to his guests. She was the most beautiful woman on

49

the place.

'Don't be a baby,' she said. ''Course he bought me. Go get your sister.'

Ben thought the command merely meant that she was going to say goodbye to them – Bandy Joe was saddling up the visitor's horse in the yard outside the stables – and considered simply running away into the *riprière* and hiding, to weep until she was gone. But by all accounts New Orleans was a big place, with lots of streets and houses, and he didn't know where in it she'd be or how he'd find her. So he ran as fast as he could to Granny Ya's, where the children too small even to clean chicken coops were kept, and found Olympe, who had already tried to run away and had been retrieved, covered with bayou mud and thrashing like a pissed-off alligator. By the time he and Granny got her to the cabin, his mother had washed and gone on up to the house. Ben had to wash Olympe himself – no small chore – and drag her up to the house, he thought, to see his mother one last time.

Two horses waited in the yard, Michie Janvier's thick-boned gray gelding (whom Ben later learned was named Gustav) and the Belle-fleur overseer's scrubby piebald. In the plantation office, his mother waited, with the white man Ben had seen around the house for the past two days: she standing, he sitting in one of the bent-willow chairs. He was a chubby little man, dark hair already thinning and cut short in the latest fashion instead of braided back in a queue. He had a kindly serious face.

'Ben, Olympe—' She dropped the words
50

almost carelessly. 'Make your reverence to Michie Janvier. He was kind enough to buy you, as well as me. We're all going to go live in New Orleans now, and be free.'

She spoke as if she had always known that it was her due to no longer be a slave. But Ben stared up at that lumpy, sallow face, those pleasant dark eyes, dazzled. He wouldn't lose her. That was what 'free' meant. And he wouldn't lose Olympe, ever...

But it came to him then that he would lose everyone else he knew.

Even at seven and a half, he knew freedom was worth it. But looking out at the saddled horses – knowing that they were leaving *now*, without even going back to gather up their belongings from the cabin (*'What the hell you think we'll need, of that trash?'* He could almost hear his mother saying it) or say goodby to his father or Auntie Jeanne or Granny Ya or his friends Quash and Rufe – he felt the tears flood to his eyes, his throat close on the thanks he knew he should utter. Grief swallowed him, like a minor chord of the music that he had not yet heard.

Olympe ran up, spat on Michie Janvier's shoes, and ran from the room as if the devil were in pursuit.

In the cramped dark of the cabin on the *Anne Marie*, January listened to the hellish roundelay of creaking ropes and squealing timbers, the muffled crash of tons of water against the frail wooden wall beside his cheek, and thought about St-Denis Janvier.

51

Dominique's father.

His mother's lover for nearly twenty years.

Among the several properties Janvier had owned in New Orleans was a cottage on Rue Burgundy, at the sparsely-settled rear of the walled town. This he sold to a free colored labor-contractor named Trouvet, who in turn presented it to Livia, it being against the law for a white man to give property to a person of color. It was also against the law for a white person to marry any person of color, so all over the city, transactions like these went on between wealthy white gentlemen and the *librée* women who 'placed' themselves under their protection. Through similar channels, Janvier arranged for Livia to be paid an annuity and had her two children put in school, Olympe in the Ursuline Convent and Ben in the Acadèmie St Louis for Boys, meaning, Boys of Color.

Ben – though wearing shoes and speaking proper French came difficult for him at first – understood and deeply appreciated these gifts. For her part, Livia Janvier – as she soon came to be called – regarded her new position as a job, and did it thoroughly. She took advice at once on proper dress and deportment, and spent thousands of dollars, over the years, on skin creams, hairdressers, a jaw-dropping wardrobe of gowns and shoes, and the finest in food, wines, and cigars for her lover when he came to visit. For the first few years he lived with her as husband and wife. When January was twelve, Janvier married the widow of a wealthy wine-merchant whose stock and business connections could be of use to the white Janvier family business, but continued to keep Livia as his mistress. This was the custom of the country. In that year of 1807 most of Livia's neighbors on Rue Burgundy were also plaçées.

When January was sixteen – in 1811 – Livia bore St-Denis Janvier a daughter, who from the moment she drew breath was the joy of his existence, the princess of his world: petted, indulged, beloved.

It still astonished January that Dominique wasn't spoiled as well. She easily could have been: she was the only one of Livia Janvier's children upon whom Livia lavished attention and care. In the cabin's pitchy blackness, January could have reached up and touched the ropes of her bunk a few feet above his face; once he heard Charmian wake with a soft cry of *'Maman...'* and, a moment later, Minou's voice, crooning a lullaby January remembered their mother singing to her, one evening when he'd been crossing the cottage yard in the dusk from his own room in the *garçonnière* above the kitchen.

Had he put out his hand to the side of his bunk, here in the blind stuffiness that smelled of lamp oil and badly-cured hides in the cargo hold and twenty voyages' worth of spilled chamber-pots, he would have touched the wall of trunks that filled most of the rest of the tiny chamber: petticoats, laces, pomades, ribbons, shawls.

As far as he knew, his pretty sister had never once expressed a wish that hadn't been granted. He wondered if she'd ever had any that she hadn't dared to speak.

For it had been understood by all, from her birth, that she was expected to become a white man's mistress in her turn.

They landed in Baltimore on Tuesday, the twentieth of March, and on Thursday took the steam-train to Washington City. As in Louisiana, the colored cars were a higgledy-piggledy selection of local businessmen, barbers, clerks, slaves, sailors and prostitutes. Charmian clung to her mother's hand and gazed about her like an Italian princess kidnapped by gypsies. On shipboard she'd taken her meals in their cabin with her nurse Musette and Thèrése, Dominique's maid, and in the saloon she'd been made much of by the other passengers. This was her first experience with the filth and discomfort of hard benches, unswept floors, flying soot and drunken cursing at the back of the car. She looked as if she hadn't made up her mind whether to burst into tears or go over and investigate.

'Pay no attention to them.' Thèrése glared at a couple of loud-voiced market-girls flirting with some sailors. 'They are Americans: drunk as holes and crazy as sticks. You are not to speak to such as they.'

When they disembarked in Washington the noise was worse. Porters shouted, passengers cursed; the squeal of brakes and the rattle of wagons and cabs beyond the platform. A long coffle of slaves passed them, chained neck and ankle: Washington and Baltimore were collec-

54

tion points for the slave dealers who traveled the roads of Virginia, buying men from the old tobacco-plantations whose exhausted soil no longer produced crops enough to support large villages of slaves. In the faces of the chained men, January read the echo of his own childhood nightmare. Some wept; the young men joked with defiant bravado: 'Oh, yeah? Well, *my* marse got nine hundred dollars for *me*...'

Most wore only the shuttered expression of silent despair.

Men loitered on the platform: rough-clothed white men whom January thought at first were waiting for work. But they didn't approach the gangs of stevedores, or speak to the bosses. Just spat tobacco and watched.

He thought it was on the black passengers that their gaze lingered.

Congress was in session, and every boarding house in town was full. Henri and Chloë – and Henri's valet Leopold and Chloë's maid Hèléne and fourteen trunks of books, dresses, waistcoats, hats, seashell collections, a microscope and a barometer – set off for the Indian Queen Hotel with an army of porters and cabs. January sought out the conductor who'd been in charge of their car on the journey, a solemn young man named Frank Preston, and handed him half a Spanish dollar: 'You know a place where my family can get lodgings?'

'I do, sir.' Preston had fetched a cup of water for Charmian during the stuffy, rattling journey and – when she'd thanked him – had replied in excellent French, *'Je vous en prie, Mademoi-*

selle.' 'It's the place I live myself when I'm here in Washington.' He signed for a porter. 'Take this gentleman's trunks to Trigg's on Eighteenth Street.'

'I don't suppose,' said January resignedly, 'that here in the nation's capital the likes of us are permitted to take a cab?'

'No, sir.' The young man's mouth compressed, but he was well-trained to his job, and part of his job, January understood, was to express no opinions while in the uniform of the Baltimore and Washington Railroad. 'But if the ladies don't mind–' he tipped his cap in the direction of Dominique, with whom he appeared to have fallen in love in the preceding hour and a half – 'I'm sure Tim and Ollie here–' he nodded to the porters – 'won't object to taking you up in their wagon.'

Thèrése looked as if she would rather walk three miles across a strange city on a warm spring afternoon rather than accept a ride in a goods wagon – and from Americans who were probably Protestants at that – but Minou at once held out her kid-gloved hands, first to Preston, and then to the two grubby porters, and beamed. 'Thank you, M'ssieux! Charmian, say "thank you" to these gentlemen—'

In her precise little voice, the child said, 'Thank you, M'sieu,' in English – she had every atom of Dominique's charm and more – and then, in French, to Preston, 'Would you please ask them to take special care of my box?' And she held it up: a flat, sturdy rectangle which Rose had given her before they'd set out, lined

56

with cotton, in which for the entirety of the sea voyage Charmian had collected and stored whatever spiders, fragments of seaweed, raveled bits of rope and chips of holystone she could find on shipboard.

Preston bowed deeply. 'It will be my pleasure, Mademoiselle.'

January, Dominique, Charmian, Charmian's doll Philomène, and the two servants followed the procession of porters and trunks out of the station and within an hour were unpacking their things at the boarding house of Mrs Octavia Trigg.

FOUR

'We has breakfast in the dining room from six til nine.' The landlady's mannishly deep tones matched her towering stature and stern, rectangular face. 'Dinner's on the table at six. I keeps some hot in the kitchen till eight. After that, you speak to me if you'll be in late and needin' somethin'. I don't have guests come into my kitchen scroungin' food in the middle of the night.'

Thérése, bred to a world of midnight suppers and after-theater coffee, rolled her eyes at these plebeian strictures, but Dominique nodded and said, *'Bien sûr, Madame.'*

Charmian, clutching box and doll to herself

57

behind her mother's skirts, tugged at Minou's hand and whispered, 'Mama, is that a lady or a man?'

Mrs Trigg's dark eyes touched the child, and a smile softened the corners of her mouth. 'Your little girl speak any English, Mrs Janvier?'

'*Un petit peu.*' Dominique's fingers and thumb measured a quantity the size of a housefly.

'You want to watch out for her.' The smile disappeared, and the gaze that met Dominique's eyes – and traveled on to January's – was suddenly somber. 'And for yourself, m'am, if I may say it. Washington's no safe town for black folks. There's four or five dealers here that don't care where they gets their stock from. Now there's railroads out to Baltimore, a man can disappear in this town and be on a boat bound for New Orleans before his family knows he's late comin' home from work. Police curfew's at ten. These days it pays you be careful where you walk in the day. Get that good-for-nothing husband of mine–' she threw a glance toward the small and dapper Mr Trigg, just descending the stair to the wide front hall – 'to show you round one day, if he gets out of bed 'fore noon...'

'Might I remind you, woman, that those days I get out of bed *after* noon is when I've been working like a ditch-digger—'

'Workin' for some rich man who don't mind if you steals his champagne.' Her smile sparkled in her eyes but didn't touch that unyielding mouth. Half-concealed behind the parlor door, four children of stair-step heights and their mother's coal-dark complexion giggled. There was a fifth

58

girl among them, of much lighter hue and completely different build – Ife, January guessed, compact and small. 'My husband is a musician,' the landlady explained, and Trigg came forward and shook hands all around. 'Seems the white folks in this town doesn't want the black ones around the streets at night unless *they* want somethin' – like a ride home, or someone to serve 'em oysters, or music for their guests to dance...'

January assumed an expression of horror. 'I have never heard of such a thing!'

Trigg grinned.

The rooms to which Trigg showed them – two large connecting chambers on the second floor – were spotlessly clean, the furniture comfortable, and – January found out that evening – the cooking was up to the best he'd had in New Orleans. A Methodist preacher and his family had a similar arrangement across the hall, the third floor being reserved for the single men: Frank Preston and two other conductors on the Baltimore and Washington line, a cab driver, two waiters, and in solitary state at the back a single white gentleman hiding out from his creditors. The four Trigg children helped serve dinner in the long dining-room (the white gentleman had his own small salon across the hall) and Darius Trigg was a fountainhead of information about the town.

'Was that who those men were on the railway platform this morning?' asked January, when the guests (with the exception of the white gentleman) gathered for tea and coffee after dinner in the lamplit double parlor. 'Slave stealers?'

'They *say*–' Trigg took his music satchel from a shelf, sat on the piano stool to sort its contents – 'they're watchin' for runaways. And given that dealers like Klephert and Birch are handing out cash for any man or boy they lay hand to, a lot of 'em *are* runaways.'

'Sometimes they'll come aboard and search the trains.' Frank Preston looked up from the *Washington Intelligencer*, issues of which lay on the parlor's round marble-topped table, along with the New York *Herald*, the *Colored American*, and school books for the children. 'City constables don't take any notice, no more than they stopped the Irish, three years ago, from burning down Negro churches and Negro businesses...'

'Congress has now adopted a ruling that legislation concerning slavery cannot be discussed in its sessions.' The Reverend Horace Perkins grimaced. 'Except of course where it involves more effective pursuit of runaways...'

Then he glanced, almost apologetically, toward his stout little wife Clarice, who sat with Dominique watching over the children as they played pick up sticks, as if to remind everyone that politics ought not to be discussed in mixed company.

Mrs Trigg had informed Dominique that *all* guests beneath her roof were welcome both at her table and in the parlor, so Thèrése – though she had little good to say in private about American Protestant blacks (and she herself, she was quick to point out, was NOT black, but *colored*) – sat a little apart, graciously accepting compliments from a growing court of admiring bachelor boarders.

Trigg took from the top of the bookshelf a leather case which contained a ten-key Steitwolf flute, and for a time he and January talked music, while Dominique started a game of euchre with the Reverend. Under cover of this chatter, January said in a lowered voice, 'I've spoken to a few runaways in New Orleans.'

More than a few, over the past year and a half, who'd spent the night in the secret room under January's house, waiting to be smuggled out of town and on to the long freedom-trail that led north.

'Have you, now?' A smile lifted one corner of Trigg's neat little mustache, as if he read the secret in his voice.

'I have.'

Their eyes met. 'Well, well ... Honored to have you under my roof, sir. I've spoken to a few runaways myself.' He turned his head quickly at the sound of a knock on the outside door. 'And that,' he said, 'will be my boys. There's a ball tonight at Mr Corcoran's – the banker, you know, or maybe you don't – and every Senator in the city will be turning up on his doorstep because his cook is the best in town except for Octavia.' He threw a glance and a grin in the direction of the dining room, now empty and lighted only by the lingering twilight in the windows and the lamp glow from the kitchen beyond. 'We make it a practice to walk over there together once dark falls, and if I was you, sir, I'd make it your practice as well.'

'I shall.' January nodded toward the parlor piano. 'Some evening when you're not stealing some white banker's champagne, maybe you and I could play a little together? That's a fine instrument there.'

Trigg settled his silk-fine beaver hat on to his pomaded hair. 'I'd be more than pleased.'

'You're seeing the town at its best,' said Frank Preston the following morning as he escorted the Janvier party – January, Dominique, Charmian, Musette, and Thèrése – down Connecticut Avenue toward the handsome houses of Lafayette Square.

'*Tiens*!' Minou gazed around her at the vacant fields. Cows grazed peacefully between widely-scattered houses, pigs rooted in roadside ditches. Even this close to the center of Washington – a roughly built-up rectangle that stretched from the President's House to a bit beyond the Capitol two miles away – the houses were countrified, set back from the unpaved streets and surrounded by chicken coops, cow barns, vegetable gardens and orchards. 'And what is it like at its worst, *enfin*? No, darling, this isn't the day we collect insects, you'll get your frock dirty—'

Charmian gazed in agonized regret at the katydid perched on a heart-shaped platform of pickerelweed, but allowed Musette to tug her back to the grassy verge.

'Honestly, Madame, you shouldn't indulge her about insects at all,' sniffed Thèrése. 'Dirty, nasty things. As if Michie Henri weren't bad enough!'

The dank river-fog that had cloaked the city at breakfast time was burning off, the morning's mellowness turning sticky-hot. Beyond the houses of Lafayette Square, a great half-built mass of masonry swarmed with workmen and wagons.

'The new Treasury,' said Preston. 'It's brought hundreds of Irishmen into town to work on it. I'm told there's fights every night, down in Reservation B by the canal, between Irish *b'hoys* and the slave gangs that haul in the bricks from the barges.'

'And what,' inquired January, 'do they plan to put into this nice new Treasury when it's finished?'

Preston looked more than usually grave. 'That I wouldn't know, sir. But Democrats from all over the country are coming into town asking for jobs there—' He extended a hand to assist Dominique over a modest puddle, which in January's fraternal opinion his sister could easily have hopped across herself.

'Those gentlemen there.' Preston nodded toward the knots of men in threadbare coats, spitting and reading newspapers on the steps of several of the grand houses of Lafayette Square. 'First thing the Democrats did, when Jackson got into office, was fire all the men who opposed him and replace them with his own supporters. Senators, and the gentlemen that head up the departments, have the disposal of jobs as well. Last fall, during the Special Session of Congress, you'd see a line outside the President's

House clear to the street.'

'When in the fall?'

'All through September, and the first two weeks of October,' the conductor replied. January guessed his age at just over thirty, and he spoke with the accent of New England. His customary gravity seemed to extend to the protectiveness he'd developed toward Dominique, and he led her along as if he feared the slightest jar would shatter her.

Having seen London, Paris, and Rome, January felt a sort of amazement at the backwater provincialism of this capital city of the country in which he'd been born. Grandiose boulevards stretched for miles, wide as processional ways and unpaved as village cart-tracks, between cow pastures and swampy streams. The brick mansions and commercial row-houses of 'downtown' were more reminiscent of a modest river-port – Baton Rouge or Natchez – than of the national grandeur frequently claimed in political speeches. As they passed the President's House and entered the more populous zones traffic was thick, noisy, and bogged in the mud of the unpaved streets; where the thoroughfares were firm, draymen black and white seemed unable to resist the urge to lash their horses like Roman chariot teams at a dead gallop, scattering pedestrians right and left.

As they sprang clear of one such speeding Jehu, January inquired, 'If a stranger were run down by one of those lunatics, where would they take him? Is there a public hospital?'

'Up on Crow Hill,' said Preston. 'That's a

64

couple of miles north of here.'

'Is *everything* in this town a couple of miles apart?' Thèrése lifted her petticoats to pointedly examine her too-tight shoe.

'What about the police department?' asked January. 'If he were shot in a tavern—'

'You don't want to get anywhere near the constables.' Preston lowered his voice and glanced back at Charmian and Musette, stopped now to gaze in wonder at a stuffed owl in a shop window. 'Nor the jail. There's only one constable to each ward here, and their job is purely and solely to keep black men from "illegally assembling". There's a dealer named Fowler who pays the constables to let him into the jails "looking for runaways". And any likely-looking man who finds himself jailed for having abolitionist newspapers in his possession, or failing to step out of the way of a white man on the street, is going to be "recognized" as a runaway and taken into Fowler's slave jail.'

Preston's mouth hardened. 'Dealers like Neal at the Central Market, and Bill Williams, have their own slave-jails – the smaller dealers pay off the constables to keep their slaves in the public jails. If your friend was a black man—'

'A white man, English. He disappeared here in October.'

'I should go to the Ministry, then. If he was killed in a tavern, the owner would pay off the constables and not report it. But if he were in a street accident, the Minister might have heard.'

Since Chloë Viellard had written to the British Minister as soon as she guessed Singletary was missing, January only nodded, and they passed on to other topics. They were now in the center of town, and the street was lined with boarding houses and hotels, oyster parlors and barber shops, harness makers, livery stables, tobacconists and stationers. At the far end of the street, above a scrim of straggly poplar-trees, the flattish copper dome of the Capitol rose above its shallow hill, like a countryman's hat.

'Last year was a short session,' Preston explained. 'They rose in March. The long sessions, they'll sit through May or sometimes June, if they've a great deal of business. After the short sessions, the Congressmen all go home – many of the foreign ministers as well.

'Most Congressmen come here without their families.' Preston waved at the façade of a grubby clapboard structure grandly named *The Virginia House*. 'Senators sometimes bring them, and gentlemen like Mr Henry Clay, or Mr Daniel Webster, are wealthy enough to rent houses for their terms. But most Congressmen live in rooms and eat around a common table like students at a college. The biggest houses belong to folk like Mr Corcoran the banker, and Mr Peabody who owns buildings all over town. They're the ones that the Congressmen go "calling" on to leave their cards ... Those, and the foreign ministries.'

'Benjamin, look!' Minou caught his arm. 'Oh, the darling thing ... That lady across the street, just look at her bonnet ... Is that Belgian lace, do you think, or French?'

'You'll want to visit Rochelle's up on K

66

Street,' said Preston with a smile. 'Mrs Perkins will take you—'

Thèrése rolled her eyes to indicate her opinion of the sartorial taste displayed by the Reverend Perkins' chubby wife. Dominique said, 'Thèrése, hush! Honestly, I don't know why I put up with you...'

As they neared Capitol Hill, the neighborhood deteriorated. Among the shabby plank boardinghouses and taverns they passed half a dozen buildings which bore signs: SLAVES FOR SALE. Chained coffles of slaves passed them from the direction of the Baltimore road, bare feet thick with gray mud. Everywhere in town January had seen dark faces, but further up the avenue the black men and women he'd seen were well-dressed, like artisans or shopkeepers. Here they wore the clothes of laborers, or the numbered tin badges of slaves. Thèrése ignored them and Dominique seemed to, but Charmian, who had been chattering brightly to Preston, grew silent, and January felt her small, lace-gloved hand tighten around his fingers.

'There.' Preston halted, and his voice sank. 'Across the street in that doorway, see 'em? The man in the green jacket, the woman in the striped skirt...'

January nodded.

To call the man's face bestial would have insulted every harmless four-footed creature God had made. It was, rather, the worst of human: hard, calm, with brown eyes like a doll's, expressionless. The long chin was unshaven, and his long dark hair unclean. He'd been talking to one of the dealers under a sign that said: SLAVES – TOP PRICES PAID – FANCIES, but he turned his head, watched Dominique, January, and those with them with calculation that made January's blood go cold. The woman's round, lumpy countenance would have been pleasant were it not for the watchful squint and the stripe of tobacco-stain down the middle of her chin.

'Mark 'em good,' murmured Preston. 'Those are the Fowlers, Elsie and Kyle. They run the biggest ring of kidnappers in town. They work with all the dealers. They have houses of prostitution, too, just across the Avenue in Reservation C. The yellow man behind them—'

January looked: a man almost his own height and powerful build, with African features, a broken nose, and a complexion little darker than a Spaniard's.

'—that's Kyle's chief driver, Davy Quent. They work with a wagon with a false bottom; two big bay horses with white feet. Kyle, Quent and their boys can knock a man out and have him under the bottom of the wagon in half a minute, tied and gagged. If you see that team or any of the three of them in a place where there aren't a dozen people about, turn around and get out of there as quick as you can walk.'

The line of slaves went by. Davy Quent didn't even glance at them. *This is our job. This has nothing to do with me.*

The Capitol's low hill rose a few streets beyond, surrounded by what was probably supposed to be a lawn of weedy grass. A gang of

68

young men – they could have been apprentices or clerks – played what appeared to be a four-cornered game of cricket: 'That's town ball,' explained Preston. 'They play it all over New England, and the year before last a couple of Massachusetts clerks at the Navy Yard got up a team. Now everyone in town's playing. It's just One Old Cat with Massachusetts rules.'

January had never heard of One Old Cat, but the game looked like what children played on Hounslow Heath, on his one visit to London in 1822. Across the street from the Capitol stood two slave-jails, and the men chained on the bench outside watched the game, and cheered when one or another of the team that was 'up' thwacked the thrown leather ball with a round stick like a cricket-bat, and dashed the circuit marked out with four-foot pegs.

Shallow steps descended from the two wings of the Capitol, where the Houses of Congress met. 'They barred Negroes from entering the Capitol years ago,' said Preston, in that carefully neutral voice he had used at the train station. 'I'm sorry for it, for I would have liked to see the laws of our country made.'

'Maybe that's why they did it,' January said.

The inevitable clumps of office seekers, waiting on the Capitol steps for the appearance of Senators or Congressman who might recommend them for work, watched the ball players, too. Now and then an elected official would emerge from the halls of Congress, dignified in an elegant coat and a tall beaver hat; the office seekers would surround him, practically wagging their tails.

The representatives of Life, Liberty, and the Pursuit of Happiness passed down the steps and within twenty feet of the chained men on the benches without so much as a glance.

Many of them, January reminded himself, had probably seen slaves sold before.

But as they walked away from the legislature of their nation, January found himself remembering the story of Jesus' visit to the Temple: how he had become so enraged at the moneylenders who'd set up shop in its courtyard that he'd taken a whip to them, overturning the tables, scattering the coin, and driving their sacrilegious greedy asses out into the street...

And got nailed to a cross for his trouble.

Jesus, thought January, *where are you now?*

FIVE

'I would not,' said January to Darius Trigg, later that afternoon, 'want your good wife to have wrong ideas about my sister. Hers is a common arrangement, the custom of the country in Louisiana. Henri Viellard has been my sister's protector for eleven years. It isn't...'

He hesitated, seeking a word, leaning in the doorway of the shed where he'd found his host cutting kindling for the next morning's fires.

'It's like a marriage,' he finished. 'For many

70

men in New Orleans, it *is* marriage – they never take white wives. It drives their families insane,' he added, with a certain satisfaction.

'You know–' Trigg drove the hatchet into the block – 'if I had the choice to be rich and white, and barred from ever marrying Mrs Trigg ... I don't think I could do it.'

January thought of that formidable woman, six feet tall and square and solid as a drystone chimney, and smiled at the light in the smaller man's eyes. 'I feel the same way about Mrs Janvier,' he said. 'The *real* Mrs Janvier, back in New Orleans. I was asked to pretend Dominique was my wife, for the sake of appearances, on the voyage out here ... If that kind of arrangement was good enough for the patriarch Abraham in the Bible,' he added gravely, 'it should be good enough for us regular folks.'

'Except that Abraham pretended his wife was his sister,' Trigg grinned, 'not that his sister was his wife ... And I don't care if he *did* have some kind of special deal with God, that business with the Pharoah always sounded fishy to me.'

'Me, too, but I got hit with a ruler by Père Antoine for asking about it.'

'I think we musta gone to the same school.' The landlord rubbed the back of his head reminiscently, then bent to gather up the kindling. January fetched the big willow basket from beside the door. In the yard, eight-year-old Mandie Trigg called to her sister to stop chasing those chickens before she got pecked, and help her with the eggs. 'And this M'sieu Viellard's here in town?'

71

'At the Indian Queen Hotel. With his wife –
who seems to have no objection to the arrangement—'

'If he dies, can I marry her?'

'You wouldn't like it.' January recalled Chloë
Viellard's prim humor and astringent tongue.
'She's often said that she knows she couldn't
make M'sieu Viellard – or any man – a comfortable wife, and that it isn't his fault their
families insisted on the match. And she knows
my sister makes him happy.'

Trigg grimaced. 'I guess it's better than
everybody sneaking around making each other
miserable ... I'll let Mrs Trigg know.'

Upon their return from their tour of the city,
January had found two letters on the table in the
hall, addressed in Henri Viellard's tiny, unread-
able hand. One was to Minou, advising her that
his carriage – hired, coachman and all, for their
stay in the capital – would call for her that
evening, to take her to a house in Georgetown,
also rented for the evening from a Mrs Arabella
Purchase. It was this which had prompted
January's quest for his host, not only to make
sure that Mrs Trigg understood the conventions
inherited from French society which might not
be viewed in the same light by Americans, but to
ask about Mrs Purchase. The memory of
Preston's words about Kyle Fowler and his hol-
low-bottomed wagon lingered unpleasantly.

'Oh, she'll be perfectly safe,' said Trigg, when
January – a little circumspectly – mentioned the
evening's program. 'I know Bella Purchase. She
knows her business depends on a good

reputation and repeat customers. That's the custom of the country here in Washington.'

They climbed the two rear steps to the kitchen door: like the new American houses in New Orleans' Second Municipality, those here in Washington had kitchens built into the back part of the main house, rather than as a separate building across the yard. 'Men are in and out of town all the time. Most of their families are back at home, especially if they live in some God-forsaken place like Wisconsin. Some of 'em just go down to Reservation C if they need their ashes hauled, or visit places like Mrs Newby's over on Louisiana Avenue if they've got the money. But a lot of gentlemen take regular mistresses. Ladies who're maybe married to somebody else.'

He set down the kindling basket beside the wide hearth. 'So there's folks in town who run "houses of accommodation". Nice little cottage, quiet neighborhood, servant or two who know how to keep their mouths shut. Gentleman books 'em for an afternoon, or an evening, same as you'd book a church hall. For a little extra, they'll even arrange to find you a lady. The owners have their regular customers, some of 'em for years.'

'Considering how the overseer of the place I was born on went about getting *his* greens,' said January drily, 'I'm not going to throw stones at any man who commits adultery like a gentleman. Besides,' he added, 'anything that'll put a Senator in a kindlier frame of mind before he goes into Congress is all right with me.'

73

The second note from Henri contained a request that January accompany himself and Chloë to Georgetown the following afternoon, to meet with Rowena Bray, who had had tea with Selwyn Singletary shortly before the elderly mathematician's disappearance.

Georgetown (according to Trigg) was an older community than Washington, slightly upriver on the other side of the wooded gorge of Rock Creek. From what January could see from the driver's box of Henri Viellard's extremely stylish landaulet on Saturday afternoon, it was also a more prosperous one. No cows browsed in its vacant fields, no pigs rooted in its lanes. When the landaulet rumbled across the wooden bridge at P Street and out of the trees, it was as if they had entered another world.

Handsome houses of mellowed brick lined streets of cobblestone or gravel. Further up the bluffs along the creek, January glimpsed a paper-mill and a couple of grist-mills, half-hidden among sweet gum and sycamore just coming into spring leaf. As they turned on to Monroe Street, he saw another group of young men playing 'town ball', shouting like schoolboys: Frank Preston had evidently been right that everyone in town was playing it this year. At supper last night, it had been clear that his host (to Mrs Trigg's outspoken disdain) was captain of a team known as the K Street Stalwarts, who regularly trounced the Alexandria Conquerors, the Georgetown Knights, and even sometimes the formidable Centurions from Judiciary Square. ('Like grown men don't got better things to do...')

'I thought any "assembly" of Negroes is illegal in this town,' January had asked, and Trigg had merely grinned and made a gesture as if counting out coin.

According to Darius Trigg, Luke Bray was a Kentucky planter's son who had been appointed assistant to the Secretary of the Navy by President Jackson, in spite of having never set foot on a boat in his life. His house on Monroe Street boasted a peach orchard on one side and a hedged rose garden on the other, both in the slight state of dilapidation that told January that either there were not quite enough servants, or that the servants weren't being kept to their work.

A liveried slave led them into the parlor, where Mrs Bray – sylphlike, worried-looking, and dressed in a plain dark-blue gown whose sleeves were several seasons out of date – came forward to greet the Viellards in exquisite boarding-school French. 'I was horrified to receive your letter, Madame. Oh, please,' she added, turning her wide green eyes on January, who had remained standing beside the parlor door when the slave bowed himself out. 'Do have a seat, Mr January. My husband and his father will *die* of outrage if they learn of it, but I will *not* turn myself into one of these frightful Democrats for their sakes.'

She clasped Chloë's hand, drew her to the sofa.

'Poor Mr Singletary called on me twice – in fact he was supposed to take tea here again with me on the eighteenth of October. When he didn't

75

come I simply thought he'd forgotten. He's shockingly absent-minded, you know. He said he'd write me when he reached Charlottesville, and I should have worried earlier. It wasn't like him to forget completely, but it *was* like him to forget for awhile, I'm afraid.'

'Do you know where he was staying, M'am?' Being welcomed to sit in a chair was one thing, but January was certain that it was his inclusion in the parlor which accounted for the absence of a tea tray. As on the *Anne Marie*, one could accept blacks with every sign of equanimity, but one would never risk having it said that one ate with such people.

Particularly not if one's husband was ambitious for advancement in the Department of the Navy.

Or was the son of a tobacco planter in Kentucky.

'The National Hotel, I believe he said, though I may be misremembering.'

'How well did you know him?' Chloë leaned forward. 'It sounds strange to say so, but though I feel I've known him half my life, he and I have never met face to face.'

'That sounds *so* like him.' Mrs Bray was, January guessed, a year or two younger than Rose – twenty-five or -six – and not precisely pretty, though there was great vivacity in her thin face. 'He's been in and out of Papa's bank since I was quite a tiny child. Such an odd man, like a big gray bear, at a time when nobody in the City–' January could almost hear the capital letter, as she spoke of London's banking district – 'ever

76

wore a beard. But I never spoke to him – he's very shy. Only when Father wrote to me that Mr Singletary would be passing through Washington on his way to take up this teaching post, of course I invited him to tea.'

She chuckled, amusement turning her face beautiful, like sunlight on marble. 'Mr Bray was here the first time Mr Singletary called and hadn't the slightest idea what to make of him. In many ways my husband is ... I suppose what you in New Orleans would call a *Kain-tuck*, though you could search the earth and not find a nobler heart.' She frowned for a moment, as if troubled at some thought concerning her husband.

Then she gave her head a little shake and went on gaily, 'And of course Mr Singletary, having no more small talk than the kitchen cat, proceeded to explain to him the principles of double-entry accounting, with an aside into methods of converting Turkish lire into pounds, poking at him with his eyeglasses all the while...'

Her smile faded. 'What do you suppose happened to him?'

'I spoke to the Chief Constable yesterday.' Henri straightened his spectacles and fished in his vest pocket for his notebook. 'He said that no – er – body has been found bearing anything that might be identified as his, although I must say the constabulary did not impress me. At the coach office, the clerks said they had no record of anyone of his name purchasing a ticket to Charlottesville, and I can't imagine why he would have done so incognito. Now that we have some idea of what he looked like we can inquire at the hospitals...'

'Surely if he'd been taken ill,' protested Mrs Bray, 'the hospital would have written to me. I know he had my card. In any case–' her dark brows knit – 'when it became clear that Mr Singletary was missing, Mr Oldmixton at the British Ministry – Sir Henry Fox's secretary – sent a clerk to make enquiries along the stage route to Charlottesville. It was then,' she finished simply, 'that I wrote to you.'

In the silence that followed, the voices of slaves drifted from the kitchen, then dimmed as the door closed, which divided the small office at the back of the parlor from the kitchen quarters behind. The long parlor, looking on to the rose garden at the east of the house through three tall French windows, was suffused at this hour with a gentle dimness that would turn into twilight soon. January guessed the two marble busts – one of Athena, the other of a young woman with a hairstyle of fifty years ago – had been brought by this soft-voiced young woman to her marriage; probably the handsome spinet piano as well.

Chloë asked, 'And he spoke of no one else that he might have seen here?'

Mrs Bray shook her head. 'Though conversation with Mr Singletary was always a bit problematic. I wish I'd insisted that he take Mede with him to Charlottesville...'

'Mede?'

'Ganymede, my husband's valet. His Good Man Friday, he calls him – when he's not order-

78

ing him about quite shockingly. An invaluable young man. But Mr Bray wouldn't hear of it.'

Through the long windows January glimpsed a flurry of movement as a groom ran out to meet the horseman who'd come up the drive at a canter on a horse that easily could have cost a thousand dollars. The man who leaped from the saddle was tall, wide-shouldered, and moved with feral grace. Honey-colored hair, straight, clear features ... he sprang toward the front stairs and January heard him yell, 'Mede! Where the hell are you, you lazy savage...? Get my bath ready...'

An expression of tightness fleeted across Mrs Bray's face.

But Henri, his thoughts pursuing other tracks, asked suddenly, 'Should we be inquiring about Mr Singletary's friends? Or asking about his enemies?'

'Enemies?' Mrs Bray looked startled. 'I shouldn't imagine the poor old man had an enemy in the world! What makes you say that?'

Henri frowned, clasping and unclasping his kid gloves in his plump, ink-stained hands. Like his tiny wife, he was nearly blind as a mole, and behind thick spectacle lenses his enormous brown eyes usually had a bovine mildness that most people took for stupidity. 'I took a walk yesterday afternoon along the marshlands where the canal flows into the river,' he said, 'and saw a cerulean warbler and at least three different varieties of *Limenitidinae*, by the way ... But it occurred to me that the Potomac isn't at all like the Mississippi. It's all mudflats hereabouts. If a

79

man were knocked on the head and dumped into the river from the bank, he wouldn't be swept out to sea unless this occurred at the very flow of the tide. Or else, he'd have to have been taken out to midstream on a boat, or dropped from the middle of the Alexandria bridge, which I've observed is closed at night. And both of those procedures sound like a great deal of trouble for casual robbers.'

Mrs Bray looked baffled; Chloë, suddenly thoughtful.

'It's actually quite difficult to completely dispose of a human body, isn't it, Benjamin?'

'That's true,' January agreed.

'I think both of you have been spending entirely too much time listening to Dominique.'

Henri looked disconcerted – as well he might, January reflected, coming from his wife – but he himself only said, 'Maybe. But M'sieu Viellard is correct, Madame. And put in that light, something about the completeness of Mr Singletary's disappearance is ... odd.'

The parlor door flew open; the tall gentleman from the drive stood framed in it. 'Rowena— I'm sorry, I beg your pardon.' He bowed, flustered. His face was older, January observed, than the boyish energy of his body, lined about the eyes and with a kind of settled tiredness in the corners of his mouth. His voice had the soft up-country accents of Kentucky, reminding January of Abishag Shaw's.

'Madame Viellard, Monsieur Viellard,' said their hostess as Henri and January rose, 'my husband. And this is Mr January,' she added, 'who is helping them look for poor Mr Singletary.'

'Good Lord, is he *still* missin'?' Bray yanked off his glove, held out his hand first to Chloë, then to Henri, and then to January, with no sign of sudden death from outrage. 'I do beg your pardon, m'am ... Mrs Bray, is it tonight we're due at that shindig at the Arlington House? There anythin' else beforehand?'

'Dinner,' she said patiently. 'At Mr Creighton's—'

'Damn! Dang,' he corrected himself, with an apologetic glance at Chloë. 'I meant dang, m'am. If you'll excuse me ... Mede!' he yelled, and retreated into the hall. 'Mede, God damn you—'

'It sounds as if you have a busy evening before you.' Chloë rose and gathered her point-lace shawl about her. 'I cannot thank you enough for taking the time to see us. If you recall anything else about M'sieu Singletary – anything he might have said to you, or anything odd about his behavior ... given the general context,' she added, with a quirk of her brows, 'please do send me a note. We're staying at the Indian Queen Hotel.'

Mrs Bray's eyes grew wide. 'You don't honestly think...?'

'I don't honestly think a thing yet. But Benjamin – and Henri – may in fact be right ... and it may behoove us to learn a good deal more about who else M'sieu Singletary might have known in Washington, and how he spent his time here.'

SIX

The following afternoon – after walking out to Georgetown to Mass in the morning, there being no Catholic church in Washington itself – January was inducted into the K Street Stalwarts and the mysteries of town ball.

As January had observed at supper on Friday evening, particularly since the great Virginia slave uprising six years ago, there were statutes on the books forbidding any 'assembly' of blacks, for purposes of playing ball or anything else. ''Fraid the Abolitionists are going to come around handing out pamphlets and fomenting another insurrection,' said Trigg as they left Connecticut Avenue and waded across fields of marshy grass. 'Like we need a bunch of New England white men telling us slavery is bad.'

'Well,' sighed January, 'I guess some of us niggers is so stupid we haven't figured that out yet.'

'And the riot back in 'thirty-five didn't help anything. But as long as we stay out here–' Trigg gestured to the empty pastures that stretched along the stream called Reedy Branch above L Street – 'we're pretty safe. Besides, Madison Jeffers – he's Constable of the Second Ward – brokers the bets on our games and takes a cut.'

Four wooden stakes had been driven into the ground to mark out a sixty-foot square, and an assortment of old goods-boxes and broken fence-rails lined up for the team that was 'up' to sit on while waiting for their turn at bat. Though it was only March, the new grass had already been worn into pathways between the 'bases', and bald circles had developed where the thrower and striker habitually stood. Another game was in progress on the other side of the avenue, and by the shouts of, 'Plug that Whig whoreson!' and, 'You show that tar-heeled skunk!' January deduced that Northern clerks were ranged against Southern ones.

'I suppose it's better than getting in duels,' he remarked to Dominique, who had come out with Clarice Perkins, whose husband, Sabbath or no Sabbath, was an enthusiastic member of the team.

'Or spending all their days in some *salle d'armes* practicing for one. Don't go too far, dearest!' she called after Charmian, who had darted away in quest of the pale-pink trillium that starred the long grass. 'I suppose they're bored,' she added wistfully. 'It's easy for boys, you know, to find things to do in a strange city – even if they aren't hunting for purple emperor butterflies or missing mathematicians. The Reverend Perkins said I might help him teach the children some evenings.' She didn't add, *When Henri is at parties*, and didn't need to. They had seen Henri and Chloë at Mass, sitting in the front pew of Holy Trinity Church with the scattering of clerks and secretaries from the

French, Spanish, and Italian ministries: the rest of the little church had been crammed with Irish b'hoys from the construction crews. That afternoon, the Viellards had joined the rest of Washington society in paying calls.

'The Reverend is nice,' Minou added after a moment. 'He is not how I thought a Protestant preacher would be. Though I don't think I am how he thought a kept woman would be.'

'Has anyone called you that?' asked January sharply.

'Oh, P'tit,' she sighed. 'They don't have to. Madame Trigg has been very kind, and I think she talked to Madame Perkins a little...' She shook her head. 'But it isn't the same here. At home, everyone I know, practically, is *placée*. Or else they're like Rose, or Odile Gignac the dressmaker: their mothers were *placée*. Here, there is nothing between a married lady like Madame Perkins and those ... those *salopes* we saw on the steam train.'

Around the thrower's circle, Trigg and the Reverend clustered with several of the Georgetown Knights to toss a coin for 'first up'. Talk and laughter drifted in the air. It was true, reflected January, that he'd been accepted as a teammate and a brother. That he could seek community anywhere he pleased in this city, while a woman, with her octoroon child...

Minou tucked her hand into the crook of his arm, smiled up at him. 'And I think it *infamous*,' she added in a jesting voice, 'that poor Rose should have to stay home and cook and keep house and visit friends and family, and sit on her

84

own gallery in the evening – all those things I would commit *murder* to do! – when she wants to travel with you and hunt for a man who's vanished off the face of the earth without a trace ... Oh, *look* at that little dog! Such an adorable ... Do you think Henri would get me one? Or should I get a parrot instead?'

'I think Henri would assassinate you,' said January, 'if you got either one. And if he didn't, I would, the minute you brought it into the cabin on the ship going home...'

She made a face at him, then turned her brilliant smile on Trigg as he came back in their direction, swinging the long striking-stick – like a round cricket-bat – and gesturing for January to try a few hits.

'I meant to introduce you to Tice Byrd,' said Trigg, after he and the others on the team had patiently coached January in the art of striking. 'He's the piano man who usually works with me. Now Dan–' he nodded at the tall and extremely handsome waiter who was the best hitter on the team – 'tells me Tice's gone and broke his wrist—'

'He all right?' January knew what broken fingers, broken wrists, or – in his own case a few years ago – dislocated shoulders could do in the midst of a season of entertainments. *The one thing worse than angering a wealthy white gentleman by being right about his fighting nigger...*

'It's a clean break,' said Handsome Dan. 'He was trying to get that sorry brother of his up the stairs to his rooms and the man started to fight him – drunk, of course – and they both went ass-over-teakettle down the whole flight. And of course the brother's just fine...'

'We're taking up money for his wife and kids,' said Trigg. 'But that still leaves me short a piano man Thursday night—'

January flung up his hands. 'Say no more. I'm your man—'

'That's mighty white of you, Ben.'

Amid the laughter of the team, January glanced back in Dominique's direction, saw her standing alone – Thérése had settled on one of the goods boxes complaining about her feet again – watching her child stalk butterflies.

Minou, Charmian, and their little entourage returned with Clarice Perkins to the boarding house as the sun began to set; the Stalwarts and the Knights (and the Patriots and the Panthers, across the way) remained playing until it was too dark to see. 'You just get a little more practice in,' said Charlie Springer – the head waiter at Blodgett's Hotel – encouragingly, 'and you'll be fine.'

'I'll be fine if standing out in the field is what you want to do all day,' sighed January, but there was a chorus of good-natured rebuttals – *No, give him a few games, he'd be fine*! And it was very good, he reflected, to be out, hitting (or trying to hit) balls and running around in the long grass on a spring evening.

Behind him, Handsome Dan said something to the Reverend Perkins that made January prick up his ears: 'What's that about a *National Institution for the diffusion of knowledge*?'

'Congress is trying to put it together,' said the Reverend. 'I think it a laudable scheme.'

'Bet me,' said Trigg, 'that that *knowledge* is going to get *diffused* to white men only.'

'Who in Congress?'

'John Quincy Adams,' said Dan, in his purring South Carolina drawl. 'See, there was this Englishman name of Smithson died ten years back, and he left half a million in gold to the United States, to found an *institution for the diffusion of scientific knowledge for the benefit of all mankind*. And of course the Congress turned around and used it to fund state banks—'

'Which lent it out and then closed their doors and defaulted,' added Springer.

'And Adams,' finished Trigg, 'stood up in Congress – this was a couple of years ago – and said, no, Congress had to put the money back to the original terms of the bequest.' They paused in the darkness opposite the fire station, the dim lights of the scattered houses blurred by the river's rising mist. 'You a scientist, Ben?'

The team split into twos and threes, Trigg, January, the Reverend and Seth Berger the cab driver proceeding along K Street.

'My wife is,' he replied. 'But the man I'm looking for – Mr Singletary – is a mathematician, and it sounds to me like he'd have an interest in this Mr Smithson's Institute. I'd be willing to bet he's written to Congressman Adams about it – maybe even called on him here in Washington.'

Staggered at the temerity of the idea, Berger said, 'You're gonna call on *John Quincy*

Adams?'

'He's a public official.'

'He used to be President of the United States! He's not gonna give you the time of day!'

'He's been fighting for years to get that gag rule about slavery rescinded in Congress,' said Trigg thoughtfully. 'I bet he would, too, give you the time of day, quicker than some other used-to-be Presidents I could name. He's also trying to get the slave trade banned here in Washington—'

The Reverend Perkins' hand clamped suddenly on January's shoulder. Hooves clopped in the thickening mists. Berger whispered, 'Speak of the Devil...'

The men halted in their tracks. 'It's the Devil, all right,' breathed Trigg.

They stood in silence, hidden – January hoped – in fog and darkness as the wagon creaked by. Lanterns on its high front caught the white-furred hooves of the team, outlined the round, motherly face of Elsie Fowler on the box. Glinted on the cudgels of the men sitting in the wagon behind.

In his years in New Orleans, January had several times gone to voodoo dances: seen the gods take the bodies of the celebrants, speak in their voices, handle fire in their bare hands or summon the dead...

And nothing he had seen raised the hair on the back of his neck, as did the sight of that half-glimpsed wagon in the fog, the sound of the creaking harness. *There could be a man in the hollow beneath the wagon bed*, thought January.

A free man, drugged, beaten, tied, gagged and maybe awake enough to know what's happening to him.

At the back of the wagon sat Davy Quent, pock-marked face pale in the lantern-glow, a rifle across his knees.

Or there might not.

And if I ran to the wagon, leaped on it, tried to free that man ... What? I'd be shot and Rose would spend the rest of her life struggling to keep a roof over her head.

And the wagon might be empty.

Mists swallowed the wagon. Like the Devil's eyes, the lanterns mocked him in the wet darkness, then slowly faded away.

Back on Eighteenth Street, dinner was on the table. Afterwards, Trigg got out his flute, and an impromptu dance ensued as he and January familiarized themselves with each others' tricks of rhythm and timing. Not a gentleman passed up the chance to dance with Dominique, with Thèrése, with Musette and fat little Mrs Perkins and the four giggling little girls; even Octavia Trigg got tugged into a waltz by the Reverend. When January and Trigg played 'The Moon', Minou and Octavia sang a duet, voices mingling in the low topaz radiance of the lamps. Glancing through the open door, January saw in the doorway of the opposite parlor, solitary and rather lonely-looking, the white gentleman boarder standing to listen, his dark head bowed.

Tea was brought in, and the children packed off to bed; Mrs Trigg carried a small pot across

89

the dark hall, to serve to her white boarder in his kingly isolation. When she returned, she fetched the letters from the top of the piano and handed two to January.

One was from Henri Viellard, on the stationery of the Indian Queen Hotel.

Mr Janvier,

Enquiries at the National Hotel reveal no record of any Selwyn Singletary having stayed there, either in October of 1837 or at any time before or since. The register does not list his name, nor is the hand on any other name in it familiar to myself or to Madame Viellard. The manager, a M. Breckenridge, disclaims any recollection of an Englishman of Singletary's description.

However, the British Minister, Sir Henry Fox, informs me that M. Singletary left a card upon him on the 12th of October and was to have come to call on the 20th, an appointment which he did not keep. Sir Henry's secretary, a Mr Old-mixton, is as Mrs Bray attested well acquainted with Singletary. Madame Viellard and I will dine at the Ministry Wednesday night, and inform you of all we learn.

Yours respectfully,

H. Viellard

The second note was written in kitchen-pencil on extremely fine paper, in a hand at once firm and unpracticed.

Mr January,

My name is Ganymede, valet to Mr Bray. The last time he came to the house your friend Mr S left his notebook in my care and said keep it

90

secret from every living soul no matter who. I have not known what to do with it. Would you meet me at the Paper Mill Bridge where P Street runs over Rock Creek tomorrow afternoon at four? Mr S said that he was in fear of his life.

Yr ob't s'vt

Ganymede Tyler

SEVEN

'Why did he leave this with you?' January turned the notebook in his hands. It was old and much thumbed, red Morocco-leather, stained and flaking.

Mede glanced over his shoulder, where the road ran into the wooded bluffs that hid George-town from the bridge. 'First time he took tea with Mrs Bray, he'd walked out here from town, sir.' His voice had the soft inflection of Kentucky, but January didn't need that to know that Luke Bray's 'Good Man Friday' was one of the slaves he'd brought with him from his father's plantation.

Mede, some ten years his master's junior, was almost his double. His complexion was a generation or two more dusky, his hair the hue of molasses rather than honey; the blue of his eyes tinged with the turquoise-gray familiar to January from the *sang mêlé* community of New Orleans.

91

Mede Tyler was Luke Bray's brother. His father's son, by one of his father's slaves.

'When it came on to rain, she asked me to drive him back—'

'Where was he staying?'

'I don't know, sir. As we were coming down Pennsylvania Avenue, he asked, would I take him on to the Capitol instead, so he could look at the Library. On the way he asked me about my family, and Red Horse Hill Plantation ... Not prying,' added the young man, as if anxious to absolve the old Englishman of nosiness. 'You know the way some Northerners do. He asked as if I was just anybody he'd met on a train. He was a funny old gentleman, sir, but a very kind one.'

January opened the notebook. The first half was filled with what looked like jottings, page after page of what January recognized as 'magic squares' – mathematical puzzles in which all numbers in the rows of a grid added up to the same sum – interspersed with formulae and calculations. Some of these were in pencil, others in various colors and strengths of ink, made over the course of months or years. The last six pages, however, had all – by the appearance of the ink – been made at the same time. Two columns of numbers side by side ran over all six pages, and at the bottom of the last page, a thick block of numbers.

17
21   Ø6191425   Ø7   Ø5
Ø720171316232001151722131623   Ø821
Ø6241424   Ø323101113   Ø1221124   Ø3
Ø8101210202 520

17151814 Ø42419 Ø120251420 Ø4 Ø125
Ø121 Ø7201924 Ø3201622 Ø11219 Ø6 Ø3 Ø4
Ø22014 Ø12224 Ø8

171519241Ø232521202516 Ø1 Ø61925 Ø8
Ø4 Ø8 Ø3 Ø81225 Ø12212 Ø2 Ø62119141219
Ø71324102217121913 Ø6

171521 Ø5 Ø6 Ø712 Ø11321 Ø22120191413
Ø424121324 Ø3 Ø221221920 Ø713 Ø612
Ø32025

'I think he was one of those people who really
doesn't see if a person is white or black or a man
or a woman,' Ganymede went on as January
flipped the fragile pages. 'Like I was a nun
behind a curtain in a convent, and he couldn't
see who or what I was at all. So he'd forget I
wasn't free to do the things he did, or he sort of
assumed everybody in the world understood
arithmetic or liked cauliflower. To tell the truth,
I felt a bit sorry for him. What's the good being
a free man, if you have no friends and no family?
I'd never have said so to him,' he added quickly.

'Then when he came to the house the second
time, he came early, and Mrs Bray was out. I
brought him in some tea, and we talked a little
more. He was all wound up, pacing like a dog
in a windstorm. I asked him, was something
wrong, and he said someone was trying to kill
him; that someone had broke in and searched his
rooms the night before.'

'He have any idea who it might have been?'

The young servant shook his head. 'But he was
scared, sir. He said he woke in the night and
someone was there, moving around in the dark.

He cried out and the intruder shoved him over and fled; he said in the morning he found a knife on the floor that wasn't his.'

Mede was silent. Beneath the bridge, the creek purled over its stones.

'That's why I'm giving this notebook to you, sir,' he said after a time. 'It was starting up to rain again when he left, and I walked him with an umbrella to where Jem had brought his chaise. When we got to the chaise he put this book into my hand and said, "Keep this for me. I'll send you word where to send it, but don't let anyone – not a living soul – know you've got it." Then he got in the chaise and drove off fast.'

Daylight was fading already: January had reached the Paper Mill Bridge just before four, but the young valet had not arrived for nearly forty minutes. 'Did he speak of anyone else he knew in Washington?'

'He did, sir. That first time, he said he should call on Dr Woolmer at the Potomac School, so I guess he hadn't yet. And he spoke of Mr Adams – the gentleman that used to be President – and of Mrs Bray's friend Mr Oldmixton that works at the British Ministry. But I thought—' He ducked his head, unwilling for a moment to admit what he'd thought, and it went through January's mind:

He was afraid they were in on it.

Or would talk to someone connected with the intruder.

'When we were in the chaise that first time, sir,' Mede went on after a moment, 'Mr Singletary also spoke of Mr and Mrs Viellard in New

94

Orleans, who he said were his friends. Lodie –
Mrs Bray's maid, sir – said Saturday that Mr and
Mrs Viellard was here, looking for Mr Singletary, and that you were with them and looking,
too.'

'Lodie listens at doors, does she?'

Mede let a little silence lie between them
without answering, then said, 'You – nor Mr and
Mrs Viellard – weren't here in Washington when
Mr Singletary disappeared, sir. And if they came
all the way here to look for him, they can be
trusted. I hope so, sir, because before God I don't
know what else I can do.'

'Did you look in it?'

'I did, sir, yes, that night, after I'd got Marse
Luke settled. I could make nothing of it.'

The light was nearly gone. Ganymede looked
over his shoulder again, and January guessed
that the valet had stolen away from his master's
house. He wondered if 'Marse Luke' beat his
valet, brother or no brother.

What was it, he wondered, about those tiny,
regular figures that caught his attention...?

'I told him,' Mede went on, 'it could be just a
robber. Thieves break in hotels all over town,
looking for a gold watch or a silver pen—'

A pen.

'He had a pen.' January looked up from the
notebook's pages. 'One of those new reservoir
pens—'

'Yes, sir. He showed it to me on that first ride
to the Capitol, told me how it worked. I couldn't
make heads or tails of it.'

The ink lines don't change shape as a quill's

do...

That's why all those tiny numbers look different.

A friend had showed him one in Paris some years ago. It had bled ink like a stuck pig.

'Silver?'

'Yes, sir. I'd never seen one before. Marse Luke takes steel-nib pens from the Navy, for his office upstairs, and Mrs Bray has a gold one downstairs, for doing the books.'

'And had he a gold watch?'

'He did, sir. He looked at it as I was driving him.'

'Could you describe it? Initials? Design?' And, when Ganymede shook his head: 'Anything else of value that you remember? Fobs? Fob chain? Pin?'

'He had a pin, sir. He wore an old-fashioned stock, like Marse Luke's grandpa.' The young man grinned a little, at some memory of that old man back in Kentucky. 'What Grandma Bray calls a baroque pearl. Not round, but lumpy. It looked just like a tiny fist clenched up. He had a fob seal, but I never saw what it was. The top of it was shaped like a little chess-piece, when they don't want to make a whole little soldier for a pawn, but just a ball on the top. More than that I don't remember, sir—'

'That's enough.' January thrust the notebook into his pocket. 'And thank you, Mede, more than I can say, for coming out here to meet me like this.' He clasped the young man's hand. 'Now head on back, before you get into trouble with Mrs Bray.'

'Will what I told you help you find him?' The valet's expression told January more than words could have, about the old man's friendliness and concern for someone he didn't have to pay attention to at all.

'After all this time I may not be able to find him,' January said. 'But if one of those items turns up in a pawn shop, I may be able to find the man who took them off him.'

Not even the twinkle of lamplight shone in the formless distance as January quickened his step across the bridge. He followed the curve of the road up the uneven banks of the creek, aware of how isolated this spot was. The moon had not risen and no light penetrated the shadows beneath the trees. He hoped the creak and rustle away to his left was a fox, or one of the capital's ubiquitous pigs. He strained his eyes, seeking the movement—

A fragment of breeze brought him the mingled stink of tobacco spit and dirty clothes.

It was gone an instant later, but his heart froze in his breast.

The breeze had come from his right.

To his left, another rustle, which stopped the instant after his own footfalls did. Harness jingled somewhere as a horse tossed its head.

Oh, Jesus...

He turned back toward the bridge and saw a shadow for a moment on the pale trace of the road.

It disappeared into the trees, but he knew it for a man.

*The wagon in the black mists of K Street. The
glint of lantern light on the barrel of a gun.*

He reached down and slipped from his boot the
knife that he would have been arrested for
carrying. What good it would do him, he didn't
know: there were at least three of them, possibly
a fourth somewhere in the dark woods.

He'd stood too long. Feet crunched the leaves
to his right. He wondered if leaving the road and
striking out cross-country would save him. He
could at least get up a tree, if he could locate one
suitably large in the dark. Against the blackness
of the woods he saw movement, closing in on
him...

'*Ben*!' shouted a voice, and a lantern flashed
on the road ahead of him.

January swung around, startled at the sound of
his name—

'Ben, goddamit, when I sent you to take those
books to Mr Smith's this afternoon I told you not
to be all goddam day about it!'

The man striding up the road toward him, lantern held high, was Mrs Trigg's white boarder.

January immediately gave the guiltiest flinch
he could manage and scurried toward his bene-
factor – kidnappers would carry off any free
black they could find, but a white master would
make serious trouble to recover a piece of
property worth fifteen hundred dollars. 'Marse
Poe–' he was astonished he remembered the
man's name – 'I swear I wasn't just foolin' away
the time! Marse Smith wanted me to move some
bookshelves for him—'

'Marse' Poe caught January by the arm – he

98

was a good eight inches shorter, slender and elegant despite the shabbiness of his black greatcoat – and shook him. 'Don't you give me your excuses!' In the light of the upraised lantern their eyes met, Poe's warning: *Play along*...

January nodded very slightly, and Poe thrust him roughly back in the direction of Washington.

'I swear...' he began again.

'And I swear I'll wear you out with the buggy whip next time you go off on your own,' retorted 'Marse' Poe, and he stalked away up the road, January scurrying meekly at his heels.

Behind them, the woods were silent.

They'd gone about fifty yards before Poe breathed, 'They still back there?'

'They're not following us.'

'Well, thank God for small favors, anyway.' His soft voice had the accent of Virginia. 'I apologize if I spoke insultingly, sir. Had I leaped to your defense shouting, "You shall not drag this poor nigger into slavery!" they'd probably have shot me.'

'It was damn quick thinking, sir. Thank you. But I fear I've disrupted your evening's plans – you were on your way to Georgetown, I think?'

'No great matter. One of those gatherings at which one barely knows one's hostess but tries to insinuate oneself into an introduction to another of the guests. A disgusting practice, but apparently how things are managed in these degenerate days, and beggars can't be choosers. Outwitting slave stealers in the woods has infinitely more appeal than convincing some

Western Congressman of what a good post-master I'd make.'

'I'm grateful,' said January simply. 'And a little amazed you recognized me at that distance in the dusk. I don't think I'd have stopped if you hadn't called my name.'

'Well, at your height you are difficult to miss.' They were coming clear of the trees. The first lights of the Washington houses had begun to twinkle, far off to their right. Behind them January heard the clop of hooves, the creak of harness, and stepped quickly aside. A wagon came past in the gloom: four men, dark against the paler sky. Dark horses, white feet.

Whether the men looked down at him and his 'master' as they passed, he couldn't tell.

'You think they've caught some other poor devil?' whispered Poe.

'They may just have given up for the night. It isn't a frequented road.'

But the thought of how close he'd come to lying bound in that coffin-like space, listening to the sounds of Washington's streets around him and knowing what he was going to, made him shiver. He said again, 'Thank you, sir. You didn't have to do what you did.'

Poe shook his head. 'I'm no abolitionist, but I'll not stand by and watch someone who's legally gained his freedom have it taken away from him – certainly not by the likes of some of the scum one sees lollygagging about this town.'

They turned down one of those long, pointless avenues that stretched from nowhere to nowhere in Washington, surrounded on all sides by empty fields and thin woods. 'And your playing has given me a great deal of pleasure.'

'I think that might be a case of "turnabout is fair play".' Poe glanced back at him, and January nodded toward the ink-stains on the man's frayed cuff, where the lantern's light showed them up. 'You wouldn't be Mr *Edgar* Poe, who writes for the *Richmond Intelligencer*, would you?'

'The same.' He looked both a little shy and tremendously pleased.

'My wife and I both are great admirers of your reviews. And your poetry is some of the most astonishing I've read. And I'm not saying that,' he added with a wry grin, 'just because you rescued me back there. Whenever we can get the *Intelligencer* in New Orleans, we look for your work.'

'You're most kind, sir. It's always gratifying to hear that one's work is appreciated – particularly that far afield. I had hoped – indeed, it has always been the aim of my life – to be the first American to make his living solely by his pen, as Pope and Johnson did, though of late it's been borne upon me that this might not be possible. America is less than – kind – toward those from whose work money cannot be gleaned. Hence this evening's quest for an introduction to the Right Honorable Representative Thumbtwiddle of Ohio, or whatever the man's name is.' A note of grimness edged his voice. 'Still, one lives in hope.'

They reached the Western Market, lanterns moving about its brick arches like fireflies where a final few vendors packed up their goods. To the south, among the larger houses, more lights glimmered, and carriages proliferated as the business of the government went forward at dinners, receptions, balls. The wealthy bankers, landowners, planters who dwelled in Washington spread feasts of Virginia ham and plum tarts for Senators wearied of boarding house fare, and ambassadors whose ancestors had ridden with Richard the Lionheart bowed respectfully to the dapper little son of a New York tavern-keeper in the White House. Men in shabby greatcoats and beaver hats a few years out of fashion attended gatherings put on by would-be political hostesses, in the hopes of insinuating introductions to someone who could recommend them for a paying job.

Other men, dressed more shabbily still, drew rein in the alleys behind the slave pens down near the Capitol and unloaded mutely-struggling cargoes from beneath false wagon-beds, or half-carried stupefied men into brick cells by the light of shaded lanterns.

'And you, sir?' asked Poe. 'Are you also here in Washington on business?'

January slipped his hand into his coat pocket and touched the worn binding of the notebook Ganymede Tyler had handed him. 'In a manner of speaking, sir. In a manner of speaking.'

EIGHT

By Thursday afternoon – Henri's note informed January – Chloë had inveigled an invitation to the reception and musicale being given that night by the Right Honorable Representative from Massachusetts, John Quincy Adams, at which January, under the aegis of Darius Trigg, was scheduled to play.

From the dais at the end of the ballroom, January saw them enter the handsome house on F Street: Henri in silver-gray bore exactly the appearance of a whale escorting a mermaid. Mrs Adams – a delicate Englishwoman some ten years January's senior – greeted them with great politeness, but Mr Adams was effusive, expressing – in fluent French – the hope of speaking to them at length later in the evening.

As he played Schubert's Leider, operatic barcaroles and the sentimental ballads of Moore on the Adams' Broadwood grand, January observed the guests, to whom he was – he knew – for all intents and purposes invisible. In this new city he might not have his mother's gossip to rely on about everybody's family background, finances, and extramarital escapades, but this lack was more than offset by the knowledge that these were the men about whose policies and foibles he'd been reading for years in political broadsides. Between glees and serenades, Trigg or Blair Langston, the elderly violinist, would pass information to him in a whisper: 'Tall gentleman's Mr Clay of Kentucky – handsomest man in America, my wife says ... and flirts something shocking, if I do say it of a white man! That lady there is Mrs Corcoran, that's daughter of Commodore Morris the Navy Commissioner. She run off with Mr Corcoran a few years ago – that's Mr Corcoran over there. Richest man in Washington ... Fellow in the green uniform's Mr Vorontsov, that's minister from Russia – I don't know who that lady is he's with, but it sure ain't *Mrs* Vorontsov...'

January wondered if he'd be more impressed by this parade of notables had he been permitted to vote. But even the sight of Massachusetts Senator Daniel Webster – for whom January would have voted, had it been possible, in the last election – only served to remind him of all he'd seen in his week in Washington: muddy streets, slave pens twenty feet from the Capitol. Frank Preston saying, 'They barred Negroes from entering the Capitol years ago...'

A wagon creaking by in misty darkness.

If you'd been elected, he wondered, watching the Senator's square, commanding form cross the reception-room toward the punchbowl, *would you have tried to change these things?*

Or would you have argued that it was 'inexpedient' to offend the Southern states, and let the situation stand?

But since it was, perforce, not his business, he

104

let his mind slip back into the pleasure of the music. The Adams' piano had clearly been pampered like a racehorse, and the keys responded to the lightest touch. Prior to supper, the reception was an occasion for talk and pleasantries in the ballroom, with the fashionable alternatives of card-playing and billiards in the library across the hall. The host – a diplomat from the age of fourteen – might be notoriously prickly, unsociable and incapable of political compromise, but he made sure he spoke to every man and woman in the room, inquiring of Henry Clay how his son's racehorse was shaping up and complimenting the President's dapper son on his engagement to a wealthy planter's daughter. He even flirted a little with Dolley Madison, still vividly pretty despite rouge and embonpoint.

'*Ma chère Madame Viellard!*'

Mrs Bray, flower-like in rose-hued silk and masses of blonde lace, detached herself from her husband's arm and fluttered over to Chloë, hands outstretched in greeting. Luke Bray made a beeline for the junior Congressmen, clerks, and attachés clumped around the punchbowl, and within moments January could see by their gestures that town ball was the subject of the conversation.

'Better if you throw it side-arm-around–' he demonstrated the grip on an empty punch-cup – ''stead of underhand...'

('Ten cents says he forgets and throws that thing,' whispered January to Langston the fiddler, who nodded agreement without missing a note.)

'Can you *do* that?'
'*No*—'
'Who says?'
'Everybody says.'
'The rules says.'
('Think they're going to get in a fight over it?'
'They will if one of the Massachusetts Whigs comes over...')

A cluster of ladies – including the vivacious Widow Madison – descended upon Chloë and Mrs Bray, and January caught wisps of talk about the ministries, Senatorial receptions, who must be conciliated and who cold-shouldered. The invisible magic behind politics, January was well aware from his days playing for the restoration nobility of Paris; the decisions made outside of Congress, and the women who engineered meetings or prevented them. Rowena Bray, he observed, for all her air of dewy-eyed helplessness, knew everyone, and in the course of the evening made the rounds of the room, as surely as her host and Mrs Madison and Henry Clay and the President's son, speaking to everyone, unerringly recalling everyone's name and face and interests.

If some turned away from the English Minister, with hard words about the Canadians' right to fight for their own freedom ('We should have marched up and took 'em when we had the chance!'), Mrs Bray's marriage to an American seemed to have softened at least some of the animosity. ('Why should you care, sir? You want us to shed our blood so you can force the Canadians to send back your escaped slaves?')

The only person, in fact, who didn't seem to be arguing politics, discussing town ball, or seeking an introduction to someone in quest of a job was Henri Viellard, working his way through lobster patties, crème tarts, and marzipan on the buffet with the steady inevitability of an ox pulling a plow.

'Not to worry,' Trigg reassured the musicians as they filed off the dais. 'If Sir Henry–' he nodded back in the direction of the British Minister, deep in conversation with Mr Clay – 'was to announce that England was sending troops into Canada *tonight*, I don't think anybody would have the nerve to pick a fight in Mr Adams's house.'

With a glance at the delicate, smiling, steely Mrs Adams – and at the cold sharp eyes of the Right Honorable Representative from Massachusetts – January guessed that Trigg was right.

In any case, Sir Henry Fox was clearly not about to announce invasion that night or much of anything else. Already visibly drunk, he disappeared almost at once into the gaming room. It was his secretary, a sturdy, pink-faced gentleman attired point-de-vice in a long-tailed coat and knee-smalls, who intercepted questions from irate New Englanders about the rebellion in Canada, and who smoothed the feathers of a much-ruffled Secretary of War.

'You think we'll really go to war over Canada?' asked January as they descended the narrow stair to the kitchen – suffocating with the stink of lamp oil and onions and jostling with servants as they organized the supper's opening

107

course.

'What the hell else we gonna do?' demanded Phinn Mudwall, who doubled clarionette and cornet in the little orchestra. 'Wring our little hands and say, "Oh dear"? They came across the Niagara river, seized one of *our* boats on *our* side, *burned* it, and sent it over the Falls with all hands—'

'I heard there was only one man killed.' The musicians edged around the turmoil, ascended the stair that led to the yard. The night air was cold, and fog held in the smoke of the cressets that burned in the yard, where a dozen carriages – their teams snugly blanketed – were ranged between the house and the stables.

'That makes it better?' Mudwall drew himself up, hugely indignant for a man who wasn't allowed to vote. 'One dead man or a dozen—'

'The ship was taking supplies to the Canadian rebels. What would we have done, if the French or the Spanish sent guns to the Cherokee a couple of years ago when Jackson had them run out of Georgia?'

'That's different!' boomed Mudwall. 'That's a completely different issue!'

A voice from the depths of the kitchen called up that sandwiches and beer were ready for the musicians. At the same moment, around the corner of the house, reflected light from the torches caught in rectangular spectacle-lenses, and January said, 'Save me a sandwich, would you?' as the others went back into the door and down the stairs. He crossed the porch as the rotund silhouette detached itself from the corner of the house.

'Did you speak to Mr Adams, sir?' January said as Henri stepped into the glow of the lantern above the porch. The mere fact that Henri would make himself late for dinner – particularly in light of the reputation of the Adams' cook – argued a deep concern indeed for his missing friend.

'I did. You were quite right: not only had M'sieu Singletary corresponded with M'sieu Adams for years, but he visited him on October tenth. M'sieu Adams says they spoke of astronomy and the respective school systems of the United States and Britain, of the proposed Smithsonian Institution, and of the contents of their libraries. No mention whatsoever of mutual acquaintances in Washington, and certainly not of anyone who would wish poor Singletary harm.'

'But someone seems to have.' January produced the little red-bound notebook from his pocket. 'Singletary gave this to Ganymede Tyler – Mr Bray's valet – on the fourteenth because someone had broken into his hotel-room the previous night. Someone he feared was not a thief, but a would-be murderer.'

Henri's brown eyes widened as if he'd read bad luck in the pulling of daisy petals and moments later had witnessed a comet destroy Washington.

'Murderer?'

'According to Tyler.' January wondered if Tyler had been the surname of Mede's mother, or if he'd later chosen it for himself. 'And it sounds to me as if Singletary suspected the danger might be coming from someone he knew or might know. It may pay me to make the journey down to Charlottesville—'

'Oh, that's hardly necessary.' Henri looked up from peering at the notebook's pages in the glow of the nearest cresset. 'We also spoke with Mr Oldmixton – Madame Viellard and I did – the secretary from the Ministry who sent a clerk to make enquiries along the Alexandria–Warrenton road about whether the body of a traveler had been found. Have you any idea what these numbers might be?'

January shook his head. 'But the two long columns there at the back aren't precisely identical. In that second column there'll be a set of about a dozen numbers identical to the first, then one that isn't in the first, or sometimes two or three ... then another set of a dozen that are the same.'

'The writing is different.' Henri moved his chubby thumb down the page. 'Look how the numbers in the first column slant and run together, while those in the second are neat and wider-spaced.' He frowned up at January, standing above him on the step. 'Might they have been written on different occasions?'

'No reason to think they weren't.' January studied the small differences in the hand. 'I'm guessing they're simply *aides-memoires*, the context of which Singletary understood. That short block of numbers at the end with a seventeen at the top, I have no idea what it means.'

'Would you be willing to make a copy of this?'

110

Henri riffled the pages of magic squares, his fair brows drawn down over his nose. 'I'm not certain Madame Viellard would be able to make more of it than yourself, but she's far cleverer than I with numbers.'

'I'll do that.'

'If our poor friend handed the book to a servant rather than to his hostess – with whom he'd been taking tea moments before...' He glanced worriedly at the lighted windows of the dining room. 'You don't think he feared *her*?'

'More likely someone she might speak to of the matter.' January reflected on young Mrs Bray's constant airy chatter and the way she clung to the arm of the British Minister or his secretary. 'And she's the daughter of Singletary's employer. If he learned something to the discredit of Hurlstone and Ludd – or if he came to be mixed up in something that would damage the firm – he might hesitate to tell her about it. Even a comment in a letter to her family back home might be enough to topple a house of cards ... if a house of cards is what Singletary was building.'

Across the yard a gust of laughter came from the stables, where coachmen and grooms diced by lantern light.

'At this point we can't know, sir. But Mede gave me a description of Singletary's watch, pin, and watch fobs, so with your permission I'll ask around at the pawnshops—'

The kitchen door opened, and Trigg put his head out. 'I can't keep Phinn's greasy hands off your sandwich much longer, Ben. You better get in and eat it 'fore he kills his brother over your beer.'

'Tell 'em I'll drown the both of 'em in the rain barrel if they even think of takin' it!'

He glanced back to the driveway, but Henri was gone.

January was aware that the 'musicale' portion of the evening – which customarily meant the little orchestra of piano, flute, cornet, violin and violoncello playing for various of the female guests to sing – was always something of a mixed bag. But he knew also that the point was the pleasure of the singers and their personal friends and relatives, not the excellence of the performance, and in any case many of the young ladies who participated were quite good. Mrs Bray sat with Mr Oldmixton of the British Ministry, as neither the British Minister himself nor Luke Bray would desert the card tables of the library to listen. But when the dancing started at eleven, the younger clerks and secretaries from the Navy Department and Treasury emerged from the smoke-filled chamber with the news that a challenge had been issued by a ball team made up of their opposite numbers in the various foreign ministries.

'You got to play, Stockard!' proclaimed Luke Bray in a loud and slightly drunken voice, clinging to the arm of the Right Honorable Junior Representative from the State of Alabama. 'The honor of America is at stake!'

'The honor of America and my twenty dollars—' added a slight and rather chinless young gentleman whom Langston had earlier pointed out as the son of a prominent local planter.

'Hell, Luke, Miss Russell says she'll kill me if I don't come to this tea-squall her ma's giving Saturday.' Stockard was a little older than his teammates, broad-shouldered, curly-haired, and resplendent in a waistcoat embroidered with hearts and skulls.

'A woman who don't enter into her husband's interests and concerns – let alone keeps him back from upholdin' the honor of his country – is no bride for a Congressman, Stockard.'

'What the hell do Frenchies know about playin' ball, anyway?'

'I dunno,' opined somebody else. 'That feller Lenoir can knock that ball clear across the Canal.'

'They're nancies—'

'The Warriors can rub 'em out, same as we mopped up them snot-nosed abolitionists from the Treasury last week—'

January smiled as he followed the lead of Trigg's flute through the figures of the Quadrille. Silk petticoats whispered, dancing slippers patted on the waxed oak of the floor. Gas flames bent with the passage of the dancers: jeté and rigadoon, chassé and pas de basque. The pacing differed from the more sedate New Orleans style, with a sort of peasant verve. Chloë Viellard danced every dance, with Henry Clay and Daniel Webster and Brom Van Buren, and even coaxed Mr Adams out on to the floor – probably talking to him in French about astronomy the

113

whole time. Henri, no matter what longing he may have felt for a quiet evening with Minou, crème caramel, and his butterfly collection, danced also, with surprising grace for a man of his bulk, deftly squiring the formidable leaders of Washington fashion like Mrs Madison and the elegant Sophie Hallam, and shy matrons like the lovely Mrs Lee.

Rowena Bray danced not at all. Her husband would now and then blunder, red-faced with liquor, from the gambling tables in the library, then return almost at once to his cronies. He was still there when the guests began to call for their carriages, and Mr Adams and his wife bowed and shook hands and acknowledged a hundred variations of, *Thank you so much for having us, we have had a splendid time...*

At four, the musicians packed up their instruments. The fog was now thick outside. Rugs were pulled from the backs of the carriage teams; servants sent to the yard, or out to the square where a dozen equipages had been forced to wait all evening beside makeshift bonfires. Since all the musicians lived above K Street, they waited together on the narrow back porch while Trigg collected their pay from the Adams' major-domo. Around the corner of the drive January heard Luke Bray shouting incoherently as his friends led him down the steps to his carriage.

'—not fucken drunk! Everybody in this goddam town acts like a bunch of Christly Puritans if a man takes one goddam drink—'

'You watch the step here, Mr Bray,' said a

voice with a Northern twang to it, and January, stepping to the end of the porch, saw a lean-faced young senior clerk assist the Right Honorable Representative Stockard in getting Bray down to the drive.

'Don't you goddam tell me what to do, Noyes, you goddam suck-arse abolitionist!' Bray swung at him; Stockard grabbed Bray's arm, and a dark figure sprang down from the footman's perch of the carriage.

'Now, Marse Luke, it's nothing to get yourself in a conniption over,' said Ganymede Tyler's familiar soft voice. 'You just sit here for a spell – no, up here, where it's soft – and you'll feel better by and by...'

The stocky form of Mr Adams appeared on the porch, Mrs Bray leaning on his arm.

'Are you sure you wish to ride with him?' the Massachusetts Congressman asked. Adams had the reputation of a cold-fish intellectual, but there was genuine concern in his voice. 'His Good Man Friday seems well able to see him home. I can have Dick put the horses to in a moment, and Mrs Adams will be glad to accompany you...'

'Thank you, Congressman – and please thank Mrs Adams for me. It's most kind of you both. But I think it's best that I stay with Mr Bray. He ... Sometimes when he gets like this, he has said things...' She shivered and drew her cloak about her. 'Things that lead me to feel that now, of all times, he ought not to be left alone.'

Adams was silent. His head tilted slightly, as if he were thinking about deeper meanings of the remark, and Mrs Bray quickly pressed his hand – 'I'm sorry,' she said. A few years ago, January recalled, the Congressman's son had either fallen from a boat en route to Washington while drunk ... or had thrown himself overboard.

But Adams said only, 'Quite all right, Madame.'

She turned to the servant, said, 'Thank you, Mede,' and climbed into the carriage.

Luke Bray could be heard, still shouting drunkenly, as the vehicle rolled away into the darkness.

NINE

Over the next four days, January visited every pawnshop in the District of Columbia.

Georgetown boasted two. He visited them on Saturday with Henri Viellard and noticed that the proprietors gave greater attention to the white man's tale of a fictitious brother who had come to grief in Washington than those few in Alexandria, on the other side of the river, did to his own quest for the effects of a missing friend.

Most such establishments, however, seemed to be in Washington City itself. Evidently, many of those office seekers who cluttered the Senatorial steps or buttonholed the President whenever he put his nose out of his office door underestimated the cost of living in that city while Congress was in session. January and Poe visited a dozen in the course of Monday afternoon, and the poet seemed to grasp instinctively – as Henri didn't – that a man who waltzed into a pawnbroker's with a list of missing items in his hand was simply asking to be lied to. January would have sworn he saw the glisten of tears in Poe's soulful dark eyes as he spoke of: 'A silver reservoir-pen and a gold watch ... I know my brother was in Washington last fall, and he had nothing in his pockets when his poor body was found in Baltimore. His widow begged me to make enquiries...'

'I suppose it's because my parents were actors,' Poe said as they emerged from Bronstein's on Judiciary Square. 'I never knew them – my mother died before I turned three – but there is something in the blood ... A fact which horrified my stepfather, I might add.' Old bitterness mingled with wry, exasperated affection tugged at the corner of his mouth.

The disclaimer of any knowledge of silver reservoir-pens would be followed, in every establishment, by perusal of the shelves of shoes, watches, tiepins, earrings, musical instruments, birdcages, needle cases, dishes (individually or in sets of up to forty), and ten thousand other items—

('What the devil *is* that?'
'Obstetrical forceps, sir.')

—and a murmur of, 'I'll just look around a little before I go...'

The day was chill and cloudy, the smell of rain blowing from the east. On the previous afternoon – pawnshops being closed on the Sabbath – January had had the pleasure of walking out to the fields along Delaware Avenue and watching the Warriors of Democracy – mostly Democrat clerks but including the sons of two local planters and the Right Honorable Representative from Alabama, Royal Stockard – get their American honor soundly trounced by the Invaders...

A pleasure, because on Trigg's advice January had unpatriotically bet two dollars on the foreign ministry team and could afford to buy Rose a very fine Swiss spyglass at a pawnshop on Constitution Avenue, and a well-thumbed copy of *Don Quixote*.

Monday, in the course of quartering the thickly-built blocks between Judiciary Square and the Tiber Canal, they found – in addition to the spyglass – half a dozen ball-topped seals which bore initials that did not include the letter 'S'—

('He might have kept someone else's seal out of sentimental attachment.'

'A father's or a brother's would still have "S". It isn't something that's usually passed outside the family.')

—at least fifteen cravat-pins decorated with round 'orient' pearls but no baroques—

('If that's actually a pearl then so is the knob on my bedpost.')

—and a white linen handkerchief bearing the embroidered initials 'S.S.'.

'A woman's,' said January.

'It's perfectly plain.'

118

'A sensible woman's.' January held the fragile square up to the light of the old-fashioned window's small panes. 'One who doesn't need lace all over every square inch of her possessions – unlike my sister. A man's handkerchief would be at least two inches larger, and of heavier fabric.'

'You're an observant devil,' remarked the poet as they returned to Capitol Street. 'I shall have to use that in a story.'

'Be my guest.' January sprang out of the way of yet another empty goods-wagon whose driver imagined himself in the Circus Maximus. 'I grew up among people who lived by watching others. Is the overseer rumpled and angry, with a shaving-cut on his chin? Walk soft. Is Madame storming up and down the house with her hair down? She's mislaid a comb and in a minute she'll decide someone stole it. Is one of the carriage horses starting to cough? Start praying, because somebody's going to get sold to buy a new one, and it might just be you.'

Poe said, 'Hmn,' and looked uncomfortable, as whites frequently did when the subject of getting sold came into the conversation. *No wonder they don't want to mix socially with us.* But he only said, after a time, 'My stepmother would have it that Negroes had "second sight" and could divine things white men could not.'

'Sure would have helped.'

The Virginian was silent for another few moments as they passed a couple of slaves unloading hay in the gate of a livery-stable yard. But his writer's curiosity got the better of him: 'You were born a slave, then?'

119

'On a sugar plantation near New Orleans. My sister and I grew up playing in the woods – another place to learn to observe what's around you, because it was easy to get yourself lost.'

Poe's dark brows pinched together as he studied January, as if trying to align the well-dressed, well-spoken (and obviously well-read, if he appreciated Poe's poetry) musician with a people considered too superstitious and simple-brained to be anything more than laborers.

January let him think about this as they walked on in the direction of the Capitol, wondering how a Southern man of letters would ultimately deal with the conundrum.

Probably by deciding I'm the exception to a known rule, and that most black men can't tell their right hands from their left...

Or maybe he just knows what his editors will buy.

They were in the district of shabby boarding houses and taverns that surrounded the Capitol's low hill, a neighborhood of mud-wallow alleys that swarmed with children – black or Irish, never both in the same alley – stray dogs, and wandering pigs.

Gryme's – one of the largest pawnbrokers in the city – stood just south of the Capitol, between a shop selling watches and Cullie's Slave Exchange. Poe had the grace to look discomfited as they walked past men and women in ankle chains on the benches in front of Cullie's.

Once inside, however, the poet's moving saga of a deceased brother and a distraught widow brought forth a silver reservoir-pen immediately.

120

January, wandering among the glass-topped cases in the center of the great wooden barn of a store, at the same moment spotted the cravat pin with the little blue-gray fist of a black baroque pearl. 'Ben! Come tell me if this wasn't your master's!' called out Poe, and January caught his eye for an instant, then came over and held the pen to the light of the dirty windows.

'This his, sure enough, Marse Eddie.' January had taken Gryme's measure the moment they entered and assumed his most humble stance and language. 'I seen it in his hand a hundred times.'

'What did the man look like, who brought it in?' Poe asked Mr Gryme.

'That I don't know, sir,' the pawnbroker responded smoothly. 'It was one of my boys in the shop that day. But he did say he was a Virginia gentleman, like yourself.'

Poe covered his eyes with his hand in stricken grief. 'Did he bring in anything else? A watch? He had a tiepin, with a black baroque pearl—'

These objects were produced, along with a half-dozen fobs and watch keys, a pair of spectacles in a cheap shagreen case, a card case of the same material, a gold signet-ring, a pair of kid gloves, and a cane with a silver head. January strongly suspected that not all of these had been Mr Singletary's property – the signet-ring bore the initials W.H. and was clearly the most expensive piece of male jewelry in the store – but nodded, very slightly, at the exorbitant price quoted. It was, after all, Chloë Viellard's money.

'Wretched thief.' Poe turned the cane in his hands as they regained the plank sidewalk.

121

'Right here on the head: *To CONGRESSMAN Peter Vhole from his friends at the Eagle* ... Faugh! *"A Virginia gentleman like myself,"* indeed!'

'Walk on ahead, sir,' said January softly, and fell back a pace to the men along the bench outside Cullie's Exchange. He slipped a silver quarter-dollar from his pocket, asked, 'What time does Gryme go to dinner?'

'Anytime 'tween four and four thirty.' One of the men nodded toward the massive ornamental clock in a window beside Gryme's. Flurries of rain rattled on the shop awnings, and a stout man in a green coat turned into the pawnbroker's door. January hoped he'd keep him busy.

'He lock up, or leave a boy?'

'Leaves a boy, sir,' said a woman, in the clean, bright calico gown that dealers gave their female slaves to make them look more 'likely'. 'Name of Tim.'

'He smart or stupid?'

The first man grinned. 'He ain't so smart as he thinks he is.'

January grinned back, paid his informants, and hastened his steps to catch up his 'master' lest Mr Gryme should look out through his window and observe the transaction.

Trigg's parlor was empty at the pre-dinner hour. January penned a swift note to Henri Viellard and ducked into the kitchen to enlist twelve-year-old Ritchie Trigg to carry it (for a consideration) to the Indian Queen, then returned to the small oak table beside the front window where the light was best.

Poe was already holding the card case to the rainy gray panes to examine every scratch on its finely-pebbled surface. From his pocket January produced the magnifying lens Rose had lent him before leaving New Orleans, came around to Poe's side and studied the silver pen. 'What do you make of it?' he asked.

Poe opened the case, brought it close to his eyes, to see the delicate hinges, then drew back sharply. 'What do *you* make of *this*?'

January handed him the pen, took the case, and flinched back.

'Where's it been?' asked the poet.

While January gently extracted the bloated, mold-glued rectangle of pasteboard from within, Poe went to the escritoire beside the other window and searched the drawer for another magnifier. It was easily found: there was no clutter in any drawer, box, or cupboard in the house of Octavia Trigg. The top card within the case was inscribed, *W. Milliken, Bookseller*, with an address in Boston, but when January gently prized the cards apart with a penknife, it proved that Selwyn Singletary had the habit of storing cards he was given in his case. The last six cards in the case were Singletary's. The other cards included another bookseller in New York, a Baltimore importer of hats, a Mr Deaver who operated a bookstore in Charlottesville, Dr Clarence Woolmer of the Potomac School in Georgetown, Dr Applegrove of the University of Virginia, Charlottesville, and John Quincy Adams. On the back of one of Singletary's own cards, in the unmistakable, even line of the reservoir-pen, was scribbled the address of Luke Bray.

The cards stank. The hinges of the case – and of the spectacle case, which contained a pair of round reading-glasses in the strength that an old man might need – were gritted slightly with dirt, which, when January poked a few grains free with a pin on to a clean sheet of notepaper, stank too. More of this earth was caught under the hinge of the watch case.

January fetched a back issue of the *Inquirer* from the kindling box by the hearth and spread it on the table. On it he laid the cards and card case, the spectacle case, the pen, the fob, and the cravat pin. The signet he put aside, along with the gloves – which smelled only of camphor and dust – and the cane, all of which he judged to have been added to the order by Gryme to raise the price. Poe tried without success to write with the pen, then carefully unscrewed its thick silver body and examined the gummed residue of the ink.

'What does it smell like to you?' January asked. For three ghastly summers he'd worked in the cholera wards in New Orleans, and had, every spring, gone with his mother, his sisters, his wife to the St Louis Cemetery on the Feast of All Saints to clean and decorate the tombs. He knew the smell.

Poe replied without hesitation, 'These things have come out of a grave.'

TEN

Dominique insisted on being the maidservant. *'P'tit*, I'm absolutely going out of my *mind* with boredom in this *execrable* village, and if I don't have some entertainment I will throw myself into the river!' She turned from January to Henri, who had arrived with his wife shortly after the conclusion of dinner. 'We have a *fabulous* mystery, a *fearsome* murder – though I am of course most sorry about poor M'sieu Singletary – and we're on the trail of grave robbers and villainous pawnbrokers and who knows what else, and you tell me to stay here at the boarding house and ... and read a good book! I feel like I have read every good book in this *city*!'

'I fear you cannot argue with the lady there,' put in Poe in his excellent French. 'If God picked up Washington and shook it like a carpet, I doubt that more than a score of volumes of literature of any sort would drop out.'

'Besides—' Minou widened her beautiful eyes and put a hand over Henri's protesting lips. 'You know Chloë cannot act.' She turned to the younger girl. 'Isn't that so, dearest?'

'She's quite right, Henri.' Chloë slipped her arm around Dominique's waist. 'I think you would make a *splendid* maid, darling.'

125

Because of the children's lessons – and the general business of two families and several single men on a rainy Monday evening – Poe and January had retreated to the 'white gentleman's parlor' upon the arrival of the Viellards, to lay out the evidence on the small marquetry table there. Both Henri and January were inclined to object when Dominique included herself in the conference, and both had been put sharply in their place by Madame Viellard: 'After she has been good enough to come with us all this distance–' Chloë as usual made no reference to *why* Dominique and her child (and her two servants) were part of the expedition – 'surely she has a right not to be kept out of things. Besides,' she added, 'Minou may see things that we do not.'

So far the only observation that Minou had made concerned the superiority of orient over baroque pearls and the poor quality of pearl earrings available at Law's Emporium on Capitol Street (*'Honestly*, darling, they couldn't hope to fool a *blind* man! They were flaking even as he took them out of the box...') but that, January understood, wasn't the point.

'If Minou is to do the talking while Chloë sobs discreetly behind a widow's veil,' he pointed out now, 'we need to bear in mind that she doesn't speak English very well.'

'I do, yes!' protested his sister in that language. 'I speak *magnificent* English!'

Chloë picked up the reservoir pen and turned it in her thin little fingers, as if mentally comparing the metal tip with the even line of the handwriting she had seen on so many letters, and behind her thick lenses her gaze was like frozen aquamarine. Tears had gathered in Henri's eyes. In Chloë's, January saw the anger that avenges in cool blood, without mercy.

'If I may advance an opinion,' said Poe, 'and I very much hope Madame Viellard will forgive my observation, I should say that a woman who can weep on command can be taught English phrases, but that one who knows English can not necessarily register convincing grief. My apologies, Madame—'

'None are called for, M'sieu.' Chloë gave him her precise smile. 'Indeed, I made a complete disgrace of myself at my father's funeral. For though I credit him with many Christian virtues and a sound business-sense, I had no respect whatsoever for his character, nor any good memories of his treatment of me – and no success in pretending otherwise, even in circumstances which called for it. Therefore I doubt my abilities to summon tears for a fictitious husband who allegedly drank himself to death in the streets of Washington.'

'Then it's a good thing you'll be wearing a veil,' declared Minou.

Accordingly, at three the following afternoon, Henri Viellard's closed carriage halted in front of the boarding house on Eighteenth Street, and January and Dominique mounted the box. The coachman – a different one than January had previously seen, who introduced himself as Esau – then guided the vehicle through mud and

127

traffic equally thick down Pennsylvania Avenue to the Capitol district. They stopped just opposite the Capitol to lift down Dominique, clothed in calico and a headscarf like a servant (any servant except Thèrése), and to let Chloë alight. Chloë might be incapable of weeping on demand, but she clearly shared Poe's sense of the believable. Swathed in inky mourning and veiled to her knees ('And, dearest,' Dominique said later, 'I am *eternally* grateful that I was able to borrow Musette's dress, because crape stains *everything* it touches, and Thèrése would have *killed* me if I'd gotten black all over her muslin!'), she was as invisible as a Turkish woman in *burqa* and *hijab*.

As Mr Gryme's stocky form disappeared along the street in the direction of the taverns on the other side of Capitol hill, the two women picked their way across the rutted muck of last night's rain with every appearance of casualness and disappeared inside. Esau guided the carriage to the edge of the Capitol's so-called 'lawn' at the end of a rank of vehicles. Men emerged from the doorways of the two wings of the white brick building, surrounded at once by job-hunters petitioning for attention. A few greeted them. Others simply strode off in the direction of the nearest café, trailing their entourages behind as a butcher's wagon trailed dogs.

Discussing the impending crisis with Canada? January wondered. *Is Congress REALLY going to get us into a war with England in the hopes of taking everyone's minds off the ongoing rats-nest of financial disaster?*

128

He wouldn't have put it past them.

The Right Honorable Junior Representative from Alabama – Luke Bray's crony Royall Stockard – strode down the steps and plowed through the weeds to where a couple of the Warriors of Democracy had gotten up a game of One Old Cat, in the absence of an opposing team. January smiled at the recollection of their defeat on Sunday. There had been a moment – with darkness falling, and the gap between the Warriors' score and that of the Invaders becoming more and more obviously unbridgeable, though neither team was anywhere near the one hundred points required for a clear win – when he'd thought the Americans were going to go after their opponents in the time-honored American fashion with their bats, bowie knives, and the torn-up pegs from the field.

He glanced across the street at Gryme's, but the shop door remained shut. The spring afternoon was cooling.

In the closed carriage below him, did Henri Viellard also watch the pawnshop door, behind which his wife and his mistress chatted away like sisters? Or had he buried himself in the pages of Thomas Wyatt's ponderous *Manual of Conchology*, which he'd brought along to contemplate while waiting? Eleven years of association with Dominique had evidently taught him: *Bring a book*.

From his own pocket, January drew Selwyn Singletary's red-backed notebook, familiar to him now with close study: he had spent the past three evenings copying every page so that Chloë and Henri could examine it at their leisure. Some of it obviously bore no relationship to its owner's disappearance: lists of laundry, prices of cabs in London, ratios of height to breadth of every building on Throgmorton Street and how far each one was from Hurlstone and Ludd's bank (in paces, inches, millimeters and cubits), expenditures on lobster-and-lettuce at the White Tree, the names of all his fellow-passengers on the *Beaufort* appended to strings of nearly-identical numbers (28081837, 30081837, 02091837) that he realized after a moment's puzzling were dates during his voyage, presumably marking a conversation or a first encounter. There were also infinite sets of tally marks, all dated and some labeled: *cockroaches, cats, crossing-sweepers...*

But what of those two sets of columns, on six successive pages, one set hastily scribbled and the other in a more deliberate hand?

And what of that thick, short block of numbers at the end of the book?

The door of Gryme's shop opened. Maid and mistress emerged. A bulky man in a mustard-colored coat, whom January had seen a few moments previously emerge from the halls of Congress, paused on the sidewalk and removed his hat to address Chloë, then tenderly escorted the black-clothed 'widow' across the goop of Independence Avenue to the carriage.

January dismounted the box, bowed deeply to Chloë as he helped her inside, lifted Minou up to the driving seat and sprang up beside her. Chloë waved a dainty hand at her escort as the carriage pulled away in the direction of the Indian Queen Hotel. 'You were right, *P'tit*!' exclaimed Dominique the moment the vehicle was in motion. 'Those things – oh, look at that lady in the pink over there. Do you suppose her hair is *really* that color? But the style of it is *adorable...*'

'What happened?' asked January.

'In the pawnshop? Shame on you for doubting! Chloë was *marvelous*! She just stood with her head bowed and spoke to me in a soft voice in French, and I'd turn to the young man behind the counter ... Such a *grubby* boy, with a face *just* like a weasel! And the most *frightful* tie, embroidered all over with yellow skulls, which I'm afraid just pointed up the fact that his face was all over with spots ... And tobacco! He had a stripe of it, practically, down the middle of his chin—'

'Did he tell you anything?' January had long ago learned that the only way to get any information out of his youngest sister was to interrupt her ruthlessly.

'But yes! Of course! Chloë said – through me translating, though her English actually is as good as mine—'

It was in fact much better, but January wasn't about to interrupt her to say so.

'—that she would pay *three dollars* for information that would lead her to her poor husband's grave ... You were absolutely right, *P'tit*! Those things *did* come out of a grave, and that horrible boy with the spots didn't deny it. He said they were brought in by a man named Wylie Pease,

131

and even the offer of another three dollars didn't get him to tell us where he lived, so the boy probably actually didn't know. Oh! And I bought this wonderful book, *Zuliemia, or, The Prisoner of Saragosa*, for only fifteen cents. Frank says that reading novels destroys a woman's character, but this one...'

'Did he say how one might find this Wylie Pease? Or anything about him?'

'Only that he's a grave robber.' Dominique looked up from attempting to unwrap the extremely fat volume she'd purchased from its enclosing paper. 'So I expect if you read the obituary columns and attended the next funeral in town, you'd find him quickly enough.'

For all the impression she frequently gave of not having a brain in her head, Minou had an excellent sense of where the shortest line lay between two points.

Darius Trigg knew all about Wylie Pease. 'He's in the resurrection trade, all right.' The landlord grimaced as he collected his music satchel and his flute. Mandie came scurrying out of the dining room, where the supper table was being cleared off, to fetch her father his hat; her tiny sister Kizzy, trotting at her heels, fetched January his. January had become a great favorite with the children of the house.

'You wouldn't happen to know where I could find him?' January rose from the round marble-topped table where he'd been perusing the *Washington Intelligencer.* A Mrs Horace Kelsey, wife of a well-known Washington tavern-keeper, would be laid to rest in the Washington Parish burial ground on Thursday afternoon. January hated himself for his feeling of satisfaction at seeing this news.

But Trigg shook his head: 'All I ever heard of him was his name.'

January took up his own music satchel, bowed grave thanks to four-year-old Kizzy, and followed Trigg out into the gathering dusk.

'And his trade,' Trigg went on as they turned their steps along K Street toward Rock Creek. 'Half the surgeons here in town have used his services, one time or another, and some over at Columbian College as well. The going rate's supposed to be fifty dollars.'

'Fresh or ... not?' inquired January, only half jesting, and Trigg gave him a slantindicular grin.

'If they was too fresh I'd start to wonder.'

'When I was studying in Paris,' January went on, 'the Senior Anatomist at the Hôtel Dieu had an assistant named Courveche. I don't know if he ever studied formally or not, but he probably knew more about the subject than some of the surgeons on the staff. Every few months a rumor would go around among the students that there was going to be a "gathering" at some barn outside of town, in places like Montmartre or Louveciennes. We'd all sneak out like conspirators before the city barriers were closed for the night ... This was back in 1818 or 1819. At the Hôtel Dieu we didn't see a dissection more than once or twice a year, with a hundred of us crammed into the galleries of the operating theater trying to see down to the table—'

Lights twinkled in the scattered houses along Reedy Branch. Cow bells clanked as children drove the animals home through the dusk.

'You think it's right,' asked Trigg – curiosity rather than disgust in his voice – 'for doctors to go cuttin' up a dead man?'

'When I sit down to play that new mazurka we're going to try out tonight,' returned January mildly, 'won't you be glad I'd played through it a couple of times this morning on a real piano, rather than just watching somebody else play it from thirty feet away?'

'So you cut up dead men?'

'Cut up live ones, too,' said January. 'They were glad I'd had the practice.'

Trigg laughed shortly. They crossed an elegant circle, laid out like a dropped carpet in the midst of the fields, and ahead of them saw the handsome residence of the British Minister against the woods along Rock Creek. Cressets burned in front of its shallow steps, and a red carpet had been laid from its door to the carriage block, in defiance of the wet clouds rapidly obliterating the stars.

'First time I went into surgery,' January added quietly, 'I wished I'd been able to pay the hundred and fifty francs that was the going rate – that was my rent for six months! And half the time we did get to Courveche's "gatherings" I'd have paid that much again – if I'd had it! – just to have a cadaver that was fresh.'

'Now *that*,' protested Trigg with a grin, 'is more than I want to know about *that*!'

The Mudwall brothers joined them then, and

the talk turned to other matters as they crossed through the open field beside the Minister's house and circled around to the warmth and light of its kitchen door. But during the course of the evening, as January played German quadrilles and light-footed waltzes, and watched the top couple in the country dances work its way down the set and back, the horror of those evenings in Louveciennes barns and ruined cottages out in Passy returned to him, the sickening reek and the peculiarly slimy touch of rotting flesh beneath his fingers.

And he remembered, in coming and going from the dissections – and mostly he and the other students had to spend the night in a hayrick or a stable, since the city barriers weren't open again until first light – he would sometimes see the anatomy assistant Courveche in quiet converse in the shadows with furtive, unshaven men whose peasant clothing always smelled of grave-mold.

Looking out at the sweeping silk skirts, pink and gray and bronze and green – at the gentlemen with their pomaded hair and embroidered waistcoats – at Henry Clay who owned five hundred slaves, and Dolley Madison who had fled from Washington before the invading army that he, Benjamin January, had helped defeat in New Orleans – at all those others, young and old, hungry for fame or sick of its demands...

Each was after all only a set of lungs, a pair of kidneys, a tangle of guts and arteries and nerves.

Bring me the fairest creature northward born, says the dark prince of Morocco to Portia in *The*

135

Merchant of Venice; and let us make incision ...
to prove whose blood is reddest, his or mine...

January could himself attest that he had never seen the smallest difference between a white man's flesh and a black man's, between the blood and organs of a vaunted 'European' and those of the men they'd said were 'childlike', 'animal', and happy in their slavery.

After every dissection, he recalled, he'd gone to confession, and the priests had told him that what he'd done was a grave sin. Every time, he had argued that for every dead man he cut up – *and they're dead, they're DONE with those bodies!* – his chances of saving a living man's life or arm or eye or livelihood increased a dozenfold.

It doesn't matter, the priests always said. *We must accept on faith that the councils of the Church know more than we do of these matters...*

The way Congress knew more about slavery than did a man chopping cotton in some other man's field?

He turned his heart back to the music, light and precious as fairy gold, lest by looking into the darkness, he should come to hate humankind.

ELEVEN

And, of course, with a third of the nation's men out of work and the possibility of war looming with Britain, all anyone talked of that night, in the ballroom at least, was Sunday's defeat by the Invaders of the Washington Warriors of Democracy.

Most of the Warriors were there, from Royall Stockard down to Chilperic Creighton, the seventeen-year-old scion of a local planter family who clearly demonstrated by the cut and color of his waistcoat that he wanted to be Royall Stockard when he grew up, and all of them protesting that they had been robbed. Since Messrs Gonesse and Lenoir – clerks of the French Ministry and co-captains of the Invaders – were likewise present, it took all the combined tact and authority of Senator Clay and Mr Old-mixton of the British Ministry (Sir Henry Fox being, for the most part, absent in the gambling-room) to prevent violence. Only the unilateral promise by Secretary of the Navy Dickerson that any man who issued a challenge would be fired from his position in disgrace warded off a series of duels being arranged at a later date.

'How many duels you think will come of it?' whispered January, under cover of unfurling the music for the Varsoviana, and Trigg immediately said, 'Three.'

'That all?' protested Phinn Mudwall. 'I say five at least...'

'I'll cover that...'

'How'll we tell?'

'Say, in the next two weeks...'

The musicians hastily straightened themselves up and played an opening bar, as M'sieu Pageot – chargé d'affaires of the French Ministry and, like Mr Oldmixton in the British establishment, the actual power there – took the two French ball-captains like a couple of puppies into a corner near the musicians' bower and threatened them with murder if they behaved like school-boys here in the very mansion of the British Minister.

'I know Pageot's coachman,' whispered old Langston the fiddler. 'I can find out from him if either of 'em gets in a duel...'

But when supper was called, and the musicians descended the narrow stair to the underground kitchen, they found there – among the flustered scullions – the young Frenchmen Gonesse and Lenoir themselves, accompanied by a long-limbed young man in an extremely American coat, and Signor Baldini, the rather youthful secretary of the Minister from the Kingdom of the Two Sicilies ... last seen throwing the balls that the Warriors of Democracy had shown themselves ultimately unable to hit.

'Monsieur Trigg?' inquired Gonesse, a bright-eyed Gascon with extravagantly-cut lapels to his swallowtail coat and three waistcoats in different

138

colors on underneath. 'Have I the honor to address the Captain of the Stalwarts?' He held out his hand.

Trigg stepped forward and shook it firmly. Behind him, Phinn Mudwall whispered, 'Well, I'll be dipped in shit.'

'Might I present my colleagues, sir?' said Trigg. 'Mr Blair Langston; Mr Phineas Mudwall; Mr Phileas Mudwall; Mr Benjamin January. Mr January is the newest member of the Stalwarts.'

'And I am Jules Gonesse. M'sieu Andreas Lenoir, Mr Caldwell Noyes of the Navy Department, and Signor Baldini—'

'I had the honor, Signor–' Trigg bowed to Baldini – 'and the pleasure, I might add, of watching the truly excellent way that you made the Warriors look no-how last Sunday.'

'You were there?' Gonesse's grin flashed in the gloom of the oil lamps. 'M'sieu Noyes has only informed me this evening, M'sieu, of the existence of the Stalwarts. I had been told that it was against the laws of this city for men of your race to play ball.'

'So it is,' replied Trigg. 'But as long as we play out on the far side of town – and as long as the city's constabulary goes on betting on our games – they're happy to accept our bribes just like they accept everybody else's in this town.'

Pecunia non olet,' January said, quoting the words of Vespasian, Emperor of Rome and inventor of pay toilets, and all four of their guests laughed and applauded.

'I had the pleasure of telling our European

colleagues,' said Noyes, in the nasal accents of New England, 'that the Stalwarts are accounted one of the strongest teams in Washington.'

'That's very kind of you, sir,' replied Trigg. 'I think we can beat most of the other colored teams, more often than not – but not a great deal more often. It all depends on who's having a good day.' With the genial dignity of an ambassador – or a boarding-house-keeper – he turned to Gonesse. 'I'm guessing you've learned already that every game's a different game, and every day's a different day.'

'Spoken as a gentleman and a sportsman!' Gonesse beamed. *'Jove lifts the golden balances, that show, the fates of mortal men, and things below.'*

With a slow grin, January quoted the next two lines: *'Here each contending hero's lot he tries, and weighs, with equal hand, their destinies.'*

'And would you and your teammates–' Gonesse inclined his head to Trigg – 'cast your fate into Jove's golden balances against us, M'sieu, say ... two weeks from this Saturday? Like Achilles, we seek glory, and the more worthy the opponents, the better we are pleased.'

'Then we shall strive to please you, sir.' Trigg bowed in return. 'And if you gentlemen will forgive my impudence in the name of sport, my teammates and I will whip you soundly and send you back to your embassy in honorable defeat.'

'Eh bien!' The French captain beamed. Eph Norcum back in New Orleans, January reflected, would have struck Trigg for being 'uppity'. 'So *you* say, sir! But the master of all victories is

140

fate!'

The skinny New Englander Noyes applauded again, almost glowing with triumph. An abolitionist, January recalled suddenly, was what Bray had called him a few nights ago. And as such, merely in bringing the game about he had challenged the southern Democrats, be they clerks or planters' sons.

There was – he knew immediately – going to be trouble.

News of the upcoming game reached the white folks' supper room even before the dancing resumed. January could feel it as they took their places on the dais again, like the heat-dance above fire on a day too bright to clearly see the flames. Could hear it in the crackling *sotto voce* whispers; see it in the way Congressman Stockard grabbed the sleeve of this teammate or that. But he was also aware of Congressional secretaries, clerks and assistants stepping behind curtains and into doorways to exchange money and write down wagers: *Damned foreigners – goddam insult...*

Luke Bray's voice surged from the door of the gambling-room: 'Hell yes, they can beat 'em! We was goddam robbed by them Frenchy cheats—!'

Florid-faced Senator Buchanan led Mrs Bray from the dance-floor with as much gallantry as if he hadn't been 'married' for years to the darkly handsome Senator King from Alabama: 'Your husband seems to be more than usually exercised over a game of ball, M'am.'

'My husband is drunk.' Her lovely peridot

gaze touched the door of the gambling room with distaste. 'And it isn't merely a game of ball, sir. It's the honor of America.' Contempt glinted from her words, as from the facets of a diamond.

Three hours later, as the musicians ascended the kitchen stair to take their leave into the foggy blackness, the honor of America manifested itself in the form of Bray, leaning heavily on Congressman Stockard's arm as he staggered down the driveway and into the yard. 'Trigg!' Bray yelled, and almost veered under the hooves of a departing carriage. 'Trigg, goddamit, you gotta let my boy Mede into that team of yours!'

'Luke, for God's sake—' Stockard was laughing.

'I mean it!' insisted Bray. 'Mede – where's that boy?'

One of the Ministry servants dodged among the carriages at a trot, Ganymede Tyler at his heels. The young valet's breath puffed softly in the light of the lantern over the kitchen door: 'I'm here, sir—'

'You gonna join the Stalwarts.' Bray grabbed the startled Mede by the shoulder and thrust him at Trigg. 'Best goddam thrower in the District,' he announced. 'I take him out to help me practice, and he can throw fast, slow, whichever way, an' put that ball wherever he wants. Can't NOBODY hit what my Man Friday throws! Just goes WHOOSH! Right past 'em!'

His extravagant demonstration nearly spun him off his own feet.

'I heard all that and more, sir,' replied Trigg.

'But the fact is, sir, you know it's only free men that's on the Stalwarts.'

'Told you that, Bray.' Stockard shook his curly head, obviously well aware that after a certain point in the evening there was only so much you *could* tell Luke Bray. 'You know there's no slave nigger ball teams.'

'How about if I set him free, then?' demanded Bray. 'That satisfy everybody?'

Ganymede, who had borne the discussion of his prowess and slave status with a kind of embarrassed detachment – more, January suspected, on behalf of his master than himself – now froze as still as an animal startled in the woods, and January heard the hiss of his indrawn breath.

'Set him free!' stated Bray, still more loudly, and yanked his arm away from his friend's supporting hand. 'That'll show them cheatin' foreign nancy-boys! They want to play niggers, we'll *give* 'em niggers! Show 'em even our *niggers* can beat cheatin' foreign arse-suckin' nancy-boys!'

Mede turned startled eyes on Trigg: wide, shocked, and wild with a hope that he dared not utter.

Trigg shrugged casually. 'I guess we'll take him if he's free.'

'Don't be a damn idiot, Luke! That nigger's worth two thousand dollars if he's worth a dime—'

'And what's the good name of America worth, hunh?' Luke swiveled on his friend, chin thrust belligerently. 'Two thousand dollars? Ten thousand dollars?'

'Luke, for Chrissake, you already lost seventeen hundred tonight playin' poker—'

'You think seventeen hundred, or twen'y-seven hundred, means fuck-all to me, compared to the honor of America?' He jabbed Stockard's waistcoat with his forefinger. 'Hell, I bet fancier niggers'n him in poker games! Mede!' He spun again, shook a finger in his valet's face. 'I hereby declare you *free*!'

Stockard rolled his eyes, as if this were a child's game rather than a legal issue that would alter a man's life forever.

'Now you join up with the Stalwarts and you show those suck-arse foreigner bastards that even the NIGGERS in this country can whoop their sorry behinds!'

'Yes, sir,' Mede whispered. 'I'll do that, sir.'

'Now go find the carriage.' Luke Bray shoved him in the direction of the dark confusion of vehicles in the adjacent field. 'Mrs Bray gonna kill me, keepin' her waitin' when she has a headache...'

'She *always* got a headache, Luke,' grinned Stockard, and Bray laughed owlishly.

'And, Mede! Stop an' get yourself a drink to celebrate!'

Mede whispered, 'Yes, Marse Luke.' The look he threw toward the musicians, still grouped in the dim glow of the oil-lamp that fell through the kitchen door, was that of a sailor overboard gazing at wreckage, hoping he could reach it before the waves drove it off again. And like men on a half-foundered ship, they could only return his gaze, praying he'd make it without the

144

slightest ability to help.

Behind January, a quiet voice spoke behind him in the kitchen door. 'Might I have a word with you, M'sieu, on the subject of Mr Selwyn Singletary?'

TWELVE

It was Sir Henry Fox's secretary, Mr Oldmixton.

He'd heard the man's voice a few minutes before from the direction of the pillared portico of the house, bidding farewell to departing guests and making witty excuses for the fact that the Minister himself had been helped up to bed some hours previously. Even in the dank gloom of the kitchen stair, Oldmixton's exquisitely simple London tailoring was a polite rebuke to the bright waistcoats and gold watch-fobs of the American Congressmen who'd filled the house all evening.

He shook January's hand, said, 'Madame Viellard suggested that I take the opportunity to speak with you.'

January had glimpsed Chloë Viellard in the ballroom, exquisite in Italian silk, under the aegis of the Adams party. Henri had very properly departed from the boarding house that afternoon with his wife, after the expedition to Gryme's pawnshop, and an hour later his carriage had arrived – with yet another of the livery stable's hired drivers, Esau having gone off to supper – to take Dominique to Mrs Purchase's house in Georgetown.

'That's very kind of you, sir—'

They stepped out of the doorway and moved to the darkness at the far end of the loggia that stretched across the rear of the house. The Ministry servants – purchased, January guessed, from local planters – continued to move from the back door to the pump in the yard: January guessed they'd be oiling knives and washing punch-cups well into daylight.

'Madame Viellard suggested that I give you this.' Oldmixton produced three folded sheets of foolscap from the inner pocket of his coat. 'It's a copy of the report that Glover – my clerk – made up, of his enquiries for Mr Singletary along the Alexandria–Warrenton road.'

January unfolded the yellowish paper and angled it toward the reflected light from the lantern above the door. Mr Glover had made his investigations between the twelfth and seventeenth of November, in that six-week hiatus between the end of Congress's special session and the beginning of its regular meetings in December. Appended to the notes of who he had talked to, where, and when, the clerk had added his own expenses for the journey: *Dinner at the Queen of Prussia, rump steak, fish, eggs, cold fowl, pies, puddings, tea, and coffee – $1.50. Brandy and spirits free. Bed with clean sheets at Cayle's Tavern in Orange, seventy-five cents.* January wondered how much it would have been with dirty sheets.

His glance went to Oldmixton's face again, trying to read anything behind that bland façade. It was the British Ministry that Singletary was going to visit, just before his departure from Washington on the twentieth of October.

'You'll see he made enquiries not only at the regular post-inns on the route – the Queen of Prussia in Warrenton and the Orange Hotel in Orange.' A rich voice, with something of Poe's theatrical inflection. A man who understood how to manipulate words to target or to conceal. *Keep this for me*, the frightened Singletary had said; *don't breathe a word to anyone*...

'But because there's no record of Singletary having taken the stage, Glover asked at the smaller inns in Manassas, Warrenton, and Culpeper as well, and of the local sheriffs, as to whether a body had been found.'

Spoke with Lewis, sheriff Prince William County. Body discovered 12 October, Negro man. Spoke with Puser, sheriff Fauquier County; no bodies reported...

'Your clerk put a great deal of time and effort into this search.'

'Mr Glover is a very thorough young man,' agreed Oldmixton. 'I became extremely fond of Singletary when we worked together in the Home Office. He was a queer old bird but he impressed me as being very lonely. The last few years I was in London I made sure he joined my family for holidays, Christmases, an occasional Sunday ... He didn't always come. He was shy of people, and with good reason; he had a devouring curiosity about them and would ask any damn question that came into his mind, everything from how old my aunt was to how ladies went about acquiring underdrawers. It was as if humanity were a different species. I told Glover to leave no stone unturned, and to be frank,' he added with a grin, 'I suspect Glover thoroughly enjoyed his exploration of the Virginia countryside.'

The sudden elfin expression faded. 'But I would not like to think that poor old Singletary had come to harm.'

As January slipped the folded sheets into his pocket, his fingers touched the silver pen, the battered card-case, like the skull fragments of the dead. 'No,' he said. 'Nor would I.'

'Is Mede that good a thrower?' asked Phinn Mudwall as the five musicians made their way along the now-silent K Street toward the great, empty circle in the fields. Fog trapped the stinks of stale smoke, ill-tended privies, green weeds and thousands of horses and cows into a soft and heavy murk. Here and there across the empty fields a window glowed like a bleared drunkard's eye, but the men walked with their lanterns shuttered and kept their voices low. It was long past curfew and nobody wanted to risk being shaken down by the constables, always supposing that the constables were sober enough, at that hour, to stumble forth from the barrooms.

And there were worse things than the police afoot in the vaporous dark.

'God, yes.' Their voices were barely a whisper as they crossed the mouth of an alley, between a row of three brick shops – standing isolated like an abandoned dollhouse – and the Globe and Eagle tavern on the corner of Twenty-Fourth Street, likewise closed for the night. 'I seen him throw. That boy can make a ball do whatever he wants to; I seen men swing and miss at throws you'd swear were pure candy—'

Trigg halted at the corner and listened. Even in fog and darkness, Irish b'hoys would take advantage of the emptiness of the long, straight streets and whip their teams to full gallop. Not a week went by that some late-walking market-woman or sailor was injured or killed.

'So Luke Bray's let go of his Good Man Friday for the honor of America,' marveled January, 'and cost himself two thousand dollars, when he'd scream bloody murder if somebody suggested that he and his friends *truly* honor America by setting them all free.'

'White man's logic at its finest.' Little Phil Mudwall shook his head. 'Let's hope—'

January raised his hand at the sound of a team of horses approaching in the fog. The creak of wheels.

The musicians melted back against the corner of the tavern.

Blurred lantern light in the fog, barely visible. But the set of the two lanterns and their height from the ground, the squeak of harness, brought back to January the vision of Fowler's wagon a few nights ago, on the road through the deserted woods. As the black bulk passed them, almost invisible in the blackness, the smell of tobacco was the same.

Dim away to their left, a slurred voice asked, 'Where are we?'

'Don't you worry, friend,' soothed a reply. 'I'll get you home. Not far now.'

A lantern flickered, coming up Twenty-Fourth Street.

Without a word traded among them, the musicians worked their way back along the shuttered wall of the Globe and Eagle to the alleyway, reeking like sin of piss and garbage. The lantern glow drew nearer. The slurred voice said, 'Marse Luke said ... Marse Luke said I was to get myself a drink, come right on back...'

'That's where we're headed,' replied his companion. 'Back to Marse Luke.'

'I'm a free man now.' Pride rang in Mede's voice. 'Marse Luke set me free.'

'That was mighty good of him.'

They came opposite the mouth of the alley. January saw that the man with Mede was Davy Quent, but he'd felt in his skin already who it had to be. Silently, he slipped his knife from his boot, stepped from the alley for the instant it took to seize Quent by the arm and put the knife to his throat and then step back: 'Not one sound,' he breathed.

Quent dropped the lantern and pissed himself with shock.

Freed of Quent's grasp, Mede stood weaving on the muddy verge of the street. Trigg scooped up the lantern, shut the slide, drew Mede into the alley's blackness.

'What the fuck you doin'?' Quent gasped, and January, behind him now and holding his arm in

150

his massive grip, cut him a little. Old Blair Langston – January could smell his pomade – came up on their right and took whatever weapon Quent had in his right-hand pocket. Quent's voice was squeaky with panic. 'He just drunk, man, I'm just takin' him home—'

A momentary glint of yellow light. Trigg opened the lantern slide long enough to look at Mede's eyes, then shut it. 'He ain't drunk. His eyes is pinned—'

January said, 'Opium.'

Quent twisted in his grip, tried to stomp his foot, his hand shooting down to grab at January's groin. In his panic Quent missed, and with a single quick jerk January cut his throat – he'd known from the beginning he was going to – and shoved the body away at once, before any of the blood could spray on him. The smell of it, and of Quent's bowels releasing, filled the alley.

Trigg blew out the lantern. January groped for the leg of Quent's trousers and cleaned the blade of his knife. This really was jail-worthy behavior, and without a word exchanged among them they left the lantern beside Quent's body and returned to Twenty-Fifth Street at a casual stroll that did not hesitate. They turned back down to I, crossed through a field deep in weeds and smelling of cow dung and took refuge in the blackness behind somebody's stables. Only then Trigg opened his own lantern just enough to examine January's sleeves and coat-front.

There was blood on his right sleeve and shoulder – 'Damn, I liked this coat...' – and on his gloves. He tried to sound casual, but though he felt not the slightest remorse over killing a man who'd dragged hundreds into slavery, he had begun to tremble, and felt dizzy, as if he'd run a long way. When they returned to the Ministry, he remained far back in the darkness with the Mudwall brothers, watching Langston and Trigg approach the pillared front porch as if it were a lighted stage.

Most of the carriages were gone from the yard and from the adjacent field. On the porch, Mr Oldmixton was bidding as warm a farewell to Mrs Madison and her niece – always the last to leave any gathering – as if it weren't nearly three in the morning. The former Presidentress chuckled with genuine delight at Oldmixton's account of his new Queen's numerous suitors: 'Well, what's the poor girl to do, when sweeping her off her feet could get one of them clapped up in the Tower? She's a sentimental little thing but she isn't about to share power with anyone. The first thing she did when they told her she was queen was tell that frightful mother of hers that she wanted her own room—'

Mrs Madison sniffed. 'What did she think the girl was going to do in a room of her own, have clandestine *affaires* with the footmen? Why, hello, Mr Trigg—' She smiled and extended her hand as Trigg stepped up to the porch. 'I thought you'd gone home an hour ago ... Good heavens, it *was* an hour ago and here we are still standing, and poor Anne–' she touched her niece's shoulder – 'wanting to get to bed! John, I am *covered* with shame—'

Oldmixton returned her smile, even as he

turned to Trigg.

'Excuse me bothering you, sir, m'am.' Trigg bowed. 'But we found Mr Bray's manservant wandering over in the circle, and it looks like he's been taken ill—'

'Good heavens!' Oldmixton peered through the fog to where Langston stood with Mede on the edge of the dim zone of light from the porch lanterns. 'Mr Bray cursed a good deal – he seems to have had the idea that his Good Man Friday took him at his word and went off to get himself drunk ... I shouldn't imagine he has much head for it; he's the soberest young fellow I've ever met. Is he all right?'

'Quite all right, sir.' Trigg glanced in Mede's direction, and, January thought, to where he and the Mudwall brothers stood in the darkness. 'Just a touch of fever. He should be right as rain in the morning.'

'I can put him up here for the night,' offered Oldmixton. 'There's a spare bed in the grooms' dormitory over the stable, if you're certain it isn't anything catching. Or I'll have Clayton put down a pallet in the tack room. We'll send a message to Mr Bray in the morning.'

And seeing through the well-schooled stillness of Trigg's face, he added, his own voice neutral, 'Mr and Mrs Bray left nearly an hour ago.'

'That's very kind of you, sir,' said Trigg, 'but no need to trouble. We'll take him on home with us.'

THIRTEEN

On the following afternoon, Mrs Howard Kelsey was buried in the Washington Parish churchyard, near the banks of the river.

In between cutting January's bloodstained coat into pieces small enough to be burned, Trigg had written to Luke Bray, informing him that his former valet had been taken ill on his way home and would return to Georgetown before nightfall. No one was going to breathe the words 'slave stealers', for there was no way of knowing who knew whom in the white world, or where chance words might end up. 'Generally,' the landlord told January as young Ritchie set off to deliver the note, 'the constables don't spend too much time askin' about dead niggers, 'specially those that met their destinies after curfew in alleys. But Kyle Fowler's done a lot of favors for the constables over the years, so we'd better walk a little careful here.'

It was fortunate, January reflected, that he'd just made the round of Washington pawnshops and knew where he could acquire another long-tailed formal coat in more or less his own massive size. When he returned from this errand, Mede – who had spent the night in one of the modest bedrooms on the third floor – had wakened and returned to his master's house.

154

At just before two, then, January arrived at Christ's Church, clothed in the rough tweed jacket and corduroy trousers of an artisan or craftsman: a tavern-keeper's wife wouldn't have black gentlemen in well-cut frock-coats and silk vests seeing her to her grave. The white men gathered at the gray, Gothic-style church were dressed all up and down the social ladder, from the high beaver hats and well-fitting coats of Senators and bankers, down to the rough – though decent – jackets and work pants of teamsters, drovers, builders and laborers who had clearly known Mrs Kelsey over many years of buying her husband's beer. The benches at the back of the church were crowded with black artisans and grocers dressed much like himself, and a fair number whom January guessed – by the old-fashioned cut of their clothing – to be slaves in the wealthy houses of the capital.

Men whose lives this unknown woman had touched. Men she'd spoken cheerfully to after a day of back-breaking work in heat or cold.

Men who thought enough of her husband to stand with him as he saw her to her grave.

Mr Kelsey himself, a tallish, stooped gentleman in his sixties, was guided to his pew by three young men – sons or sons-in-law? – but moved like a man who'd been struck over the head, seeming neither to hear nor see. January almost couldn't look at that terrible lost-dog expression in his eyes.

Did I look like that, when Ayasha died?

Even at a distance of six years, the pain was as

155

vivid as if he had come home only yesterday to find her dead.

Will he go home and box up everything she owned and throw the trunk into the river, lest the sight of it tear the soul out of his body?

He averted his eyes and did what he'd come there to do: watched for a man who *didn't* go up to comfort the widower.

He spotted him almost immediately. The slouchy fellow with the bald head, who stayed at the back of the crowd. If Kelsey or the young men around him seemed about to come in his direction, he slipped away.

As a musician, and an active member in the Faubourg Tremé Free Colored Militia and Burial Society, January had attended hundreds of funerals. Even allowing for differences in the way things were done in the American portions of the United States – such as women not attending – there were some things that remained the same. Things that were part of the human experience of loss, and friendship, and common decency.

Is your Pa going to be all right?

What can I do to help?

I sure am sorry to hear of your loss.

What time's the wake?

This man did none of these things. He took notice, not of the people around him, but of where in the churchyard the grave was dug.

If that's not Wylie Pease, reflected January, studying the narrow, furtive face, *it's someone who can sure as hell tell me where to find him.*

The Washington Parish cemetery lay near the

156

river, distant from the center of town. It covered a good ten acres, lavishly planted with trees and shrubs after the newest fashion in Europe. A brick wall surrounded it, new enough, and high enough, to require a ladder and a confederate. January made a mental note of the larger monuments and groves, and as the funeral guests made their slow way from the graveside toward the gates, he lagged farther and farther behind. Mr Slouchy, as he dubbed his man, slipped out among the first and didn't linger.

The rest of the mourners clustered around Kelsey and his sons, talking in quiet voices. In New Orleans, the uptown blacks – American-raised Protestants, slave or freedman – would shake their heads when the Catholic funerals of the downtown *gens de couleur librés* would form up processions at the cemetery gates; when the music would turn from solemn marches to the slow, proud strut of joy, of triumph – *You took the one we loved, Baron Cemetery, Mr Death, but you can't make us cry. You can't break our hearts.* The parade would come down Rue Orleans from the gates of the chapel, the women waving their scarves and twirling their parasols, the men dancing as they marched.

This standing around in sorrow, though he understood it to the bottom of his soul, seemed to him very strange. White folks' funerals were just so *gloomy.*

When you've crossed over to Heaven, do you really want to see your friends back home weep?

People talked a little, then walked back toward town through the cold patchy brightness of the

157

cloudy day. Only Mr Kelsey and a small handful of others had carriages, or had rented the black ones from the undertaker, with their sable teams and nodding plumes. No music played them on their way. January guessed there'd be none at the wake.

How did white people stand loss, on those terms?

January himself stood in feigned contemplation of the headstone raised by the King of Prussia to his ambassador – who had had the misfortune to die in Washington – then wandered off toward the line of stumpy granite cenotaphs that represented Congressmen whose remains had later been taken away by their families. In the deep weeds behind one of these, on his way in, he had cached a satchel containing a sandwich, a water bottle, a heavy knit pullover, his new copy of *Don Quixote*, a dark-lantern and a couple of extra candles.

At a guess, as the afternoon drew on, the cemetery watchmen would keep an eye on how many people entered the place, and count how many departed. With the leave-taking of the last of the mourners, January sought out one of the groves at the far end of the grounds. Later, as dusk deepened and fog moved in, he shifted his post to the shrubbery that surrounded the cemetery's public vault on three sides, and from there watched the solitary watchman make a thorough patrol of the place just prior to closing the gates at sunset. At the funeral he'd observed one of Kelsey's sons give this man some money, probably far less than a private guard would charge.

158

In theory, a private guard would protect the body of the deceased in some specific grave until it was beyond the state where it would be acceptable to a body-snatcher's customer ... Obviously, reflected January, these were people who didn't know the buyers associated with the Paris medical schools.

Or the guards who were sometimes in league with them.

How long shall a man lie in the earth, ere he rot? Hamlet had inquired of the jovial grave-digger...

Get thee to my lady's chamber and tell her, let her paint an inch thick, to this favor she must come...

After passing through a truly unpleasant intermediary stage.

As a surgeon in Paris, he had visited the crowded rooms of the very poor, to find the corpses of family members six and eight days dead, laid out upon tables: *We can't pay to hire a guard, sir, and we didn't want to risk...*

The fog thickened with the clammy dark. January donned his knitted pullover, but remained where he was beside the half-buried brick vault. He knew he'd have plenty of time. Body-snatchers generally didn't even start work till after midnight, when chilled watchmen grew sleepy after a few too many nips of rum, *To keep me warm...*

The moon was waxing, a day or two from full. Its ghostly pallor diffused faintly through the mists without making anything easier to see. When he heard the clocks of the Christ Church steeple strike two, January moved among the graves toward the remote section where Mrs Kelsey would be sleeping alone for the first time, perhaps, in decades. Her husband's tavern would be closed up but beyond a doubt its upstairs room would be warm and bright, tables spread with food brought by all those wives who hadn't come to the funeral, voices getting louder. As with their funerals, it had always surprised and puzzled January how tame white folks' wakes were, compared to the dancing, gay music and howling grief that he was used to. His landmarks loomed with malevolent suddenness through the blackness: a round-topped head-stone here, a row of cenotaphs just beyond. Past that, a modest obelisk watched over the grave of *Clara Teller, 1813-1815. She is not dead, but only sleeping...*

Now and then the small vermin of the riverside – foxes or rats – made the black vapors stir, but as long as it wasn't alligators, such as one might encounter in the low ground at the back of New Orleans, January wasn't much concerned. He'd worked too many cholera wards in the murky New Orleans summers to be disconcerted by fog and a few headstones. Despite a rigorous European education he didn't precisely disbelieve in ghosts, but he would have been happy to encounter any number of dead Congressman in preference to the men who'd been waiting for Davy Quent to steer his victim to them last night.

He passed a tomb of whitewashed brick, just tall enough to enclose a coffin. A Lilliputian turret surmounted it, containing a bell, though the rope which had at one time extended, through discreet holes in tomb-top and coffin, to the corpse's hand had fallen away. Fearful as people were about being clandestinely exhumed after they were dead, there seemed to be almost as much morbid terror of interment before they were quite ready for it. January had seen three or four of these tombs in the cemetery, equipped with bell turrets or other escape features. The medical students at the Hôtel Dieu had taken ghoulish delight in trading tales of corpses exhumed with screams frozen on their faces, or fingers lacerated by attempts to claw their way out of the coffin when they'd waked from a coma in the enclosed darkness, but January had personally never encountered such a case. It was always and inevitably something that someone had heard from someone else.

In New Orleans, where tombs lay above ground and the fissures frequently opened between the cracked bricks, everyone could see the crawfish that crept in and out, and the monstrous black roaches. Nobody in that city was under much illusion about how quickly a corpse would be reduced to its bones.

Don't bother about the bell; Grandma's definitely dead.

The moon moved above the fog. January held his chilled fingers against the hot iron of the closed lantern. The Christ's Church clock sounded three.

A yellow blink in the darkness. Not the watchman: that light would be steady. Wylie Pease – or whatever body-snatcher it was, making his way from the wall through this moist, lightless world – was doing precisely what January had done, slipping the door on his dark-lantern just long enough to orient himself on the next landmark.

January shifted his cramped knees.

The rustle of clothing, and the woody knock as shovel handles scraped within burlap. Light again, close enough to outline two shapes, one leading with the lantern and the shovels, the other following with a rolled-up stretcher borne like a rifle over his shoulder.

Good. Only two.

Let's hope there isn't a third concealed somewhere in the dark...

They put the lantern against a headstone nearby, shielding the light from the direction of the distant church. The feeble gleam showed January the face of the slouchy little bald man at the funeral, the long ferret-like nose, the close-set eyes and pouting, girlish rosebud mouth. They laid a blanket over the grass nearby, heaped on it the flowers that had been left on the grave. Beside these they made a neat stack of the turves: *You don't want the vestry confronted with a mess. Out of sheer self-defense they'd have to hire more watchmen, or lose the two dollars they get for each plot here.*

January slipped his knife from his boot.

The soil was loose and easily shoveled. Yet sixty-six cubic feet of earth is a great deal to move, and the need to work in silence, and the narrow confines of the dug grave and easy excavation, made the men work in shifts. The other man – so far as January could make out in the misty gleam of the lantern – was a large youth, whose dark hair and snub nose made it unlikely he was a relative. He protested when Pease – if it was Pease – signed him to start the digging, and got a sharp, 'Hsh! You want old Malvers over here?'

Malvers being the watchman, presumably, huddled with his flask in the shelter of the church porch.

The youth looked surly, and with a kind of defiance he pulled a bottle from his pocket and took a protracted gulp. Pease spat a long string of tobacco and said nothing. The youth glared at him and drank again, as if daring him to speak, then capped the bottle and with a kind of lagging deliberation got to work. Pease turned away, unrolled the stretcher, took out a bottle of his own. Had a drink – and then another – and, after a watchful glare at his assistant, pocketed the bottle and moved off into the darkness unbuttoning his flies.

As he had last night, January stepped around a headstone, put a hand over the man's mouth and the blade of his knife against the man's throat, and yanked him away into the fog.

'Make a sound and you're dead.' Even as he said the words January knew he wouldn't do it. Not even the thought of Mr Kelsey's bewildered eyes, the vision of the body that poor man had loved being carved open – the uterus that had borne those sons dumped out on to a dirty table-top, the heart whose kindness had brought all those mourners to see her on her way – was

163

enough to rob a man of life.

Compared to Davy Quent, he was nothing.

Still, Pease didn't know this, and he shuddered with terror like a plump little woman in January's grip.

'Six months ago you got spectacles, a watch, and a silver reservoir pen out of a grave,' January whispered. 'Where was it?'

He slipped his hand from the man's mouth, and the grave robber stammered, 'I don't know nuthin' about it – I never saw them things in my life...'

At the same instant January heard the fleet swish-swish of striding feet in wet grass and shoved his captive around as a shield, as a blow connected with the back of his shoulder with force that felt like a bullet's impact. *Damn it, there WAS a third man...*

He staggered, ducked sideways and heard something whiff past his ear. A sap or a club— Pease grabbed his wrist, twisted in his grip. *He'll have a knife...*

He kneed the smaller man in the belly, wrenched loose as the man behind him blundered into him, his right arm numb and useless. At the top of his lungs he bellowed: 'CHEAT ME WILL YOU, YOU FUCKING BASTARD?!?!' and prayed that the watchman hadn't been bribed or drugged...

He evidently hadn't, because Pease – if it was Pease – and the formless black shape of his late-arriving rescuer fled with the promptness of startled cockroaches. A crash and clatter from the direction of the grave told January that

164

Sullen-Boy had dropped everything and taken to his heels as well – something which he himself proceeded to do, pausing only long enough to scoop up his knife from the ground.

Clearly, they expected the watchman to come running at the slightest sound.

January didn't remain anywhere near the grave, so didn't know whether the watchman did in fact come running or not. He only knew what three such men would do if they found themselves in possession, not of a corpse worth fifty dollars, but of a black man – albeit with a slightly cracked skull – worth three hundred to such individuals as Kyle and Elsie Fowler. He spent the remainder of the night crouched in the laurel bushes along the cemetery wall, which he found after considerable blundering, gingerly flexing and straightening his right arm as the feeling slowly came back into it. When the Christ Church clock struck six, he followed the wall around to the gate, the black fog graying around him and the wet trees looming like home-going ghosts.

As soon as the watchman opened the gate and walked back to his little booth by the church, January slipped through. He walked the three and a half miles back to Trigg's boarding house, chilled to the bone, his shoulder aching as if it had been broken, and arrived in time for breakfast, to find Ritchie Trigg just carrying a very small bundle of clothes and shoes upstairs – 'It's the new boarder's, sir...' – and Ganymede Tyler, looking a little overwhelmed, sitting at the long breakfast table at Dominique's side.

165

FOURTEEN

January slept most of the day. Waking, he found letters from Rose and from Hannibal Sefton – forwarded via Dominique through Henri, to whom they'd been sent at the Indian Queen – and passed the evening writing back to them, though he knew, and they knew, that by the time a reply to his letter reached Washington, he would almost certainly be on his way home.

Still, it was wonderful beyond measure to read that Rose had gotten a few small commissions to translate Thucydides for a bookseller in Mobile; that the first of the strawberry-sellers had begun to promenade along Rue Esplanade singing long, wailing songs about their wares; that Hannibal had yet another new girlfriend, a tavern-keeper on Girod Street named Russian Nancy.

At supper Mede Tyler announced, rather shyly, that he'd been taken on as a waiter at Blodgett's Hotel.

On Saturday morning, January took the steam cars north to Philadelphia and sought out the Catholic church in one of the small alleyways near Chestnut Street that Frank Preston had told him of. There he confessed to killing a man in defense of the life of a friend – 'A black man, Father, not a white one' – and bowed his head under the German priest's troubled recommendation that he turn himself over to the police at once.

'If your cause was just, my son, you should have nothing to fear.'

'De man I kilt wuz frien's wid de po-lice,' said January, in the coarsest field-hand English he could produce. 'He workin' wid de slave stealers, that kidnap free men, an' take 'em to livin' hell.' From Preston also, January knew that at least one such ring operated on the docks of Philadelphia, not far from this church. 'You know there ain't no justice, fo' such as we.'

The priest was silent for a long time after that, and when he spoke at last it was in the tone of a man forcing himself to repeat what he has been told is right. 'It is not for us to judge these things, or to pick which parts of the law we will follow. I will give you absolution, my son, but remember that only God truly knows whether you are in fact forgiven or not for your sin. He will tell you what is right.'

The penance was heavy – daily prayer and fasting for a year – but January left the church and walked back to the train station feeling cleansed.

He returned to Washington in time to walk out to the fields of what had once been the Jenkins farm, to watch the ball game between the Stalwarts and the Judiciary Square Centurions ... and to observe that Ganymede Tyler's inclusion in the team would indeed make the difference, in the contest next week, between victory and defeat.

Mede Tyler was everything Luke Bray had claimed for him, and more. He had a strong sidearm pitch – which engendered a good deal of argument along the sidelines about whether this method of throwing was admissible or not—

('That ain't how it's done in Massachusetts...'

'Well, since we AIN'T in Massachusetts, you can't help but be right about that...')

—and a graceful way of lobbing slow under-hand tosses that looked like they were coming straight at your bat ... until they weren't. The Centurions had a couple of devastating strikers, and had hitherto had things pretty much their own way, so it was gratifying to see them retired to the field after missing those deceptive throws.

'You need a couple extra men, for the game with the French?' Luther Jones, captain of the Centurions, came over to Trigg and the little group of Stalwarts supporters, gathered to one side of the field. 'Fip Franklin can knock any-thing that comes at him – 'cept that new boy's throws,' he added ruefully with a nod toward Mede. 'And Red Vassall can run like the devil. That'd bring you up to fourteen—'

'Do it,' urged January, when Trigg hesitated. He knew what was in his landlord's mind, re-calling his own pitiful performance in last Sunday's practice game. 'We've got the honor of America to uphold.'

'I'm not takin' any of my boys out of the line.' Trigg looked at Jones rather than January, though it was pretty clear that nothing personal had been meant by the offer.

'Oh, hell, no...' Jones hastened to disclaim.

'Hey, I know the point of the game is to hit the ball, not fan around it,' January joked, and they all laughed. 'You can't tell me the French aren't recruiting strikers from the Redcoats.'

'You don't worry about it.' Trigg jabbed a finger at him. 'You get some more practice in, and by next Saturday, you'll be knockin' 'em clean into the woods. We'll take 'em,' he added, turning back to Jones. 'We'll show those—'

Movement from among the spectators drew January's eye. *Police?* Despite the word that most members of the constabulary had bet heavily on the game, it wasn't impossible...

A high-wheeled phaeton yanked to a halt at the edge of the crowd: a man in a blue coat sprang down. January didn't know whether it was the way he moved, or the golden hair beneath the stylish high-crowned hat he wore, that let him recognize, even at a distance, Luke Bray.

Ganymede, sitting on a packing box talking with Frank Preston, turned his head.

You didn't expect him to leave your roof when you signed his freedom papers, did you? January motioned to Trigg, and both men moved inconspicuously in Mede's direction. The young valet got to his feet, waited while his former master strode up to him.

A slave doesn't speak until spoken to.

Face distorted with rage, Bray boxed him hard on the ear, yelled, 'What the hell you mean, boy, creepin' out of the house yesterday mornin' and settin' up your own place? Who the hell'd you think was gonna get my things together this morning? Or run Mrs Bray's errands for her?

169

You even think of that? Just 'cause you're a free man now don't mean you ain't got duties – what the *hell* was you thinking? You sneak your things out of my house like a thief, you don't say a word to anyone about where you're going or that somebody else gonna have to do your work for you ... Here I am comin' in late at the Navy Yard, with everybody grinnin' behind my back 'cause that suck-arse Stockard been sayin' I'd gone and throwed away the best nigger in the District...'

Mede stood, eyes downcast, as the words poured over his head like a poisoned mill-race. For a moment January remembered the stink of the yard behind the Turkey Buzzard, and the fighter Gun lying on the bench with a face like ashes.

'If I'd meant you to quit valetin' for me and go sneak out of my house AND get yourself a room someplace like you thought you was a white man, don't you think I'd have made that *clear*? Just 'cause you're free don't mean you quit bein' my valet, and don't NOBODY quit me without a word, like a thief creepin' off in the night—'

Bray paused, out of breath, and struck Mede again. 'Don't you got anythin' to say for yourself, boy?'

Mede said, very quietly, 'No, sir.' Their faces, so close now, were mirrors of each other, weathered marble and bronze, made of the same mold.

Bray took him by the arm. 'Then you get the hell on that carriage box and come home.'

'No, sir.' Mede braced his feet and settled his weight against the peremptory jerk of Bray's hand.

The Kentuckian's expression would have been comical, had it not been for the grief in Mede's face. 'What?'

'No, sir,' the young man repeated. 'Wednesday when I came home to your house you said I was a free man. You signed papers that I was no longer a slave. Not bein' a slave means I can live where I choose.'

Bray stared at him for nearly a full minute, disbelieving, shocked as if the earth had opened beneath his feet. Then he shouted, 'You ungrateful cur-dog! You mealy-mouth bastard sneak!' January could smell the liquor on him, from where he stood. 'I didn't free you so's you could go off livin' how you choose! All those years of: "Whatever you think best, sir," and: "However makes you comfortable, sir," and now you turn around and run off on me? You get in that goddam carriage 'fore I take the hide off your worthless back—'

'I won't, sir. I'm sorry. I did lay your things out for your Thursday morning before I left, and polished your boots last night—'

'What the *hell* does that have to do with anything? By God you're the stupidest, orneriest nigger I ever— Get in that carriage!'

'No, sir.'

Bray slapped him a third time, then strode off in the direction of his phaeton. January caught Mede by the elbow and steered him into the nearest group of spectators – *does he think Mede's going to stand and wait for him to come back with the whip?* – which congregated around

171

them as if they'd been rehearsed. Someone pulled Mede's jacket off him; someone else handed
him another one of a different color and cut. His
cap was snatched from his head and replaced
with a slouched and tatty beaver. Dominique –
who'd come along with Clarice Perkins – put her
arm through Mede's and smiled up into his face
in a wifely fashion, and the Perkinses, Preston,
and January fell in around them, to make up a
family group as they walked off down Seventeenth Street.

Bray passed them in his phaeton, glaring
furiously right and left with his whip in his hand,
and didn't give them so much as a glance.

When they reached the boarding house Mede
was still trembling.

'You have your papers?' January guided the
young man into a chair in the parlor. Mrs Perkins
herded the children from the room; Dominique
looked as if she might speak, but Preston gently
put a hand on her back, steered her out into the
hall.

When Mede nodded, January continued, 'It
might be you'll want to go North. Preston can
recommend you to the manager of the Baltimore
and Washington, and you can certainly get work
on the trains.'

'I can't—' Mede took a breath, trying to steady
himself. 'I don't want to do that right now, sir.
Thank you,' he added.

'He know you live here?'

'I don't know. He could find out easy enough.'
He raised his head as January drew breath to
speak, went on, 'I can't leave him, sir. He's in...'

He stopped himself – *from saying what? That he's in trouble?*

'I had to get out of that house.' Mede picked his words carefully. 'But I need to be where I'm close.'

'So he can hit you again?'

Mede wiped the blood that trickled from his cut ear. 'He's drunk this evenin'.'

In the silence that followed, January heard Minou's voice in the hall, low and troubled, and Preston saying something in reply.

'—it would not have happened,' she said, and Frank answered, his own voice tired.

'In Louisiana a man frees the children of his free plaçée. Does no man father children on his house women and pretend that they aren't his?' And when Minou did not reply, into her silence he went on, 'Do you think even the French there aren't being drawn into the American way of doing things these days?'

Her voice was sad. 'It is not as it was.'

Daylight faded from the windows. In the dining room, someone lit the lamps. China rattled softly as Octavia Trigg took it from its cupboards. When the door beyond opened, January could smell onions, biscuits, stew.

'He's been very good to me,' Mede said after some time. 'When I was little – three years old, four years old – and my mama died, he'd let me tag along after him. Would take me up on his horse when he'd go hunting. Got Old Marse Luke to have me taught my letters, and made his valet.'

January let his breath out in a tiny sigh. On

Bayou St Cecile, just upriver from Bellefleur, he remembered M'am Gertzer had taken up a pretty little girl from the quarters as a pet: fed from her own plate at table, dressed in pretty calico, taught to fix hair and run about after her carrying her sewing box. And Michie Paul, thirteen-year-old son of the master of Lac Mort Plantation along Bayou St John, had done much the same with a boy out of the quarters: *Hell, P'tit Roux'll follow me anywhere...*

Another custom of the country.

'He ever put you up in a poker game?' January remembered what had eventually happened to *P'tit* Roux, and to M'am Gertzer's pretty little maid-girl.

'He paid two thousand dollars to get me back the next day.'

As if that made it all right.

'And he was drunk.'

'Like this evening.' Outside the window, Trigg and the Reverend came across the yard, bats on their shoulders, reliving each strike and run and throw.

'That sounds stupid, doesn't it?' Mede raised his eyes to him. 'For me to care about him? He's a good man, Mr J. You've seen him at his worst.'

Does he have a best?

How many years since YOU'VE seen it?

'I can't leave him. Not flat cold, get-out-of-town leave. He's in trouble—'

'What kind of trouble?'

The young man shook his head.

'Do you think you can get him out of it?'

'No, sir. But even if I'm free, I'm still his Man

174

Friday. I won't leave him in it alone.'

'It have anything to do with why you had to get out of his house?'

Mede hesitated for so long before replying, as if weighing incidents and impressions, that January thought he wasn't going to answer. At length he said, 'I can't say that, sir.'

Did Mrs Bray put her hand on your thigh some afternoon when the two of you were alone in the house?

Did Luke?

'I don't—' Mede broke off, thought about his words. 'I don't rightly know what to do, sir. I do need advice, but I don't ... I don't know how to go about getting it, without someone getting hurt.'

Bright, soft voices in the dining room: little Olive Perkins, and Mandie Trigg. Mrs Trigg's deep alto: 'No, honey, the blade of the knife got to turn toward the plate, 'cause you don't want to be pointin' the edge of a knife at your guest...' Trigg's voice and Perkins' in the hall, and a moment later the front door closing: 'Evenin', Mr Poe, sir. Can my wife make you a cup of tea, 'fore dinner's ready?'

'Thank you, sir, I would take that most kindly of her, if it won't be any trouble.'

January thought Poe's footfalls hesitated a moment before the big parlor door, before they crossed the hall to his small and privileged sanctum opposite. Because he'd seen that January was in conversation with a man of his own race? Or because it didn't behoove a white man to go ask a black one how the investigation was proceeding?

Mede seemed to hear none of it. Only sat looking into the neatly-swept fireplace, where logs
and kindling stood ready to warm the chilly
room.

Everyone Mede knew, January recalled, was
back in Georgetown. Maids, cook, stableman ...
Or else back in Kentucky, where 'Marse Luke'
had been so kind. January well remembered his
own sense of isolation, that first year in New
Orleans. He had cried every night because he
missed the other members of the hogmeat gang,
desperately missed his father and his aunties and
uncles, missed every dog and mule and kitchen
cat on the place where he'd been beaten, starved,
and lived every day of his life in terror that he'd
lose his family and friends at a drunkard's whim.

And ashamed that he was so weak as to cry.

Trust has to be earned. It was years before he'd
found anyone he could speak to.

'It's all strange now.' He lightly touched the
young man's back. 'Took me years to get used to
it, and I was just a kid – and a field hand at that.'

Mede glanced up at him, as if startled to find
that someone else – someone free and who
seemed to know his way around – had started the
same road from the same place.

'That was a good game you played this afternoon. Settle a bit, and get some sleep. But don't
go back to him.'

'No, sir. I won't do that.'

FIFTEEN

Sunday after Mass, January, Poe, and Henri met in the 'white folks' parlor' and divided the surgeons in Washington up amongst them. More accurately, January, Poe, and Chloë each took a list of surgeons from the City Directory, but as it would be wildly improper for a lady – be she never so married – to go visiting the offices of medical gentlemen without a male escort, when they sallied forth on Monday, she went on Henri's arm, to observe the reactions of those gentlemen to her husband's carefully-conned questions.

The tale – invented by Poe in the face of the obvious fact that neither he nor Henri could convincingly pass himself off as a medical student – was that M'sieu Viellard (or 'Mr Allan') was an aspiring artist, disbarred from the Pennsylvania Academy of the Fine Arts, the American Academy of the Fine Arts, and the National Academy ... 'Out of jealousy! Sheer jealousy!' went the story, in tones which would, it was hoped, imply that overfondness for wine and women had more to do with his expulsion than his ability to out-paint the likes of John Trumbull. Mr Allan (or M'sieu Viellard) sought instruction in anatomy in order to paint in the muscular style of Michelangelo and was willing to pay *extremely handsomely* for lessons in the specific attachment of muscles, and the arrangement of tendons, organs, and veins.

Since the idea of a black man being either a professional artist, or wealthy enough to pay handsomely for anything, was almost as ludicrous as that of a well-bred white woman visiting surgeons' offices by herself, January worked in partnership with Poe. 'You're a credit to your parents, sir,' he observed on the way down the rather grimy steps of the office of Mr Clunch, on D Street, after that gentleman had informed them in no uncertain terms that if *dissection* was what Mr Allan was hinting at, he, Bernard Clunch, had nothing further to discuss, not for a hundred dollars or a thousand.

'My stepfather would suffer an apoplexy to hear you say so, sir.' Poe sounded pleased at that prospect as he straightened the lapels of his black greatcoat. Despite his preference for black, he had also – when Henri had given him the money for a new waistcoat in the interests of verisimilitude ('You need to look as if you *could* hand them a hundred dollars to show you how to cut up a corpse') – chosen a dandyish jonquil-yellow garment to further his role. 'God knows,' he went on with a grin, 'I'm sufficiently familiar with the breed to do a creditable imitation of the would-be Michelangelos I've met ... Actual working artists are in general very businesslike fellows, you know.'

'That's my experience as well,' agreed January. 'Mad as hatters, of course—'

'Oh, God, yes!' He paused as they emerged on to the street, and January ticked Mr Clunch's name from the list.

'And jealous as schoolgirls, some of them...'

'Most artists are.' Poe considered the list, and then the sky, which was gray and threatening rain. They were in the heart of the town, near the city hall and Judiciary Square; the streets were a gumbo of mud, the air redolent with the cursing of Irish teamsters, the cracking of whips.

'In our heart of hearts. I don't know if musicians are the same,' Poe said. They turned their steps along the plank sidewalk toward the neighborhood known as Reservation B – swampland on the so-called 'Mall' that had been sold off for commercial development. 'God knows I'm eaten with envy when I see another man's poem in print, when mine has been passed over: how *dare* they? Terrible when it's better than mine, because I wish *I'd* had the talent to write that well—'

'*Desiring this man's art, and that man's scope*,' January said, quoting the greatest of poets who'd ever gnashed his teeth over another's success, and Poe laughed.

'Yes, at least I'm in good company.' He shoved his hands in his greatcoat pockets, against the sharp chill of the river breeze. 'And it's ten times more maddening when it's some abominable effusion by a Gothic rodomontodian whose entire repertoire of human experience has been gleaned from other peoples' novels. At least that conceited puppy "Mr Allan" is trying to get himself cadaver drawing-lessons by inquiring for

179

grave robbers. The infuriating ones are those who write execrably and refuse to listen to a breath of criticism: mightn't it be a trifle *unlikely* that the exchanged baby daughter of a French duke should be the *one* flower girl whose wares are bought by a disguised Prince seeking his long-lost father in the slums of New York?'

January pretended deep thought. 'Could happen...'

Poe made a face, as if he'd bitten sour fruit. 'The author's husband called me out.' They halted before the shabby line of clapboard shops given as the address of Mr Nicholas Wellesley, Surgeon; there was a note of weary bitterness in the poet's voice. 'Well, not immediately. First he attempted to sue me. I believe his lawyer pointed out to him that the publication of a book – even if one's husband pays for it – places that book in the domain of a public document, open to criticism by those who are paid by the newspapers to read and criticize books. *Then* he called me out. When I refused to meet him – I *do* have a family to support, who unlike his would be left quite destitute by my martyrdom to the principle of literary verisimilitude – I was warned that he'd paid three of his employees – he is a building contractor – to teach me a less formal lesson in keeping my opinions to myself. I thought it best to leave Baltimore for a time.'

'If you'll pardon the liberty, sir–' with whites, even friendly ones, it was always well to be careful – 'I did wonder what you were doing in Washington.'

'It isn't only that.' The young man stood for a

180

moment in the mouth of the passway between that building and the next: a sign pointed down the mucky slot with the information that Mr Wellesley's office could be found further along. 'The incident brought home to me the fact that it might, perhaps, be a trifle quixotic of me to attempt to make my living entirely by my pen. Quixotic, and detrimental to those who depend upon me for shelter and food.'

After a few moments' thoughtful silence, January said, 'I can't argue with you there.'

Cold wind skirled down the wide avenues of Washington, whipped the black skirts of Poe's shabby greatcoat. Flecks of rain bit like the promise of sorrow to come.

'Well.' Poe sighed and straightened his shoulders. 'In the meantime, I comfort myself with the reflection that to an artist, no experience is ever wasted – and I must and will have an interview with a bona fide grave-robber! *Allons-y*, Benjamin.' And with that curious inward reconfiguration characteristic of actors, he ceased to be a wryly intelligent poet, critic, and observer of human nature, and became the arrogant and self-obsessed would-be Michelangelo Mr Allan. 'Come along.'

A good and humble valet, January said, 'Yes, sir, Marse Eddie,' and followed him along to the surgeon's door.

'Of course I have no dealings with such people myself,' Mr Wellesley hastened to explain.

'No, certainly, sir, I would never mean to imply...'

'But one does hear things in my profession.' The stooped gray-haired gentleman cast a sharply calculating eye over his visitor ... *His WHITE visitor*, January observed. The large valet who had accompanied Mr Allan into the outer room of the surgery was, of course, no more regarded than the hat his master had handed him. 'I believe I could get in touch with someone who could provide us the – er – *facilities* you require ... though I warn you now, a hundred dollars...'

'The hundred dollars is for your services, sir,' replied 'Mr Allan' loftily. 'Naturally, I understand such people charge for their – ah – goods.' He produced a twenty-dollar gold-piece from his pocket and laid it on the corner of the surgeon's scarred desk. January took note of how Mr Wellesley's eyes flared. Judging by the disused look of the office, enthusiasm was understandable. Surgeons cost money. Poe was far from the only man in Washington with a family to support.

'Approximately how long should your enquiries take, sir? I can return Thursday, at about this hour...'

'That should give me time.' Mr Wellesley's skinny fingers nipped up the coin as if he feared Poe would change his mind and take it away again. 'Farcy uses an accommodation address, but he's generally fairly quick to reply...'

Since Henri was no more an actor than he was a medical student, it had been agreed that it was Chloë who would be the besotted and ambitious wife, and who would do all the talking. Like

182

Poe, she had sufficient experience with over-bearing French Creole matrons to personate one with terrifying accuracy.

'I only hope I shan't be obliged to actually assist at a dissection,' fretted Henri that evening when they reassembled in the boarding house parlor. 'I'm not sure that I could – well – sustain the role to that extent.'

'No reason why you should have to, sir,' returned January bracingly as he spread his list and Chloë's on the table in the small parlor. 'Remember, you're a *poseur*. You only *think* you're a second Michelangelo. This may be the first occasion you've ever been in the same room with a corpse.'

'If you faint dead away, I'll have smelling salts on hand,' encouraged Chloë heartlessly.

'*Cher*—!' Dominique put her arms protectively around Henri, who had turned slightly green. She looked tired and fretful, as if the day's inclement weather bore upon her nerves. Like Mede Tyler, thought January, she was separated from almost everyone she knew – her friends, the little household she kept on Rue Dumaine, the familiar rhythms and activities of her community. She might assist the Perkinses with teaching the children, or cut and stitch clothing for her own child, or shop – accom-panied by her maid – in such facilities as Wash-ington offered women of color, but the fact remained that she was uprooted and alone in a strange town.

'In any case,' soothed Poe, 'we will have made our contact with our resurrectionist – and gotten from him Mr Pease's direction, if he isn't Mr Pease himself – long before the proceedings start.'

'*Bleu.*' Chloë looked up from considering the lists over January's shoulder. 'I have never seen a dissection – don't look like that, Henri ... I don't suppose there's a way that I can come along and watch, M'sieu Poe? Oh, all right,' she added as January and Henri both shook their heads. 'How many took the bait today, and who must we visit tomorrow?'

'Benjamin and Mr Poe – if Mr Poe would be so good as to continue his efforts on our behalf – could take Alexandria all in a day, I dare say.' Henri took up the papers, on which January had underlined in kitchen pencil the surgeons willing to "make arrangements" and had further noted the names mentioned by the surgeons in question, if any. 'But if you recall, my dear, you and I will be paying a call on Dr Woolmer at the Potomac School.'

With this, Chloë and Henri departed, and Poe ascended to his own spartan chamber to change shirt and waistcoat before setting forth for another Washington 'at home' in the hopes of encountering some department head in quest of a clerk. 'And I can only pray that none of the other guests there is one of the surgeons we've visited,' sighed the poet as he came downstairs, adjusting his best black silk cravat, to encounter January in the hall again. January had changed clothes also – a coarse mechanic's shirt made of ticking – and bore four long 'pegs' and his bat on his shoulder.

'I shouldn't worry, sir,' returned January cheerfully. 'What would a surgeon be doing at such an event? He's already *got* a job.'

The afternoon's sprinkly showers had ceased. A sufficient number of the Centurions were assembled in the field beside the Reedy Branch in the gray end of afternoon to ensure a ball game, but the atmosphere was more helpful than competitive. 'Hell,' said Fip Franklin of the Centurions as he took January aside to give him a little extra practice at hitting the ball, 'every man on the team got money on you boys, against the French.'

January picked out Gonesse and Lenoir in the crowd along the fringes of the field – quite a gathering, this evening, particularly for a Monday – observing the game. With them he recognized Mr Noyes, the lanky young abolitionist clerk who'd come down to the kitchen of the British Ministry Tuesday night.

'He's captain of the Eagles,' Trigg identified him, coming over to January while the other Stalwarts lined up into ragged order behind the striker's position, halfway between two of the pegs. 'New England boys – Whigs.'

'I didn't know there were any in Washington these days.'

'More than you'd think. They've got a game going Saturday against the Warriors, but I'm told the betting on it is nothing to the money on ours.'

Hence, reflected January drily, the relative pallor of the crowd. All the sporting Senators and youthful Congressmen, jealously gauging not only the actual prowess of the black team and the foreigners, but what their strength *should* be, in whatever universe of race nobility or degeneration existed in their heads and hearts.

Should Frenchmen be able to beat Americans – even if those Americans were black?

Or was there no such thing as a black American? Did Trigg, and Mede, gangly Reverend Perkins and January himself, count only as transplanted Africans, a lesser and degraded race?

There's a dilemma for you, gentlemen. Are you ready to put good money on what you feel SHOULD be?

Reason enough to ride out to the far end of the Second Ward to see Ganymede Tyler throw.

His gaze passed across the crowd – as usual, January was the tallest man present – and he picked out curly-haired Royall Stockard in a fancy gig, with young Chilperic Creighton, the planter's son, beside him. Close by, a little surprisingly, January saw Frank Preston – fresh from the Baltimore run and still in his neat blue conductor's uniform – with Dominique, Thèrése, Charmian and Musette. Thèrése, in an extremely fashionable plumed bonnet, looked bored, as usual, by the absolute American vulgarity of the gathering, but Minou was arguing animatedly with the young conductor about something on the pad of paper that he held.

'I hear tell,' put in Handsome Dan, 'there's folks got a *thousand dollars* on that game.'

'That's ridiculous.' Trigg looked almost angry at the words. 'It's a damn *game...*'

This was all the commentary he had time for, because Luther Jones threw a high sidearm lob to Reverend Perkins, who knocked it straight at the feet of the Centurion behind third base. The Centurion picked it out of the air on the first bounce and neatly plugged Seth Berger, sprinting from the second peg to the third, and that was that.

Not that it made a difference, with Mede pitching. The Centurions were out in the field again before some of them had time to find places on the boxes.

'I just hope Bray leaves Mede alone until Saturday,' remarked January, swinging his bat experimentally and hoping he'd actually hit something when he came up to position. 'The last thing we need is for him to be put off his game by the kind of scene we had Friday.'

'As I understand it—' Trigg glanced in the direction of Stockard – 'Bray's been warned to stay away from Mede, for just that reason.'

As Mede stepped up to the striker's zone, he too scanned the crowd worriedly, the setting sun transforming him into a slim long-limbed young god. Then he returned his attention to the Centurion thrower, the bat held above his shoulder, gauging the toss not as a move from an enemy, but simply as a job to be done, and done to perfection.

Why? January wondered. *Because of a love for the game, or for these comrades he'd known for so short a time?*

Or because his former master – his brother – had ordered him to win?

And where would he go from here?

It wasn't until the night before the game that Bray was heard from.

It was Good Friday, and January – who, mindful of the Philadelphia priest's penance, had fasted all day – walked out to Georgetown with Minou, Charmian, and the servants to Mass. They had barely been home an hour when Henri's rented carriage arrived and Dominique departed again, with Thèrése, whom she generally took along to Mrs Purchase's to make coffee. Everyone else in the boarding house went to the I Street Methodist Chapel (colored) to hear Reverend Perkins preach and returned just before dark, to tea and jam cakes in the parlor, and a late dinner of cold meats and cheese. The Reverend and January read the Bible to the children in the parlor, and Mede then helped Clarice herd the little ones up to bed.

Mrs Trigg had just begun to clear up the cups when knocking clattered at the front door.

Talk in the parlor silenced at once. All eyes went to the clock.

It was after curfew. At this hour, a visitor's knock never boded well.

Trigg's footfalls sounded loud as hammer blows on the oak planks of the hall.

Hurried voices. Returning feet.

'Mede?' Trigg came back in, followed by a skinny youth in a coachman's caped greatcoat.

Bray's coachman. January knew his face, from brief glimpses by torchlight.

The boy was ashen with shock.

'Jem—' Mede started forward toward him.

188

'It's Marse Luke, Mede,' said Jem. 'He's tried to kill himself.'

SIXTEEN

'Has a doctor been sent for?'

Jem shook his head. 'Miz Rowena said no-body's to know—'

'Will you come with me, Mr J?'

In Mede's turquoise eyes, January saw that Luke's Good Man Friday knew that Luke's wife wouldn't send.

'Mrs Bray—' Mede bit off whatever he had to say about his master's wife. 'Will you come?'

Luke Bray's phaeton waited at the end of the gravel drive. The youthful coachman scrambled up into the high rear seat, and against every city ordinance from Maryland to the Sabine River, Mede took the reins of the sleek black team. *And let's hope the city constables are too drunk to be watching...*

Jail was not where January wanted to end up tonight.

The moon was just past full, and though fog lay thin toward the river and the canal, as the vehicle swept up Nineteenth Street, most of it was left behind. January breathed a prayer of thanks for those racecourse thoroughfares.

'What did your master do?' he asked over his

189

shoulder to Jem. 'How did he do it?'

'He cut his wrists, sir.' The boy's accent was local – Virginia or Maryland rather than the rougher inflections of Kentucky. 'Miz Rowena says he was drunk. An' he *was* drunk, sir, when he came home, drunker'n I've ever seen him. Peter – that's his new valet, sir – put him to bed. Then just about midnight he rang his bell, an' Peter went in an' found him, with his wrists cut an' blood all over the room.'

'Did Mrs Bray bandage up his wrists herself? Or have one of the servants do it?'

'Herself, sir. She sent Robbie – that's the gardener, sir – for that Mr Oldmixton at the British Ministry, that's a friend of her father's. But she said, *Nobody else*. She said, Mr Luke's reputation couldn't take the scandal.'

'*Her* reputation, she means.' Mede's voice was tight.

'Do you know any reason why he would have done it?' January glanced to the young man beside him.

Mede kept his eyes on the pale smudge of the road. 'No, sir.'

The woods by Rock Creek cut out even the glimmer of moonlight. Jem sprang from his perch to lead the horses across the Paper Mill bridge, the smell of the creek cold and ferrous in the blackness below.

Curtains masked all trace of lamplight behind the shutters of the Bray house. In the rear yard a shiny English brougham was drawn up, its horse rugged against the cold and its coachman seated in the kitchen drinking coffee with the cook. As

190

they came into the dim oil-lamp glow of the kitchen Mede asked, 'How is he?' and the cook spread his hands.

'Sleepin'.' Like Jem, this man had the slurry lowland accent of Virginia. January guessed they'd both been purchased at the same time as the house. 'Miz Rowena keeps sayin' how he'll be all right, but he sure lost a bucket of blood. Mr Oldmixton up with Miz Rowena now.'

'Has a doctor been sent for?' January held up his satchel. 'I'm staying at the same house with Mede, my name's Ben January. I trained as a surgeon in Paris. I came in case—'

Some of the tension went out of the cook's round face, and he rose to shake January's hand. 'Lord bless you for comin', sir. I don't know if Mr Oldmixton sent for anybody, and neither does Tommy here—' He nodded toward the strange coachman. 'But Miz Rowena keeps sayin' how Marse Luke don't need no doctor just for a *fool accident* with a *saber*.' His glance moved toward Tommy the coachman: *He doesn't know.*

And the British Minister's coachman returned the look with tired eyes that said, *Oh, the hell I don't.*

January followed Mede up the back stairs.

Luke Bray slept in the sort of chamber that was referred to in polite circles as 'the gentleman's dressing room', lest anyone be prompted to faint with horror at the thought that the master and mistress of the house didn't sleep in the same bed the way honest yeoman farmers were supposed to. Among the French, Spanish, and

African Creoles of Louisiana, houses of any size were divided into the men's side and the women's. January routinely slept in his wife's room and bed, but had his own bedchamber and study on the other side of the parlor, and the American arrangement struck him as school-girlish.

Like many such chambers – including January's back on Rue Esplanade – Bray's was small and plainly furnished, containing the obligatory single bed, a washstand, an armoire, a single chair, and not much else. The chair had been moved over beside the bed and bore three lamps, only one of which was now alight. Bandages, scissors, pins and sticking plaster piled a corner of the washstand. The bowl and ewer were missing – *carried to the scullery to be rinsed?* The bedlinen had been recently changed, too, but when January lit the other two lamps, the brighter glow showed smudges of blood on the wallpaper. The whole room stank of it.

Bray's face was wax pale and filmed with sweat. His breath rasped through gray lips, and his shut eyes had a sunken look. Mede whispered, 'Oh, dear God!' sank to his knees beside the bed and took his brother's hand. 'I'm here, Marse Luke. Your Good Man Friday's here.'

Both arms were tightly bandaged.

'Can you do something for him, Mr J? Give him something?'

January brought the lamp nearer and retracted the patient's eyelid, saw that the pupil was barely a pinpoint in the blue iris.

Oh, indeed?

There was no sign of a laudanum bottle anywhere in the room.

'When he wakes he'll need water. Broth, if it's
available. Can you go down and ask the cook to
make some? Beef or chicken, it doesn't matter ...
And bring me some water on your way up, if you
would. Where would his valet – Peter, Jem said?
– put his clothing?' Even as Mede darted from
the room, January saw coat, trousers, waistcoat
folded beside the washstand. When he went to
look at them he understood why they hadn't
been replaced in the armoire. They reeked of
alcohol, as if someone had emptied a bottle over
them.

In fact, he thought, very much as if someone
had emptied a bottle over them.

He went through the pockets quickly. Money,
visiting cards – dumped in loose, not stored in a
card case – a handkerchief in the coat. More
visiting cards and a watch in the vest. January
opened the watch, and saw that a piece of notepaper had been folded small and jammed tightly
into the case.

He unfolded it.

Magic squares.

'What the—?'

January turned. Pitcher in hands, Mede stood
at his side.

'It's them things that were in Mr Singletary's
notebook.'

'They are,' agreed January. 'But this isn't a
page from the notebook—'

'No, sir, I know. That's Mrs Bray's stationery
from her desk. I get sent to buy it from Moffatt's

all the time. But that's Mr Luke's hand, the way he shapes his numbers, with the four open at the top.'

'Did he ever see Singletary's notebook?'

'No, sir. He never even spoke to Mr Singletary, but the once. And then afterwards he's laughing about him – not mean, just shakin' his head over him goin' on the way he did about French money and Turkish money to a total stranger he'd never met before, in a lady's parlor. And it was kind of funny,' added Mede, with the tiniest ghost of a reminiscent grin.

Voices in the stairwell outside: '—isn't any reason for you to remain,' said Mr Oldmixton, like coffee-brown velvet. 'I shall be leaving the moment Congress adjourns and won't return until December. I can easily escort you back...'

'It's kind of you to offer, sir.' Rowena Bray's voice was faint, but steady. 'But I think we both know that my place is here. It's just that I'm afraid—'

Mede stepped quickly to the doorway of the chamber. 'Mrs Bray—'

'Mede!' Through the half-opened door, January saw Mrs Bray run from the top of the stair and clasp the young valet's hands. 'Oh, thank God you've come!'

'M'am, please forgive me if I've done what I shouldn't. I brought a fellow who stays at the same boarding house as me, a surgeon, Mr January. He trained in Paris—'

Mrs Bray looked startled, as if trying to work out what a black man was doing staying in the same boarding house with a surgeon, but Old-

194

mixton clapped Mede on the shoulder and said, 'Good man! Quick thinking!' He strode into the little bedchamber as January tucked all the cards, and the sheet of notepaper, into his vest pockets, and stepped away from the folded clothing.

'Mr January—' Oldmixton paused on the threshold, his hand extended. It wasn't an American's frown of startled disapproval (*What's this Negro doing in Mr Bray's bedchamber and where's this surgeon Mede spoke of?*), but only the momentary puzzlement of unexpected recognition.

And then, 'Good Heavens!' as he clasped January's hand. 'I'd never have thought ... You play like a professional, sir.'

'I *am* a professional, sir,' January replied. 'You don't think anyone in this country would hire a black surgeon, do you?' He turned back to the bed. 'How long before anyone found him?'

'Not long, I don't believe.' The Englishman knelt beside the bed, studied Bray's slack face in the lamplight. 'He's lost a shocking amount of blood, of course. Isn't there some new operation they're doing now in cases like these, to infuse the blood of a healthy man into the veins of one who's lost a great deal?'

'Is that true, sir?' Mede's eyes blazed with such hope that he looked almost foolish. 'Can you do that?'

'It's been done,' said January. 'But in at least half the cases the patient dies.'

In the doorway, Rowena Bray made a small noise, like a sob, and pressed her lace-mitted

195

hand to her lips.

'I won't know anything for certain until I can see Mr Bray in daylight,' January went on. 'But I think if he's lived this long, he'll survive. I've seen men survive worse after battle – or duels.' He turned to the woman, dressed, he noticed, in a day-gown of blue delaine. Even her hair had been neatly combed, braided and coiled on the back of her head.

Probably in the hour between the discovery of Bray's attempt and the arrival of Mr Oldmixton. Such, he supposed, was the strictness of a girl's upbringing, that even crisis must not discover her in her own home undressed.

'Do you feel able to talk about this, M'am?' he asked. 'Or would you rather send for Mr Bray's valet? I understand it was he who found your husband.'

'It was...' She caught the jamb of the door as if to support herself, groped in her pocket for something, probably smelling salts.

Oldmixton shifted the lamps to the washstand and brought the chair around for her to sit on, then gathered the medical detritus and bore it out into the hall.

'We had spent the evening at Mr Pageot's. Mr Bray passed most of the evening gambling with the other gentlemen, for shockingly high stakes, I'm afraid. Mr Bray was ... was severely intoxicated, worse than I've ever seen him. In the carriage he kept saying over and over again that we were ruined. I don't know—' She fought to keep her voice steady. 'I don't know whether this is true or not. He's said this before.'

She passed her hand briefly over her mouth, as if in thought but, January suspected, to keep anyone from seeing how her lips trembled.

'I was ... I was exasperated with him and went to bed. I knew nothing more until I heard Peter shouting. I ran into Mr Bray's room and found him lying...'

Her voice pinched off, but her eyes went to the corner nearest the bed, where a thick ribbon of cloth hung down, ending in a seedy tassel. Blood smudged the wall, stained the floor beneath. She fumbled again in her pockets, found the vinaigrette this time. Her hands shook so badly that she could barely get the top off.

'He'd emptied his pockets. There were notes of his gambling losses all over the floor. I'm afraid I fainted—'

'I've added up the notes.' Oldmixton returned empty-handed to the room. 'They come to about fifteen hundred dollars, which is not a shocking amount, given the stakes that men play for in this town. Hardly enough to slit one's wrists over, if one were in one's right mind.'

January looked for a time at the still face against the pillow linen, at Mede's molasses-colored curls resting beside it.

Mrs Bray took another whiff of her phial. 'I knew we were often without money. Last month he sold two of the carriage horses, and – and one of the maids. It's been my impression that the situation has been worsening.' Lamplight glistened in her tears of shock and mortification. 'And in these last few months he has been ... He has not been himself. He acts the part among his friends, and with the men he knows at the Navy Department, but I know him. He's been deeply troubled in his mind, prey to moods of terrible despair. I've spoken to you—'

She reached toward Oldmixton, who took her hand reassuringly. 'Every time I speak to him about gambling, he puts me off. He says that in this country a man must gamble, and must show himself game and unafraid. I have feared...'

Her voice thinned to nothing, and she sat trembling.

'Forgive me for asking this, M'am,' said January at length. 'But did your husband have money on this ball game that Mede is playing in this afternoon?'

Mede's head came up sharply. 'I couldn't—'

'If you don't,' January said, 'I think it may make the situation worse, as far as Mr Bray is concerned.'

'He does,' the lady whispered. 'How much, I have no idea, but ... a great deal, I think. Oh, Mede, *can* you play? *Could* you?'

'Of course, M'am,' responded Mede at once. 'He gave me my freedom, for me to play this game.' He turned to January. 'I'll be at the field at four. Mr Springer at Blodgett's gave me today off...'

'If you'll be playing–' January laid a hand on Mede's shoulder – 'especially now, you need as much rest as you can get. Please excuse us, M'am,' he added, as Mrs Bray began to speak, and, rising, led the younger man into the hall.

'He needs me.' Mede said this as if it explained everything.

198

January lowered his voice almost to a whisper. 'It may be that's what someone counted on. Did Mr Bray ever take opium? Or drink laudanum?'

'No, sir!' Mede sounded shocked.

'Did you ever know him to get so drunk he spilled liquor on his clothes? I didn't think so – but his clothes smell too much. As if someone took him aside and sprinkled him.'

Mede only stared at him, not understanding.

'I don't think Mr Bray got himself that drunk,' said January softly, 'and I don't think Mr Bray slit his own wrists. He doesn't sleep with Mrs Bray, does he?'

Had the light in the hallway had been better, January guessed he'd have seen blood flush up under the young man's skin. 'No, sir. Not for the longest. Sometimes when he's drunk he'll ... But she keeps her door locked.'

'So someone knew if he got falling-down, stinking drunk at the Pageot's soirée he'd be in his bedroom alone.'

'Who—?'

'Someone who had a thousand dollars bet on today's game? Slitting a man's wrists isn't the way to kill him, Mede. As suicides go, it's a poor choice, and an even worse one for murder. It might be that someone did this simply to make sure *you* weren't in fit shape to play. Either because you hadn't had any sleep ... or because you'd be coming across the Paper Mill bridge late tomorrow afternoon by yourself.'

Mede stared at him, appalled. 'For a *ball game*? Ben, that's insane!'

'Not a ball game,' said January quietly. 'For a

199

thousand dollars? Or two thousand? Or three thousand, depending on what the odds are?'

Or maybe for the honor of America?

Mede only shook his head. A country boy, thought January, when all was said and done. Raised in the peaceful hills of Kentucky, a bucolic world of horses and deer and the grinding rigors of agricultural labor. Exhausting and unfair, but straightforward, like Robinson Crusoe's island.

'I don't believe it.'

No, thought January. *Neither do I.*

In his pocket he fingered the fragile notepaper, scribbled with magic squares.

So what IS going on?

SEVENTEEN

'There's nothing further you can do tonight, Rowena.' Mr Oldmixton's voice was soothing as he led Mrs Bray from the bedroom. The upstairs hall formed a sort of gallery around the main stairwell, which descended to the center hall downstairs. On the other side of that dark gulf a lamplit door stood open, though Oldmixton didn't approach it closer than the head of the stair. 'I shall remain with Luke tonight. In his current state of mind I don't think he ought to be alone...'

A maid appeared in the bedroom door. Mrs Bray clung to her friend's hand, and very softly, January breathed to Mede, 'Delay him.'

He slipped back into Bray's room. It was ridiculous on the face of it to think he'd be able to see anything useful by the low amber gloom of the lamps, but he took one up nevertheless, crossed to the window which looked east over the neglected lawn, and examined the casement around the latch.

Back in New Orleans, Abishag Shaw – January reflected drily – would take one look at the chipped old paint, the ill-fitting frame, and pronounce, *Forced open with a penknife not later'n midnight, I reckon, by a left-handed man what used to be a sailor...*

Damn him.

January himself could see nothing. Whether the scratches in the paint on the latch were new or old was a mystery to him and probably would be so even in full daylight. He undid the latch, opened the casement inward, and looked at the corresponding latch on the shutters. There was nothing there either that screamed at him, *This was forced!* but he had no idea what such a mark would look like. The brass had been treated with a dark stain of some kind – his brother-in-law, Paul Corbier the upholsterer, would have been able to tell him what – and it was liberally scratched all around where it fitted into its slot on the other shutter.

But it was a latch, not a bolt. It could have been easily forced.

The wood between the shutters was worn pale

by the nightly friction of being opened and closed.

And our wrist-slitter – if there was one – could have entered through any window in the house and tiptoed up here. Everyone was asleep.

A pallet bed was rolled up in the corner. Presumably, the new valet Peter hadn't been required to sleep in his master's room, if Bray could slit his wrists in despair and privacy: the pallet was probably Mede's. Many men – and women, too – held to the old custom of keeping their servant nearby. A country planter, even a young one, might well have been raised to think it indispensable. He'd talked to ex-servants in both Paris and London who'd told him of aristocratic masters who'd adhered to the same habit, either because they feared an intruder or because they simply couldn't conceive of not having someone at their beck and call every second of the day.

Did Mrs Bray – a banker's daughter – require her maid to sleep at the foot of her bed?

He doubted it. The modern way was to give servants a room in the attic, but enough people still followed the old custom to make him wonder, *Who knew there would be no servant asleep in the room?*

Everyone in Washington, of course, would have heard from Bray that Mede had forsaken him *like a thief creepin' off in the night.*

And a great many would know that Bray would not be in bed with his wife.

Oldmixton's firm tread creaked the waxed floorboards of the hall. Close by the door Mede spoke: 'Is there anything further I can do, sir?'

January returned soundlessly to the bedside and replaced the lamp on the chair. From his satchel he drew his stethoscope, knelt to place the flared muzzle of the long cherrywood tube to Bray's chest.

'Any change?' Oldmixton's shadow bulked against the candle flicker of the hall.

'The heart's action is a little slower. That's a good sign.' January returned the tube to his bag. 'I've asked Mede to have the cook make broth. Keep him on fluids – clear broths and juice – for the first day or so. His digestion will be weak. Marrow or meat jelly is good. No alcohol of course—'

Oldmixton, who had knelt at January's side to study Bray's face in the honey-gold light, turned his head to regard him for a moment, then asked, 'What the *hell* are you doing playing piano for your living, sir?'

'How long have you lived in the United States, sir?'

The secretary laughed mirthlessly. 'I do beg your pardon. But—' He shook his head, and January held up a hand.

'I was a surgeon in France for six years and never made enough to wed, or even buy myself a new waistcoat,' he said. 'When I took up a profession considered more suitable for a man of my race, I was able to do both. And,' he added, 'I'm a very good piano player. If you believe that joy has value, it isn't as much of a waste as you fear. Will Mrs Bray be all right?'

'Married to a drunkard who runs up nearly two

thousand dollars in gambling debts in an evening? I doubt it.'

January was silent.

'I'm sorry,' Oldmixton apologized at once. 'Shockingly bad form, but— I feel responsible. I fear I played Cupid in this match. She met him in my house, three years ago, on a visit to Washington with her aunt. He's some connection of Mr Pointsett's – the Secretary of War – and seemed promising to go far. I hope Mrs Bray will accept my offer and return to London with me once Congress rises – Washington in July is beyond frightful. Like Hell without the Devil's conversation to enliven it. If for no other reason than because if something does ... happen ... she'll hear of it second-hand, and after the fact.'

'You think he'll make another attempt?'

Or someone else will?

'Mrs Bray says she has feared this for some time. She knows her husband better than anyone. I should call in a nerve doctor, did such a thing exist in this benighted country, but the only specialist of the kind is that ghastly wretch in Alexandria. Aside from the fact that I wouldn't send a rabid dog to that man's asylum if it had bit me, Mr Bray would never consent to be seen. It would be the end of his career with the Navy Department...'

'And the end of Mrs Bray in decent society?'

'It sounds heartless to say so,' agreed Oldmixton quietly, 'but yes. The world is monstrously unfair to women who are so unfortunate as to marry good-looking scoundrels.'

He rose from the bedside and walked with

January down the wide stairway to the front hall, Mede following quietly with a lamp. *Trust an Englishman, reflected January, not to have it cross his mind that a black man, be he never so much a surgeon, ought not to be permitted to use the main stair...*

'Has she family in England?' The single lamp barely made a dent in the blackness that filled the tall space around them.

'Oh, heavens, yes. Hurlstone and Ludd is one of the five largest private banks in England. But I suspect she married Mr Bray – quite aside from his undoubted comeliness – to disoblige her parents. Her father is one of the most horrid men I've ever encountered, and there was a reason she chose to come with her aunt to America when she finished school rather than return to his house. There isn't a great deal to choose between living as a grass widow beneath her father's roof and stultifying on a two-by-six tobacco-farm in Fayette County, Kentucky. She deserves better than either.

'She's a woman of great promise,' he added as they reached the outer door – a portal through which no butler in the United States would have permitted January to pass, much less Mede. 'And she likes Washington. As you've probably seen, she's a born political hostess. But I fear that, married to a man like Bray, it's only a matter of time before disaster strikes.'

Movement at his side drew January's eye. He glanced sidelong, to see Mede looking into the distance with a face like stone. Only when the great front door had shut behind him did the young man say softly, 'He wasn't that way before I left.'

'If he can't take you becoming a free man,' said January, 'is he worth going back to?'

Jem had brought the phaeton around to the front of the house. He looked both sleepy and rather nervous about driving back to Washington at this late hour, and no wonder. The moon had set, and the mist had grown thicker. The glow of the carriage lamps was absorbed by a softly impenetrable black wall, as light is by velvet. In this dead hour, January guessed there would be little chance of meeting slave stealers, but getting safely across the bridge and through the marshy land north of town would be a matter for great care.

Mede took a deep breath and shook his head. 'No. But that don't change it, that I've left him alone.'

'We all get left alone,' said January, 'one time or another in our lives. And I still believe that whatever your master felt about you leaving him, he didn't do this himself. And if he got drunk to the point where he couldn't protect himself – if you're thinking that you should have been there, sleeping on the floor of his bedroom like a dog, to protect him – it's time he grew up.'

And you, too, he didn't add.

The carriage moved off slowly into the darkness.

Mist, like old ashes, still lay thick on Washington when January woke. Breakfast was over – just as well, since the sight of everybody else

206

consuming bacon and sausage was, as the Philadelphia priest had intended, a sorrow and a
burden to him – and he had to sweet-talk leftover
porridge from Mrs Trigg. At ten he sallied forth
with fifty dollars of Henri Viellard's money in
his pockets, in quest of a half-dozen of the surgeons on his list, in various corners of the
District. He spent a tiring day, paying 'earnest
money' to open negotiations with the potential
suppliers of cadavers – being careful to remember whether he was acting for 'Mr Allan' or
M'sieu Viellard – and then striking up conversa-
tions either with the surgeons themselves, or
with their servants if they had them, which
eventually led to the question, 'You think this
man would be willin' to take on a helper?'

'Fact is, sir–' or *Bill*, or *Lou*, as the case might
be – 'I know other gentlemen, friends of M'sieu
Viellard–' or Mr Allan – 'that's in the same case.
They can't pay so well, but if I could speak to
this resurrection man myself, I think maybe
somethin' could be worked out.'

Two of the surgeons he asked put him off:
'Does Mr Allan–' or M'sieu Viellard – 'know
you're about asking this?'

Neither Bill nor Lou – the surgeons' servants –
were able to give him the name of the grave
robber with whom their masters dealt, but Lou –
a solemn elderly man with a crippled leg – put a
hand on January's shoulder and said worriedly,
'I know it might not be my business to say it,
Ben, but you sure don't want to go mixin' yourself up with folks like that. Sure, they makes a
pile of money, diggin' poor folk up outta their

graves. But leavin' out what it'd do to your soul, if you cares about such things, you lettin' yourself in for more trouble than you know. They are evil men, an' care no more about the livin' than they do for the dead.'

Bill, on the other hand, contracted with January for the sum of a dollar to find out the name of the resurrectionist, half of which would be paid immediately, which January did.

He then returned to the boarding-house, feeling only moderately besmirched by the day's business, to change his clothes for the ball game against the Invaders.

The fog had thinned away all morning while January tramped the streets around the Capitol, and had finally burned off around two. By four the bright air was sweetly hazy, the weather balmy, and the field along Reedy Branch thick with spectators. In addition to the usual friends and families of the Stalwarts (and of the two or three Centurions who had been added to their ranks), neighbors, workmates, and total strangers had turned up, some of them with flat-bed wagons in which makeshift benches had been installed, with seats for sale at a nickel apiece. French and Neapolitan and English clerks arrived from the embassies, Prussian and Bavarian and Russian, boisterous at the Invaders' earlier victory over the 'Yankees' and shouting to see how the 'legions of Ethiopia' would play.

One of the first faces January recognized when he, Mede, and Darius Trigg waded through the trampled grass from Connecticut Avenue was that of old John Quincy Adams, perched in a gig.

208

'Good Lord, January, there's a dozen of us from the House here,' the old man replied to January's exclamation of surprise, blinking down at him with his huge pale-blue eyes. 'And the clerks and secretaries of a dozen more – Southerners who won't admit an interest in the proceedings but want to know the outcome ... or have a bet on it.'

'*I'll* admit an interest, all right,' added the lanky Mr Noyes, who stood by the horse's head. 'After hearing nothing for months in the Department, except how any white man created can trounce a dozen Negroes – and I should dearly love to see Mr Stockard attempt to trounce *you* – I have a powerful academic interest in seeing how white shall stack up against black after all.'

'What you shall see, sir,' replied Trigg, 'is how men stack up against men, on this particular day, in this particular light ... And that is all you shall see.'

'Oh, I think should our friends the Stalwarts win,' said Adams, with a creaky chuckle, 'we'll be treated to any number of interesting expressions on the faces of the Southerners present – and that's what *I'm* here to see. I dare say they don't know who to "root" for: the Invaders of their soil, or defenders who they have claimed repeatedly shouldn't be able to defend. You behold me–' he flung up his kid-gloved hands and waggled his fingers like a schoolgirl – 'all a-twitter with anticipation.'

Trigg laughed and strode off to meet Jules Gonesse beside the worn dip in the grass that marked the thrower's position in the middle of

the square. The three referees were chosen –
Charlie Springer of the Stalwarts, one Invader (a
Prussian secretary who'd been in Washington
for years and spoke excellent English), and
Perce Inkletape, one of Senator Webster's clerks
known for his fairness and his abolitionist
sentiments.

The Stalwarts won the toss and took their
places on the line of goods boxes to await their
turn at bat.

'You think he's here?' Mede whispered to
January.

No need to ask who he meant. Or to guess at
how much sleep the young man had had, judging
from the drawn look around his eyes.

'I doubt he's even awake.'

Mede nodded. *Of course. I should have
thought* ... 'I'll go there once the game's done.
He'll want to know,' he added, as if he heard
January's thoughts, 'and it's what a friend
should do. I'm still his Man Friday, even if I am
free now. He shouldn't be alone.'

No need to ask, January reflected, whether a
man with his wife at his bedside and a family
friend like Oldmixton at hand was to be considered 'alone'. He'd had friends in Paris, after
his wife had died. 'Alone' was not something
reckoned by how many other people were in the
room.

'You still think he did it himself.'

'I still think he might have.' Mede's eyebrows
tugged together. 'If what she says is true...'
Again, no need to define who *she* was. January
could almost hear a capital letter on the name:

She. The only *She* who mattered, in that household or in the small, closed circle of Mede and his master.

'If what she says is true, he's changed so ... Debts never used to trouble him. Yes, he gambles too much, and he did sell off two of the horses ... but he sold Caro because she stole Mrs Bray's earrings, not because he was desperate to pay what he owed. But he laughed about the horses, and his friends joshed him something terrible.'

Mede fell silent, picking at a splinter on the box with his thumbnail.

Remembering the times when Luke would haul him along to practice, would make him throw thousands of 'good' tosses that he and his friends could swing at?

Or thinking of that ravaged face by the lamplight, the big hands – duplicates of Mede's own – lying empty on the coverlet, swathed in bandages to the wrists?

'Even this trouble between him and Mrs Bray,' he continued hesitantly. 'Her turning cold on him, locking him out of her room ... He'd no more harm himself over that than he'd ... than he'd become a monk, sir! I know him! I *did* know him...'

Hoots and curses yanked January back to the present. Red Vassall – one of the Centurions who'd been loaned to them as a 'sure-fire' striker – had taken a swing at the Frenchman's pitch and missed, putting the team out. On the way out to the field the kidding was good-naturedly fierce: 'You swattin' flies there, Red?'

'Whoa, he saw Miss Prissy standin' in the crowd—' Miss Prissy was Vassall's sweetheart of the moment.

'No, he's tryin' to impress his mother...'

'Don't worry about it.' January gripped Mede's shoulder reassuringly. 'Mr Bray's fine. He'll sleep through the day and won't know anything about this. You know he wants you to win. That's all you need to know right now. The rest is for tomorrow.'

'Tomorrow,' said Mede softly, and walked to the striker's position, straightening his shoulders in the silvery light.

And within moments January saw that his worry over the young man was totally needless. Mede threw like a demon: changeable, tempting, tantalizing, and devastating. Gonesse, Baldini, and a young man named Djemal from the Turkish embassy managed to hit every ball Mede threw, and scored a respectable number of tallies, but the rest of the foreign team was at his mercy. They swung at deceptive slow-balls. They lashed and swatted at fast sidearm flings. A dozen arguments ensued among the three Referees about whether the striker *could* have hit the ball instead of simply standing there and letting it go past, in order for the fourth throw to count as a knock, and the game became one of gnawing attrition. The Invaders went out earlier, and more often. The Stalwarts got a slim lead, held it, widened it. When they reached fifty tallies, to the enemies' thirty-five, even the Southerners in the audience started cheering.

Tomorrow, thought January. When the game

was over, and the 'honor of America' saved or lost ... Did Luke Bray really think his Good Man Friday was going to come back to him?

Did Mede really think the young planter capable of being friends with a black man who had formerly been his slave?

From his waistcoat pocket he unfolded the small sheets he'd taken from Bray's watch, studied the five little diagrams. The notepaper itself was clean, the creases fresh-looking in the waning evening light.

And what about this?

He took out the red-backed notebook that never left him. Page after page of magic squares, including these five. *Why copy these?*

And from where? There had never been a time, so far as January could tell, when Bray had had access to Singletary's notes.

If Mede goes back tomorrow, can I go with him and ask Bray where he found these?

And if I did, would he tell me the truth?

The Invaders rallied when Trigg took Mede out into the field for a time, to let his arm rest, but they never managed to close the lead. When, at seventy points to forty-five, Mede walked back to the throwing mark, the shouts and whoops were deafening.

By that time the sky was nearly dark, and fog was beginning to rise. The distant houses back in the direction of K Street were speckled with light. Mede put out the first French striker without effort, and after the French regained the offensive by plugging the Reverend Perkins on his run from third base to fourth, put them out

213

again on his first throw.

At that point the referees called the team captains together, and Gonesse conceded that there was no way the Invaders could recover the lead.

The game was declared for the Stalwarts.

Shouts, shrieks, howls of triumph. Gnashing of teeth, too, thought January, if people really had bet a thousand dollars, that whites – even Frenchmen – were better players than blacks. A phaeton – led by a groom at the team's head – worked its way toward them through the crowd, and January was astonished to see Luke Bray sitting up in its high seat, chalk-white and clinging to the polished brass rails for support. As it came near Mede cried, 'Marse Luke!' and shoved his way forward, reached the vehicle even as Luke – with the assistance of the disapproving Jem – climbed down, his face aglow with his smile.

'You did it, Friday!'

The two men embraced, Mede's strength holding his former master on his feet.

'You shouldn't have come!'

'I don't need you nursemaidin' me, Mede.' There was deep love in his voice. 'It's worth it seein' you standin' up there like an oak-tree puttin' them French pussies in their place. Worth it seein' those polecats from over at the Treasury coughin' up money they didn't have any better sense than to bet—' He swayed on his feet.

Both January and Royall Stockard sprang forward out of the press to support him. Stockard scrambled up into the phaeton, said, 'Pass him

214

up to me, boy,' and January and Mede lifted him to the high seat. 'Dumb idiot,' Stockard added affectionately, and hugged Bray around his shoulders. 'You didn't have to come down here – good *Lord*, Dickerson said you'd had a fall from your horse but he didn't say you'd half killed yourself! You didn't have to come down here to know even our niggers could whip a bunch of Frenchies!'

'Knew they could,' gasped Bray, still grinning from ear to ear. 'By God, I wanted to see it ... Wanted to see my boy.'

From the other side of the phaeton, Mr Noyes raised his sharp New England voice. '*Even* your niggers, Mr Stockard? I seem to recall it was those same Frenchies whipped *you*.'

Stockard turned his head. The other Warriors who had gathered around the phaeton grew silent, and the silence spread like blood in water.

The young Congressman climbed down, stood four-square before the abolitionist, the other Warriors of Democracy grouped behind. 'What are you sayin', sir?' he inquired in a soft and deadly voice.

'I'm saying ... *sir*–' Noyes' pale eyes sparkled with a holy warrior's gleam – 'is that if the sons of Africa have proven themselves better men than the white sons of France, isn't it time that you – and these other *honorable* sons of Virginia, and South Carolina, and the other states of this Union whom you disgrace before the eyes of the world with the blight of slavery – admit that these men who have, in your own words, "saved the honor of America", *are* men? Men like

215

yourselves?'

Someone in the crowd shouted, 'You know fuck-all about it, Yankee!'

And the abolitionists who had quietly assembled behind Noyes shouted back, 'You can't have it both ways!'

'They are men, sir,' Stockard replied. 'But if you weren't a fucking fool pur-blind on abolitionist drivel, you'd see by lookin' at 'em they aren't men like ourselves. They are niggers.'

'Then give us a chance to see what kind of men *you* are,' returned Noyes, in a voice pitched to carry over the whole of the crowd. 'Mr Trigg, will your men be ready, in two weeks' time, on this spot, to let the sons of Virginia, the sons of South Carolina, the sons of Maryland test their *honorable* manhood against you in an honest game?'

'I will, sir.' Darius Trigg stepped forward out of the crowd, and the Stalwarts moved in around him: weedy Reverend Perkins, Frank Preston, Handsome Dan. January stepped back from the side of the phaeton and stood behind the flute player. 'Two weeks from this evening we'll be here on this field waiting for you to defeat us, Mr Stockard, sir.'

He spoke humbly: three years ago whites had rampaged through Washington burning black men's businesses and every black school in the city. But the challenge was there. Before Stockard could retort, a loud-voiced Indiana Senator bellowed, 'I got a hundred dollars says the Warriors'll take 'em!'

'I'll see that—' somebody yelled, and a pan-

216

demonium of betting swept the crowd.

Mede started to walk toward his teammates, and Luke Bray held his whip down from his seat on the phaeton, blocking Mede's path with its whalebone shaft. For a long minute their eyes met.

Don't you fucken dare...

Gently, Mede slid his shoulder past the whip and walked over to stand beside January.

Bray fumbled for the reins, then sagged back with a gasp. Stockard, his face like stone, leaped back up to the high seat, snatched the whip and the reins, and without a glance at Jem – who had stood all this time at the horses' heads – lashed the team with a crack like lightning. The startled horses sprang straight at the Stalwarts, who leaped aside, and the whole crowd, black and white, had to scramble out of the way.

January looked around him, as if only then he became conscious of the shoving, shouting men. Yells of, 'Six to one ... Three to one ... Dammit, they can beat them...' hammered him from all sides. He felt slightly short of breath, aware he'd seen something unprecedented, unheard-of. Though carefully phrased in the humblest of language, black men had challenged white ones to combat.

It was as if poor Gun, back in New Orleans, had risen from his bench and broken Eph Norcum's well-deserving nose.

'No fucken way white men gonna play against niggers...'

'You think they can't win?'

'I think it ain't right...'

217

'I got ten dollars says they can't win...'

He looked around, glimpsed Frank Preston hurrying Dominique, Thèrése, and Mrs Perkins – who was shouting imprecations back over her shoulder – away in the direction of Connecticut Avenue. To Mede he said, 'We'd better get out of here.'

It was only a matter of time before some outraged soul ran to call the constables...

If the constables weren't there already.

Or some enthusiastic Democrat came to the conclusion that the way to avoid the whole issue was to beat the living crap out of the Stalwarts...

A hand touched his elbow; a voice said, 'Ben.'

He turned and found himself looking at Bill, the sweeper-up in the offices of the surgeon Charles Date.

Bill held out his hand. 'I found your grave robber for you. Feller name of Wylie Pease.'

EIGHTEEN

Easter morning. There were Masses at Holy Trinity in Georgetown at noon and two as well as in the morning; January knew in his bones that Mede shouldn't visit Luke Bray alone.

'Might I beg you to wait a few minutes?' When she came into the kitchen to meet them, Rowena Bray didn't look as if she'd slept much last night. By the activity around the work table – the

218

cook working pastry, and a girl in a housemaid's calico dress pressed into service cutting up fruit – there would be company for dinner that afternoon, despite the illness of the master of the house ... Or perhaps as a means of showing Washington society that he was not so very ill? 'I fear Dr Gurry is a Southerner, and these Americans...'

She hesitated, seeking tactful words, and January gave a wry smile. 'You mean he'd walk out in a pet if he thought someone had called in a black surgeon to look at his patient? M'am, compared to what went on at the ball game yesterday afternoon, that strikes me with about the force of a bread pellet.'

She ducked her head and made a tremulous sound almost like a laugh.

'Thank you for understanding, Mr January.' In a gentler voice, she added, 'I shall tell Luke you're here also, Mede. Though I warn you, he was ... I have never seen him as he was, when Mr Stockard brought him home yesterday evening.'

'I expect he's angry at me.'

'I don't even know how to describe it.' She passed her hand over her brow, with a wince of dread. 'That blackness of spirits, that look that haunts his eyes ... I thought after yesterday's excursion he must sleep through the night like a ... I would say like a baby – that's the expression, isn't it? Only babies never *do* sleep through the night! He was exhausted when Mr Stockard brought him in, but his sleep was tormented, all night, by nightmares. Please do come in—'

She shook her head, as if to clear away night-mares of her own, and led them toward the door at the other side of the kitchen. 'Curses upon these Americans for not putting servants' halls in their houses – and I will *not* make you wait in the kitchen! Would you much mind sitting in my office? I shall have Dacey bring you coffee—'

The tiny office contained no more than a desk, a chair, and another straight-backed chair for the tradesmen for whose visits the chamber was designed. The household account-books ranged on a shelf: butcher, grocer, dealers in coal and wood and hay. Another green-bound book logged the daily running-expenses of the house; yet another concerned the expenses of the slaves. Folders held the receipts, tied up with tape: the meticulous track of every penny, into the household and out again. A clean-washed slate occupied a corner of the desk, chalks neatly set in a tray beside the ink pot, standish, and pens. Rose hated doing the bills almost as much as she hated sewing, but a lifetime of near poverty had trained her in the skill. She and January took turns at the chore, as they traded off washing the dishes, scouring the chamber pots, and sweeping the hearths.

January couldn't imagine trying to run a household that included a man who'd bet a thousand dollars on a hand of cards. Planters lived from crop to crop: Luke Bray must have grown up in the systole and diastole of debt and credit. And in fact Rowena Bray had been quite right when she'd repeated Luke's argument that a gentleman *must* bet. It was a way of demonstrating that one *was* a gentleman, generous and not clutch-fisted. The worst one gentleman could say about another was that he was stingy.

Newspapers lay on the desk: the *National Intelligencer*, the *New York Times*. Beside them, a stack of small notes, crumpled and straightened again. Blotted, January saw, with the brown stains of blood.

As if someone bleeding from both wrists had pawed through them in drunken delirium, hoping the sums on them didn't really add up to all that much.

When the housemaid brought in the coffee, Mede followed her back into the kitchen to ask news of his friends, so January also rose, and looked at the top note of the pile:

Stockard. $50

The cost of food for a month, for himself, Rose, Baby John, Zizi-Marie and Gabriel.

The price of a lady's silk shawl. A laboring man's wage for a month and a half; the purchase of a horse, or that horse's upkeep for three months.

The cost of the body of a dead man, to a surgeon desperate to increase his skills.

He fingered Bill's note in his pocket.

Now, THERE'S a fit occupation for the feast of the Resurrection.

Voices in the hall. January cursed the curiosity that made him pry like a nosy child into the affairs of a woman who treated him as a human being in this land of slavery and prejudice, and sat down again. 'A most serious malady, Mrs Bray.' Through the door that led to the main hall, he saw a tall gray-haired man in a physician's frock coat and top hat descend the stair with Mrs Bray. 'Assuredly, the Poet knew whereof he spoke when he penned the words, *Melancholy is the nurse of frenzy*. You did well to summon my aid.' A light voice and a mellow South Carolina accent. 'With care and proper treatment – I am myself a strong proponent of the water-treatment for vexations of the mind – the tenor of your poor husband's thoughts can be restored. He must have complete care by responsible experts.'

'Of course, Dr Gurry. But his position in the Navy Department—'

'One must never permit the mere prejudices of one's neighbors to bar the golden road to mental health, Madame. Your husband is in a very serious case, very serious.' Dr Gurry pulled on his expensive kid gloves. 'The violence of his discourse, and his oscillation from the agitation we observed to the depression which you have described, indicate to me a most grave condition. Moreover, even the brief examination of his skull which I was able to accomplish made it clear to me that his organs of melancholia, combatativeness, and destructiveness are dangerously overdeveloped, while the areas of hope and equanimity are so attenuated as to be almost non-existent.' He adjusted his pince-nez and regarded Mrs Bray with fatherly severity.

'You do him no favor, by allowing your wifely concern for mere *reputation* to override all the signs of a condition which may well result in disaster. You – ah!' He paused as a knock on the

222

front door was answered by the maid who slipped past them to open it. 'Mr Spunge.' He bowed to the trim little gentleman in the flowered waistcoat who entered the hall.

Mrs Bray offered the newcomer two fingers in the English fashion. 'Mr Spunge, I presume you are acquainted with Dr Gurry—'

There was a general murmuring among all present at how pleased they were to encounter one another in Mrs Bray's front hall. Mrs Bray saw Dr Gurry out the front door, then hastened to escort Mr Spunge – January recognized his name from the list of surgeons Henri and Chloë had visited – up the stairs.

Dacey had left the door open between the parlor and the kitchen, and through it he heard Mede's account of the town ball game, and the cook's tale of their master's determination to see that game despite his wife's orders to Jem not to take the phaeton out. 'No, he's pretty much his old self,' said Dacey the maid. 'That gruel your Mr January had us make for him yesterday, he took an' flung it, bowl an' all, at Peter's head ... The cursin' he done when M'am brought up that Dr Gurry to see him this mornin' was mighty fine. I ain't heard such cursin' since I worked for Marse Stackpole in Charleston...'

'He does try to keep up the appearance of good spirits before the servants,' said Mrs Bray, when she came into the office from seeing Spunge out the door. 'It's one of the most unnerving things about this melancholia that comes over him. It's like watching him turn into another person, when he thinks no one can see him. This morn-

223

ing I passed his door and heard him weeping like a child—' She turned her head, as Mede came quietly in from the kitchen, and closed the door behind him.

'I'm so sorry, Mede.' She took the valet's hand. 'He said, "If freedom's what he wants, let him have it, then, and see what it is to be a free man." He turned his face to the wall at the sound of your name.'

It was a kindly gesture, and January was interested to see that Mede endured her touch in stony silence.

She looked back at January, exhaustion darkening her eyes. 'And he said he'd have nothing of a – a physician of your race,' she finished. 'I suspected as much, when I sent for Mr Spunge, and for Dr Gurry, though it was exceedingly good of you to come back. And to tell you the truth—' She lowered her voice with a glance toward the empty hall behind her, as if Mr Spunge's ghost lingered, listening. 'I trust your remedies – and your discretion – a great deal more than I trust theirs. Which is why I want to ask you – and you, too, Mede – if he said anything to you, or spoke of anything...'

She hesitated. 'I know you and I haven't always gotten on, Mede,' she went on quietly. 'And I know your loyalty to Mr Bray. But if there is anything...'

'I don't know what you mean, m'am.'

Rowena Bray hesitated, as if forcing herself to leap into cold water. 'I mean, for some time I've suspected that Mr Bray was being blackmailed.'

January's eyes went immediately to Mede's

still face. The valet didn't gasp, *Blackmail!* Or, *That's ridiculous!* Didn't demand, *Who would do a thing like that?*

Just waited, silent. January was reminded of how a cat, turned out of a box in an unfamiliar room, will crouch motionless, rapidly figuring out which way it can bolt.

'I do the accounts in this household, Mr January,' she went on. 'Sheer terror at the magnitude of my husband's gambling has made me something of a spymaster, estimating how much he tosses away each night. And the amounts don't add up. He seems to be losing an additional two to three hundred dollars every month that I can't account for.'

'Have you spoken to him about this?'

Dark curls swung against her pale cheeks as she shook her head. 'He claims it's all gambling money, and not as much as I seem to think. But the way he drinks—'

Mede's lips parted as if he would say something, but good slaves did not contradict whites – particularly white ladies – and no sound came out.

'—I'm not sure he would remember how much he's lost. He has no recollection of cutting his wrists, you know. None. But he generally does gamble with the same people, at least so far as I know...'

'It's one explanation,' said January carefully. Like Mede, he'd had it beaten into him at a young age what a black man could and couldn't say to a white woman, no matter how English she was or with what fairness she had regarded

225

him. 'Another one might be an irregular establishment.'

She averted her face for a moment, either in shock or in shame. 'You mean, is he keeping a mistress?' Her voice trembled. 'I think I'd have heard of it. Washington teems with women who love nothing better than to pass along gossip, only to bask in the reaction they provoke. And as an Englishwoman...'

Quickly and surreptitiously, she wiped her eyes. 'It's one reason I'm trying to ... to get to the bottom of what *is* going on. Of what drove him first to that degree of intoxication, to the point that he didn't know what he was doing, and from there to despair. Because I'm afraid of what I might find out. What others might find out. May I count on your help?'

'At any hour of the day or night.' January bowed.

'Mede—'

'Of course, M'am. You know I would do anything for him – except remain a slave.'

'Nor would he want you to,' she responded, and smiled warmly. 'Not in his better moments. I will send word to Mrs Trigg's, if his condition changes.'

They walked in silence across the Paper Mill Bridge. Beneath the canopy of hickory and oak the air had a moist mildness that reminded January poignantly of New Orleans. January had had another letter from Rose and one from Olympe, and his heart ached at the memory of the indigo shade of the marketplace arches, the smell of the river and the long, melismatic wailing of the charcoal sellers in the streets. 'Why didn't you and Mrs Bray get along?' he asked at length.

'She's mean to him.' Mede's boots scuffed last year's brown leaves with a muffled swishing, like the scattering away of memories that might or might not be true. 'She's sweet as wild strawberries, when anybody can see her,' he went on, after a long time. 'All that time he was courting her, she was like a kitten, pretty and playful, hanging on his arm. When nobody's around she's got a mouth on her like a cat o' nine tails.'

January tried to imagine what his calmly matter-of-fact Rose, or his cheerily sensual Ayasha, would have said to him if he'd lost a thousand dollars over a hand of cards.

'Thing is, Mr J, Marse Luke's never been happy here in Washington. He hadn't been here a year, workin' for Mr Pointsett, when he knew he'd had enough of livin' in this town. He was never made for copyin' some other man's words in his best handwriting, and riding to an office every day, when the wind's soft off the river and there's fat rabbits stirring around the woods. He said living here made him feel like he was all alone on a desert island. It's why he called me his Man Friday.'

He glanced across at January a little shyly, hoping he understood.

'Friday was Crusoe's friend,' said January, 'as well as his servant. The only man he could trust to guard his back.'

'So he was, sir. Marse Luke couldn't wait to

227

get back to Fayette County. But by then he'd met Mrs Bray.'

A born political hostess, Mr Oldmixton had said. A woman who didn't want to go back to her father's house.

If that was almost three years ago – January counted back in his mind – Jackson would have been President. And Jackson, still aching from his own bereavement, was always susceptible to playful, kitten-pretty young ladies begging for a favor...

And always ready to give a valuable job to a bluegrass boy.

He could just imagine what a 'born political hostess', bred in London and used to the amenities of daily newspapers and decent opera in season, would have to say to the suggestion that she retire to a modest tobacco-plantation a day's ride from the nearest village.

The stream purled in its rust-brown bed as they climbed up the road where January had almost been kidnapped, at his first meeting with this young man almost three weeks ago.

'*Is* he being blackmailed?'

Mede didn't answer for a time. *An answer in itself*, January reflected. Though the morning was warming, the young man walked with his shoulders hunched and his hands in his pockets, like an Israelite longing for the fleshpots of Egypt where at least he'd had the illusion of safety.

'When a man's being blackmailed,' asked Mede at last, 'does he get letters written in numbers instead of letters?'

'Numbers instead of letters?'

'I saw one on his desk, clear last spring, when I came into his room unexpected. He locked it up quick and I never saw it again. But it was just lines of numbers, right across the paper like you'd write a letter or like the printing in a book.'

'Did you notice the paper?'

'It was that yellow tablet-paper, which everybody uses in the government offices. I never spoke of it. Dacey talks like birds in a tree and Lodie – that's Mrs Bray's maid – carries tales to Mrs Bray. And it wasn't my business to be noticing what Marse Luke has on his desk. But blackmail is about secret writing, isn't it?'

'It could be,' answered January slowly. 'If I were blackmailing someone I'd be damn careful about what I put into writing. Last spring?'

'Yes, sir. Long before he could have seen those number squares from Mr Singletary's notebook ... and I still can't figure how he got hold of them.'

'Unless he knew them before. Did Luke ever write in code to anyone?'

Mede laughed softly. 'Mr J, Marse Luke doesn't even write to people in regular handwriting. He hates writing, and figuring, and numbers. It's why this job he has at the Navy Yard is like a chain on him. He's said to me he'd rather chop cotton than copy documents—'

'There speaks a man who's never chopped cotton.'

'Well, true.' Mede grinned again, as briefly as before. 'Not that I've ever done field work, 'cept

229

once when his daddy got mad at me when I was ten, for covering up when Marse Luke rode out to meet a girl his daddy didn't like. Marse Charles put me out in the tobacco fields for a day and a half, 'cause I wouldn't tell.' He shook his head, then let the memory go: the hot stink of dirt, the thirst and the ache in back and arms and hands ... January knew them well.

And remembered the pride and love in Luke Bray's voice: *It's worth it seein' you standin' up there like an oak tree...*

'*Does* he have a mistress?'

Mede shook his head. 'Not regular, no. There's houses down near the Capitol, on Maine and Missouri Avenues, close enough to the Navy Yard that him and his friends will stop there early of an evening, after an oyster supper. But I don't recall him ever speaking more of one girl than another, and he never could keep their names straight. And he never went in for the nasty stuff, or the strange stuff, like some of the Congress gentlemen do. Sure, nothing he'd pay somebody two or three hundred dollars a month not to talk about.'

'You know this?'

'Like I know myself, sir. I hear the girls downtown like him. Back home there was four of the girls on our place that he'd screw regular, but he wasn't ever mean. And he'd give 'em presents, and not just for puttin' out for him. At other times, just to be nice. I don't think I ever heard of him forcin' somebody who didn't want to go, like a lot of men do.'

Given the malicious hell a planter's son could

make for any bondswoman who didn't 'consent', this wasn't saying much, but on an isolated plantation, January was aware that even this token forbearance qualified Luke Bray as a Galahad.

And yet ... reflected January. *And yet.*

People sometimes found surprising things about themselves, once they reached a city and learned what was available.

And since he'd been employed at the Navy Yard, Luke Bray had, for the first time in his life, not been under Mede's observation for the greater part of the day.

Again his hand sought in his pocket the folded sheet of magic squares, the link between Luke Bray and a shy, odd, fussy gentleman whom he had supposedly met only once in his life.

There was definitely something odd going on.

NINETEEN

In New Orleans, Easter was the start of the starving season for musicians.

Planters and their families would be returning to their plantations, to make sure the cane was in the ground – if it was going in that year – or to supervise the planting of the cotton, before the summer's onflowing heat drove them to the little towns of Milneburg and Mandeville on the lakeside. January reflected upon the hundred and

231

fifty dollars he'd left in Rose's hands, and the forty or so that he'd accumulated here in Washington playing at balls and sent on to her, and was comforted.

May Eph Norcum catch fever and die.

The direction written on Bill the sweeper's note was that of the King's Head on C Street, in the insalubrious district between Pennsylvania Avenue and the canal. Guised as a laborer – and keeping a very sharp eye on his back – January made his way thence on Easter Monday afternoon and loafed around the neighborhood, scraping acquaintance with a slave named Pancake, who was sweeping the board sidewalk in front of a cheap grocery across the street from the tavern, and helping the slaves at the livery stable next door for a dime. He said his name was Lou Grima and that he was in Washington looking for work.

'None around, unless you likes waitin' on white men,' returned Boston, one of the stablemen. 'Even then, 'bout half the hotels buys fancy niggers to work their dinin' rooms, rather-'n hire free men.'

'I heard there was work on that new Treasury buildin',' protested January in a pained voice.

'They's all Irish. They better not even catch you askin' is there work.'

'Animals,' opined Jerry, the other raker of soiled straw. 'Don't even hardly speak no English. Papists, too.'

January spotted Wylie Pease almost at once and recognized him as the bald ferret-nosed man from Mrs Kelsey's funeral. He emerged hatless and blinking from the King's Head – the sign above the door was of a royally robed figure with nothing above its ermine-clad shoulders but a bleeding stump – in what looked like a nightshirt tucked into grimy trousers, looked around him at the street, spat, and went in again.

The livery was so situated that from its gate, January could see both the front door of the tavern and the mouth of the alley beside it. Like many Washington alleys, this one was built up with tiny houses, converted sheds, and the occasional garden-patch or cow house attached to the dwellings on the nearby streets, and swarmed with the children of the poor. He made no comment until he'd finished his shoveling and raking, and had helped haul water and hay for all fifteen animals, but in that time he observed the clientele of the tavern: carters, cabmen, tough-looking Irish b'hoys. He thought he recognized the sullen-faced youth from the cemetery, also in déshabillé. A lodging house on the premises, then.

Even in an ordinary boarding house, there was always someone around. A tavern would, however, guarantee where most of its denizens would be for most of the evening ... and increase the chances that they would be in an unobservant condition.

'They're not taking any work across the way?' He nodded at the grimy frontage of unpainted boards. 'Place sure looks like it could use a little sprucin' up.'

'You don't want to go inside any tavern in this neighborhood,' said Boston firmly. 'Nor around

233

their back doors neither. That feller over there?'

January followed his nod and recognized the slave-stealer Kyle Fowler as the tall man stopped to trade words with one of the Irish draymen emerging from the nearby grocery.

'He got three–four men workin' this neighborhood regular. You want some liquor, you go over to one of the groceries on K Street, or Bissell's on Madison Alley, or Singer's on Naylor's Alley. They's safe, and run by freemen.'

''Sides—' Jerry waved toward the tavern as Pease appeared in the doorway again, wearing a waistcoat this time and smoking a cigar, and carrying a bucket that slopped a brown horror of mucus and spat tobacco over his shoes that could be smelled across the street. '—Miz Drail got herself a boyfriend there regular who does all the sprucin' she can stand.' Pease tossed the contents of the bucket into gutter, went back inside. 'Nasty piece of work.'

Boston laughed and inquired in a voice squeaky with mock wonderment, 'Now, what *would* a modest lady like Miz Drail see in him?' By the way Jerry laughed, January guessed everything he needed to know about the saloon's owner even before that lady put in an appearance, diminutive, brass-haired and cursing as she shoved a youthful Irishman out into the muck of the street with a bloody nose.

January finished helping with the chores, collected his ten cents, bade the men goodby and went on his way with wishes for good luck and a great deal of the same advice that Trigg had given him about not drinking with friendly strangers. He remained in the neighborhood long enough to walk the streets all around the King's Head, taking note of alleys, shops, and open lots. In childhood he'd scouted every foot of Bellefleur Plantation for hiding places and escape routes, for those occasions on which his master had had a few too many whiskies, and knew what to look for.

He was back on K Street well before the mild spring twilight drew on.

'Is it like this farther North?' he asked his hostess after dinner as Minou and Clarice Perkins herded the younger children into the parlor for lessons and Frank Preston turned up the lamps. 'Always looking over your shoulder?'

'Depends on how far north you get,' said Mrs Trigg.

'It used not to be,' Preston amplified. 'But even in Boston or Providence, it's getting harder for a black man to find work. If an Irishman or a German wants a place in one of the new factories ... Well, one of these days he'll get citizenship, and vote. So the local Democrat ward-bosses help him apply. Then they'll go to the factory owners and shop masters, and tell them, "I have a friend who needs work." A black man is never going to be able to vote, so he's of no use to the bosses. And now they've got the railroads through from Baltimore and Washington to pretty much anyplace in the North you can name, we get "special deputies" coming around, looking for runaways.'

'Or anybody who looks like he might be a runaway.'

'That's it, I'm afraid.' Preston tilted his head a little, to listen to the women's voices through the door: Thèrése's teasing laughter as she twitted one of her beaux, Dominique's bright chatter of pomade and the price of coffee that broke off to praise Charmian when the child located a hidden letter-block.

Octavia Trigg started to gather up the silverware. 'You thought it'd be different in the North, Mr J?'

'Not really.' January stood also and collected the few plates that remained on the table: Ritchie and Mandie had already made their first sweep and could be heard in the kitchen in a way that reminded him achingly of his own kitchen, of Gabriel and Zizi-Marie...

'I've been to Mexico, and I lived in France. Both places where slavery doesn't exist, and it still all comes down to money, and power, and what color your skin is.'

The landlady's coal-dark eyes rested on him for a moment, as if reading in his words things that he wouldn't say. 'Why'd you come back?'

'My family is here,' said January simply. 'When my wife died – the wife I married in France – I was willing to live with things as they are in Louisiana, so that I could be with my kin.' *Like Mede*, he realized suddenly, *drawn back toward slavery by love of his brother...*

'You don't know how alone you are,' he went on, 'until something like that happens. I had friends in Paris – good friends. But it wasn't the same.'

'No.' Mrs Trigg took the dishes from his

hands. She had a face like black rock, except for the kindness in her eyes. 'No, there is nuthin' the same as that.' And she moved past him through the kitchen door.

January gathered up his coffee cup and made to follow Preston into the parlor, where new newspapers had been brought in that morning and were being shared around by the boarders as Minou read to Olive and Charmian, Kizzy and tiny Jesse. But a thought took him, and he set down the cup and moved instead through the right-hand door into the hallway – softly gloomy with its single lamp – and to the half-open doorway of the opposite parlor, likewise glowing with muted amber light. Through the opening he could see the room's sole occupant, slouched in a chair, a whisky bottle on the table before him, full and corked. An empty glass.

Poe's head was sunk on one hand, like a man for the moment unable to go on.

January tapped at the door.

'Come.' The poet straightened and beckoned him to the other chair. 'How goes the Problem of the Missing Mathematician?' He sounded sardonic and infinitely tired, but his eyes brightened when January dropped Bill the sweeper's note on the marble tabletop.

'Desperate deeds are in order.'

'Ah.' Poe shoved bottle and glass aside. 'So you've come to the most desperate man in Washington?' The tone jested; his eyes didn't.

'Well,' said January in an apologetic tone, 'I thought of having Mr Viellard back my play at gunpoint when I go after grave robbers in their

237

nest, but somehow I don't think Madame Viellard would approve.'

'Lord, what I'd give to see Madame Viellard do it, though!' Poe gave a crack of genuine laughter. 'Dress her as a boy, put up her hair under a cap...'

'Mr Viellard really would kill me, if harm came to her. My sister also, I suspect.'

'True.' He picked up the note, studied it with the lamplight gleaming in his dark eyes. 'And I would hesitate to run afoul of the beautiful Dominique. You're really going to flush the grave robbers in their nest?'

'I'm going to try. The problem is, I need someone to go in and start trouble in the King's Head.'

'At last!' The poet sprang up and smote his chest dramatically. 'I thought this moment would never come. I shall finally have the occasion to use some of what I learned best at West Point – starting trouble. I am, my dear Benjamin, your man. Or—' He mimed hesitation. 'Or are *you* supposed to be *my* man?'

'I'll be your man. You be my man next time.'

'Very good. On we go!'

They sent Ritchie Trigg to Turvey's Livery stable a block away on Connecticut Avenue to hire a gig, and then drove through the pitch-black streets of Washington to the Fountain House Hotel on Pennsylvania Avenue, January perched on the back like a good servant. From the Fountain House they walked to within a few streets of the King's Head, January's heart

238

pounding at the prospect of being on these streets at this hour alone. It was close to eleven, a rare, clear night with dull orange lamplight gleaming in the taverns and bordellos and dark figures passing, briefly illuminated by the glow of the windows. The tinkly rattle of out-of-tune piano-music mingled with voices from the doorways: 'Fook ya's fer a fookin' Orangeman, them dice is loaded!'

'Is it callin' me a liar ye are?'

'Damn, and me luck's gotta turn sometime...'

You HAVE to be drunk, thought January, *to believe THAT...*

Now and then a man would stagger outside to piss against the wall. Sometimes a woman would speak from the shadows, and a man would go into the dark between the buildings with her – January wondered whether anyone actually believed such an encounter would end in copulation instead of a thwack over the head with a slung shot.

'I'll need a half-hour.' January kindled his dark-lantern and closed the slide. 'An hour, if you can cause trouble that long without getting pitched out.'

'My dear Mr January,' drawled Poe, 'the very idea! I'm not going to cause trouble. I am merely – with all apologies to your good family and friends – going to harangue the crowd on the subject of abolitionism – *contra*, not *pro* – and encourage every man present to express himself as well. After three drinks, no man I have ever encountered can resist the sound of his own voice, and I predict that men will run from all points of the compass to join in the general airing of grievances ... Trust me. And watch your back.'

'And you watch yours, sir. I'll meet you back at the Fountain House, with whatever evidence against the man I can find.'

It was hard to tell, as January crossed the street toward the alley that ran behind the King's Head, whether he was being watched or followed: he didn't think so. He wasn't sure whether he feared the slave stealers more, or the police. The alley was pitch-black and stank of raw sewage. Something flittered along the ground in the blackness ahead of him. Eyes flashed – rats. Raised voices shouting agreement ('...it's the goddam abolitionists that's causing the problem! The niggers was fine until they come along!') amply identified the back of the King's Head, a four-square black block of a building dimly traced by bits of leaked window-light from the street in front of it.

There was a privy in the back but no lantern on the porch. January couldn't imagine how anyone found their way from the back door to the facility. By the smell of it, nobody bothered. It was as much as his life was worth to slip the slide on his lantern out here, so he fumbled his way by touch to the porch. Once achieved, it was easy to slip under the railing and locate the un-locked back door. No light underneath; it would open into a hall of some sort. If Miss Drail and Mr Pease had any sense, they were in the bar-room dispensing drinks and keeping their attention riveted on the crowd, which could turn violent in a heartbeat.

January doubled back long enough to scrape his boot soles carefully on the edge of the porch – a ritual he doubted many customers bothered with – then slipped inside.

A hall, as he'd thought. Doors gave into the barroom and what was presumably a storeroom, padlocked. Light leaked under the inner door, and the noise was a hundred times louder. Poe's beautiful deep voice, slurred as if with alcohol, soared over the general din: 'Gentlemen, you cannot convince me that these actions are not a *deliberate plot* against this nation, a concerted effort by those who seek power for its own sake to undermine and destroy the *manhood*, the *livelihood*, the *moral force* of the men whose courage and strength they could not otherwise vanquish!' The cheering would have drowned January's footsteps even if he'd stood on one foot and hopped.

Gingerly, he felt along the walls until he located a narrow stair. At a guess, the proprietress and her sweetheart would live above the back room where the liquor was stored, leaving to the 'guests' the front of the building. Presumably, there was a kitchen down here someplace as well, but he wasn't going to hunt for it.

In the shelter of the stair he slipped the lantern-slide a bare quarter-inch, then moved swiftly upwards. A short hall at the top communicated with two rooms, corresponding as far as January could tell to the storeroom down below and the hypothetical kitchen. The one above the storeroom was the bedroom shared by Miss Drail and Wylie Pease. No door communicated to the front part of the upstairs. To get there, one would have to descend, go through the hall, through the barroom, and presumably up whatever stair ascended from there. Though inconvenient, the arrangement would certainly cut down on the nuisance created by inebriated guests.

January opened the lantern fully and made a search, not difficult save for the comprehensively unclean state of the bedchamber. Rats whisked behind a jumble of trunks. One contained a reeking tangle of dresses, skirts, petticoats and underclothing, none of which had been washed or cleaned, apparently, since the Jefferson administration. In the other two were folded a mix of garments, a few ladies' dresses, a couple of the new frock-coats and several of the more old-fashioned cutaways, a dozen shirts and assorted cravats, corsets, stockings and shoes. There were also three halves of petticoats, roughly scissored up the sides. Familiar with the ooze of fluids from the bodies of the dead, January understood what had been cut away. There were no trousers.

In a corner of one trunk lay two coils of hair, one of them brunette and as long and thick as his arm, the other blondish, shorter, but still enough to make a fine wig.

How dare you. For a moment he could feel in his fingers Rose's curly torrent of hair, Dominique's dark mane, and his hands shook at the thought. *How DARE you?*

He had dissected the bodies of the dead, knowing where some of them had come from. He'd pushed aside the knowledge that the naked cadavers delivered to the surgeries in the dead of night were not the only source of income to the men who provided them.

Guilt rose in him like the vomit of sickness, and like sickness he forced it back.

Now is not the time to feel.

A desk stood between the room's two windows. In one of its drawers January found seven wedding-rings and three gold lockets, two containing miniatures of women and one of a young man. There was also the framed picture of another man. The most elaborate of the lockets he thrust into the pocket of his jacket, and left the others where they were. *No sense giving the man the alarm before I can get at him.* There were also five small rounds or ovals of ivory, two bearing miniatures of children – a boy and a girl – and the rest only faintly stained, where the watercolor images had been scrubbed off. Three more miniature portraits – like the ivory rounds, unframed – painted on vellum lay at the back of the drawer.

January pocketed one of each, and the only one of the wedding rings which bore an engraving, though the tiny glow of the lantern was far too dim for him to read what it said. It struck him for the first time as curious that Singletary's pen, watch, and card case had been buried with him. In ordinary circumstances these were things that would have been held for the family of the deceased, not taken to the grave, but if he'd been murdered, why bury these effects, for Wylie

243

Pease to dig up?

The drawer also contained, like trash, dozens of wisps of hair of various colors, dumped out, presumably, from earlier lockets. Each wisp was the echo of a name, testimony to a love too precious to be surrendered even in death.

Footsteps thumped in the storeroom below. A woman's voice shouted instructions back through the door into the barroom, a ten-word sentence of which six words were obscenities. *Fetching more liquor...*

The window was closed but the shutters unlatched: *Good.* He closed his lantern, opened the window, checked – in the dim starlight – that the ground below was clear of broken boxes or encumbering rain-barrels, slid out and, half-sitting on the sill, closed the sash as far as he could before slithering down to the length of his arms. Reaching up with one hand he closed the rest of the sash, then let himself down again and dropped, praying he wouldn't break an ankle after all his trouble.

He didn't.

Listening behind him, around him, wary in the darkness as a scared rabbit, he made his way by the quickest and most public route he could find back to the Fountain Hotel.

And now comes the chore, he reflected, *of ambushing and blackmailing Wylie Pease.*

TWENTY

'I can't see a thing!' protested Henri, when Chloë removed his spectacles to tie a sinister-looking satin mask over his round, good-natured face.

'The only other person in the carriage is going to be Benjamin,' Chloë explained firmly. 'So just point this–' she handed him a long-barreled cavalry pistol, which he immediately dropped in horror – 'at the person who isn't six feet tall and black.'

'It isn't loaded, is it?'

'No, sir.' January retrieved the weapon from the floor of the Trigg parlor. 'It's perfectly safe.'

'What if Pease is armed?'

'We'll disarm him before he gets into the carriage.'

'What if Pease shouts for the police?'

'In that neighborhood?' January's eyebrows lifted nearly to his hairline. 'None of his neighbors would ever speak to him again.'

'That's the beauty of the plan, sir.' Poe's dark eyes sparkled as he pulled on the many-caped coachman's greatcoat that Seth Berger had lent him. 'Pease knows perfectly well that in that neighborhood–' he brandished the other pistol that would be his part in the melodrama – 'if I *was* to shoot him dead in the street in broad daylight, nobody would much care.'

'In any neighborhood, I should say,' remarked Chloë. She set her satchel on the marble-topped parlor table and withdrew a traveling chess-set and a volume of Suetonius. It had been agreed that she would wait at the boarding house for the results of Pease's abduction, and Chloë was not a woman who was ever unprepared.

'Why can't Poe be the Master Villain?' pleaded Henri.

'Because Pease might recognize me as the man who kept the whole tavern in an uproar for an hour and a half last night.'

'And we are *not* the villains of this piece!' added Dominique firmly. 'We are the ... the terror of wrongdoers, the avenging angels who survey the hearts of the wicked and see all!'

'I'm glad someone can see something!' complained Henri as his fellow-conspirators hustled him out of the boarding house to where his rented carriage waited for him in K Street.

'You don't have to, darling.' Dominique slipped his spectacles into his breast pocket. Standing on the gravel path that led from the door to the street, in the pale noon sunlight she had far more the appearance of a wife, in her spring gown of jonquil muslin with its bright green ribbons, though neither he nor she would ever have touched hands, or given the smallest sign of physical intimacy, in Chloë's presence.

Chloë, in her plain, elegantly-cut white linen and thick spectacles, resembled nothing so much as a schoolgirl sister – except that Henri's four sisters all resembled Henri, like large, plump, amiable sheep.

'Just sound stern and fierce and clever, as if you really had broken into the King's Head and found those things in that horrid man's desk drawer...'

'Pretend you're playing Shylock,' urged Chloë. 'You do an excellent Shylock.'

'Lord, yes!' Poe stroked his mustache like a stage villain. 'A fat and oily spider who knows all, sitting at the center of his web...'

'Oh, all right.' Henri clambered up into the coach and shut the door. 'But I thought we brought Benjamin along to do things like this.'

'And I have racked my brains,' agreed January patiently, 'for a method by which a black man can hold up a white one at gunpoint in the streets of Washington and force information out of him, and have arrived at the conclusion that it cannot be done. And I thank you, sir,' he added sincerely, 'for taking it on yourself to help me in this. For I think we're closing in on the riddle of what became of Mr Singletary. When we find his grave, it may tell us a good deal about who put him there. The trail may be cold, but at least we can talk to the man who saw his body just after his death.'

He pulled his wide-brimmed hat more closely down over his eyes and climbed up to the old-fashioned footman's stand on the back of the coach. Poe, muffled in a scarf that the chilly air made more convincing, flapped the reins, and the rented team trotted out smartly into Con-

247

necticut Avenue. Out here there were few wagons and foot-passengers – grocery carts, a milk wagon, and now and then a more fashionable tilbury bound to or from Georgetown – but as they crossed K Street traffic thickened. Around Lafayette Square, Poe steered between the smart, closed broughams of the diplomatic and Senatorial wives – out performing the *de rigueur* duty of 'leaving cards upon' one another – and the cursing teamsters en route to the Treasury site, then made his way down Pennsylvania Avenue through the heart of the town.

At this hour, the saloons south of Pennsylvania Avenue were opening for business. Rough-clothed men loitered around the doors or lounged on the benches outside, chewing, smoking, and reading newspapers as they waited for the day-labor that the saloon-keepers brokered for them with carters and construction bosses. Whether one sought employment driving mules or copying Navy lists, finding it was largely a matter of who one knew.

Poe drew up the carriage a dozen feet short of the King's Head and dismounted the box, an anonymous figure in slouched hat, scarf, and high collar against the cloud-flash of the heatless sun. January walked to the saloon's door.

'Mr Pease?' he called into the dark cavern – he knew better than to walk through the front door of any establishment that catered to white men. 'Gennelmun here to see you, sir.' He saluted with his whip: *See, I'm an innocent coachman, and the gennelmun outside is wealthy enough to keep such a thing.*

Within, he observed, a solid wooden bar stretched the entire width of the room. A hall on the north side – there was a door to his left on the outside wall – probably communicated with the stairway that led to the lodgers' rooms. Another door from the barroom led into it, and a third, as he had observed the previous night, gave access from behind the bar into the hall and thence the storeroom, an arrangement that meant that whoever was behind the bar could keep the patrons away from the good liquor.

'He'll come out when he's finished his goddam chores,' retorted Miss Drail's brazen voice. She stood behind the bar, washing glasses in a tin basin.

'To hell with you, woman.' Wylie Pease threw the broom he wielded into a corner, kicked it when it bounced off the wall and fell in his path, and untied his apron as he strode to the door. 'Who is it?'

'Mr Wellesley, sir.' January named one of the surgeons they'd encountered on their rounds. 'This way, sir.'

Evidently, going to speak to surgical gentlemen at their carriages was no new experience for Pease. He followed January without a blink.

Poe opened the brougham's door, and as Pease got near it, stepped neatly behind him and shoved a gun into his ribs under the cover of his many-caped coat.

'Get in the carriage,' snarled Poe, 'and you won't be hurt. We just want to talk to you.'

Pease blenched, tried to pull away, and January

took his arm in a grip like an anaconda. He thrust him into the carriage and climbed in after him, pulled the door shut behind them. Poe swung to the box and started the team at once. Pease started to squeak, 'What the hell—' and Henri raised his pistol.

'Ten short minutes of your time is all we ask, Mr Pease. We mean you no harm.'

Masked, and in the gloom of the coach with all its shades drawn, Henri managed to look surprisingly sinister, a huge gray form with the gun in one plump white hand. 'Ten short minutes, and a little information.'

He did indeed sound like Shylock.

'You are Wylie Pease, the grave robber—'

'Never! If it's that stinking liar Fowler that told you so—'

'I haven't the pleasure of Mr Fowler's acquaintance – yet.' Henri cocked his head a little, just as if he actually saw the man sitting opposite him instead of an indistinct blur. 'But you're either a grave robber or receive goods from one...'

Without varying the pistol's line in the slightest, with his free hand he produced the gold locket and one of the ivory portraits from his pocket. 'I found these a few nights ago in your desk drawer—'

'I don't know who put 'em in there, Mister! We got all kinds of bad customers coming through the tavern, and many's the time I've had to—'

'What, through that storeroom and up your private staircase? That's a pity,' Henri went on

250

smoothly. 'My client has authorized me to pay twenty dollars for information which we were led to believe that you might possess.' He laid locket and portrait on one chubby knee, reached into the breast of his coat – a lifetime of short-sightedness had given the young planter a surprisingly sure touch with finding things – and brought out first a twenty-dollar gold piece, which he placed on the seat beside him, then Selwyn Singletary's silver reservoir-pen, card case, and spectacle case.

'And don't pretend you've never seen them before.' He managed a surprisingly sinister sneer. 'I haven't the slightest objection to your disgusting occupation. I'm not going to peach on you–' he tapped the ivory portrait with the end of the pen – 'unless you insist upon making me do so. Why would Mr Fowler take the trouble to slander you, I wonder...? And him so popular with the constabulary of this city.'

'Why d'you think?' demanded Pease sullenly. 'He's beat me out of a dozen stiffs this year, him and his boys. He's a greedy bastard, wanting a piece of everything in this town – and a traitor in the bargain.'

'But it was you who found these things, wasn't it? All I want to know is where.'

Pease hesitated – Henri still held the gun on him ('If the gun really were loaded,' he confessed to January later, 'I wouldn't have taken it off him for a second, would I?') – then picked up the pen.

'Oh, this stuff.' He frowned, and his hard little eyes flickered from Henri's face to January. 'If you'd offered me gelt in the graveyard, Sambo, 'stead of grabbin' me, Jimmy wouldn't a' slugged you. You ain't going to believe this, sir—' he turned back to Henri – 'and God knows I got no way of provin' it, but I swear you it's true. I found it in the grave of the French minister's secretary.'

Henri looked nonplussed, as if Shylock had suddenly been given Macbeth's cue. January snapped his fingers like a man suddenly enlightened, cried, 'Didn't you say to me, sir, how funny it was that a man'd be buried with his pen, 'stead of a locket like them others you found?'

'Er – I did indeed.' Henri made a stab at sounding suave and villainous. He raised his pistol and Pease flinched. 'Surely you aren't going to attempt to convince me that the French Minister's secretary picked Mr Singletary's pocket before he died?'

'I dunno nuthin' about this Singletary jasper. But the stuff wasn't on the Frenchy. It was tied up in a handkerchief and buried a couple inches deep at one side of the grave, like somebody'd just scooped a little hole in the loose dirt after the grave was filled an' poked it in. They put the cut turves back over the soil when they close up the grave, but it's nuthin' to push one aside.'

Henri looked wildly at January, there being nothing that he could imagine a fat and oily spider in its web would say to this information.

January produced his notebook from his pocket and asked – as if it were his job to do so, which in fact it was – 'When was this, sir?'

'What, Frenchy's funeral? Last fall sometime.'

'Was Congress still in session?'

Pease glanced at Henri as if protesting that he didn't owe a black man any answers to anything, and Henri – who appeared to have recovered his sangfroid – grated in a steely voice, 'Answer the question, you wretch.'

The grave robber replied sullenly, 'Musta been, 'cause there was a hell of a funeral. Old Van Buren himself spoke over him: this was a cousin of that Frog that married Old Hickory's niece, and every Democrat in Congress showed up to shed tears. They put a guard on the grave for a week, but there was a cold snap. I knew he'd be pretty fresh still. Only reason I got to him, too. Fowler doesn't know a thing about the business,' he added with a sneer. 'Thinks after a week nobody'll take 'em. You might not get fifty for him, but there's them'll pay twenty-five.' He glanced at Henri again. 'That's all I know, mister – sir. I swear it on my mother's grave.'

'I expect that was the first one you robbed,' retorted Henri loftily.

'Did you keep an eye on the grave yourself?' asked January. 'Watch it to see how long the guards remained?'

'With that rat-bastard Fowler hanging around ready to get in ahead of me? You bet I did, Sambo. I wouldn't put it past him to bribe the guards – pay 'em to help him dig, if I know Fowler.'

'Did you see people visit the grave?'

'There's always people will visit a grave, that first week or two.' Pease spread his hands. 'Pomercy – and I didn't get but twenty dollars

253

for him, on account of the delay, though he was fresher'n anybody had a right to expect ... Pomercy was related to half the Frogs in the District. There was somebody coming every day to snivel over the dear departed. I'd look over the churchyard wall, couple times a day. The grave's about fifty yards from the church, but it's around the back and there's trees in between it and the gate, so you can't see it from the road.'

'So anybody kneeling beside the grave could have moved a turf aside, scooped a hole with his hands, and shoved these things–' January gestured toward the artifacts – 'down inside.' He sat silent for a moment while the carriage jogged through the rutted streets around the Capitol, trying to identify the feeling that tugged at the back of his mind. The feeling that he was missing something, looking in the wrong direction.

'Easy as takin' candy from a baby, Sambo.'

You'd probably know.

'His Lordship's client–' January nodded at the startled Henri – 'is seeking news of a large man – about His Lordship's stature – burly, bearded, graying, and last seen wearing English clothing.' He pretended to be reading this from the notebook. 'He came to grief between the fourteenth of October and the sixteenth.' He picked the gold piece from the seat beside Henri and placed it in the grave robber's hand. 'Has such a body been found, in any grave? Or in any unorthodox spot? The money is yours, whether you answer yes or no. We only seek the truth.'

Pease shoved the coin immediately into his waistcoat pocket. 'God's honest truth, I ain't

254

heard of any.' He continued to address Henri, as if it were inconceivable that the questions would originate in any brain but his. 'Rusty McClain – works as a churchyard guard these days, but used to do a little resurrectin' – he's with Fowler now, but he'll come in and have a drink for old times' sake. I'd have heard it from him, if there'd been anything funny turn up. And if it's an Englishman you're lookin' for, Fowler would have told 'em at the Ministry.'

Henri merely looked puzzled, but January said, 'That's Christian of him.'

'Christian my arse.' A spasm of anger crossed the resurrection man's ferrety face. 'Told you Fowler's a goddam traitor. He works for that Limey bastard Oldmixton. Collects information for him – any goddam thing. That stink-arsed sister of his runs three whorehouses down in Reservation C, and you can bet they send in a report to Oldmixton, about which Senators use the one that don't peddle girls. If a Congressman fires a secretary that's been readin' somebody else's love letters an' pokin' his nose in the dirty laundry, you bet that secretary knows Fowler'll pay him for whatever he's found.'

Pease sniffed. 'Police in this rotten town get all over a poor man for turnin' an honest dollar – and Fowler's got them in his pocket, too! You bet he does! – and then shut their eyes when the likes of Fowler goes sellin' whatever information he can get to this slick Limey nancy. No wonder this country's going to the dogs.'

Henri paused in gathering up Singletary's modest grave-goods and returned to his character as Shylock as he regarded Pease. 'And are you so poor, Mr Pease?'

Pease smiled, like the First Murderer from Macbeth. 'I am that, sir.'

'Well, we'll have to see what we can do about that.' Henri fished in his pocket and held up another gold piece. 'I think two can play at Mr Oldmixton's game. Can I trust you to make enquiries – and I'll want the truth, now; my client only wishes to know where his friend lies buried – about this large gray-bearded gentleman who met with an untimely end sometime in October of last year? I shall send Ben here for word.'

He returned the coin to his pocket and gestured with the pistol. 'And I trust you'll see to it that he returns to me safely.' He took up his cane and thumped the roof of the coach, and in a few minutes – January guessed they'd simply gone back and forth along Pennsylvania Avenue – the vehicle came to a stop, and the door opened.

January sprang out and let down the step – though remembering the coils of shorn-off hair in Pease's trunk the impulse was strong to trip Pease as he got down. They were in the market square near the canal. Beyond its smelly water, low-lying woodlands and swampy pasturage stretched for almost two miles from the river to the Capitol on its little hill, and, southward from the canal, those splendid, weed-grown, unpaved avenues extended amid woods and occasional farm-lots to the river and the hills of Maryland beyond.

Anywhere in that bucolic wilderness, he

reflected despairingly as he swung himself up on to the footman's stand again, Henri and Chloë's wandering Englishman might be resting in a shallow grave...

Or not, he thought as the carriage pulled into motion again.

Or not.

TWENTY-ONE

'You're a surgeon, Benjamin.' Henri pulled the satin mask from his face and for a moment appeared as Minou must often see him: fair, fine hair ruffled in a hundred directions, bovine brown eyes blinking myopically as he took a seat on the small parlor's sofa and fished his spectacles from his pocket. 'How might a body have been disposed of, other than by burial or throwing it in the river?'

Dominique and Chloë cleared from the marquetry table the remains of the hat that the latter had been watching the former trim. From the dining room came the music of dishes being set out, as beyond the curtained windows Mandie, Kizzy, and Charmian raced to the chicken run to search for eggs.

'Don't rule out throwing in the river,' said January. 'An unweighted body might stand a good chance of being washed up on a mudflat, but between the Treasury, the Post Office, and the canal docks this town is hip deep in unguarded building-stones. You can steal a stone during the daytime but the body has to go into the river at dead of night, when a wagon is noticeable—'

'Always supposing the constables are sober.' Chloë looked up from polishing her spectacles. 'But you're quite right. Bodies are found every day in the back alleys of Washington...'

Including Davy Quent's, January reflected, with an inner sigh for the loss of bacon and eggs. It was the only regret he could yet feel for removing the man from the world, and that, he supposed, was the point of the penance.

'The crux of the question,' Chloë went on, 'seems not so much who murdered M'sieu Singletary, but who would want to obliterate all trace of him?'

'Exactly.' January leaned against the door jamb. 'Anyone kneeling at poor M'sieu Pomercy's graveside for fifteen minutes with his back to the church could dispose of the pen and the card case. It's safer than the river – scavengers work the mudflats, you know. But why would you? Why not sell them, unless it was to prevent any chance of recognition? That doesn't sound to me like the act of a stranger.'

'They do say, don't they,' put in Poe, 'that something like half of all murder victims know their killer?'

'I should certainly be happy to murder at least half of the people I know.' Chloë put her spectacles back on.

'But poor M'sieu Singletary knew no one

in Washington,' pointed out Dominique. 'Or almost no one. Myself, I cannot picture M'sieu John Quincy Adams slugging him over the head and burying him in the garden.'

'For one thing,' added Chloë reasonably, 'the servants would see, not to speak of Mrs Adams. Although Mr Adams is quite strong enough to lift a big man's body unaided.'

'Really?' Minou's beautiful eyes widened. 'That is strong – it's getting so I can barely lift Charmian, she's grown to such a big girl! And him President of the United States!'

'Former President,' Henri corrected.

'I'd like to see Van Buren sling a corpse about,' remarked Poe. 'He'd be the sort who'd pay someone else to do it, I expect ... and then pay three times as much in hush money.'

'And that's precisely the problem.' January lifted his hand to retrieve the attention of his erratic fellow sleuth-hounds. 'Whether you bury the body in the woods or throw it in the river with a fifty-pound segment of the United States Treasury building attached to its feet or cut the flesh off and burn it – in which case you still have the bones to worry about, as well as tell-tale smoke and a tremendous amount of fire-wood to be accounted for ... All those problems go away if you just kill him and let him lie. So why didn't they?'

'In this town,' mused Poe, 'it can't be from fear of arrest.'

'No.' January let the word sink in. 'No.'

'If he had been ambushed in the woods—' began Minou, and even as she said the words her voice tailed off.

'I suppose you could drag him into the woods to bury him,' pointed out Henri. 'But you would need to bring a shovel out there with you. And if you buried him anywhere near the road, you'd run the risk of encountering Mr Fowler and his merry men lying in wait for some poor Negro. You'd certainly run the risk of *them* coming upon an informal grave and peddling its contents, and according to Brother Pease that hasn't happened.'

'The problems multiply further,' continued January, 'if the murder took place at whatever hotel or boarding house Singletary was staying at...'

He sat silent for a moment, turning over again the thought that had come to him as he'd stood by the canal that afternoon.

'What if Singletary isn't dead?' he asked.

In the startled silence, Octavia Trigg's heavy tread creaked in the hallway: a squeal of door hinges, a murmur of voices, then the landlady's step retreated into the big parlor opposite...

'You mean he's fled?' Henri frowned. 'But *why*?'

January shook his head. 'We know almost nothing about the man,' he pointed out. 'The only person in Washington – in the country, apparently – who knows him well is Mr Oldmixton, who seems to be running a spy ring—'

'You'd believe the word of a man like Pease?' Henri's pale eyebrows shot up. 'Or Fowler, for pity's sake?'

'I don't suppose the Secretary of State would,'

agreed January. 'Or whoever it is who's in charge of trapping spymasters. Oldmixton sounded extremely concerned about Singletary, but that may just mean that he's as skilled an actor as you are, Marse Eddie...'

'He'd scarcely be a successful spy if he wasn't,' observed Chloë. 'And it does put a different context to M'sieu Singletary's fears for his life. Mrs Bray could have dropped some remark about Oldmixton over tea that revealed the extent of Singletary's danger ... But if he is alive somewhere, why hasn't he retrieved his notebook?'

'Perhaps he's being held prisoner?' suggested Dominique, eyes aglow.

'My dear Minou, where?' asked Henri sensibly. 'In the attic of the Ministry? The man's been gone for six months! You can't keep someone locked up for that length of time without the servants suspecting something!'

'Only four years ago,' January pointed out, 'a very respectable Creole lady in New Orleans was discovered to have been keeping seven slaves imprisoned in her attic and torturing them daily, and nobody in town was the wiser.'

Henri turned pink. 'That situation was rather different.' The Viellards were related to the respectable Creole lady in question.

'And there are people locked in pens and back rooms not fifty feet from the Capitol,' added Dominique, her voice very soft, 'and kept drugged, some of them, so that they do not cry out over the walls to passers-by that they are free men.'

'Well, my dear—' Henri looked excruciatingly uncomfortable – 'one can hardly think that poor Singletary has been kept in blackface for six months.'

'In any case,' added Chloë, 'who in their right mind would have hired Singletary as a spy to begin with, when they have so many more useful villains like Fowler skulking about? By all accounts he doesn't sound capable of finding his way around Washington unaided, much less—'

'An asylum,' said Poe.

They all looked at him.

'A madhouse. Whoever had him admitted drugs him – which solves the problem of getting him into a vehicle – and arranges with the doctors there to keep him drugged. The mad have no more rights, and their protestations of wrongful imprisonment are no more heeded, than those of slaves. Of course a slave will proclaim that he's really free, and of course a madman will claim that he's actually sane ... You've described the man as being eccentric in his behavior—'

'Is there a madhouse hereabouts?' asked Chloë.

'Alexandria,' said January at once. 'Run by a man named Gurry.'

Still struggling with the idea, Henri repeated, 'But think of the risk! Why not simply kill him?'

'That's something we don't need to know,' said January. 'What we do need, right now, is to ascertain whether he's actually there, and if he is, how to get him out. Because whoever put him in,' he went on grimly, 'you can be sure that it isn't under the name of Singletary.'

There was a practice game that evening, out in the meadow by Reedy Branch. An even larger audience turned out to watch than last night, and a larger percentage of that audience, January noted with uneasiness, was white. He spoke to both Darius Trigg and to Charlie Springer – who as head of the local Prince Hall Masonic Lodge knew most of the free colored population of the District and a large number of the slaves – and gave them a description of Selwyn Singletary.

'Deke Bellwether works as a cleaner for Gurry, doesn't he, Charlie?' asked Trigg.

'He lives out in Alexandria, but he's in the choir of my church. He's one of the basses – got a voice that fills the hall. He said he'd be here today ... Here's our boy,' Springer added, waving as Mede Tyler strode through the long grass from the direction of Connecticut Avenue, still in the neat white jacket of his waiter's costume and carrying his rougher clothes, and the bat that Fip Franklin of the Centurions had whittled for him, in a bundle. At his approach, a half-dozen white men separated themselves from the edge of the crowd, teamsters in plug hats and corduroy jackets. With a prickling sensation on the back of his neck, January started in that direction, trailed by Trigg and several others. As they got closer January saw that several of the whites had clubs in their hands, and one of them, what looked like an ox chain.

'Think you're good enough to be playin' a white man's game, boy?' one of them called out as they spread in a line between Mede and the playing field.

'Want to see what kind of games white men really play with uppity fookin' niggers?'

Mede paused, moved to his left to go around them, and their line stretched to meet him.

'One thing just makes me retch, it's a nigger that don't know his place...'

January reached Mede's side. The players – Stalwarts and Centurions – grouped around them, unarmed, but outnumbering the whites three or four to one.

'We're just out here to play a little ball, sir,' said Trigg, in his most pleasant voice. 'It's just a game. I'm most sorry if our friend spoke out of line to you.'

The man with the chain spat tobacco on to Trigg's foot. 'Your friend is breakin' the goddam law,' he said. 'It's against the law for niggers to play ball. Against the law for niggers to assemble. There's one thing I can't stand, it's a law-breakin' criminal nigger—'

'There's one thing I can't stand,' retorted a soft voice as the whites – who had begun to close in around them – parted. Kyle Fowler slouched forward, tall and dirty, with two of his own 'boys' at his back. 'And that's a man that makes a bet and then tries to fuck with the contest beforehand. You bet on the Warriors, O'Hanlon?' His voice was soft and high, almost womanish, his eyes expressionless a reptile's.

Without answering the question, O'Hanlon spat into the grass again. 'These fookin' niggers are breakin' the law.'

Fowler looked over at the crowd around Mede,

then back at the whites. 'Shame on them,' he said. 'You want to come down to the station house and swear out a complaint. I think Constable Jeffers has money on that game, too. He'll want to hear what you have to say.'

January's hand closed silently around Mede's elbow, drew him back into the crowd, which closed around them like water. As they walked back toward the worn square of the playing field, he said softly, 'If Fowler wants to arrest us – are those fellows with him part of the police-force? – he'll come over. I take it the Hibernian gentlemen have bet on the Warriors like he said?'

'They wouldn't be trying to stop Mede if they'd bet on us,' returned Trigg grimly. January could feel Mede shivering.

After a moment Trigg added, 'It's a goddam *game*!'

'No,' said January quietly. 'It's the honor of America.'

That evening's game – a practice match against a scratch team of mixed Knights and Centurions – wasn't notable for anyone's good playing after that. The one exception was Mede, whom, it appeared, very little could shake once he got into the thrower's circle. Most of the men – waiting for trouble of one kind or another, either arrest by the constables with Fowler, or attack by the Irish teamsters who'd bet on the Warriors, or even the outbreak of general riot between those teamsters and the Abolitionists – could barely hit the ball, and no wonder, reflected January.

Watching Mede in the worn patch of grass, he was struck with how exposed the young man looked, and his eyes went to the line of trees that bordered one edge of the field.

'Would you send a man over there?' he whispered to Trigg. 'It'd be an easy shot, for someone with a rifle.'

'It's a goddam *game*—'

'I'll go.' Preston jogged away in that direction.

A few minutes later Noyes came to where the Stalwarts stood, with the news that O'Hanlon and his boys had taken themselves off. 'Fowler and Roberts – that's the assistant constable with him – are still here,' he said softly. 'They say Constable Jeffers has a couple thousand bet on the game, besides a percentage of bets he's brokered for just about everybody in the ward. Lots of men don't want to admit they've bet on black men to beat white ones, but with Bray still out of play – he's one of the best strikers the Warriors have – it's pretty clear you boys are going to win.'

'A win is never clear.' Trigg turned from watching Mede – with the effortless perfection of a machine – put out yet another Centurion, and the men started to come in from the field. 'That's what games are. Not something to make you scared to play them.'

January was the striker for the next round and missed the ball totally. With his mind still running on the O'Hanlons of the world, and rifles in trees, he doubted he could have hit a watermelon on a tabletop. He took his place in right field – where he could do the least harm to his own team's cause – for the few minutes it took Mede to put out the next striker, and when he came back toward the line of boxes, he found Charlie Springer there, with a short, jolly-looking man with features that January identified as Ibo.

'This's Deke Bellwether, Ben,' Charlie introduced them. 'My choirman, who works out at Gurry's madhouse.'

'Dr Gurry be first to correct you, sir,' replied Bellwether, in a deep voice like black velvet and the slurry, profoundly African English of the coastal islands. 'It a Asylum, he say – a place for people for to take refuge.'

'And did a man come in to take refuge there last October?' asked January. 'He'd be an Englishman, probably close to six feet tall, gray beard, gray hair, heavy through the chest and shoulders.'

The attendant cast his mind back for a moment. 'No English bukra,' he said. 'Some been come last fall – planter from Charleston name Criswell, Boston bukra name Leland. None been come that description.'

Damn it.

And yet...

The perfection of Poe's solution tugged at January's thoughts: *Where else COULD a white man be kept prisoner?*

He turned toward the empty fields, the few scattered farmhouses that were all that stood on this end of Washington. *He could be held in any of them...*

But then why dispose of anything that would identify him?

'Is there another lunatic asylum in the District?' he asked. 'Or over toward Baltimore?'

'There the state asylum in Baltimore,' rumbled Bellwether. 'Dr Gurry he always slangin' them mad-doctors there, say they imbeciles. And there another private asylum in Manassas, Dr Blaine run.'

'It's thirty miles to Manassas,' put in Springer. 'And you'll want to be careful, walkin' that by yourself, Ben. They talk of puttin' a railway line through there, but it ain't happened yet.'

'Could you get me into Gurry's, Deke?' January asked at last. 'As your assistant, or your cousin, or something, for an afternoon?'

'Gurry gonna gone Thursday,' said Bellwether, nodding. 'You do carpentry? Or plastering? You know fixin' sash windows? Kumbayah, I make sure somethin' broken—'

'You have a piano?' asked January. 'I can tune one of those, and I saw the tuning equipment in a pawnshop just last week.'

'That we do.' Bellwether grinned. 'But I tellin' you, ain't no English buckra there, with or not with no big gray beard.'

It wasn't the best ball any man present had ever played, and they split up and went back to their homes while the sun was just touching the tops of the woods along Rock Creek. On fine spring evenings like this one, the teams played until it was too dark to see. But though O'Hanlon and his b'hoys had taken their leave, nobody liked the idea of walking home in the darkness. Mede, Trigg, the Reverend Perkins and January were

escorted back to the boarding house by a size-
able crowd of neighbors and friends.

'It ain't what a game is supposed to be,' said
Trigg angrily, when, by the warm lamplight of
the dining room, he helped hand around the
plates of chicken stew and potatoes. 'Sure as
gun's iron, when that game's over and those
white gentlemen settles their wagers, the constables are going to come down with the letter of
the law and our children won't be able to even
get up a game of One Old Cat. And not from
anything *we've* done. Just because *they* was
made to look at something they didn't want to
look at.'

'You ever heard of white teams playing black
ones further North, Frank?' January turned to the
conductor.

'Once or twice.' The young man, who had
maneuvered a place beside Minou, helped Charmian to a chicken leg. 'Or there'll sometimes be
a black player on a white team. That's usually if
he's just about the only black man in town. I
think it makes them nervous, seeing us in
groups.'

'Not as nervous as it makes me,' returned
January, 'seeing *them* in groups.'

'And what will you do, Mede,' asked Dominique, 'when this game is done? It is in a sense
the payment for your freedom, is it not? What
will you do, when that payment is made?'

'I don't know,' said Mede quietly. 'My whole
family is on Red Horse Hill Plantation. My
mama, my sisters, my little brother...'

Not to speak of the white side of your family,

269

reflected January. *The brother you love. The father who brought you up as a slave...*

'But now I'm a free man, I can't go back to Kentucky. Once a man's been freed, he's got to leave the state. It's the same here in Virginia, isn't it? I can't just go back to Lexington and take a job.'

He ducked his head. 'You know, after all my life, Marse Luke calling me his Good Man Friday, I read that book it comes out of. And Mr Crusoe's Man Friday went back to England with him in the end. As if there wasn't anything in his own world to return to; as if he couldn't even imagine being free, or doing anything else with his life, except tag along after his master. Now it looks like I can't even do that.'

He rose from his place with a bow to Mrs Trigg – 'If you'll excuse me, m'am.' Picking up from the sideboard the envelope that had been brought for him that afternoon, he passed into the hall. The lamp there shone briefly gold on his hair, before he ascended the stair into shadow.

It was January's last sight of him alive.

TWENTY-TWO

'But if these men who were admitted to the asylum in October bear no resemblance to M'sieu Singletary,' argued Dominique as she untied the strings of her daughter's bonnet the following morning, 'what do you seek in M'sieu Gurry's madhouse, *P'tit*? Show Uncle Benjamin what you have found this morning, darling—'

Charmian carefully opened her specimen box, to display, on its filling of felt and cotton wool, the leaves, buttons, stones and feathers she'd collected on this morning's walk.

She would have gathered dead bugs and cigar ends as well, had her mother permitted it. Like Henri – to Minou's horror and January's secret amusement – everything in the world fascinated Charmian to an equal degree.

'I seek a look at his daybooks.' January squatted down to study someone's lost rosette of ribbon, the bright leaves of dogwood in the box. 'A man could have been admitted any time after October...'

'If they waited to admit him, where did they hide him in-between-times?'

'A cellar,' said January promptly. 'An attic. A sickroom under drugs. That's a very beautiful beetle, *P'tite*, where did you find it?'

'Beside the stream by Eighteenth Street,'

specified the child precisely. 'It has long feelers.'

'So it does. I don't think I've seen such an insect at home in New Orleans, have you?'

Charmian thought about it for a moment, then shook her head.

'But why?' demanded Minou. 'The whole thing is absurd!'

'And he could have died, at any time between his admission and now.' He stood and ran a gentle hand over his niece's mahogany-red curls. 'I don't think there's a soul in creation so completely at the mercy of his jailers, as a lunatic in an asylum,' he said. 'At least not in the United States. Even in prisons, the warders and guards are accountable for it, if a prisoner dies. And slaves, God knows, are worth money to their owners. But in a madhouse, a man – or a woman – may be dosed with whatever medication the mad-doctors consider effective that month, from salts of mercury to ipecac. They may be bled, blistered, stood naked under douches of freezing water, puked, purged, and opiated to the point of death in the name of "calming their nerves" or "shocking them back to their senses", and no one will ask or argue or suggest that the mad-doctors mightn't know what they're doing. They could be tarred and feathered if some savant writes an article about how it stimulates the nerves.'

'You spoke to the man from Gurry's, then?' Poe emerged from his parlor, where his breakfast tray lay on the table in the watery sunlight. He was immaculately dressed in his usual black – presumably in preparation for yet another day

272

of waiting in some Senator's office in the hopes of convincing him to use his influence to get him a job – and looked, January thought, haggard and grim. But his dark eyes came alive as he inquired, 'Will you need a respectable family member to demand a sight of the madman?'

'Possibly later,' said January, rising. 'Depending on what I can find in the daybooks. I'm guessing whoever locked Singletary up – *if* he was locked up – has made arrangements to hear of it if someone comes around asking questions. Right now I'm feeling my way in the dark.'

In the dining room, the clock struck half-past eight. Dominique said, *'Peste*— Come along, dearest. Let's get you changed before Madame Trigg locks the doors on us and casts us out without breakfast—'

They went upstairs, passing Seth Berger the cabman on his way down; Thèrése and Musette hastened from the dining room in their mistress' wake.

'There's a state asylum near Baltimore,' January went on, and Poe nodded.

'Yes, I've visited that one. A friend of mine – a lad I went to school with – had the ... misfortune ... to be incarcerated there, for drinking and addiction to laudanum. A horrifying place.' Shadow crossed the back of those dark eyes: shadow and fear. 'I still have nightmares of being locked up ... At least if a man has money, he can go mad in comfort.'

'There's evidently a place out in Manassas too, and I may beg your company, if it comes to that—'

273

'My dear Benjamin, given the choice between kicking my heels in quest of a job I don't actually want, and breaking into a madhouse in search of—'

'Benjamin!' Dominique appeared at the top of the stairs.

The note of shock in her voice had January vaulting up two steps at a time without asking why. Whatever it was, it wasn't good.

When he came close – Poe at his heels – she said, very quietly, 'It's Mede. He's dead.'

And as January turned toward the stair – Mede's room was on the third floor – she caught his sleeve. In the shadows of the stairway her face looked like a cut-out of ivory, slashed with eyebrows startlingly dark. 'I wanted to ask him about going to Blodgett's tonight, before he left...' She swallowed hard. 'Someone cut his throat.'

There were no vines, no drainpipes, nothing that would serve for a handhold on the whitewashed brick side of the house. It was twenty-seven feet from the window sill to the ground. 'How could they have got up?' Poe asked at once, looking down.

January shook his head.

The shutters and sash had both been open when he came into the room: he and Poe had gone straight to the window. Directly beneath the sill, the room's single ladder-back chair lay on the floor on its side. January examined the chair's joints and angles, and almost at once he found a thread of cotton caught in one, where a rope had looped around it to permit someone to descend from the window on a doubled line, which could then be pulled free.

Only then did he turn and approach the bed.

Mede lay on his back, naked under the light blankets. Sheets, pillows, mattress were soaked in blood, but the young man's eyes were closed and his face peaceful, as if someone had simply bent over him and slit his throat in his sleep. One hand lay at his side, the other arm was extended, doubled back and tucked half under the pillow. There were no cuts on either hand. He hadn't struggled. He probably hadn't even woken.

The smell of the blood brought back the alley behind the Globe and Eagle, and the man for whose sake he was to fast on Lenten rations until Easter of next year ... The man who had tried to kidnap Mede into slavery on his first night of freedom.

All that struggle for nothing.

All the anguish it cost Mede to pull himself free of a master he loved. To take the harder, colder road that led to manhood.

It's a damn game...

Flies were beginning to circle the bed and settle on the clotted slash.

Children's voices on the stairway. Musette said sharply, 'No, stay away, that isn't for you to see.'

A shadow darkened the doorway. Trigg said, 'Jesus Christ—!' He came in and shut the door. 'How could they have got in the house?' he asked. 'I locked the place up good after that hoo-rah at the game. And I told Mede to make sure his shutters was bolted fast.'

'Mine surely were.' January walked to the window again. 'This's how he got out. Ran a double length of clothes-rope, it looks like, around this post of the chair-back. With the chair taller than the window is wide it just braced against the frame. He climbed down, then pulled the rope down after him.'

'Still doesn't tell us how he got in.'

The door opened a crack, more than filled by Octavia Trigg's towering shape. 'We gotta get him outta here.'

January half-drew breath to begin a sentence containing the word *constables*, then let it, and the thought, dissolve away.

In New Orleans – at least in the French Town, where everyone knew who was who and the free colored owned property – it was still possible to deal with the City Guard and have some assurance that one wasn't going to be comprehensively sorry you'd called them in. But as if he'd opened the door to the future and looked down a lighted vista populated with inescapable events, he saw Kyle Fowler with the second ward constables; he saw men stinging with disappointed rage at the loss of their bet money; he heard those rough American voices: *Arrest 'em all, one of 'em's got to have done it.* And then, *We gonna lose our bet money, they owe us to make it up...*

And saw Kyle Fowler, and George Klephert, and every other one of the dozens of slave dealers operating in the District walking through the crowded cells: *I recognize that one, he's a runaway ... Yeah, that wench is a runaway too...*

Rage went through him like a poison.

He took a deep breath, let it out. Closed his eyes. The brotherhood of man, the fatherhood of God, for that moment jeered back at him, an obscene jest.

God, guide me...

Don't let me go down that road.

First things first. 'Get the children out of the house,' he said, and opened his eyes. 'Octavia, can you tell them Mede's suffered an accident and needs to be taken to a hospital? We'll need a couple of quilts, laid on the floor here for the blood. We can keep him in the cellar till it gets dark—'

'Bury him there,' said Octavia calmly. 'Under the coal bin, so's the children won't find his grave.' And, when her husband opened his mouth in protest: 'Constable Jeffers got money on the game. If word gets out Mede's dead he'll ask why, an' God knows what kind of answer he gonna come up with.' She turned to regard Poe with somber eyes. 'That sit with you, sir? You know what happen to any black man or woman that end up in a jail in this town?'

Poe started to answer, then closed his mouth again and thought about it. Quietly, he said, 'I have no objection to the program, Madame. I'm only sorry that...' He looked down at Mede's quiet face. 'That it can't be otherwise than it is. He deserves much better.'

'Lot o' men do, Mr Poe,' she returned. 'Lot o' men do.' Through the window January could see Musette, Minou, and Clarice Perkins hurrying away with the children in the direction of the open fields.

277

Trigg stepped into the hall; Seth Berger's voice came muffled: 'Damn, not even a Christian grave—'

'Better men have gone to worse graves,' responded the Reverend Perkins' rather thin tones. 'God no more cares about that than you'd care about what inn you spent a night at, on your way home. I'm sure our brother Mede doesn't care.'

'You sure 'bout that, Reverend?' asked Harrison Winters, one of the railroad conductors. 'He ain't gonna walk, is he?'

And the waiter, Lunn: 'It's just, there's kids in the house...'

'He will have as good a burial as any Christian man,' said Frank Preston. 'Men don't walk after that.'

January stepped to the door, half-opened it where the men stood in the shadowy hall. 'We'll find the one who did it,' he said softly. 'As long as he knows we're looking, no, he won't walk.'

As the men came into the room January looked around again. The chamber was starkly bare and simple: bed, a small dresser, washstand, a rag rug on the floor. Mede's white jacket from Blodgett's dining room, his dark 'good' trousers and white shirt, lay on the floor in a heap. The killer had dumped them to take the chair ... Yes, there was a smudge of blood on the shirt. His 'other' shirt – the one he'd been wearing when he walked out of Luke Bray's house – hung on a peg on the wall, with his 'other' trousers. The bat that Fip Franklin had whittled for him stood up in the corner.

It's a damn game...

Grief like a knife, at the memory of that young man standing in the sunlight like an oak tree, beating white men at an honest game. Showing the white men who'd come to watch that it could happen.

Good Man Friday, with his feet on the road that led to the rest of his life.

The dresser drawers contained nothing but a single clean shirt, a few pairs of under-drawers, some socks, and in the bottom drawer a shoe-shining kit. A small stack of coins, amounting to about three dollars, stood on the corner of the dresser, with a second-hand clothes-brush and a comb. Nothing else.

January's eyes narrowed as he understood what had happened.

'Mr Poe,' he said quietly. 'Would you come with me, please?'

Frank Preston had fetched an improvised stretcher from the kitchen, made of clothes poles and a sheet. As he, Berger, and Trigg moved Mede's body on to this, January and Poe slipped out into the hall. 'It'll take most of the day to dig a grave deep enough to contain the smell,' he said as they passed along the narrow hallway between the rooms of the single men: Berger, Preston, Winters and Lunn. 'There's half a ton of coal in that bin—'

'Might it not be quicker to bury him upright in the wall, as disobedient nuns were interred in the Middle Ages?' inquired Poe. 'I've been in that cellar; there's space between the piers that hold up the house. Surely the brickwork would be enough to keep it from stinking.'

'It wouldn't,' replied January simply. He picked up a lamp from the hall table – not yet cleaned, contrary to all habit of the house. 'You might do something like that in a catacomb or a deep wine-vault, where no one is going to come for months at a time. But under a regular house, even if there were seepage from the cesspit into the cellar – enough to make it smell – rats, or a cat, would scent meat. If they did so while there was anyone in the cellar of a suspicious nature, it would give the game away.'

'And do you think–' Poe scratched a lucifer, held the flame to the wick – 'that gentlemen of a suspicious nature might come asking to have a look at Mrs Trigg's cellar in the near future?' He cocked a worried eyebrow up at January, who had already thought of this possibility.

'Proving a murder would prove that the betting had been tampered with.' He opened the narrow door that led to the attic's lightless stair. 'It would be cause for people not to pay. If that's why he was killed.'

'What other reason would there be?'

The attic – like all such spaces – was crowded with trunks and boxes. Yet it was scrupulously neat, without cobwebs or the smell of mold. January almost laughed. Of course Octavia Trigg's habitual cleanliness and order would extend to places in the house where no one went. There was no such thing, in her world, as 'out of sight, out of mind'. No broken chairs or household utensils too worn to be used, and every cardboard box was labeled: *Quilts. Sheets. Good dishes. Winter clothes.* The piles of newspapers

280

were recent and clearly only in temporary storage before serving as kindling or wrapping paper or for service in the jakes. Dismantled bedsteads – January counted five of them – stood neatly in one place along the wall, awaiting an occasion for use downstairs. Though dusty and already growing hot, the room had a feeling of openness under its low, slanting rafters.

There were no obscure hidey-holes.

He moved systematically to the darker corners, holding the lamp low to the floor. After watching him in silence for a moment Poe darted down the stairs and returned a few minutes later with a second lamp, as if he guessed the kind of thing January was looking for.

As if he understood suddenly how the killer had gotten into the house.

'There.' January held the lamp down almost to the boards, in a sort of nook between *Church Banquet Linens* and a half-dozen empty mattresses rolled up in holland sheets.

Poe brought his own lamp close.

It wasn't much. A couple of fragments of half-dried mud, the right angle of two sides cleanly defined, still damp enough to adhere together.

'From the inside angle of somebody's shoe sole.' January turned his own foot sideways to demonstrate. 'Between the instep and the heel. Somebody who was up here – sitting here out of sight – yesterday. You can see it's still damp. Mrs Trigg—' He swiveled on his heels as the landlady's heavy step creaked the floorboards. 'Somebody came to the house yesterday afternoon with a note for Mede, didn't they? I heard your voices in the hall – and I didn't see that note in his room.'

'White boy,' she answered promptly. 'Fifteen, sixteen I'd say. Dressed pretty rough.'

'You leave him alone in the hall when you went to look for Mede with the note?'

She nodded, confirming January's recollection. 'When I come back he gone. The front door was open, lettin' the flies in—' Her eyes widened. 'You ain't sayin' instead of leavin' he come up here?'

'I think he did.' January pointed down to the fragments of clayey mud. 'I think he had a razor and some candles in his pocket and fifty feet of clothesline rope wrapped around his body under his shirt. He came up here, found the darkest corner he could, and sat quiet until the dead of night when the house was asleep ... Look.' He passed the lamp close to the floor again.

Three spots of white wax – fresh and untouched by dust – dotted the floorboards near the tell-tale chunks of shoe dirt.

'Was he dark or fair?'

'He wore a cap, pulled down 'most to his eyebrows. His eyes was green.'

'Were they? Hazel-green, or green-green?'

'Light,' she said, 'like new leaves. His brows was dark, an' so's the little bit of hair down by his ears—' With her own thick fingers she fluffed at the place.

'Thin boy, fat boy?'

'Husky in the body, but his face was thin. So was his hands. They was dirty, too—'

January was silent for a moment, thinking.

Expensive wax – that didn't smell as tallow did. And not a stub of match left behind ... 'What about his voice?'

'Sort of low and rough, but it hadn't broken. He spoke like an Irish.'

An easy accent to mimic. 'Could it have been a girl's face? A woman's?'

Her brows drew sharply together. 'It surely could. Not a pretty gal, but delicate.'

'This boy didn't happen to say who the note was from, did he?'

'He say, he had to be sure it went straight into Mr Tyler's own hand, though I'd already told him Mr Tyler just left for Blodgett's. He might catch him up if he ran, I says. He says, was I sure about that? 'Fore he went off runnin' only to find himself runnin' all the way to Blodgett's in front of the man he was supposed to catch ... I went an' checked in the kitchen,' she added as they descended the attic stair, moved along the thin carpet of the upstairs hall. 'When I come out, he's gone.'

'But not to deliver the note?'

'No, that note was in my hand when I went in the kitchen.' As they descended to the second floor January heard the quiet voices, the shuffling footsteps as the furtive pall-bearers descended the main stair before them. 'So I put it on the sideboard, for Mr Tyler to get when he come in for supper.'

'Which he picked up,' said January thoughtfully. 'I saw him carry it out. Who was it from?'

'By what that boy say,' said Octavia Trigg, 'it was from Mrs Bray.'

TWENTY-THREE

'But why on earth would Rowena Bray want to murder her husband's ex-valet?' Henri's voice had a plaintive note, as if to protest that he'd allowed himself to be dragged two thousand miles from his butterfly collection to search for a missing friend, not to solve a murder – and a black man's murder, at that.

Before descending to the cellar to move coal and dig Mede's grave – tasks which had not concluded until long after dark – January had sent a message to the Viellards at the Indian Queen, requesting a rendezvous at the Mockingbird Inn above Rock Creek on the following day. Trigg had recommended the place: private, respectable, and with a separate entrance to its private parlor, so that none could see who came or went. One could only speculate, in Washington, who else had need of such facilities.

'It's absurd,' fretted Henri. 'I'm terribly sorry about young Mede, of course – he seemed like a quite personable young man, and even if he weren't, it's still a frightful way to die...'

The Viellards had been told that Mede's body had been 'taken away secretly', though the reason January had given them for doing so had been truthful: Henri had murmured, 'Oh, surely not...' but had not pursued his objections further. Chloë, sitting at his side, had said nothing, her blue eyes speculative and crystal-cold, as if she were working mathematical sums in her head.

The Reverend Perkins had read the burial service over that narrow grave before they'd put the coal back, and Octavia Trigg had sacrificed four cups and a couple of flowerpots, to provide enough fragments of broken pottery and china to surround the grave with the traditional hedge of teeth. The shards had been buried completely, lest by any chance anyone dig down under the coal and find the grave outlined. But they were there, to keep ill ghosts away from Mede's secret bed...

And to keep Mede himself from staggering forth like a sleepwalker in quest of vengeance.

'But is it really any of our business?' He cast a pleading glance at his wife and, receiving no help there, at Minou.

'No.' Minou folded her hands – she had threatened violence unless she was included in the conference. 'It isn't. Nor is it yours – nor Chloë's, really – to go three weeks in that *awful* ship to this *frightful* town looking for a man neither of you has ever met. But you did it because poor M'sieu Singletary has no family, and no friends, and no one else to look for him or to care whether he lives or dies. You did it because he deserves better than to lie in an unmarked grave and be forgotten by everybody.'

It had been Dominique's idea, January had learned later, to take the children to the house of Charlie Springer, who rented out his barn loft for everything from dances to Masonic meetings. Springer had been given a tale of feared exposure to scarlet fever, Thèrése and Musette had been sent back to the Triggs' for food and quilts – it was Musette who had gone with the note to the Viellards at the Indian Queen – the children had 'camped out' in the barn under the supervision of Clarice Perkins, Minou and the two servants, and a splendid time was had by all.

But returning to the house that morning, and walking out to the Mockingbird Inn with January and Poe, Dominique had been unwontedly quiet.

'Madame Bray is entertaining tomorrow evening,' spoke up Chloë unexpectedly. 'Mostly, I believe, to convince people that her husband merely suffered a bad fall from a horse. If I send Madame Bray a note this afternoon begging for an appointment to go driving – pleading the need of her advice—'

'Dearest—!'

'Be still, Henri, we cannot expect M'sieu Janvier to burgle the house by night. He might miss something. We already know the household is short a maid, so all the servants will be downstairs polishing silverware and rearranging the dining room. No one will go upstairs after ten o'clock, I should say, until Madame Bray returns to get dressed – at four, to judge by the way I've seen her turned out at the British Minister's. There's a French door from the garden, though you may have to pick the lock, Benjamin.'

'Dearest—!'

'And I will go,' added Dominique, 'to break
286

the news to the other servants in the kitchen that poor Mede has disappeared, and to give them all the details of the fracas at the ball game Tuesday—'

'Excellent, darling!'

'—and the scarlet-fever scare last night—'

'Dearest, I beg of you—'

Chloë turned to regard her husband, her small hands folded primly on the tabletop in the dappled sunlight. That evening, January knew, the Stalwarts would be out practicing by the creek, and given the probable presence of O'Hanlon and the Irish teamsters, rumors about Mede's disappearance would be flying by dark.

'I have been seeking a good reason,' Chloë went on, 'to have someone go in and search Madame Bray's establishment for some days now.' From her reticule she plucked the copies January had made for her of the notebook, and of the paper he'd found in Luke Bray's watch, and unfolded both on the table. 'I've had tea with Madame Bray three times and have spoken to her at a dozen different entertainments. Likewise have I spoken to M'sieu Bray when I could catch him on his way to the gaming rooms. And neither of them is of a mathematical turn of mind.'

'So why did Bray copy those five squares?' Poe, who had been standing by the chimney breast, came to the table, turned the papers over in his long, ink-stained fingers. 'There are close to a hundred squares in that notebook. Why only those five? And why only five in the order of five?'

'They all add up to sixty-five.' Dominique

287

leaned around his shoulder. 'Is there significance to sixty-five?'

'It's the only number you can get on a square of the order of five,' said Poe. He had volunteered to help in the grave-digging and coal-moving yesterday evening, but Mrs Trigg had posted him instead in his little parlor with a cup of coffee and orders to intercept any white men who might come to the door. He'd remained on guard until past midnight, when all the shovels had been cleaned and everyone had bathed and gone to bed, and January felt that he was slightly disappointed that absolutely nothing had transpired.

'Then what is the importance of five? Were these the only squares of five in the notebook?'

'No.' Poe shook his head. 'There were near a dozen of this order.'

'They are the *last* five squares of the order of five in the notebook,' provided Chloë. 'But they are not all written together. Three were together, one was on a page with squares of orders from three up to eight, and one was on a page with a scheme – I don't know if it was his idea or something he'd heard – to relieve traffic congestion in Leicester Square by running underground tunnels underneath it with carriages pulled by pit ponies, as they have in mines. But he was fascinated by magic squares. He used to write to me about them when I was little.'

'And it is understandable,' said Poe. 'There's an eerie quality about magic squares; an incomprehensible persistence, that whichever way you add up the numbers, the answer is always the same. Like those dreams in which you keep asking a question – of the face in the mirror that isn't yours, or a bird with a demon's eyes – and it answers with an answer that you cannot comprehend but which you know to be true. You say, "What is sixty-five?" and it answers, "Sixty-five."'

'We have too few pieces of the puzzle.' January's mind returned again to Ganymede Tyler, as they'd borne him down to the cellar wrapped in quilts. Like Selwyn Singletary, a person that no one would miss and no one would look for ... possibly not even his brother-master, Robinson Crusoe infuriated and hurt at his Good Man Friday's departure. *Of course he'd run away, ungrateful nigger, after all I done for him...*

He deserves better, Dominique had said: certainly better than a secret grave beneath three-quarters of a ton of coal. *He has not dealt with us after our sins*, the Reverend Perkins had read over the grave last night, *nor recorded us according to our iniquities...*

And it crossed his mind suddenly that this was why the priest in Philadelphia had consigned him – without any means of enforcing the penance or even knowing if his supplicant paid heed – to fish, porridge, and water for a year: so that every day he would remember that though he had acted in what he felt to be a good cause, he had still taken the life of another person.

Whatever had turned Davy Quent's steps to being the man he had become, January guessed he'd remember him a lot longer than Kyle Fowler would.

His days are as grass ... the wind passeth over it, and it is gone; and the place thereof shall know it no more.

'Mede asked me once about blackmail,' he said slowly. 'About a letter that was written completely in numbers, which he found in Mr Bray's desk. But I've found,' he went on, 'in solving these puzzles, that if you start with *why*, it's hard to get anywhere. People kill one another for stupid reasons, or for no reason at all. People kill in drink, or because one man's black and another is white; or because some small irritation, rubbed at constantly, seems on a hot day, when the wind is blowing from the wrong direction, justification enough to end a man's life...'

He shook his head. 'What we need to find out is who *could* have spent the night in that attic. Minou—' He turned to his sister. 'While you're keeping the Bray servants enthralled tomorrow morning with an account of the confrontation with the b'hoys at the ball game, I trust you'll find out for me whether Mrs Bray was home on Sunday night.'

There was a judas hole cut in the wooden gate marked 'Bray' that opened from the service alley behind Monroe Street. Through it, January watched Dominique loaf her way up the gravel path, like a slave who knows that the completion of her errand is only going to get her set to some other task. In a neat calico dress borrowed from Musette, her hair bound in a slave's headscarf, she was a far cry indeed from the exquisite courtesan who graced her protector's arm at the

Blue Ribbon balls in the Orleans Ballroom.

In the quiet of the spring morning, January heard her tap at the kitchen door, heard the voices of the Bray cook and maid. Heard the door open and shut.

In one of the stables a little further down the alleyway a couple of grooms were harnessing a handsome team of chestnut geldings. He set down his satchel, thrust his hands in his pockets, gazed idly around him – *I'm just waitin' on my friend who got an errand here...*

The coachman leaped to the box, drove away up the alley. The grooms were already turning back into the stable gate. January caught up the satchel – carpentry tools purchased yesterday after the conference at the inn, from the same downtown pawnshop where he'd acquired a piano tuner's kit – and slipped through the service gate. He dodged through the rose garden, slipped along the hedge toward the garden door that Chloë had spoken of.

As Chloë had surmised, the garden was deserted, the gardener pressed to service shifting furniture in the house. January worked his way along the hedge, found the glass French-door, and let himself in. It wasn't locked. He wore the rough corduroy jacket and scuffed wool trousers of a workman and had both explanation and attitude ready, in case of discovery: *The man tol' me go on in an' fix the window upstairs...*

He doubted anyone would believe it, but it might give him time to make a break for it. The thought of burgling the house by daylight appalled him, but Chloë was right. To do a proper search of Rowena Bray's bedroom he needed daylight. A candle's glimmer wouldn't suffice.

And the more he thought about it, the more he concurred with Chloë Viellard. Mrs Bray's room needed to be searched.

The obvious places – the small desk, and under the mattress of the bed – were swiftly disposed of. A well-trained English lady would keep the servants at their work, and that included turning the mattress regularly and painting every crack and joint of the bed frame with camphor and turpentine twice a year. Though servants made life easier for the wealthy, every servant was a stranger under one's roof: a stranger who had goals and intentions never spoken of to the master.

Doubly so, if that servant knew that he or she could be sold to cover poker debts.

That left the floor, the walls, the chimney, and the armoire.

He found no false backs to any of the drawers in the bottom of the armoire, and nothing pinned or tacked to the bottom of the tall cupboard itself. No woman in her right mind would simply hide things under the shelf paper, but he checked anyway. The armoire towered above his own six foot three, its pediment of carved leaves coming within a few feet of the tall ceiling. A glance at the waxed floorboards revealed no tell-tale scratches where it had been moved, or where a chair had been placed to stow things on top of it. The top – when he placed the chair himself and checked – was clean of dust. The servants really were kept to their work.

Neither did the floor reveal scuffs or scratches to indicate that the desk had been shifted to give access to a loose board. From his satchel he took a sheet he'd borrowed from Mrs Trigg, laid it over the hearth, took off his jacket, and ran a cautious hand up the chimney – something a lady could only do, he reflected, if she was in her chemise, and even then she'd have to account for the soot in the water on the washstand after she'd cleaned it off her arm...

At least the hearth was cold. The spring day was a warm one. The windows stood open, and he heard the buzzing of a fly that blundered into the room, amplified as it bumbled its way into the open armoire.

January turned his head.

Why would a fly go *into* a cupboard?

He got to his feet.

As a child growing up in the slave quarters, January knew well the ways of flies. Hot afternoons, in the long, sticky summers, he'd observed them on the walls of the cabin, when all the boys and his sister Olympe would have contests as to how many they could kill.

Flies go to warmth, and to light.

A second fly had found its way there by the time he'd crossed the room to the massive piece.

Both insects were crawling around on the underside of the huge cupboard's top, glossy green-brown in the shadows.

And to blood.

It occurred to him, almost without conscious thought, that the high carved pediment around the top of the armoire could easily be concealing

293

space above the top shelf, like an attic. There was a long crack between the two halves of that whitewashed underside where the flies crawled, and he pushed gently up on it. It yielded easily to the pressure, revealing a space five feet by almost two and a half, and nearly a foot deep.

Groping in that space, he found a small pair of laborer's brogans, a pair of britches splattered across one thigh with blood that looked two or three days old, a man's calico shirt with blood on its front and a corduroy jacket whose right sleeve was splattered, as it would be if the wearer had cut the throat of a man lying asleep in bed. A brown woolen cap, of the sort the Irish laborers wore. A coil of clothesline rope. A razor and the stumps of two white wax candles.

Damn the woman to hell...

Four bottles of patent medicine – he sniffed them and shrank from the reek of opium – and a little box containing ink and a couple of steel-tipped pens. There was also what looked like a very long-barreled iron key with two wards, diametrically opposite one other, so that, looked at face-on, it resembled a circle with a bar across its equator, projecting from either side. Two pairs of cheap cotton gloves, one clean, one much dirtied with soot, and a folded sheet, also sprinkled and smudged with soot.

Very like, in fact, the sheet that he himself had borrowed from Mrs Trigg.

He returned to the hearth, knowing now what he had to look for. A foot-square section of the hearth bricks, beneath the fire grate itself, contained a round hole with projections that exactly matched the key. Inserted in the hole and turned, it proved to be not a key but a detachable handle, with which he lifted up the whole section of bricks, to reveal a space about two feet deep beneath.

There were four packets of papers within. Each packet – he could see at a glance – included what looked like a bank book. But his eye was drawn to the paper folded on top, which bore the now-familiar magic squares. He lifted it out, and though, like most people, his memory for a random grid of twenty-five numbers was not good, he thought the two that were immediately visible were the same.

He had no time to unfold the paper to see all of them, however, because at that moment footfalls creaked the board immediately outside the bedroom door. January dropped the paper back into its hole and replaced the bricks, scooped the sheet together and thrust it under the bed even as the doorknob turned, and rolled after it as the door opened.

'Goddam bitch,' whispered Luke Bray's voice.

TWENTY-FOUR

January held his breath.

The decision to go under the bed had been a split-second choice and it precluded any alternative explanation. Anyone, black or white, concealing himself under the bed of the mistress of the house was *ipso facto* Up To No Good. Moreover, the counterpane didn't extend entirely to the floor. Had Bray bent down and looked under the bed they'd have been nose-to-nose.

But Bray didn't.

He crossed at once to the desk, opened the drawers – by the sound of it, pulled them entirely free of the body of the desk – and rifled through them, muttering a *sotto voce* string of imprecations against some woman, presumably his wife, as he did so.

Reason enough, thought January, *to have those little hidey-holes under the hearth and on top of the armoire constructed, even had one NOT done murder in disguise.*

'Goddam lazy wenches...' Bray turned to the armoire. January had replaced the false ceiling but hadn't shut its doors. He heard the master of the house take the drawers out of the bottom, as he himself had done, and systematically look under the shelf paper. January could see Bray's

296

feet, shod in polished half-boots, such as an assistant secretary to the Secretary of the Navy would wear in pursuit of his duties. He even brought over the same chair that January had brought from the desk, and stood on it, as January had done, to look on the armoire's top, though it evidently never occurred to him – no more than it had occurred to January – to measure the distance between the top of the armoire and the 'ceiling' above its uppermost shelf.

What the hell am I going to say when he looks under the bed?

Jus' unner here checkin' de flo', Marse Luke...

When Bray crossed to the bed January shrank himself – as much as a man six feet three inches tall and powerfully built can shrink – into the very center of the space, arms close to his sides. Bray yanked up the counterpane, not to look under the bed but to run his hands under the mattress, cursing all the while: 'Thinks she can put one over on me ... Her and her goddam Limey nancy...'

'Marse Luke, sir?' The butler's deep voice – a Virginia accent, like the cook and the maids. Mede had said at supper one night that he alone had come out from Kentucky with his master, had shared a boarding house room with him until he'd married and had to set up an establishment worthy of a London banker's daughter.

'What you want?'

'A nigger gal's here, asking to see you, sir. She say she has a message from Mede.'

Minou. She must have seen Luke Bray ride up, invented a message that would bring him downstairs long enough for January to make his escape.

Whispering blessings on his sister's supposedly empty head, January slid from beneath the bed the moment Bray's footsteps and the servant's retreated down the stairs. He darted to the armoire long enough to slip the key back into its secret attic, shoved Mrs Trigg's sheet back into his satchel – which Bray apparently hadn't even noticed on the floor behind the desk – stepped into the hall...

He knew he should lose not a single second in retreating down the service stair.

Yet quietly in his ear he heard Mede's voice: *Is blackmail when they send letters all written in numbers?*

Half a dozen strides took him around to Bray's room. He pulled open the desk drawer there, dug through jumbled drafts of Navy Department correspondence and half-finished 'fair copies' of letters from Mr Dickerson to everyone from President Van Buren to the French ambassador ... Nothing.

The other drawer contained a crumpled disorder of bills, gambling-markers, scribbled notes. Beneath this January found a sheet of foolscap, bearing what he guessed Mede had seen – strings of neatly-written numbers.

11 Ø Ø Ø9 Ø Ø Ø317 Ø Ø1837 Ø Ø24 Ø924221624 Ø25 Ø621 Ø7152022252116 Ø522241425 Ø72021 Ø1192511 Ø3252120221513 Ø317252120 Ø31410 Ø72213 Ø914 Ø12114 Ø1192224162020 Ø120 Ø71513222417 Ø31024 Ø22112 Ø51025

Ø514211221 Ø4102014 Ø6 Ø324 Ø22113 Ø5
Ø82119251418 Ø71920 Ø725211115 Ø9 Ø7
Ø21412111412 Ø22119131913 Ø5 Ø217 Ø8
Ø817 Ø124 Ø71522 Ø721 Ø72224 Ø425 Ø92421
Ø118 Ø114 Ø8202214 Ø521 Ø2 Ø31825231211
Ø913 Ø522 Ø722221420161013 Ø71518
Ø120102114212514 Ø52214142114251725
Ø911 Ø22511 Ø520 Ø32221222418221516251
Ø911

As he thrust this in his pocket he heard Bray's
voice in the stairwell: 'What the hell is it to me
that he's gone? Ungrateful bastard's nothing to
me! I gave him his goddam FREEDOM to play
in that goddam game, and what the hell could
you expect of a goddam NIGGER?'

Soundlessly, January crossed to the window,
made sure no one was in the garden below, hung
from his hands from the sill, and dropped.

No matter what Royall Stockard and John C.
Calhoun and every other Southerner liked to say,
slaves were not simply 'property like any
other'...

Whatever the hell was going on in the Bray
household, Mede had seen enough of it to cost
him his life.

'But what *was* it?' Poe dropped into the chair
beside January's at the great oak table in the
main parlor, where January had spent the afternoon studying the 'letter', the sheet of magic
squares, and the enigmatic red notebook. The
windows were now blue with evening; a few
minutes ago Dominique had gone scampering up

299

the drive to where Henri's rented carriage waited for her in the dusk, and whenever the kitchen
door opened the scent of biscuits wafted through.

'What did he learn? I don't suppose Mrs Bray
is going to tell the police...'

'Mrs Bray,' returned January wearily, 'isn't
even going to *see* the police. Officially, Ganymede Tyler isn't dead. He's simply "disappeared". And if we inform the police that he's
dead and that we know who did it, do you really
think they'll arrest a white woman in preference
to every person in this house?'

Poe's lips tightened, his face suddenly pale
with anger.

'The bloodied clothing may not even be there
by the time the police search, *if* they search. And
who is the witness to finding them there? A
black man? A member of the same ball team,
who might have money on the game?' January
turned in his fingers the chalk he'd borrowed –
along with Mrs Trigg's kitchen slate – to scribble
numbers and calculations that went nowhere.
'From what I've seen of the woman, I'm guessing she'll accuse me of planting the garments
there in order to incriminate her. The police will
be more than happy to shut me up, "to prevent
scandal", as they say. It's not something I can
afford to risk. And I hope,' he added, watching
the other man's face steadily, 'that it's not something you'll feel moved to report because you're
sure that the police couldn't be *that* corrupt.'

'No.' Poe's dark eyes smouldered. 'I have little
love for the police – I think they're damned
fools, for one thing – and I've spent a few too

300

many nights in the cells myself to believe they're the guardians of anything except each other and their own pocketbooks.'

January had heard Poe's dragging steps almost pass the parlor door and had recalled he'd been meeting with an Indiana congressman about the possibility of a postmaster's job. But at the sight of January he'd come in, and as he'd listened to the précis of the afternoon's events he'd seemed to come alive again.

'But what *can* we do, then? Surely this wretched woman can't be allowed to get away with it—'

'Not if I can help it.' January pushed across to him the papers he'd been studying since he and Dominique had returned, late and footsore, from Georgetown that afternoon. 'Personally, I don't care what we get her on, so long as it's damning.'

The Reverend Perkins came into the parlor, hung up hat and coat and kissed his wife, who came hurrying downstairs with a proud account of their daughter's progress at reading. A moment later Trigg came in with Seth Berger, worriedly discussing the events of ball practice, which had evidently included further interference from the Irish. At a glance from Poe, January collected the litter of papers and slate, and the two men crossed the hall to the smaller 'white folks' parlor'. A fire had already been kindled against the nip of the evening, and the lamp lit.

Poe shut the door against the noise. 'What have you so far?'

'Not a great deal.' January spread the papers on the marquetry table. 'I thought the magic squares might be a cipher key. The alphabet can be written into a square of five, if you count I and J as a single letter, and you can see there's a distinction made between an open zero and one that's crossed. The message starts with the number eleven and then two crossed zeros, and if you'll notice there are no crossed zeros – no independent zeros at all, in fact – in any of the magic squares.'

'I'd assume the crossed zeros are place-holders.' Poe studied the thin sheet of notepaper close to the lamplight. 'Or dividers. How would you know if ten-one-two means a thousand and twelve, or a hundred and one and then two? But if you mark off a single-digit number – one through nine – with a crossed zero before it, there's no confusion. Two crossed zeros together would act as a space.'

January studied the paper. 'So the message begins with eleven, followed by three crossed zeroes – marking the number out as something important. Eleven is the top left-hand number in one of the five squares. Bray must have found these squares in his wife's desk and copied them, suspecting something but not knowing what they were. It would make sense to tell the recipient which key to use at the outset ... Only, I've attempted to transpose letters with numbers with all five of the squares and have gotten only gibberish.'

'No, it isn't a simple transposition.' Poe picked up the fine notepaper – from Mrs Bray's desk, the same as that found inside Bray's watch. 'Not a regular transposition, anyway. I'm assuming the original message was written in English – although there's no reason Mrs Bray wouldn't code her letters into Latin first, or French or German or Tahitian for that matter. It would certainly thwart any attempt from her husband to decode it. Simple transposition is always given away by recurring letters and patterns. In English the most commonly used letter is E, followed by T, A and O – this applies to any substitution, whether you've got numbers in your five-by-five block or something else. A five-by-five block works just as well with letters of the Greek alphabet, or astrological symbols, or whatever you can think of. You're still fairly safe in assuming – if your sender is an English-speaking amateur – that the most common symbol is going to turn out to be an E.'

'You sound like a man who's studied this.'

The poet looked a little self-conscious, like a schoolgirl who's been given a compliment. 'Well, one of the mathematics masters at West Point also taught cryptography, to the very few of my classmates who had the turn of mind for anything beyond the simple logistics of murdering our nation's foes. I've always been fascinated with codes – my friends and I came up with dozens as boys. He said – Professor Larson, that is – that the way to defeat this business of letter frequency is either to treat whole words as single units – which is what one does in a book code – or to keep changing the transposition.'

'I've seen transpositional tables,' said January

303

thoughtfully, 'that alternated which letter was substituted depending on which line of the document one was reading. Sugar planters use them to communicate with their agents.'

'Who have the keys. And the use of random numbers has the advantage that most people don't remember long sequences of numbers. It looks like Mrs Bray – and whoever she's sending messages to, I assume Mr Oldmixton at the Ministry – uses these five-line squares, probably alternating them.'

'Indicating that they are neither amateurs,' said January, 'nor do they expect to be dealing with amateurs. Luke Bray works in the Department of the Navy.'

'Ah,' said Poe, and there was a moment of silence.

'And his wife is the daughter of a banker. She must have grown up around people who used commercial ciphers all the time. There are daughters of bankers,' he added, 'who are content to know nothing more of the matter, beyond that dearest Papa pays for their wardrobes. But I think you and I have seen proof that Rowena Bray is not such a woman. I'm wondering if she simply got the idea of using a five-line magic square as a cipher key from Selwyn Singletary, or if it's something Singletary invented, that's routinely used in the bank.'

'Either way,' said Poe, 'it has to be something that's fairly simple to learn, once both parties have the key. Professor Larson used a method – he called it "tumbling blocks" – as a means of constantly altering your cipher without changing your key.' He drew the slate toward him.

'As I said, it's simple if you have the key – and nearly incomprehensible if you don't. You say one of those squares has eleven in the first position?'

January laid it before him.

'Then we'll mark the alphabet into the twenty-five squares of our Number Eleven grid. I'm assuming that first sequence is the date – since there is no number thirty-seven in a grid on the order of five...'

'So that 1837 really is 1837.'

'I believe so. The way "tumbling blocks" works is that you divide your message up into two-letter couplets, usually inserting an X or a Q between doubled letters in words like "meet" and "butter". You find their corresponding numbers on the grid, which will give you smaller squares within the grid. You see how three – or zero-three – and seventeen correspond to E and L? Make them two corners of a square, and their opposite corners are—'

'A and P,' said January. 'April?'

'Ninth of April of last year.'

'Bray must have found a half-written message on his wife's desk last spring. He was suspicious enough to copy it—'

'But couldn't make heads or tails of it, not even when he found – and copied – the keys.' Poe's chalk flicked over the slate as he spoke, transcribing and transposing. 'Since, as the lovely Madame Viellard says, Mrs Bray is not herself a mathematician, I should guess that Oldmixton – who also knew Singletary – was

305

the one who realized that magic-squares on the order of five could be used for code-keys. They simply look like puzzles, should anyone find them, and most peoples' minds, as I said, simply turn blank when they see ... Good lord.'

He sat back, black forelock hanging in his eyes, and stared at the scribbled slate before him.

'I think that word is *President. 9 April 1837 – Emergency meeting President's cabinet...*'

There was silence as Poe finished transcribing the lines.

TWENTY-FIVE

11Ø ØØ Ap 9, 1837 Emergency meeting Presidents cabinet x Papinau Resolution rejected x Preparations for military action discussed in event of British show of force x Send regiments to Detroit, Buffalo, Presque Isle x Station Iroqouis, Inflexible at Presque Isle.

'Papineau was one of the leaders of the Canadian revolt last year, wasn't he?' asked January, after a few minutes' study of the decryption. 'I heard there was talk of the British invading Canada to crush the rebellion, but I didn't know we'd gone so far as to station regiments at the border.'

'Neither did I – nor anyone, I expect.'

'Where and what is Presque Isle?'

'It's a bay on Lake Erie. Perry launched his

fleet from there, to defeat the British on the Great Lakes during the war. The *Iroquois* and the *Inflexible* are gun brigs.'

'War with England would be just what some people in Congress are looking for,' mused January, 'as an excuse to seize the Oregon country ... if we won.'

'What, America lose?' Poe flung up his hands. 'Perish the thought!' Then he was silent for a time, turning the chalk in his long fingers. 'Are they in it together, do you think? Bray and his wife?'

'I doubt it. He'd never have freed Mede, if he knew there were things going on in the household that Mede might have seen or guessed.'

'He was drunk,' said Poe. 'God knows the blamed stupid things I've done when drunk...'

'He was sober the following morning when he signed Mede's freedom papers,' pointed out January. 'He was suspicious enough to copy the messages he found, and the keys. And he may have remembered that Oldmixton put Mrs Bray on to him.'

I feel responsible, the Ministerial Secretary had said.

And Mede: *He couldn't wait to go back to Fayette County ... but by then he'd met Mrs Bray...*

'As long as Mede was a slave in the household,' January continued softly, 'Mrs Bray was safe. Most Southerners barely notice their slaves – one of our neighbors used to have male slaves bring in hot water for her while she was bathing. But although he could never testify against her in court, the minute Mede became a free man he was away from Mrs Bray's control. And someone might listen to what he said.'

'About a foreigner, they would,' said Poe thoughtfully. 'From the country we're close to war with. She *couldn't* let him live.'

January considered the papers for a few minutes more, the blocks and strings of numbers that a man's eye would skim right over...

Unless he knew it was a code.

Or unless he was a man who saw numbers differently than did other men.

He turned to the little morocco notebook, opened it to the last page of numbers. Then he studied the long columns that preceded it, noting that the numbers were short, in two distinct columns rather than a block-like text, and that they included no Ø symbols.

'Look at this,' he said, and put the notebook before the furiously scribbling Poe. 'Both columns start with 61836. Look down them – on the first, the fifteenth entry is 71836, then further down 81836. And the numbers are roughly close: 13076 here, 12953 opposite it ... They're household accounts.'

'By Jove, I think you're right.' Poe set down his chalk, shoved the hair from his high, pale forehead with chalky fingers. 'That's June of 1836, then further down is July, then August—'

'They carry on up to 91837.' January flipped over two pages of columned numbers. 'The month that Selwyn Singletary disappeared. Now compare that second column with the first. Identical numbers, but with interpolations in the second column: 25015 here, between what I'm guessing by its size is a month's expenses for either clothing or feed for horses – 15050...'

'A hundred and fifty dollars, fifty cents. He was just in too much of a hurry to mark the decimal point or the symbol for dollars—'

'Or didn't use one if he was just making notes to himself. He knew what he meant. Still in June, another hundred and seventy-five thirty extracted, and in October of '36 three hundred...'

'The wretched girl is cooking the books!' Poe flung down his chalk and regarded January in mingled bemusement and rage. 'That twelve thousand that's the first item in June, September, and December – or a hundred and twenty dollars – that would be quarterly rent for a house that size. The next item is always somewhere between thirteen thousand and sixteen thousand—'

'A hundred and thirty and a hundred and sixty dollars,' interpreted January. 'Food for a household that includes eight slaves. But she's skimming out those extra sums – a hundred and fifty dollars, a hundred and seventy-five, three hundred, sums that she told me *Bray* was paying out in blackmail – and putting them somewhere...'

'Putting them in banks,' said Poe grimly. 'Under another name – or four other names.' He tapped the slate sharply. 'That short block of text at the end of the notebook: Rothschild's bank in Philadelphia, under the name of Rodger Allen of Water Street, Lynn; Bethmann's of New York, as Jonas Sinter of Pine Street, Providence; Barclays of New York...'

'All foreign banks.' January studied the

decryption. 'She married Bray right about the time Jackson started to dismember the National Bank. As a banker's daughter, she wouldn't trust a state bank. Rothschild's is French; I think Bethmann's headquarters are in Frankfurt. And none of those aliases hails from the city the bank is in. I was interrupted in my search of her room, but I'll go bail that's what those packets of papers were, hidden under the fireplace bricks. Bank books and letters of identity.'

'So between what she gets from selling the naval information she finds in her husband's study—'

'—to Oldmixton, I'll be bound—'

'—and picking her husband's pocket every month...'

'Our Mrs Bray,' concluded January, 'has been a busy young lady indeed.'

At that point, January considered sending a note to Deke Bellwether at Gurry's madhouse, cancelling – or at least postponing – his appointment to impersonate a piano tuner on Monday. Given the labels on the bottles he'd seen in Rowena Bray's armoire – not only opiates, but toxic salts of mercury which many physicians considered medicinal – he had no doubt what fate had befallen Selwyn Singletary, once Mrs Bray had guessed what he'd learned of her peculations.

'It must have been she, who broke into his hotel room,' said January, when supper was done and Poe had joined him in a corner of the main parlor, mostly so that January could have an

after-dinner cup of tea without violating anyone's sense of the proprieties about who was
allowed to share food or drink with whom. It
was perfectly acceptable for a white man to have
tea in the dwelling-area of black folk – as a guest
doing them a social politeness – without acquiring, even in his own eyes, the stigma of a man
who 'ate with Negroes'.

The parlor was quiet. Darius Trigg had gone
out to play at a soirée being given at the house of
Senators Buchanan and King, and the Reverend
Perkins was at choir practice. Under Musette's
watchful eye, the household children played
dominoes at the big table, and their laughter and
talk covered the quiet voices of January and his
white guest in the corner.

'She may have said something to him the
following day that made him realize it was she.
Or maybe she was simply called away and he
got a chance to look at her account books.
They're in an office just off the parlor; you can
see them from almost anywhere in the room. Or
he might have marked his assailant somehow,
and then glimpsed the mark on her.'

'He panicked,' surmised Poe. 'God knows I
would have, if I'd begun to suspect my employer's daughter was not only a very clever
thief but also a spy. He handed his notebook over
to the only person at hand he thought he could
trust, intending to get it later. Although why Mrs
Bray thought her father would object to her
doing a little spying for King and Country—'

'Queen,' corrected January, and remembered
to add, 'sir. And for all we know, Jeremiah Hurl-

stone may be a Conservative and have no use for anything that will help Lord Melbourne's government. One can never count on a man choosing – or even seeing – what's good for his country, if it will hurt the faction he wants to see remain in power.'

'You have a Machiavellian turn of mind, my friend.' Poe slowly thumbed through the various transcriptions they had worked on until the supper gong. 'And a hard way of looking at the world. I dare say you're right.'

'Spying – particularly spying professionally – is a dirty game. It isn't like it sounds in novels. At the very least it would raise a tremendous scandal with her family, especially if Mrs Bray's father was at loggerheads with her. He may have sent Singletary via Washington particularly to inquire into her affairs. Given the situation in Canada, if word got out, Mrs Bray would lose her position in Washington society and might well be faced with the choice of either going home to a family she detests, or more likely sent to ruralize on a small plantation in Fayette County, Kentucky, far from good music, interesting books, political power and the company of anyone but one or two plantation wives...'

'Much like Acropolis, Indiana, in fact,' said Poe glumly. 'The town to which I shall, it seems, shortly become postmaster ... I was offered the position today, pending my interview with Senator Thumbtwiddle on Monday. I sympathize with the woman.' His jaw tightened, and for a moment a bleak desperation flickered in his eyes. 'Or I would, had she not killed an innocent man to get out of such a fate.'

'Two innocent men.'

Poe nodded. On the other side of the room, the dominoes game had been abandoned in favor of an extensive building-project with the tiles, amid cries of, 'You're going to crash it!' and, 'When I grow up, I'm going to have a house like that...'

'You think Singletary is dead, then?'

'Once she put him into a madhouse to establish an alternate identity for his corpse,' said January, 'there's no reason she would need him to remain alive – and every reason to finish him quickly. The medicines I saw in her armoire would be more than sufficient. All she'd need – either in her own persona or in disguise as one of her banking alter egos, Allen or Sinter or whoever – would be to tell Gurry that her "uncle's" physician back home recommends that Uncle be dosed with mercury. She disposes of his personal effects in such a way that there's no chance anyone who knew Singletary will ever see them, Singletary is buried under whatever name she committed him under—'

'Merely to get out of living in Fayette County?'

'You wouldn't do it,' said January. 'Nor would I – nor would your wife, or mine, or my sister Minou, or any of the ladies of our acquaintance—'

'I wouldn't lay money against Madame Viellard.'

January grinned. 'All right, I'll give you a maybe on Madame Viellard – and I'd bet the other way on my mother, now that I come to think of it.' His smile faded. 'But we're talking about a young woman who disguised herself as a boy in order to gain entrance to this house, who hid herself in the attic, and who came downstairs and cut the throat of a young man – a young man whom she knew, who had lived under her roof for two years – while he slept, only because of what he might have seen or learned.'

Poe said, 'Hmmn.'

'Killing a man by cutting his throat,' said January slowly, 'is different from shooting him in war, or even bayoneting him in the heat of battle. And she seems to have done so without turning a hair. I think,' he continued, 'that I'm going to go to Gurry's on Monday after all. All this is purely conjecture, until I can have a look at the daybooks for October of last year. I'll send a note to M'sieu Viellard–' they both knew he meant Chloë – 'asking for a meeting tomorrow evening when I get back...'

'We,' said Poe.

'I beg your pardon?'

'We.' The poet stood up and stretched his slender frame. 'Acropolis, Indiana, may perish for want of a postmaster, and I shall bitterly weep to see it destroyed, yet I cannot and will not for any consideration pass up the chance to break into a madhouse in the guise of a piano tuner in order to catch a foreign spy. There are things which humanity cannot demand of mortal flesh and blood.'

Their eyes met.

'Nor would I dream of it,' replied January politely. 'Sir.'

* * *

Though trained as a surgeon, January had always been fascinated by the heartbreaking conundrum of the mad. There'd been a man named Tyo on Bellefleur Plantation who heard voices speaking to him from the ground, who saw things he could barely describe and which no one else could see. Though it was obvious to everyone that during his 'spells' he was not responsible for his own actions, both the overseer and Michie Fourchet – the plant-ation's owner – punished him repeatedly for disobedience, for insolence, for trouble-making.

Eventually Michie Fourchet – who seemed possessed by his own demons when he drank – beat Tyo to death.

Later in life, January had gone with the other junior surgeons from the Hôtel Dieu out to the asylums of Charenton and Bicêtre, to see the mad, though he had been one of the few who spent more time talking with the doctors about the nature of madness than watching the inmates scream and struggle against such cures as the Swing and the rotating board.

'Half of them, we don't know why they start exhibiting symptoms of madness,' one of the doctors at Charenton had said to him. 'Nor why they recover, if they recover. Sometimes the shock to their senses – from the water cure, for instance, or icing the scalp – seems to snap them back into sanity. I suspect – but I can't prove – that others simply learn what's wanted of them, and perform it, only to regain their freedom. Still others simply waste away.'

315

All this returned to January's mind as he and Poe approached the rambling brick house in the woods beyond Alexandria.

They'd set out across the Long Bridge shortly after breakfast on Monday, clothed like workmen. January bore a satchel containing a piano tuner's hammers, tuning forks, and mutes ... as well as the spyglass he'd bought for Rose, and his set of picklocks, just in case. Beyond Alexandria – a small town of brick houses, green lawns, trees in new leaf and the biggest slave-depot in the District – they stayed off the road, and only approached the house after Gurry had gotten into his carriage and departed. 'I should hate to explain to the head of the asylum that somebody called in the piano tuners and forgot to tell him about it.'

'We could always try something else,' pointed out Poe as they emerged from the woods.

January folded up his spyglass. 'Not really. Once he's seen us, we're handicapped in all else that we do. Gurry and Mrs Bray were obviously on good terms when she called him in to see her husband, and any suspicious enquiries are going to be reported to her. Now that I think of it,' he added thoughtfully, 'drugging her husband and telling her tame mad-doctor that he slit his wrists sounds like a plan to get rid of him.'

'Wouldn't that be killing the goose that's laying golden eggs?'

'Not if he's begun to suspect her. She may need time to transfer enough money into her four bank-accounts, but if he 'kills himself' next week, all anyone will say is, *We were*

316

expecting it.'

'Anyone except Mede.'

His black hair slicked with bear's grease under a workman's cap, Poe explained to the porter at the gate in an impeccable Irish brogue that sure and Mr Gurry'd hired them to tune the parlor pianna, and they'd legged it a weary mile from Washington...

They were admitted.

'Gurry the only one keep the daybooks,' said Deke Bellwether quietly, when Gurry's assistant – a very young Mr Betzer – led them to the day parlor and shooed the patients out into the garden. 'Mr Betzer and Mr Klein – them other mad-doctors works with Mr Gurry – gonna have their hands full this hour, treatin' them poor folks, so I say best I bring the books here, for let you have a look. But I done say, we ain't had no Englishman here, nor no Singletary, nor no nobody what look like what you describe.'

The attendant slipped half a dozen slender, calf-bound ledgers from beneath his smock and down into the body of the very handsome Broadwood parlor grand that occupied a whole corner of the big day-room close to the garden windows. January immediately handed him a gold double-eagle – the man would almost certainly lose his job if his part in the morning's events were discovered. 'I be back in a hour,' said Bellwether. 'You done be done with 'em then?'

January nodded and scooped the books into his satchel. The sight of them – or of anything – resting on the wires of a good instrument raised the hair on the back of his neck.

'Look for patients admitted in October who've died,' he whispered to Poe. 'And for patients whose families bring them in medication.' He set the tuning fork into its wooden base and tapped it sharply, touched middle C. 'Look for Mrs Bray's banking alter-egos: the one we know she has papers for. Allen, Sinter, Coates, or Merton...'

He inserted the mutes and checked the general condition of the piano, which was good. It wasn't badly out of tune and hadn't been abused, which raised his opinion of Gurry's establishment. Many of the mad-doctors he'd spoken to highly recommended music and singing for their patients, which made enormous sense to January. Music had always been a shining fortress for him, proof against the worst that the world could devise: slavery and mockery, fear and the death of the woman he loved. Having met a number of madmen whose senses were abnormally acute, he guessed, too, that an out-of-tune piano would be an even worse torment to them than it was to him – completely aside from the fact that Messrs Betzer and Klein, and whatever lesser attendants assisted them, would wonder at piano tuners who did their work in silence, and might come in to see what they *were* up to...

'Drat the man,' Poe muttered, 'his handwriting's like a fish line the cat's been playing with...'

Beyond the wide windows, an attendant crossed the garden with an empty basket, bound for the low brick ice-house. Elsewhere in the house,

318

a woman's voice lifted in a wailing scream. January shivered. The most diehard cotton-planter in Alabama understood in his heart why a slave would want to be free. But a woman who shrieked in protest against being force-fed emetics to 'restore the balance of her system'? Who fought when men stripped her naked and shoved her under a torrent of ice-cold water to 'stimulate her blood'? Who wept at the thought of being tied to a board and spun round and round so that her 'circulation would improve'? She was viewed as a child, refusing to accept what could only bring her good.

'I see only a half-dozen patients whose families bring them medicaments from the outside,' whispered Poe. 'Gurry seems extremely fond of opiates – no wonder his patients are docile.'

'And no wonder he has to give them purgatives on a daily basis. Any of those who've died?'

'Not as of December ... No, wait, yes. A Mr Nyeby ... His wife came in two or three times a week with medicines prescribed by their doctor in New York...'

'I can help you with that,' said a voice from the doorway.

Poe snapped the satchel closed at once. January turned sharply: a girl stood in the doorway, skeletally thin, her hair cropped to a rough light-brown fuzz on her scar-crossed scalp.

'I've tuned pianos all my life,' she went on. 'My father taught me, as he taught me to play.' She took a step nearer. 'His brother murdered him out of jealousy, and wanting to get his

319

money. They killed my mother also, and put me in here so I wouldn't inherit.'

'I'm very sorry to hear that,' said January. 'I was told specifically by Dr Gurry not to let any of the patients assist me – or I and my friend here will lose our jobs.' He nodded to Poe. 'But I'll certainly look forward to hearing you play after I've finished, to test its tone.'

A tall young man appeared in the doorway behind her. Past them, in the hall, January saw a sturdy attendant of nearly his own height and build supporting a fragile little gentleman, as thin as the girl but swaying on his feet and muttering, broken spurts of unintelligible words.

'Now, Miss Kingmill,' said the young man, 'you're not disturbing the workmen, are you?'

'I was only telling them,' responded Miss Kingmill, 'that Uncle Andrew had me put in here so that he can keep Papa's money. He's trying to have me poisoned,' she added, turning back to January. 'I keep getting sick in here, and I know it's because they've paid Betzer to poison me.'

'Miss Kingmill,' said the young man patiently, 'you know that's not true. Mr Betzer and I – and Dr Gurry as well – have only your best interests at heart. I was looking for you just now – might you please come along with me and Silas, to help give Mr Leland his treatment?'

Miss Kingmill's thin face brightened. 'Of course,' she said. 'It's setonage,' she informed January. 'Most doctors prefer it to blistering, and it accomplishes the removal of infected fluids from the body by the same principles. My father taught me how to do it. While he lived, I helped him hundreds of times. Mr Leland's relatives are trying to poison him, too,' she concluded, and allowed herself to be led away.

January went back to sounding notes and chords, gently adjusting each of the many wires. Poe went back to the daybooks.

'A woman named Wandsworth died in January,' reported the poet after a moment. 'After being given – good Lord! – forty-five grains of opium over a twenty-four hour period because she was "excited". I can't find any other deaths than Mr Nyeby at the end of December. His widow claimed his effects and arranged for his burial.'

'Where was he from?'

'That's just it, I can't find record of his admission. His treatment – and the visits from Mrs Nyeby – are listed in the October book—'

'Any record of what she was bringing for him?'

Poe thumbed his way back through the October daybook. 'Nothing. You didn't happen to make a note of the address on those bottles you found in Mrs Bray's room, did you?'

'Hunt's Pharmacy in Baltimore.'

'I know it, it's on Gay Street.'

'We'll have to make the trip there to confirm when she purchased the things. Make a note of the dates of Mrs Nyeby's visits ... if you would, sir,' he remembered to add, though Poe seemed to neither notice nor take offense at being addressed as a friend rather than a white man. By the time Bellwether returned for the books, Poe had finished looking through them and January was nearly done with the piano. Miss Kingmill did not return – evidently Mr Leland's setonage was taking more time than planned, or else they were doing something else to the poor old gentleman – but several other patients came into the parlor, the ladies dressed in calico day-frocks and the men in trousers and smock-like shirts, to listen while January played. After a time Mr Betzer arrived also – he introduced himself to Poe – and stood listening in deep appreciation as January finished the 'Rondo à la Turque'.

While January glided into the barcarole from 'La Muette de Portici' – he could no more resist a newly-tuned piano than his little nephew Ti-Paul could resist sweets – he was aware of Poe conversing quietly with the young mad-doctor. When he finished, and turned on the bench to rise, Poe said – still in his Irish brogue – 'Ben, me old scout, the good doctor here's been kind enough to ask if we'd like a bit of a look about.'

All we need, thought January, *is for Gurry to return and recognize me from Mrs Bray's...*

'I do admit I'm curious,' he said. He saw Poe slip the man a dollar.

This wasn't unusual – he was heartily glad Poe kept the payment within the bounds of what a couple of piano tuners might have been expected to have on them. He followed quietly, keeping his mouth shut, as they were taken through – inevitably – the ward of the maniacs, the most 'exciting' or 'interesting' cases: men straitjacketed and chained in darkened rooms, women writhing against the coffin-like confines of the barred 'cribs'. He saw the fragile Miss Kingmill sobbing in the hands of one attendant while another held a sack of broken ice against her shaved scalp, while in the next 'consulting room' poor little Mr Leland was strapped down and forcibly dosed with medicine from a sinister collection of black bottles.

Scarcely surprising, reflected January, *that the patients come to the conclusion they're being poisoned.*

A newer wing had been built in the back, to house the 'consulting rooms' and, upstairs, the maniacs. 'We try to make the others as comfortable as possible,' explained Betzer as he led the way along a downstairs corridor of what had once, January guessed, been a servants' wing. 'Some, of course, we can do little for, like Mrs Campbell here—' He gestured toward the judas in one door, through which January could see a woman sitting on a corner of her neatly-made bed, staring dully at the opposite wall. Like some of the others, her head had been shaved; rather than being thin, there was an unhealthy corpulence to her, bloated and pale. 'By means of bleeding and emetics, we made some progress against the uncontrollable temper and hysterical religious mania which characterized her upon admission, but even the most persistent application of the Swing, setonage, and various forms of hydrotherapy have not yet succeeded in banishing this torpor in which she now spends her days. Yet Dr Gurry has achieved some remarkable cures by cold-water baths and plunges—'

January shuddered and looked through the

judas in the opposite door.

The room was empty. Like Mrs Campbell's, it was whitewashed, small, and nearly bare of furniture; the bed was made and the chamber pot scrubbed and sitting ready at the bed's foot. A muslin screen over the window blocked all view of the outside but admitted a soft, pleasant light.

And every inch of the walls were covered with magic squares.

TWENTY-SIX

'That's Mr Leland's room,' replied Mr Betzer, when January had recovered sufficiently to ask. 'A Boston gentleman, though by his accent I'd bet he originally hailed from the north of England.'

A place whose dialect doesn't sound a thing like a Londoner's. How much experience has Bellwether HAD with the way Englishmen sound?

Would a Frenchman conclude that the attendant's throaty Gullah speech originated in the same country as Mr Noyes' New England yap?

'We used to whitewash over his drawings, but as Mr Klein pointed out to Dr Gurry, they harm no one. His nephew brought him in, but it's his niece – a Mrs Bray – who comes to see him once or twice a week—'

Bringing opiates to dose him with...

324

'Here he is now.'

Attendants led the fragile little man along the corridor. Looking at the stooped, thin shoulders, the roughly-shaved head, January felt like kicking himself: *No wonder nobody recognized his description at any of the hotels in town. The description originated with Rowena Bray.*

The old man's eyeballs were pinpoints. He staggered as the attendants eased him into his room, where he sank down on the bed and was at once asleep.

'How long has he been like that?' January cursed the fact that the daybooks were already back in Gurry's office.

'He came to us in October. According to young Mr Merton – his nephew – and Mrs Bray, he was a very articulate and personable gentleman. This condition came upon him very suddenly and has the family quite concerned.'

'Why leave him alive?' demanded Poe. Early afternoon sunlight glittered on the long tidal flats of the Potomac. Riders and pleasure carriages passed them on the road from the city, a circumstance which made January want to dive into the roadside bushes every time one went by. Young Mr Klein had described how Rowena Bray visited her 'uncle' with fresh supplies of medicine every few days: *We're expecting her today or tomorrow, in fact.*

Every pair of black carriage-horses looked like hers, and the distance from Alexandria to the Long Bridge seemed to have doubled since that morning.

'It can't take six months to establish that he'll be buried under the name of Leland.'

'She doesn't want Oldmixton to know.' January wiped sweat from his face. The afternoon, like many of Washington in the spring, was nastily sticky, in an odd way more so than the worst of New Orleans.

'Oldmixton's her spymaster. She has only to tell him she feared exposure.'

'He may not believe her. He knows Singletary, knows him well. I wasn't sure he was telling me the truth, when he spoke of his own efforts to find the man, but now I think he was sincere. Mrs Bray may have counted on him going back to England when the special session of Congress ended in October; she'd only have had to keep Singletary alive in the asylum for a week. As it is, she knows he'll be watching for any sign of a body – and from what Pease told us, he'll have Fowler watching as well.'

A chaise appeared from around a thin copse of trees ahead. January knelt and fussed with his bootlace until it had gone past.

Even if it was her, why would she look at two workmen walking along the road?

'That explains why she had to work without accomplices,' said Poe thoughtfully. 'Because – like poor Singletary – she doesn't know who might speak the wrong word to whom.'

'Oldmixton seems to be genuinely fond of Mrs Bray as well,' said January. 'But if he recruited her as his agent I'm guessing he knows exactly what she's capable of.'

They resumed their walk, through the heavy

326

heat that smelled of woodlands and the river's tidal mud.

'When does Oldmixton go back?'

'Unless war actually *does* break out, June or July. Which I suspect,' January added drily, 'is when Luke Bray's scheduled to commit suicide.'

Poe frowned at the sailboats winging like white birds along the river, at the distant gray hilltop mansion of Arlington – home of the last family of George Washington – looming above the Long Bridge. 'So what do we do?'

'We get Singletary out of there,' said January. 'Immediately – tonight if we can. If Mrs Bray gets even a hint that people have been asking about him I think she'll risk it and put something in those medicines she's having Gurry give him.'

'If Oldmixton knows her father,' reflected Poe, 'he might very well know that Singletary came here to check on her finances. For all we know, her husband's isn't the first pocket she's picked.'

'Now who's got a Machiavellian turn of mind?'

'Do we go to Oldmixton? That doesn't sound very safe to me. And personally, I share your doubts about the police.'

'Doubts?' January's eyebrows shot up. 'I have certainty – that if Fowler is taking pay from Oldmixton, probably anything we tell the police is going to get tabled until they see who's going to pay them the most. No, we do what everyone in Washington does if they really want something accomplished,' he went on. 'We go to a member of Congress – in this case, Mr Adams.

He should be able to arrange everything we need.'

'But, *P'tit*, Chloë has gone with Senator Buchanan and his *p'tit ami* to the opera in Baltimore.' Dominique unpinned her bonnet – a pink-and-parakeet fantasia of ruching and lace – and peered into the hallway mirror to rearrange her curls. 'Henri is sending the carriage for me in ... great heavens, is it only two hours? I shall let him know. She did send you a note this afternoon...'

January had seen the note already, advising him that M'sieu Viellard would be in touch with him, but unless the matter was urgent, she would speak with him tomorrow...

And of course when he'd written the note that morning asking for a meeting, he reflected in frustration, the matter hadn't been urgent.

'I am perfectly willing,' put in Poe, with a glance at the hall clock, 'to put on my top hat and fancy vest and go in and take the place by storm tonight. I suppose I should need some sort of forged bona fides proving I am "Mr Leland's" son...'

'It wouldn't answer.' January knelt and put Charmian up on to his knee; the child immediately produced a not-quite-skeletonized mouse from her pinafore pocket to show him. 'For one thing, you might be recognized as a piano tuner—'

'Oh, spite...'

'And for another, if Gurry isn't convinced – that's *quite* a fine mouse, *ma belle*, did you catch
328

it yourself—?'

'*P'tit*, don't encourage her! You're as bad as Henri!'

'—all we'll have done is alert Mrs Bray that her prisoner has been found. No, we need to emulate Frederick the Great: strike hard, fast, and without warning, and we need to succeed on the first strike.'

'Musette, dearest, would you get rid of that thing for me? Oh, and Thèrése – where is that girl? – Thèrése, I need your help with my hair at once...' She vanished up the stairs in a silvery frou-frou of taffeta: 'Oh, M'sieu Preston, *bon soir...*'

'I rather think you're right.' Poe's dark glance slid sidelong as the young railway conductor came downstairs and went on into the parlor, his face, for an unguarded moment, grim and sad.

January's eyes followed Poe's; then for a moment their gazes met, and January, very slightly, shook his head. After a moment he resumed, 'The Viellards have to be the ones who go in,' he said. 'Preferably with Mr Adams to back them up. I don't think even Dr Gurry will question a man who used to be President of the United States. And I think that means, one of the Viellards is going to have to speak to Adams—'

'And the only one of the Viellards available is—' Poe caught back quickly whatever unwise or sarcastic words were about to leave his lips. He glanced up the stairs to make sure Minou wasn't about to flutter into the hall (*He obviously hasn't clocked her getting dressed*, thought January ...), then into the parlor, where Preston

329

was reading *The Influence of Natural Religion Upon the Temporal Happiness of Mankind* in concentrated silence, and finished: ' —is likely to be occupied all evening with other matters.'

In the end, January had to be content with writing three brief accounts of his findings at the asylum and dispatching them – after a worried glance at the fast-advancing twilight – via young Ritchie to the Indian Queen Hotel, and to the Adams house on F Street. ('Don't worry about me, Mr J, I'll run all the way and won't speak to a soul...')

The reports were accompanied by requests to meet as soon as humanly possible, though January suspected, as Dominique snatched up the report to Henri from the table, that none of those missives was even going to be read until sometime the following morning.

'Nonsense, *P'tit*.' Minou tucked the paper into her gold-stitched reticule and bent to tie Charmian's bonnet ribbons in a becoming bow beneath the child's chin. Henri's rented coachman had brought a note from him that he wanted to see his daughter that evening, so Thérése, in addition to Minou's valise, curling irons, cloak and coffee set was burdened with Charmian's coat, an extra carriage-rug, the doll Philomène, and a bunch of grapes done up in paper – 'Heaven knows what sort of food that frightful *entremetteuse* has in her house ... Don't worry, darling! I shall insist Henri read your report, even before I give him a kiss ... and Chloë reads everything before she goes to bed, even if she's been out drinking champagne all evening. Yes,

Musette, I shall see that she stays warm and doesn't stay awake a moment past eight thirty ... *And* I shall make Henri come back here, first thing in the morning.'

Which will be, reflected January uneasily as he watched his sister and her child, trailed by the disgruntled maid, flutter up the path toward the dim glow of the carriage lamps, *not a moment sooner than one in the afternoon...*

But he was wrong about that.

An hour and a half later, as Octavia Trigg and the older children cleared away the supper dishes from the communal table and the talk turned – as it had all week – to whether the Warriors would actually put in an appearance on the playing field Saturday, Poe appeared in the dining-room door. 'I do beg your pardon for interrupting your supper,' he said, into the silence that fell. 'But I thought you should know, Mr Trigg, that the carriage that was standing across the roadway from this house an hour ago is still there.'

January had noticed this vehicle just before supper – a closed dark bulk in the moonlight, a pair of lamps and the momentary flash of a horse's eye. He thought at that time that it had been there for some minutes already. During the meal, Trigg twice had gone into the parlor, to tweak the curtain aside and look out.

Each time, a tiny silence had fallen on the room, though the landlord himself had made no comment. Even the children knew that something had happened last Wednesday morning, though from things Ritchie and Mandie had

331

asked him, January gathered that they believed Mede had fled because of O'Hanlon and his teamsters.

If Mede dreamed of vengeance, asleep beneath his tomb of coal, he had not so far emerged to seek it.

'Would you be so good as to come out with us, Mr Poe?' Trigg laid aside his napkin.

He didn't say, *We might need a white man for a witness*, but in any case, January guessed that the poet's insatiable curiosity would have added him to the party whether asked or not. Frank Preston and the Reverend Perkins gathered up lamps and followed them. Their feet crunched softly on the gravel; the moist night air was heavy with scents, like the breath of some strange and ancient time. The lamplight flashed on harness brass and door handle.

The coachman sprang down from the box as the four men approached, and January recognized him at once as Esau Rivers, one of the two or three that the livery would send, turn and turn about, with Henri's rented carriage.

But if something happened to Dominique why didn't he come in...?

'I beg your pardon, sir.' Rivers touched his hat. 'But is Miss Janvier going to be coming out this evening? I've been sitting here over an hour—'

'She came out.' For a moment, January could only stare at the man. It was like those dreams, he thought, when he'd encounter three or four duplicates of his old piano-teacher in various places in Paris, all giving him contradictory instructions ... 'You picked her up at just after

332

seven.'

'No, sir, I didn't get here until seven thirty by my watch. But, I know Miss Janvier's often a little late...'

This was tactful understatement – January had known his sister to put in an appearance at two in the morning, at entertainments that began at ten. How many nights, from his place behind the piano, had he seen Henri pacing and fretting, waiting for his beautiful and maddening nymph...?

His blood was ice in his veins as Preston exclaimed, 'She is indeed! I've frequently told her—'

January said, 'Shit.' And he knew with complete certainty what had happened. 'Can you take us to M'sieu Viellard?'

The coachman hesitated, it being completely illegal for blacks to ride in cabs or carriages—

'Can you take *me* to him?' Poe stepped forward. 'Ben, get on the box...'

This was perfectly legal, for a white man's servants.

'Darius,' said January, 'get up behind, if you would ... Reverend, can you get someone to take a message to Mrs Viellard, at the Indian Queen? To wait there for her, until she gets back; it may be late. Tell her we'll be going on to the British Ministry, to speak to Mr Oldmixton. Tell her that Miss Janvier has been kidnapped.'

TWENTY-SEVEN

'Kidnapped?' Henri's pendulous cheeks turned to chalk.

'Sir,' began Rivers, 'there wasn't anything I could have done! I reached the house at seven thirty—'

'I should have thought there was something amiss when the carriage came early,' said January as Henri sank blindly into the broad velvet chair of the parlor. Mrs Purchase, it appeared, gave good value for her money: the house of accommodation was set in a grove of chestnut trees on the outskirts of Georgetown, furnished with beauty and taste. In the adjoining dining room, covered dishes sheltered what was left of an elegant little supper – they had arrived to find Minou's inamorato halfway through the second course and eyeing the sweetmeats.

Candles burned halfway down to their sockets on mantelpiece and wall sconces; a fire flickered low in the grate.

'When Miss Janvier went out to the carriage,' said Preston – January guessed he had watched in despair from the parlor window – 'the coachman handed her a note. She came back in and fetched Charmian—'

Henri made a small sound, like a hurt animal.

334

'In the darkness,' January said, 'I doubt Minou got more than a glimpse of her face.'

'Her—'

'I'm fairly sure,' said January, 'that Mrs Bray did this herself.'

'That's insane.' Luke Bray looked with bloodshot eyes from man to man, of those gathered in his parlor as the night deepened to eleven. 'You're all crazy.'

'Are we?' asked Poe quietly. 'Is Mrs Bray home tonight?'

Bray shoved the hank of blonde hair from his eyes. In the parlor lamplight it looked dark against his pallor, and his eyebrows seemed nearly black. The smell of liquor breathed from his rumpled shirt and unbuttoned waistcoat; the tabletop before him was a rummage of newspapers, letters, bills, an interrupted game of solitaire and a three-quarters-empty decanter of whisky. 'None of your goddam—'

'There is no time to waste, sir,' Poe cut him off. 'If your wife engineered the abduction of Miss Janvier and the child – Mr Viellard's child – then they may be in danger of their lives. Does your wife drive?'

'That's none of your—'

'Don't argue with me, man!' Poe grabbed a handful of the drunken man's shirt, almost pulled him from his chair.

'Don't you know yet,' put in January quietly, 'that your wife is a dangerous woman, sir? Haven't you seen that?'

Bray blinked up at him. January saw the know-

335

ledge in his eyes.

He was afraid of her.

And he'd thought he was the only one.

But accusation of a man's wife was one of the things that a man must answer with blood, even if he himself suspected the accusation to be true. Bray's eyes shifted as he revolved the problem in his mind, fumbling with it as a drunkard would fumble with his fly buttons, trying to sort out whom to challenge, what to do.

Before Bray could gather his thoughts, January drew from his pocket the crumpled sheet of numbers that he'd taken from Bray's desk, held it out to him with the decoded translation and the magic-square key. 'Mede gave me this before he disappeared,' he said. 'He said he'd found the key to the code in your watch case when you were ill. But he didn't know how to decode it. Mr Poe here figured it out only this Saturday.'

Bray's wandering eyes focused as he recognized the text of the decryption. 'Mede...'

'Mede told me that he had to leave your house,' January went on. 'Not from ingratitude or from any desire to run away from you, but because he suspected Mrs Bray was mixed up in something dangerous and he didn't know how to tell you about it. It wasn't his place, he said. And he feared what would happen, if you took her side against him.'

'I never would...'

But it was clear he sought to convince himself.

Poe spoke up, giving weight to his words like Kean playing Macbeth. 'He said he'd found things hidden in her room, sir. Spoke of a secret compartment in the top of her armoire, and of a key there that would open another hiding place down under the hearth—'

January shot the poet a glance of startled admiration – he'd been racking his brains for a way to reveal this proof to Bray without opening himself to accusations of searching a white lady's room.

'He said you had loved her.' Poe dropped his voice, torn with pity and sadness. 'And, he said, he did not know who to tell, nor how he could learn if what was going on was harmful or not.'

Luke Bray buried his head in his hands. 'It sounds like him,' he whispered. 'It sounds just like Mede. My Good Man Friday, always lookin' out for me...'

He looked up, eyes hard as gunmetal in the gloom. 'She's gone out,' he said. 'I don't know where. I never know where she goes. She drives herself, most days, handles a four-in-hand better'n that lazy buck Jem ever did. This evenin' she had Jem drive her to the National Hotel, said her friends would see her home...'

Which means she can come back in a cab, and no one the wiser...

'You know where Mede's gone?'

January shook his head. 'He just disappeared, sir,' he said. 'Went out one evening and didn't come back. Left all his things in his room.'

'Bitch.' Bray's voice turned soft. 'God-damned crawling bitch. Who's she sendin' this to?' He held the papers up, with a hand that trembled. 'It's that English nancy Oldmixton, ain't it? *Fucken* God-damn spy— He put her on to me...'

337

His face twisted suddenly, and the papers fell from his hand as he suddenly pressed it to his chest. 'Damn her to hell—'

January caught Bray's bandaged wrist, then sought the pulse in his throat. It was thready and irregular. Henri's valet Leopold, who had ridden from Mrs Purchase's behind his master, stepped quickly to the bell pull and tugged it. When a servant appeared January said, 'Get your master some hartshorn,' though he guessed that the action of the mild sedative, on top of the amount of whiskey he'd consumed, would put him to sleep.

Just as well...

In the few minutes of waiting for the servant to return he glanced around the dim-lit parlor, noticed that Poe was nowhere to be seen...

The poet slipped back into the room in the wake of Bray's valet Peter with the glass. 'She's cleared,' he whispered as he knelt at January's side. 'The key was lying beside the hearth, soot everywhere. The compartment below the hearth is empty. Looks like she grabbed what she could and fled.'

Bray leaned back in his chair, his face ghastly. Peter – a middle-aged, wiry man with grizzled hair – helped his master to his feet and guided him toward the door. A well-trained servant – though, speaking no English, he could have had only the faintest notion of what was going on – Leopold caught up the nearest lamp and followed into the darkness of the hall.

'But why?' Henri turned to January like a lost dog, his brown eyes flooded with tears of shock

338

and terror. 'You say she's kidnapped Minou ... Surely she knows we'll come after her? She won't hurt her, will she? And Charmian—'

'Why take a child?' broke in Preston. 'Won't that only slow her down? She can't have hoped that we wouldn't know...'

His voice like flint – his heart like flint in his chest – January replied, 'She hoped we would know. If she wanted Minou dead she'd have found a way to kill her without alerting us all an hour later that she was gone.'

He led the way to the parlor door, and there was an awkward moment in the hall as the black members of the party – himself, Trigg, Preston and Leopold, who came running down the stairs again – turned automatically toward the rear of the house and the whites all turned toward the front door...

'She wants us to stay and search for her,' he said. 'Just exactly as if she'd cut her and left her bleeding, knowing we'd stop and save Minou and let *her* go free.'

'Cut her—' Henri pressed his fat hands to his mouth. He was shaking all over and looked worse than the fainting man who'd been led up the stairs. 'What has she—?'

'At a guess,' said January grimly, 'she's turned her over to Fowler and the slave traders.'

And clean against all custom – to the scandalized horror of Bray's butler – the entire party, blacks and whites, went out through the front door to where the carriage waited in the drive.

Chloë caught up with them – springing out of a

cab, ethereal in pale-pink satin and coruscating with diamonds – at just short of midnight on the front doorstep of the British Ministry. Sir Henry Fox was still out gambling somewhere, so Poe's peremptory knock on the front door had at least been answered. But the rest of the Ministry staff – as the Scots butler had informed Poe in frosty accents – was long since abed.

'Give Mr Oldmixton this, please,' January had said, and handed the butler the note he'd written just before leaving Bray's house. 'I think he'll see us.'

'What happened?' Chloë demanded as the Reverend Perkins jumped down from the cab driver's box and the cab rattled away into the night. 'This good man tells me—'

The Ministry door opened, and Mr Oldmixton stood framed in it, dark hair rumpled, swathed in a satin dressing-gown of gorgeous pattern and hue. 'Rowena, what on earth—?' He stopped short, surveying the assorted group of men and women, black and white, before him on the step.

'You were able to read my message, then, sir?' inquired January politely, and held out his hand for the note that Oldmixton still carried.

'*Your* message?' The Englishman made as if to thrust the note into his dressing-gown pocket, then grimaced, and handed it over.

24ᴓ02224ᴓ3162419ᴓ711ᴓ81311202321ᴓ1
ᴓ721ᴓ813ᴓ917ᴓ324242021121912ᴓ1ᴓ9
ᴓ8ᴓ92221ᴓ81013ᴓ424ᴓ8

'*Emergency*,' he quoted it, '*all is discovered* – by the mere fact that you've managed to encrypt

340

that message I see that this is in fact the case –
must see you at once. I perceive I am due for a
few severe slaps upon my wrist from Lord
Palmerston when I'm sent home. But what I've
done is no crime, you know. Our nations aren't
at war – yet. Where *is* Mrs Bray?'

'Probably halfway to Baltimore – sir,' said
January. 'Having learned, sometime this after-
noon, that we'd discovered the whereabouts of
Selwyn Singletary—'

The startled flare of hope in Oldmixton's eyes
confirmed what January had suspected, and he
went on, 'Her one idea was to delay pursuit until
she could get clean away. Since, as I understand,
you employ Mr Kyle Fowler, I think Mrs Bray
kidnapped my sister and her child and turned
them over to him, knowing we would follow that
scent rather than hers. And since Mr Fowler is no
idiot, I think the first thing he'll do is get his new
merchandise out of Washington, so I hope, sir,
that you're going to make matters easier for us
by telling us where Fowler has his headquarters
and where he'd take a prime fancy for quick
sale.'

'Come inside – McAleister!' Oldmixton shouted over his shoulder as he stepped from the
doorway to admit them. And, when the butler
appeared: 'McAleister, send to the stables and
have them saddle—' He ran a calculating eye
over the group on the steps. 'Have them saddle
Rufus and Masianello and six other horses ... I
shall be down again in a moment—' He turned
toward the steps, then halted in a swirl of purple-
and-green satin robe-skirts: 'Where is Single-

tary? Is he alive? Is he well?'

'I don't know how well he is, sir,' replied January, 'but he was alive this morning. He's been held at Gurry's private insane asylum since October – and I only trust that Mrs Bray was in too much of a hurry to get out of town to go back and poison him after she kidnapped my sister.'

'I'll go there now,' said Chloë. 'Mr – Rivers, is it?' She addressed the hired coachman. 'Mr Rivers, do you know the road out of Alexandria—?'

Oldmixton protested, 'It's midnight, my dear girl—!'

'Twelve twenty-eight.' She plucked Henri's watch from his pocket and checked it. 'If she administered poison to him at ten, I should probably be in time, if I can get in. I don't suppose you could write me a warrant, sir? Henri—'

'I'm going with Ben.' Henri turned toward his wife with sudden dignity. 'It's my doing that Dominique came with us here at all. I have to be with them. I have to—'

'Of course you do, dearest.' Chloë stood on tiptoe, to kiss his heavy cheek. 'I was only going to say, if you'll be riding – I'm going to take the carriage to the asylum – borrow a scarf from Mr Oldmixton ... Mr Poe, might I ask you to accompany me? We'll work out exactly what our relationship is to Mr Singletary on the way. Do you happen to know if she took her jewelry? No? Then I suggest you send someone back there. Dealers don't pay more than thirty percent of market value, and she won't have enough to establish herself if she suspects her bank accounts are going to be watched. She'll need something that can be converted to cash immediately. Take care of him, Ben.' She turned to January, regarded him with huge, pale eyes like a sibyl, behind the thick rounds of glass. 'And of yourself.'

For a moment something else flitted across her eyes: fear for the husband her family had pushed her into marrying? Regret, that he was riding off to rescue his mistress, even a mistress whom she liked? Or just puzzlement about how to wish someone luck when one didn't believe in luck or miracles?

Then she turned, straight as a soldier in her lace and diamonds, caught up her skirts and ran back to the carriage, where Mr Rivers had already sprung on to the box. Poe looked uncertain, but January said, 'Go,' not needing to explain that with Henri and – it now seemed – Oldmixton, they had the requisite compliment of white witnesses to whatever else the night would bring.

Like a raven in his black greatcoat Poe dashed to the carriage. The door wasn't even shut when Esau Rivers flicked the reins, and the horses – sweaty but game – broke into a gallop down the wide processional expanse of Twenty-Sixth Street, and vanished into the night.

TWENTY-EIGHT

Kyle Fowler worked out of a tavern called the Golden Calf, in Reservation C. There was a pen out back of the usual sort, with stout plank walls twelve feet tall and a shed built across one side. It was to this pen that Elsie Fowler conducted Oldmixton and his party, with a great show of indignation at being 'rousted' at a quarter to one in the morning, as if she'd been asleep instead of pouring out stale beer 'needled' with camphor to men watching two 'waiter girls' fight in their chemises for a five-dollar purse.

'We got practically no stock this week,' groused the woman, with a sidelong glance at January and Trigg, who accompanied the Englishman inside. 'Greedy goddam bastards, think we're made of money – say, you wouldn't be interested in selling those two boys of yours, would you, mister? We pay cash, three hundred on the barrel-head, no questions asked ... That big buck of yours looks like a prime field-hand, we'd go three-fifty...'

'I am the one asking the questions, Madame,' retorted Oldmixton. 'Is Mr Fowler about?'

She held up her lamp as she led the way into the yard. January followed; Trigg remained in the doorway, one hand in the pocket of his coat

where he kept a slung shot, the other hand unobtrusively close to the pistol hidden in his
waistband. January bore his own pistol and
knife, hidden as always, plus another pistol lent
him by Oldmixton, who openly carried a rifle.
An uncovered latrine pit on the far side of the
yard filled the air with its reek. January felt the
furious longing to empty his weapon into the
woman's broad calico back as she walked along
the open front of the shed with her lamp.

'Kyle's gone down to Fauquier County; he'll
be back Saturday for that ball game...'

Oldmixton returned to the doorway, and
January said quietly, 'Check the cellars, sir.'

There were four cells in the cellar, windowless
and stinking. None was occupied, but by the
smell, two had been in use recently. Again
January stayed in the doorway, Trigg on the stair.
This was no time to get trapped underground,
and there was no telling how desperate the Fowlers were, or if they thought they could get away
with murdering a British Ministry secretary to
protect themselves from a possible accusation of
treason.

Given the current state of the Washington constabulary, reflected January, maybe they actually
could. Oldmixton held the lamp he carried close
to each of the cells' walls, and checked the
masonry in the storeroom where the establishment kept beer and coals as well. The lamplight
wasn't strong, and it would be all too easy to
miss something, but at least there probably
wasn't a sub-cellar. This close to the canal, the
clayey earth underfoot squished from seepage.

The fetor was stunning.

'Let me see your stable,' said Oldmixton.

'Look, Me Lord,' protested Elsie Fowler, 'if you think Kyle and me ain't been livin' up to our side of our bargain, you just say so, and we'll—'

'I said, let me see the stable. I don't care how many laws you break but I do demand that you don't go making side deals with my other employees without telling me of it.'

'Ain't nuthin' in the stable.' The woman's face seemed to darken and sink in on itself. 'See,' she added as she led the way through a gate to another narrow yard. 'Nuthin' here.'

From the stable gate, January saw the Englishman bend down with his lamp, examining the dirt. There was, in fact, nothing in the stable – not even the two massive white-footed drafthorses. The wagon, too, was missing. The tracks leading to the outer gate looked fresh.

Wheel tracks, and the traces of many bare feet.

'Fowler's spoken of contacts in Fredericksburg,' said Oldmixton, when they regained the muddy street.

'From there they can get a steamboat down the Rappahannock to the bay,' said Preston. 'Either that, or they'll head north to Baltimore.'

There was a pause, and Henri, sitting awkwardly on the largest and sturdiest of the British Ministry's horses, made a little whimper of despair. 'What can we do? There aren't enough of us to split up—'

'We'll have to,' said January. 'Mr Oldmixton,

would you be so good as to take charge of the Fredericksburg contingent? Preston – Reverend—' He rapidly gauged strong and weak, black and white.

'I know the Baltimore road pretty well,' volunteered Trigg.

'Leopold—' January switched to French and beckoned the valet. 'You'd better come with us.' In English he continued, 'Remember to check inside the wagon bed. And remember they may be drugged. If there's trouble,' he added to Henri as they, Trigg, and the still-incomprehending valet set out at a hand-gallop through the night-bound streets towards New York Avenue and the Baltimore pike, 'stay back and don't get yourself shot, sir. You're the only proof we have that we're not rebelling slaves.'

'Shot?' Henri glanced down in panic at the rifle sheathed on his saddle, then flung January a helpless look as they left the last dark, scattered dwellings of the town's outskirts behind them. The waning moon glinted on the bottomlands of Goose Creek; here and there birds flew up, startled by their passing.

Minou, thought January, *wherever you are, Minou, hang on...*

The horses lengthened their stride.

They passed through Bladensburg over the East Branch of the Tiber; the moon was sinking. It was the season of planting-out tobacco seedlings and the night was thick with the smell of new-turned soil. More often, the formless dark that stretched on either side of the road smelled of damp weeds, of thick untended grass, for after nearly two hundred years under tobacco the soil yielded little. The planters whose brick houses could still be glimpsed in the dappled starlight now lived, more and more, by the sale of unwanted or unneeded slaves.

They pressed on. Rising, the river fog swallowed the fingernail moon, and they kindled torches, though the light made January uneasy. *They'll see us coming...*

Far ahead through the trees, where the road curved a little back on itself, he saw the answering glimmer of fire.

Hail Mary, full of Grace, the Lord is with thee...

Help us out here...

The wagon was stopped, waiting for them. Six women sat on its benches, holding small children close. Twice that number of men, chained neck to neck, ankle to ankle, grouped up around the team, so that Fowler and the two men with him stood more or less in the clear by the wagon's tail. Torches were wedged into cracks in the back of the wagon, and flecks of burning pitch dripped down to smoulder on the ground beneath.

As January, Henri and Leopold rode into the torchlight, Henri sobbed, 'She isn't here!'

'The wagon's got a hollow bed,' replied January, in the French in which the fat man had addressed him. 'She'll be inside it, drugged.'

Henri straightened his back at that, urged his horse forward. 'M'sieu Fowler—' His voice squeaked with terror. 'I'm glad we've caught you. I believe you have two women and a child among your slaves to whom you have no right.'

Fowler spat. The male slaves clustered around the wagon, the women sitting behind and above them watched in silence, eyes a wet glint of silver in the torchlight. The slave stealer stepped forward, hand held out to shake, said in his soft voice, 'And you'd be?'

Henri blushed, hastily dismounted – January wanted to shout at him not to give up the advantage of horseback – and held out his hand in response. 'I'm so sorry,' he apologized. 'My name is Henri Viellard, of New Orleans, and I'm—'

Don't get away from your rifle—!

Fowler caught Henri's outstretched hand and dragged him forward, with his other hand – a pistol held by the barrel – dealt him a brutal crack on the side of the head that dropped him sprawling. January spurred his horse forward, pulled his own pistol from his waistband, knowing already he couldn't use it: not with the wagon full of women and children behind Fowler in the line of fire. He yelled, 'Drop it!' hoping that would work, and it didn't. Fowler shot at him at a distance of less than six feet, and pain went through his side like a javelin of fire.

The next second another man sprang out of the darkness at him, dragged him from the saddle. The horse reared, squealed, toppled under the double weight. January tried to struggle free of the writhing tangle of hooves and legs and stirrup leather, unable to breathe, his vision fragmenting under the cold dizziness of shock and pain. He hit the ground hard, snatched at the legs of the new attacker to pull him off-balance. Fowler reached him in two steps and kicked him with brutal force in the belly.

Henri sobbed, 'For the love of God! I'll pay you what you ask!'

Fowler paused, looked back at him.

Lying at Fowler's feet, January had a queer, faraway glimpse of Henri held between two of Fowler's ruffians – one with a pistol, the other holding a shotgun – close by the back of the wagon. He didn't know where Leopold was – the whole scene occupied the space of instants, bloody in torchlight – but he thought, *Trigg can't shoot for fear of hitting the women...*

From within the wagon, hollow in the wooden coffin, a child's voice screamed, 'Papa!'

'Can't risk it.' Fowler spat again. 'Like I can't risk keepin' your buck here, much as it pains me to waste him.'

He pointed his pistol down at January's head.

The woman sitting closest to the back of the wagon – barely a girl herself, a child Charmian's age in her arms – reached over with her foot and kicked the nearest torch so that it fell on to the back of the man with the shotgun.

The man screamed, lurched around as his shirt caught fire, and Henri – with the slightly startled air of an actor just recalling his cue – simply took the shotgun away from him and, at a distance of five feet, emptied it into Fowler's belly.

The kick threw him backwards out of the path of the bullet that his other guard fired at him – one of the women in the wagon screamed. Henri waded forward, holding the shotgun by the barrel, and smote the man across the side of the head with it as if he were playing town ball after all. January knew there was another ruffian nearby and grabbed the pistol Fowler had dropped – the man was almost cut in half by the shotgun blast and was certainly dead as he fell – and rolled as the last ruffian fired at him. The bullet plowed the dirt next to his head, and January saw him framed neatly in the torchlight against the night, nowhere near the wagon. It was a perfect shot, and January pulled the trigger, the pain of the kick – he'd been shot in his right side – almost making him pass out.

The man fell dead.

I'm not going to confession about that one.

The horses were whinnying and shying, but the man whose shirt was burning made no sound. As January pulled himself, half-swooning, to his hands and knees he saw him, dead a little ways from the wagon, as Trigg and Leopold rode into the torchlight, holding pistols on the ruffian Henri had felled.

Trigg sprang off his horse, ran to January's side. 'How bad you hit?' He was already pulling a bandanna from his pocket, pressing it to the wound.

January shook his head, too shaken to speak. Henri fumbled, sobbing, at the back of the wagon, and from within Charmian's voice sobbed again, 'Papa! Papa!'

'M'sieu Viellard!' cried Thèrése's voice.

One of the women in the wagon said, 'Catch over there on the side, sir.'

351

Henri scrabbled at the catches, clawed them free. Unobtrusively, Darius Trigg went through Fowler's pockets and produced his keys, which he passed to the nearest of the chained slaves by the wagon. The smell of the dead ruffian's burning flesh made a choking stink in the night.

'Papa!'

Henri dragged his daughter from the hollow bed of the wagon, fell to his knees and clutched her close, then turned back. 'Minou—'

'They took her.' Thèrése dragged herself half-out of the narrow black rectangle of the entry hole, her wrists and ankles bound, her sugar-brown hair a snarled tumble in the torchlight. 'Half their men – half their slaves – they sent south into Virginia—'

Henri sobbed, 'No—'

'We'll find her.' January dragged himself to his feet and almost threw up with pain. By the feel of it the bullet had broken one of his floating ribs and was lodged between it and the twelfth rib. 'With Fowler dead his men will let her go for money. Oldmixton will know where to look.'

Henri also stood, holding his daughter by the hand. 'Fowler—' He looked in the direction of the slave stealer.

His eyeballs rolled up, and he slid to the ground in a faint.

TWENTY-NINE

'Leave him be for a minute.' Trigg put a staying hand on Leopold's wrist as the valet hastened forward with smelling salts. To January, he said, 'I know a woman in Montgomery County who'll make sure these folks get on their way in the right direction, a few at a time. Keep the chains,' he added, to a small man of about January's age, who came up with key and shackles to hand them to him. He seemed to be the leader of the slave gang. 'Let the constables think they're looking for slave stealers rather than runaways. Ben, you think you can get back to town through the woods and the fields rather than the road?'

'I can guide 'em, sir.' A half-grown boy slipped out from among the gang. 'My old marse's place was in Bladensburg. I know the ground 'tween here and Washington.'

'Good boy,' said Trigg. 'What's your name?'

'Billy, sir.'

'Billy – you know Mrs James? Has a house called Witchhazel on the Paint River?'

A grin spread over the boy's face. 'You mean Mrs James, all this time, has been—'

'You hush,' said Trigg. 'You just get yourself there after you see these folks back close to Washington.'

Billy saluted. 'Yes, sir.'

'You be all right, Ben? Can you travel?'

'I'll be all right.' The smallest movement brought on waves of nauseated agony, and the thought of riding eight miles back to town turned him sick. Leopold came to his side and offered him Henri's crystal vial of smelling salts. They helped. More practically, Trigg dug in the pockets of Fowler's coat again and came up with a flask, which helped a good deal more. He wiped the blood off it on Fowler's coat.

'I'm sorry you can't take it with you,' said the landlord as he collected handkerchiefs and rags to make a rude dressing over the wound. 'But all you'd need is for somebody to find it on you—'

'I'll be all right.' January had, in fact, serious doubts about this assertion, but it was the only thing he could think of to say. He understood that he had no choice. He had to be all right – or at least sufficiently all right to make it back to Washington – because the alternative was to be charged with that most heinous of crimes, slave rebellion.

Black men had killed white men. Not a jury in the state of Maryland would even listen to a plea of extenuating circumstance. It was illegal for a black man to kill a white even in self-defense – always supposing that any jury would entertain the idea that the black defendant wasn't lying, and the white arresting sheriff might be mistaken in his reconstruction of the so-called facts.

No. As he climbed on to a rather shaken and indignant horse, his attention grimly focused on keeping in the saddle, he knew that he simply had to make it back to Washington at whatever the cost.

Hurt? Not me, sir.

Riding around in the middle of the night with a pistol? Why, sir, there's a dozen people – including two white gentlemen, Mr Poe and M'sieu Viellard – who'll swear I was in Mrs Trigg's parlor playing Snap with the children all the evening...

With a little fancy footwork, he reflected, his hand pressed to the swelling universe of pain in his side, *we can even convince Luke Bray that we didn't come knocking at his door at ten thirty accusing his wife of being a spy...*

'Michie Henri,' he heard Leopold saying, far off in another world on the other side of darkness, 'Michie, are you well? Up you come ... Yes, sir, your horse is over here, sir...'

For a moment, January saw Charmian, clinging tight to Trigg's arms as the little man held her. Her gaze went from her father, to her Uncle Ben, to the massacred corpse of the man who had thrust her into the wagon bed, her dark eyes wide in the torchlight but tearless and unafraid.

She's Livia's granddaughter, all right, thought January.

Thèrése, for her part, sat on the ground by the wagon bed, moaning, her face in her hands. When Henri was mounted, Leopold went over to her, helped her to her feet.

Rose ... thought January, *Rose, I won't die on you. I won't let you bring up Baby John by yourself, no matter how much help Henri and Chloë promise to be...*

355

To the end of his days, January didn't know how he made it back to Washington. The first stains of daylight found them in thin birch-woods that looked the same whichever way he turned, in gray light that had neither direction nor strength. He drifted in and out of conscious-ness, aware of nothing except gnawing pain. Leopold lent him the smelling salts again, and he clung to them as to a lifeline.

During a period of rest he examined the wound as well as he could. The blood seemed too bright to be coming from his liver, the pain – severe as it was – not bad enough to indicate a perforated bowel. Once he thought he heard Thèrése say, *But surely Ben would not wish us all to be caught, for his sake* ... and wished he had the strength to go over and slap her.

Maybe it was only a dream.

Later, as they cautiously approached the out-skirts of Washington by roundabout ways, he heard snatches of the maid's account of how the boyish, dark-browed young coachman had thrown open the carriage door in the street in front of the Golden Calf, how Fowler and his men had dragged them out at pistol point.

'Maman got the whip away from the coach-man and hit one of them with it,' provided Char-mian, cuddled like a little bird in the circle of her father's chubby arm. 'The bad man slapped her, and she spat at him. What's an *enculeur*?'

Thèrése, January noticed, had by this time smoothed and dressed her hair, and straightened her torn and dirty dress.

Will Charmian remember this? he wondered as

the horses splashed through Reedy Branch and they passed the field, half-invisible under ground mists and dew, where on Saturday they would meet the Warriors. *She's not quite three – the borderland of memories. In three years, or five years, or ten, will she remember being tied up and loaded into a moving coffin? Will she find herself there in nightmares, with no sound but the creak of the wheels and the sobbing of the terrified woman beside her?*

Every now and then Henri would hug the little girl close, his face a silent mask of horror and shame. He had brought her, brought Minou, to this, only because he couldn't bear to be parted from them for three months...

But though the fat man was, in an odd sense, January's brother-in-law, it was not January's place to speak.

The smoke of breakfast fires hung in the gray air as they circled through the unscythed fields in back of the house. Working men would already have gone, leaving the neighborhood quiet. As the horses turned in at last on to the graveled drive, January saw Frank Preston and Dominique in the shadows of the porch. He saw the young conductor take Minou's hands, speaking to her with desperate earnestness. She, like Thèrése, had tidied her hair and had also apparently been brought back to the house in enough time to change her dress as well. In the simple yellow muslin, with its spreading collar of white gauze, she had never looked more beautiful.

Preston raised her hands to his lips, and Dominique gently put one palm to his cheek.

Then she turned her head, at the sound of hooves in the drive. And as if the man who had rescued her had ceased to exist, she flew down the steps, her arms outspread, and like a bird of paradise ran to Henri's side as he clambered stiffly down from his horse.

'Charmian! Oh, my darling!'

As Henri lifted the child down, she kissed her, embraced her, and with joy as simple as a song flung herself into Henri's arms.

'It was that silly girl,' said Poe, and the steam from the tea he'd brought up to January's room drifted in a languid veil around his face in the pale late-afternoon sunlight. 'The one who came in to watch you tune the piano – whose father was supposedly both a piano tuner *and* a famous surgeon? She told Gurry about our visit the moment he returned yesterday ... Mrs Bray had given Gurry some story which included a good reason for him to notify her if anyone came asking after her "uncle", so Gurry dispatched a note to the lady post-haste. Can you manage?'

January took the tisane from him. It smelled a good deal like those his sister Olympe would make, to lower fever and strengthen the blood against infection.

The black midwife who'd extracted the bullet from his ribs had given him laudanum. He knew this would make for a couple of bad days when he quit taking it, but at the moment he didn't care. She had, in addition to removing the bullet, bound up his head, which was where he'd allegedly been struck when the whole party had allegedly been set on by robbers in the woods without ever encountering Fowler's Baltimore-bound coffle at all.

If necessary, January reflected cloudily, he supposed Oldmixton could be blackmailed into testifying that he, Preston, and Perkins had rescued all three of the kidnapped females from Fowler's henchmen on the road to Warrenton last night, instead of just Minou, but he didn't think it would be necessary. As far as he could tell, Mr Oldmixton didn't much care what color one set of Americans was who'd shot another set of Americans in the middle of the woods in the middle of the night.

Poe would care. When all was said and done, Marse Eddie was a Southern gentleman. He might wink at burying a murdered man secretly in the cellar as part of a complex and nefarious tragedy, but black men killing white ones, for whatever reason, was another matter. When it came down to it, there was simply too much at stake to trust a white man.

But, as Octavia Trigg had said, as the midwife bandaged up January's head, *what he don't know won't hurt him none.*

Feeling as if he were trying to speak in a dream, January finally roused himself to ask, 'Where's Singletary now?'

'At the Indian Queen.' Chloë came in from the hall, the ruched velvet opera-cloak she'd had on last night still draped over her pink gown, though she'd gotten rid of the diamonds. He'd heard the crunch of her carriage wheels in the street just as he emerged from several hours' sleep – presumably she'd come to fetch Henri. January had the dim recollection of Dominique telling him, as he clung to her hands while the bullet was being probed for, all about Henri's sufferings, wailings, demands for tea and blancmanges and mustard footbaths and extra pillows where he'd been tucked up on the 'white folks' parlor' couch.

And January had managed to whisper, *After what he did, give him whatever he asks.*

'You were quite right, Benjamin,' Chloë went on as Poe brought up a chair for her at the side of January's bed. 'Jeremiah Hurlstone asked M'sieu Singletary to look into his daughter's activities here. He suspected she'd forged his name on documents to transfer Hurlstone and Ludd funds from a number of European banks into those of what he thought were accomplices: Mssrs Merton, Allen, Sinter, et al. She knew, you see, that the Bank of England is going to withdraw all of its assets from American banks next month, which will mean another wave of closures – I've already made arrangements for our funds to be transferred. It's what I'd have done,' she added, 'were I in her position.'

'Would you?' Poe regarded her with respectful amusement. 'You little minx. And would you have made plans to murder your husband as well, had he turned out to be a drunkard and a gambler?'

'I don't know.' Chloë folded childlike hands on her knee. 'It's difficult for a girl, you understand, M'sieu Poe. I should like to think that I wouldn't murder an unoffending old man – or an

360

unoffending young one – to ensure myself enough money to live independent of husband and family, but then I've always been wealthy. Because of the way Louisiana property law is structured, I've never been in danger of finding myself destitute ... or completely at the mercy of a man who can't control his drinking or his gambling.'

Something in those huge blue eyes made Poe flush a little, and look aside.

January asked, 'She intended to kill Singletary, then, didn't she?'

'Oh, yes. As soon as Mr Oldmixton was out of the country. Mr Oldmixton is furious, by the way – he's gone back to Bray's house in the hopes of picking up her trail, because I'm almost certain she'll go back for her jewellery. She'll need something besides what Fowler gave her, to support her while she makes sure that her other identities aren't being watched.'

'How is Singletary?'

'Not well.' For the first time, emotion fleeted across her face, both anger and pity. 'I'd like you to have a look at him, as soon as you're feeling better yourself—' She glanced worriedly at his bandaged head, in a way that told January that even she didn't know the true story of last night's events.

'He's very fragile, and I expect he's going to have a frightful time tapering off opium. Your friend Mr Sefton was quite ill when he did so, wasn't he? I have asked him to come back to New Orleans with us for a time. He feared, he said, after his room was broken into, that it might be Mr Oldmixton, or a man in his hire, who was seeking to silence him – because he suspected about Mr Oldmixton being a spy-master. But when he startled the intruder in his room, the ink on his desk was spilt, and at tea with Mrs Bray he saw the stain of it on her hand. The following day she "chanced" to meet him, begged for the opportunity to explain—'

'—and slipped something into his sherry,' guessed Poe gloomily, 'and steered him to a waiting cab when he "came over queer"?'

'It was very simple,' pointed out Chloë. 'He'd known her from a child. And as I've said, he is a naïve and trusting old man.'

'Less so now, I presume,' said Poe, 'than he was?'

In the connecting bedroom, January heard a door open and Dominique's voice ask a soft question; Musette replied, 'Oh, yes, Madame, peaceful as an angel...'

Poe turned from the window, where he'd gone to look out into the drive. 'And Mede saw something, or learned something? Or merely put two and two together in a fashion that was beyond his blockheaded master?'

'I don't think it was anything that definite,' said January. 'Though I notice when he obtained his freedom, he didn't waste an instant in putting himself where he thought Mrs Bray couldn't get at him. But as you said yesterday, everyone in Washington would be expecting Luke's suicide *except Mede*. Because he knew Luke Bray. He couldn't testify in a court, but once he was a free man, he could certainly write to Luke's father

362

and say, *I know he would not take his own life.* And he would be believed. And because he cared for Bray, he not only could, but he would.'

'No man is an island.' Poe's dark brows pulled together. 'Not even poor Singletary ... But if Mede were still a slave when Luke "committed suicide", in a town like Washington Rowena Bray could be rid of him within hours. I can only trust...'

He turned his head sharply, hearing – as January had already heard – footsteps in the hall. Mrs Trigg said, 'I think he still awake, sir, though he took a awful crack on the head—'

And John Oldmixton replied smoothly, 'So Mr Trigg has informed me.'

And presumably, thought January, *coached you in what your part in the rescue was supposed to be...*

'I won't keep him long, m'am. Thank you.'

The door opened.

'Did she come back?' Chloë asked.

'She did.' The British Minister's Secretary closed the door quietly behind him and bent to kiss her hand. 'If three-fifty was what they offered me for a hulking cotton-hand like Benjamin, I doubt they gave her more than five hundred for both Miss Janvier and her maid. She would need more. I fear–' he straightened and turned to January – 'that I come like winged Mercury, in advance of Constable Jeffers, though I've informed him how you were injured by those *robbers in the woods.*'

He cocked a dark eyebrow.

'His interest has nothing to do with my rescue

of the ladies–' the very slight emphasis he laid on 'my' went right past the others in the room – 'though I understand that the same robbers who attacked you killed Fowler and his men—'

Chloë's eyebrows shot up. Poe exclaimed, 'Well, there is a God after all!'

'Then why is he coming here?' asked January. *What kind of story has the Bray woman told, to discredit my witness...*

'He's going to want to speak to you – and to you also, Mr Poe – on the subject of your conversation with Mr Bray last night. It seems that when Mrs Bray returned to get her jewellery in the small hours of this morning, her husband was waiting for her ... and strangled her to death.'

THIRTY

'She killed Mede.' Luke Bray raised his head to regard the men who stood before him in the dismal 'visitor room' of the jail. 'She got to have, an' if you ignorant bastards had the sense God gave a day-old chicken you'd have seen that. You'd have called in the police, got them to look for his body...' He rubbed his hand across his unshaven face.

Beside him, January was conscious of Constable Jeffers's glance: inquiring. Questioning, his pencil poised above his notebook.

Behind the barred door that led to the cells, a man's voice raised in despairing howls.

A drunkard in the grips of the horrors? Or one of the slaves locked up there by an owner passing through town?

January shook his head and tried to look like a man who has, himself, nothing to conceal. 'Sir, I only know what I told you on Monday evening: that Mede Tyler left Mr Trigg's boarding house Tuesday evenin' an' didn't come home. It ain't for me to go accusin' nobody of what I don't know—'

'Well you should have known!' The young man slammed his hand violently on the cheap pine table. Tears flooded his eyes, and a string of snot elongated itself from his nose. His whole body shook. 'You should have God-damned known she hated him! Should have God-damned known she wanted to kill him!'

Awkward silence. The Constable – a heavyset man with a political hack's oily smile – scratched a few notes on his paper and sized up the witnesses before him with shrewd blue eyes: the immaculate Englishman, the pale-faced Southern poet in black, the sable giant with a bandage on his head. As if asking himself whether he'd have to take them aside later and warn them to keep their mouths shut about the suspect's unseemly breakdown.

'Sir,' January urged gently, 'I beg you to remember the Constable is here. He'll take down everything you say—'

'Fuck him!' yelled Bray. 'God-damn the lot of 'em! I killed the bitch, and I'll shout it from the goddam rooftops!' He leaned across the table, seized January's wrist. 'He was my only friend. The only person who cared about me. He was my Man Friday, the single other human being with me on this Christly barren desert island full of God-damn cannibals! How can you be so purblind simple that you don't see what she did?'

'That will be for the court to decide.' Oldmixton, sitting directly opposite Bray at the table, took from his breast pocket a single sheet of paper and laid it before the prisoner. 'In the meantime, Mr Bray, if you'll sign this, it will give me authorization to make arrangements for her burial. As a friend of the family—'

'Arrangements for her burial?' Bray leaned across the table, pulled the papers to him and snatched the pen from Oldmixton's hand. With it he scratched a huge X through the writing, scrawled, *Tie a brick on her and throw her in the river*, and signed his name. 'There's your arrangements.' He shoved the document back at Oldmixton. 'Give that to her God-damn family! As her husband I reckon I've got the right to say how my wife's to be put to rest. You can take all that secret writing of hers, and the accountbooks you say she Jewed up, and all them bankin' papers that was in her satchel when I come into her bedroom and found her dressed like a man and diggin' her jewels out from under the floorboards – and whatever you can find out from this spyin' traitor pimp bastard—'

He jabbed a savage finger at Oldmixton, whose expression was a universe of grieved pity.

'—an' you can say what you want of me. But

366

she was an evil woman, Jeffers, and she deserved to die for what she done. For killin' the best nigger I ever knew.'

And he lowered his head to his arms, not weeping, but silent as stone.

When the constable had signed to the deputy who stood by the door, and himself led the trio of witnesses from the room into the bleak corridor of the jail's annex behind City Hall, Oldmixton asked in a tone of gentle concern, 'Is he sane enough to stand trial?'

Spymaster? ME?

Jeffers studied his notes for a moment, his thick mouth turned down at one corner. 'That I don't know, Mr Secretary,' he said. 'It'll be up to the judge at the arraignment, I guess.' To Poe, he went on, 'You say he was drunk when you told him what you'd heard of his wife's crimes—?'

'He appeared to be drunk, yes, sir. There was a near-empty bottle on the table before him, and there was nothing to have prevented him from going on drinking for the remainder of the evening, until Mrs Bray returned.'

'And these coded messages he speaks of – this cipher and key – that would give at least some evidence of his sanity if they could be found. What did they look like?'

January glanced sidelong at Oldmixton, who appeared to be listening with the same expression of grave sorrow that he'd worn in the visiting-room...

Oldmixton, who had in all probability paused to pocket the decryption and the magic-square key from among the jumble of liquor-stained bills and cards on the parlor table, when he'd gone to the Bray house early Tuesday morning and the frightened servants had led him to the locked bedroom door...

He may even have gone there in quest of them, rather than of a meeting with Mrs Bray.

'That I cannot say, sir,' Poe replied. 'He shook something at us, crumpled in his fist–' he demonstrated with a gesture – 'but I did not see what it was.'

'I would venture to say, sir,' said Oldmixton, 'and I believe that Dr Gurry, who treated Mr Bray for his attempted suicide some two weeks ago, will concur, that the shock of learning of his wife's financial chicaneries, coming so soon after his quite rightful distress at his former servant's disloyalty and disappearance, simply overset poor Mr Bray's reason. Though I am, as I said, a friend of Mrs Bray's family, and was deeply fond of Mrs Bray, I do not believe Mr Bray was in his right mind; nor should he be held responsible for what he did.'

As they crossed the lobby of the City Hall towards the doors, the Second Ward constable laid a peremptory hand on January's arm, said, 'You ain't lookin' too peart, boy.'

Oldmixton turned back immediately, his brown eyes watchful, but January only shook his head. 'I'm sorry, sir. Them robbers out by Bladensburg gave me such a crack on the head, we had to turn back to town. Mr Trigg and Leopold had to carry me most of the way back.'

He felt cold to his marrow and during his questioning about the events of Monday night had struggled against recurring waves of pain. But if he collapsed, he knew, even a cursory attempt to revive him would result in the discovery of a bullet hole in his side. 'I know I should be able to shake it off,' he added. 'My momma always did say I got a head like granite–' an untruth that turned the constable's suspicion into disarmed laughter – 'but that's just not happenin'.'

'Think you'll be in shape to play Saturday?'

'Good Lord, no, sir.' January managed a wan grin. 'But if you got money on that game, I promise you, me not bein' on the team's likely to help more'n it hurts. I am truly the sorriest player you ever saw.'

'And Mede Tyler...' Constable Jeffers sank his voice. 'You think he's gone for good? Or you think he's going to show up for the game?'

With more truth than he put into his voice, January said, 'I truly wish he would, sir.'

'Hmph.' Then he smiled and slapped January in a friendly fashion on the hurt side of his back. 'Well, you get some rest, then, boy,' he chuckled. 'Guess I'll see you at the game.'

January felt measurably better by Saturday, enough so that he was able to walk out with the Stalwarts to the fields along Reedy Branch. No further questions had been asked about the five white men found dead on the Baltimore road on Tuesday morning, nor the four bodies – also identified as Kyle Fowler's men – found near Warrenton. The countryside was being combed for the slaves that Elsie Fowler testified both bands were transporting, but – according to

Trigg – she'd had nothing to say about anyone asking after her brother late on Monday night.

As a diplomat, Mr Oldmixton could not be prosecuted for buying information, but given the current situation between the United States, Britain, and the still-rebellious Canada, Miss Fowler would certainly be hanged for selling it.

Oldmixton paid a call on the boarding house on Saturday afternoon, shortly before the Stalwarts set forth for the game. January was in the parlor, bidding farewell to Poe.

'I shall be obliged to set forth before the game is over,' the poet said, 'if I'm to catch the last train to Baltimore. Aunt Muddy – my mother-in-law, I suppose I must call her now–' and the note in his voice, the flicker of a smile on his face, spoke volumes of his affection for the woman – 'writes me that Haswell, Barrington and Haswell of Philadelphia have offered me fifty dollars to adapt and compress Wyatt's *Manual of Conchology* for American readers, so I suppose we shall be going to Philadelphia for a time...'

'And the inhabitants of Acropolis, Indiana, can look out for themselves?'

Poe smiled, a little shyly. 'God help me, I probably deserve to be horsewhipped for condemning poor Ginny to live on what a writer might make – it's worse than living with a gambler, I suppose. But before God, Ben, I can't not do it. The world burns for me, with tales to tell. Would God have made a man so, if there were not at least some path for him to follow?'

'I don't know.' January took his hand and shook it. 'But speaking entirely selfishly, my

370

wife and I will both be glad that there will be more of your work to look for.'

As he spoke he saw a gig draw up in the street, and a moment later, Oldmixton's brisk, elegant form strode down the gravel path. The Englishman greeted Poe's news with pleasure and asked if January intended to go to the ball game: 'If you actually believe there will be such a thing?'

'That I don't know, sir. I don't know if white men will think it more dishonorable to engage in a contest with black ones, or to be seen by all to run from it. But if they come, I intend to be there.'

When Poe left the room at the sound of Mrs Trigg's voice in the hall, Oldmixton lowered his own voice and, stepping close to January, took his arm.

'And is it your intent – as I understand from Madame Viellard – to return with them to New Orleans next week? I could not, for instance, persuade you to remain here?'

January raised his brows.

A moment of silence lay between them.

Are you asking me what I think you're asking me?

Quietly, Oldmixton went on, 'With Fowler gone I need a man of intelligence working for me – and Fowler, disgusting as he was, was a man of intelligence, in both senses of that word. He knew everyone in certain circles in the District, something I've observed you have had no trouble in doing either, though in much different circles. You're a man of enterprise and resolution – and a man with little reason to feel loyalty

371

to a government which truckles to the demands of people who prefer that you and your family remain legally animals, in order to grow rich from your labor and your pain. I think we could work together well.'

'So do I,' said January, with a slow smile. 'And I won't say I'm not ... intrigued. But I won't live in the District – and I won't make my family live here. In New Orleans we have a certain amount of protection, among our own people, the *gens du couleur libré*. In New Orleans we have family: those we love, the world we love.'

'And how long,' asked Oldmixton, 'do you think that world is going to last?'

'God only knows,' January said. 'But it's where I belong. Twenty-three years ago I defended it against your General Pakenham.'

'And are you glad you won?'

'Not every day.'

'Oh, *treason*!' gasped Dominique's voice in the hall. 'Oh, that ungrateful ... that wicked—!'

She swept into the parlor, fizzling with rage, shaking a piece of notepaper in her small, lace-gloved hand.

'She is a traitoress!' she cried. 'A – a *salope*...'

'Who—?'

'Thèrése!' Minou stormed over to him, thrust the note at him. 'And I doubt *she* would have done me the courtesy of leaving me a message, had not that ... that *hypocrite* thought to forestall pursuit by leaving me this! Oh! The *nerve* of the man!'

January took it. '*My dear Dominique*,' he read, '*it is with deep sorrow that we are obliged to write this, knowing your feelings toward us both—*

'If they knew my feelings toward them both at this moment they would *die* of shame!'

'—and deeply sensible of how they will be wounded. Yet we pray that your kindness will forgive two hearts that have found one another in adversity, and that your understanding will one day reconcile you to our memory. Do not worry about either of us, for we will be wed as soon as we reach a Northern city where we can establish our home and our hearts in safety and peace. Yours in loyalty and love—'

'They *dare* write to me of loyalty!' stormed Minou.

'Frank and Thèrése.'

'Nothing – *nothing* is so despicable as disloyalty of this sort!' she raged. 'This betrayal – this *infamy* ... Is it not so, *P'tit*?'

January said nothing, but Mr Oldmixton, with an ironic smile, agreed, 'Indeed, nothing.'

Minou was still fulminating – very much in the fashion of Luke Bray on the subject of Mede's desertion – when they reached the field. To do her credit, Dominique did not give vent to her fury when Charmian, trotting at her side in a springtime glory of white gauze with a cherry-red sash, asked, Where is Thèrése? But when Henri appeared, driving himself in a very stylish chaise, and Minou ran to embrace him, January picked up his niece and told her, 'Thèrése has gone away with Mr Preston to be married.'

'Is that why Maman is angry?'

'Maman is angry because Thèrése didn't tell her she was going,' said January. 'I think when she stops being angry, she'll be happy that Thèrése is happy.' He hoped this was the case, anyway. 'But it's the custom, when a servant leaves someone's household, even to marry a man she loves, to ask permission, and she didn't.'

Charmian frowned, puzzled. 'Why not? Thèrése always tells me to ask permission.'

'Do you sometimes forget?'

The little girl nodded.

'She may have just forgotten, because she loves Mr Preston so much.' He hoped that was true, too – and not simply that Thèrése needed a man's escort for a time, if she was going to make her way as a free woman in the North.

At least she hadn't helped herself to Minou's pearls, which rather surprised January, actually. Possibly, Mr Preston had objected – or Thèrése had had enough sense to realize that it was unwise to court further reason for pursuit.

'Will she marry Mr Preston and be happy?'

'She will.' January smiled a little, seeing by Dominique's furious gestures that she was pouring the whole tale into Henri's ears. Never had he seen her look so much like their mother.

'If they can get married,' asked the child, 'why can't Mama marry Papa? They're in love.'

Why can't Mama marry Papa? January looked again at the couple in the chaise, as Henri talked Minou out of her anger: held her hand, joked her gently ... got her to laugh. *Saying what?* January wondered. Making what grave little observa-

374

tions that – in spite of his bug collection and his overwhelming fondness for truffles and crème caramel – tickled her sense of humor?

His gaze went across the heads of the crowd and picked out Chloë Viellard, in a handsome barouche between Congressman Adams and a frail, bent, white-haired gentleman in shabby tweeds, whom he had last seen as 'Mr Leland' at Gurry's asylum. Chloë caught his eye and beckoned him, and he edged through the growing crowd toward her; Mr Noyes and a half-dozen of the Massachusetts abolitionists were grouped around the other side of the carriage, talking eagerly with the Right Honorable Representative from Massachusetts. When January reached the place he saw Poe by the nearside wheel, bowing to Chloë: the poet had walked out to the field by himself, lest he be seen publicly strolling with the rowdy crowd of black folk, a disgrace from which neither his reputation nor his self-respect would ever recover.

'They're late already,' he heard Noyes say on the other side of the carriage. 'They could be delaying, to push the game into the hours of twilight—'

'Or they could be planning something,' retorted someone else. 'Getting the police – or O'Hanlon and his boys...'

'M'sieu Janvier.' Chloë inclined her head, and January bowed – carefully. 'M'sieu Singletary, allow me to present to you M'sieu Janvier, the man who had most to do with us finding you.'

'Sithee, then.' Singletary addressed him in thick Yorkshire English, held out one hand, disproportionately large on his narrow wrists and gloved in shabby and ink-stained kid. 'I'm that beholden to you – and they mun be needin' other words for such occasions, think on. *Thank you* is what you say for a plate of sandwiches.'

'And another expression is needed,' replied January, taking the arthritic fingers, 'to acknowledge thanks that isn't, *The pleasure is mine*. It was no pleasure whatsoever, though I'm extremely glad to see you well, sir.'

'I bahn to write Cuthbertson on t' subject,' agreed Singletary absently. 'Head of t' London Philological Society, sithee. Wrote *Syntactical Observations on the West-Country Dialects*. Lot of slum, think on, but that sound on Old Norse numismatics...'

'Sir.' Chloë laid a hand on the old man's thin arm. 'M'sieu Janvier is a surgeon of considerable skill. As Dr Gurry is of the opinion that you will need to remain under a physician's care for many months, would you consent to appoint M'sieu Janvier your personal physician, when we take ship for New Orleans at the end of the week? The *Bordeaux* leaves for home on Thursday,' she added, turning those enormous blue eyes on January. 'I thought it best to depart as soon as possible...'

Especially in the light of a general search for the murderers of Kyle Fowler and the slaves who escaped from his coffle?

January bowed again, and said, quite truthfully, 'I will be more than grateful to get home.'

Chloë gave him her wintry smile and held out her hand to Poe. 'Henri will be delighted to hear

376

you're preparing an American version of Wyatt's *Conchology*.'

Adams sniffed. 'I hope you do not live to regret your choice, young man.'

'I expect I will, sir. It shames me to say so, but storming the madhouse in the lovely Madame's company – and hunting grave robbers with Ben here – have shown me how ... how impossible it is for me ever to consider a government job in some post office somewhere...'

'My mother would have had it that a man with true strength of character would be willing to set aside his foolishness for the sake of his family.' The old diplomat regarded him with bright, pale eyes. 'But having set aside foolishness in my time, I can't say my life has been the happier.'

'Happy or not,' replied Poe quietly, 'I've come to realize that it is ... almost immaterial. It's like those magic squares of Mr Singletary's: whichever way I add up the numbers, the reply is the same. I must be as I am. I must write. It's not that I must take that road – it's that *all* roads turn out to be that road. And whether it leads to my salvation or to my destruction I do not know. Nor does it matter.'

Adams said, 'Hmph,' and Chloë squeezed Poe's hand.

'*Bonne chance, M'sieu.*'

'*Et vous aussi, Madame*. They are,' Poe added, looking at the dimming sky, 'leaving it rather late—'

Voices rose in anger at the fringes of the crowd. Noyes and his abolitionists looked as if they might go seek the cause of the trouble, but

the shouting died away almost at once as someone – who probably had money on the game –
broke up the fight.

Close-by, someone said Mede Tyler's name –
'He gonna show up, or ain't he?'

'They'll be in a heap of trouble if he does...'

'You think he's hiding out?'

'Got to be. O'Hanlon and his boys...'

It's a goddam game...

Is it all, January wondered, *a goddam game?*

He thought of Mede Tyler, asleep in his unmarked grave.

Of Rowena Bray, buried yesterday in the
Christ Church cemetery not far from where
January had lain in wait for Wylie Pease.

He looked up at Chloë, in the carriage above
him. It would be good beyond computation to be
back in New Orleans, with Rose and Baby John,
Gabriel and Zizi-Marie, his real family, instead
of this strange artificial family, assumed out of
regard for the conventions of 'good society',
which would not let women travel alone nor
white men legitimize their love for women of
color. Muggy heat would be settling in on New
Orleans by the time they returned, but Chloë, no
doubt, would go with her elderly guest to one of
the Viellard plantations along the river while
Henri retired to his cottage at Mandeville, to live
with Dominique for the summer.

Chloë lifted her head, and January thought, for
a moment, that those enormous blue eyes rested
upon his sister and Henri over the heads of the
crowd. Jealous? Wistful? Irked at the way he
held her hands, in front of half the clerks and

378

junior Congressmen in Washington? Or merely scientifically curious about the foolishness to which humankind subjected itself, when it loved?

I am not capable of making him happy, she had said once...

Shouting again, elsewhere in the mob; serious, this time. January scanned the fringes of the crowd, calculating the quickest way to get the women and children away, if real trouble started. Far off, the bells of the Presbyterian Church on I Street struck six. The light was fading.

Already, some of the women were leaving, children in tow. Henri flicked the reins of his team, turned the chaise. As they passed Musette, the fat man leaned down to lift his daughter up to sit between them. A few minutes later, Adams observed that the oncoming evening chill was not doing either of his passengers any good and turned his own team back towards Connecticut Avenue.

Across the deep grass, straggling groups of men were walking back toward town. January saw Poe stride away, carpet bag in hand, a dilapidated raven in the twilight. He thought he saw Wylie Pease and skinny brass-haired Miss Drail emerge from the crowd and stroll back toward the new-twinkling lights, hand in hand.

From the edges of the crowd, curses were beginning to drift on the damp air.

The Stalwarts hurled the ball to one another to practice striking, or trotted between the pegs, warming up their bodies, waiting for the Warriors to arrive.

Darkness fell, the Warriors disdaining to accept the challenge of lesser men.

With darkness came curfew, the time for all good niggers to be indoors.

Among the last of the groups to leave, January walked back through evening stillness and deep grass, to pack.